THE CANNABIS PREACHER

SERMON FOUR

A Financial Thriller About a Race to Solve a Medical Mystery and Escape a Ferocious Storm, While Tracking a Cunning Killer to an Explosive Finale

SABINE FRISCH

Publishing Services provided by Paper Raven Books LLC
Printed in the United States of America
First Printing, 2023

Paperback ISBN 978-1-7390706-1-8
Hardback ISBN 978-1-7390706-0-1

PROLOGUE

The fall air was already becoming chilly, far too soon. Before he knew it, it would be too cold to keep running and hiding. He would have to find a secure hideout, away from the prying eyes of the police. Haggard and filthy, he sat back, staring into the fire he had lit in a rusty old stove in a work hut forest workers had abandoned years ago.

He, who had been the CEO of a huge company, had been reduced to being homeless and on the run. He pulled a ragged blanket around his shoulders and simply stared into the flames. The darkness didn't bother him, but the hunger gnawed his insides. It was long past time to steal some food again, but he didn't dare move any closer to town during the day. Who knew how many people were out there looking for him.

Be on the lookout—armed and dangerous.

As abandoned, dilapidated, and remote as this shack was, it served his purposes for the moment. The time would come when he could enjoy the better things in life again. Meanwhile, he waited. After all, he had nothing but time left any longer.

From his pocket, he pulled a copy of a ragged piece of notepaper and read the words written in fading ink, as he had done every day for the last few months. His eyes hardly needed to find the words on the page. He knew them by heart and whispered the words to himself.

Except for the last few lines—those he always read out loud and would continue to do so until his task was done.

"Tadeo Ivers deserved to die, for everything he had done—if there's any justice in this world, he deserved it.

"If I am taking the coward's way out, so be it. I tried to avenge my father's death with his shooting, but it was not enough, not even close.

"Rest assured, I will not stop until the Ivers family who drove him into suicide are gone."

As the silence drew around him again, he sighed with satisfaction and carefully folded the note back into the pocket where he kept it. He liked the strong sound of his own voice when he said those words; they focused his mind on what he needed to do. And finally, when everything was said and done, and his father's death avenged, someone would find that note on him and know that a massive wrong had finally been righted.

From a backpack he pulled a bottle of bourbon he had stolen a while ago and took a long draft. This would warm him for now, driving the chill and the hunger from his soul.

ONE

The slanting afternoon sun drew lines of light and dark onto the snow-white walls and glinted off the chrome and glass in the posh executive offices, while two men stared at a large TV screen—one standing, bouncing on his heels with excitement, the other leaning back in a high-end office chair.

"Perfect Cannabis Products presents Perfect Points, your latest news update with our CEO, Mr. Al Ivers..."

On the screen, a man who was meant to be standing in for Al Ivers approached a silver, wedge-shaped desk against a nighttime image of the downtown area, smiled at the camera, and said, "Good evening, ladies and gentlemen," as a trumpet fanfare rose and faded away.

Al stopped the video, put down the remote, and brought his hands up to his face, palms together. His friends always told him he looked as if he were praying in that pose—praying for patience right then.

"It's..."

"Fantastic, isn't it?"

His fundraiser, Barry Wentworth, spread his arms. "We're going to film one of these every week."

"I was going to say it's a bit over the top, Barry." Al settled his lanky frame back into his chair and looked at the man across from him.

"That's exactly what we want. Over the top, splashy, memorable—legendary. News, Al. It is news, and the stock market wants news."

"Legendary, you say..." Al bit off an acidic remark.

Legendary. That word described Barry J. Wentworth all right—the man who had been hauled off to jail twice, only to be released for lack of evidence.

Once for an illegal grow operation in the back of this very building, and once for killing Tadeo Ivers, majority shareholder of Perfect Cannabis Corporation and Al's father. Barry Wentworth was in fact not guilty of either crime—and at the same time the most likely and most implicated suspect. So much so that he had stolen an airplane to evade prosecution last time.

Legendary worked as a description of him. Barry might have stepped right out of the latest issue of *GQ* with his tanned face, three-day stubble, and Italian power suit. Al knew him better and was not impressed.

"Look…"

"Al, you don't have to say much. Just the most recent investor news in an interview style format with," Barry pointed at his own chest, "moi. Easy peasy. I can even get you a teleprompter if you need one."

"Most definitely not."

"There's no shame in it, Al. We can…"

"I do not need a teleprompter, Barry. I am merely concerned…" Al spread his hands by his face as if he were trying to catch a giant ball. "There's a difference between news and notoriety."

"Good news sells shares."

"I am well aware of that." Al Ivers leaned back without speaking and finally shook his head. "I'm also not convinced I should be drawing massive attention to myself. Especially while Turner is still out there."

"Turner? As in Greg Turner?" Barry asked and waved his hand. "That loser is long gone, mark my words. He knows he will be picked up by the police the moment he shows his face around here. Why are you even thinking about that lowlife?"

"Well, for one," Al said with a derisive laugh, "the man made a vow not to rest until all the Ivers men who drove his father into suicide are gone. Ring a bell?"

"Rhetoric," Barry mumbled and looked down at his shoes, but suddenly, the mask of confidence dropped a bit.

Yes, once he had finally been acquitted of shooting Tadeo Ivers, Barry had made magic happen for Perfect Cannabis Corporation with the funds he was able to raise. Their expansion plans had become unstoppable. Apparently, investors burned to leave their money with a truly notorious, twice-found-innocent man, who could promise it would rain dollar bills tomorrow without blushing or missing a beat.

But even Barry had been oddly quiet for a little while, when it was discovered that the man who really had shot Al's father, Greg Turner, had done so because of ancient history. Stories Barry had been feeding him in order to facilitate one of his own business moves. Here and there, Al had heard some whispered comments in private conversations that Greg might have pulled the trigger, but Barry had all but teed him up to do so.

Since spreading ancient gossip—malicious or not—was in no way punishable by the law, Barry was still a free man. But Turner had not fared so well. He'd run from the law, all right, and for all anyone knew had disappeared completely from the face of the earth—but not before vowing revenge on the remaining three Ivers men: Al, and his brothers Roberto and Dante.

"I don't think much of the idea of plastering my face all over town." Al finally pulled himself out of his reverie. "Surely, we can stick with the tried-and-true method of issuing relevant news releases?"

"That's a little…"

"Traditional?"

"Old-fashioned. Boring. There's massive competition for investor dollars out there." Barry raised his arms like the preacher he had pretended to be once. "And cannabis was the hottest thing last year. Now we compete with other sectors, other projects for investor attention. Psychedelics are the new rage of the moment. So is AI. If we want to keep raising funds, we need to stick out, be hip, be young—be 'with it.'"

"I'm still not convinced." Al forked his hand through his dark hair that refused to grey, even though he was the oldest in the management group. "If it is vitally important, maybe Rafael could…"

"All due respect—people want to hear from the CEO. Everybody wants to see you. Especially after what Turner did."

Al folded his hands again, sighed with resignation, considered for another moment, and finally nodded. "Fine then, you win."

"It's not a matter of me winning, Al, although that is my preferred state of affairs. And you won't have to appear on every week's segment."

"Every week?"

Al almost shot out of his chair. "Even if I agree to do this, not every week, Barry. That's over the top."

"No, you just don't understand." Barry did get up and began pacing up and down in the office. "I know you don't like to appear in public, though you already are a minor celebrity of sorts. I know you don't like publicity, even though you need it."

"I am not a public figure, and I believe a manufacturer of cannabis should stay somewhat under the radar."

"Wrong." Barry stopped in front of Al and gestured widely with his hands. "Wrong. I spoke to your in-house Investor Relations guy—Jack, Jim…"

"Jim," Al answered automatically. "Jim Kaiser."

"Well, hire a new one, Al. His approach is all wrong. He needs to promote this company, tell people why they should buy our stock instead of somebody else's if they are going to invest in cannabis anyway. Kaiser comes across like a foot cramp—tense and uncomfortable…"

Back and forth they went. Barry preferred flash, glitz, and glamour and showing the world what they had done here. Al liked to convince in a lowkey, fact- and science-driven manner. In the end, as they always did, they settled.

Barry would get to film his 'Perfect Points' newsflash-type show, and Al would only have to make an appearance sporadically. Instead, he would pick out interesting people who worked at the company and let them tell the story from their point of view.

It wasn't quite flashy enough for Barry, but he did not let that faze him. Happily, he thanked Al and bounced off for another meeting, while Al let out a breath and massaged his temples.

He'd heard someone likening dealing with Barry to juggling 10 balls while sitting on an active volcano and singing "Hallelujah."

True enough, he thought, *just throw in an earthquake or two.* The thing about Barry, though, was his enthusiasm. If he was behind a project, he could present it to you in a way that made you wonder where this thing had been all of your life and how you could possibly have survived without it for so long.

Most people agreed there was no better promoter or fundraiser in town—some went so far as to say in the entire country.

The door swung open again, and his chief operating officer and close friend, Rafael Covin, wandered into the office and dropped into the chair Barry had vacated moments ago.

"Saw Barry leave, figured your face would look like that. Any issues?"

"Not issues exactly." Al ran his hands through his disheveled hair and settled straighter in his chair. "We just have—a different approach to things most of the time."

"No shit," Rafael said and grinned.

Of all the things Al had been looking forward to after the real murderer of his father had finally confessed, it had been installing Rafael as an official director in the company.

He'd been doing the job in all but title for the longest time. He'd been there at the very beginning, when he founded Perfect Cannabis along with Barry. Then, when Barry disappeared, he'd worked for Al's father, Tadeo, who had funded the resurrection of the company and forced him to be CEO for a while, and now, finally, for Al.

Rafael was a natural COO. He knew every corner of the company. He had designed their processes and structures everywhere, from the growing areas to packing and, finally, shipping. The only people who knew more about that temperamental little plant called cannabis they grew here were their agronomists Dante and Nick. And they usually checked with Rafael first before they suggested any changes.

Their setup was as perfect, clean, and sterile as it could get in this business, and, consequently, they achieved high yields, pure strains, and exceptionally low losses or spoilage. The holy grail in medical marijuana. Their brand was known as the best of the best in medicinal cannabis applications and, for the last few years, recreational since it had become legal.

Their expansion plans into the field of recreational cannabis and edibles was also behind their latest round of fundraising. Nick and Dante were bursting with ideas, but their current setup was almost at capacity to fill requests in the medical field. Al had been tempted to leave well enough alone and concentrate on the medical field, but the board wouldn't hear of it. Their facility was known as top rate, they argued. Why not capitalize on that reputation?

And they were the best because of Rafael. Almost every day Al fielded requests from other companies who wanted to borrow Rafael, set up a joint venture, or license the IP to their setup, if not all three.

Last month, several countries in Europe had licensed marijuana for medical applications and came knocking at their door, and Rafael was set to fly out to Malta in a few days' time, to show them how growing was done right.

"Barry has a different approach to everything from basically 90 percent of other people," Rafael now said.

"Normal people."

"Possibly. Probably. But much as I try, I can't argue with his success. His fundraising company is like the hottest thing in the area. I hear he has a complicated screening process for new clients and a waiting list as long as your arm."

"How nice for him," Al grumbled, seeing himself on that news screen.

"They say any company that makes it through his application process and gets him to work with them already has it made. Done deal." Rafael rubbed his hands as if he were washing them.

"I'm glad he found his niche, Rafael, because he was making a mess of things here when he was trying to run PerCan. Now he wants to film a weekly fluff news program called 'Perfect Points,' and I'm to be starring on it. The mind boggles. Aside from that—what can I do for you?"

"Nothing, really, just came to check on you. You still don't really look great."

"I'm fine, Rafael, but thank you for asking. Just a little under the weather."

As if to prove his point, he coughed discreetly into his elbow, and Rafael wrinkled his brow.

"You really don't sound good, Al. I know you're stubborn, but you should really get this thing checked out. You're too pale to be well, and you've been dragging this around. You lose any more weight, and I could shove you under the door without having to bother opening it."

"Again, thank you for your concern, Rafael, but it's really nothing that a bit of rest over the weekend and plenty of hot fluids won't fix. Why don't you tell me how the plans for Malta are going?"

"Malta is fine," Rafael said dismissively and studied his friend's face. "You worry about Turner too much. Is that it?"

"Greg Turner?"

"Do we know any other Turner around here? Yes, Al, Greg Turner, the man who shot your father, confessed, and then disappeared, vowing not to rest until you, Dante, and Roberto were gone. That Turner."

"No need to get tetchy with me." Al arranged the papers on his desk in front of him, aligning the edges perfectly and perfectly square to the edge of the desk.

"To answer your question—no, I don't think about him."

"Liar."

Al hid a smile behind his hand. Rafael could always read him like nobody else, and, because of their friendship forged while working to save this company against his father's sometimes manic ideas, he said what was on his mind. Straight talk, laced with a generous dash of cusswords where appropriate.

"Fine," he said. "There are—moments I think about him. Short moments. Nothing serious, I assure you."

"You forget that I know you. The man threatened to kill your entire family. I, for one, would be terrified—maybe even walk around with a gun."

Al attempted a laugh, which even to his ears sounded hollow and contrived, and shook his head with a smile.

"Thank you, Rafael. No guns, please. I am truly honored that you are concerned about me, but I am sure Turner is a delusional individual. He is going to have his hands full hiding from the police, who are looking for him as we speak. Your friend, Detective Robertson, sends me regular updates on that search. It is quite the net they are casting for him."

"Couldn't be wide enough," Rafael grumbled, only slightly mollified. "And if he ever decides to show his ugly face around here…" He struck his palm with a closed fist. "No guarantees…"

"Rafael, that kind of talk…"

"Does no one any good and got me in trouble before, I remember. I just wish they would get on with arresting him already, so I can stop looking over my shoulder every time I walk around the place."

"Don't hold your breath." Al settled back and rubbed his chilled hands. "He may have just grabbed a page out of Barry's playbook and taken off for some faraway place with no extradition agreement, for all we know."

He coughed again and shivered.

"What's going on with the furnace anyway? For the last couple of days, it's been freezing in my office. Know anybody who could fix it?"

Rafael frowned and got up to check the electronic thermostat by the door and the furnace outlets, cleverly hidden in the baseboards of the room. Shaking his head, he went to the thermostat again, called up an app on his phone and compared the readings, and shrugged.

"Nothing. Temperature is at perfect comfort setting in here, just as it should be. Al—I don't like this. Something is seriously wrong with you. Will you please…?"

"Go to the hospital for a small cold? No thank you. I appreciate your concern, Rafael, really, but I am fine."

"You're not fine."

"Thank you, Mother. I might have caught a cold at that investor conference at the Baltimore Hotel. The crowd sure was large enough to catch something."

Rafael didn't look happy with the answer, but kept his mouth shut.

"Besides," Al continued, "as despicable as he may be, even Greg Turner has not figured out how to give you a cold that will go on to kill you, but when he does…"

"I'm sure we'll be the first to find out," Rafael finished bitterly. "All right—have it your way. And please don't use words like 'kill' when I'm around. It makes me…"

"Thank you. Now, tell me how your preparations for Malta are coming."

Rafael smiled a little because there was nothing he liked more than to talk about the setup and processes within a cannabis manufacturing plant.

He'd been on the right track when Tadeo Ivers, Al's late father, had tasked him with pulling PerCan out of the trash heap and making it the best it could be. Right then, he had decided to treat the enterprise like a large pharmaceutical lab, since he'd recently been involved in the construction of just such a plant.

From then on, he focused on efficient, clean, sterile environments and processes, and it worked. A large part of the process could be automated, leaving out the human equation and so many chances to introduce infections to the cannabis grow pods.

Finicky little suckers, he called the cannabis plants lovingly. But under the care of Al's brother Dante, and Nick Armstrong, a master grower from Colorado, and coddled and protected by Rafael's closed environments, they thrived.

And now, everyone wanted in on Rafael's secret. A well-protected and patented secret they were willing to pay top dollar for.

"Coming along," he said dismissively. "They've sent me plans for the area where they want to grow, and of course, they have it all wrong." He rolled his eyes to the ceiling and grinned. "That's what this trip is all about. Get to know one another, sniff the other guy, see if he's OK, and get them on the right track before they sink one spade into the ground."

"Indoor or outdoor grow?"

"Greenhouse," Rafael said, a little pained. Greenhouses were not his favorite. *I want to be God to those plants* was one of his favorite lines. *I decide when they get light, water, or fertilizer. That's the only real way to control a grow.*

"The climate is good enough in Malta—sunshine, stable temperatures, I worried about hurricanes, but they told me they don't really get any."

"That's a relief, I'm sure."

"Yeah." Rafael shrugged. "Given the cost of power over there, it would be prohibitively expensive to build an isolated indoor grow, as we do here, but…" He pursed his lips. "I'll work it out once I get the lay of the land. I'll put together a really nice greenhouse op for them."

Al smiled and let his friend go on about his Malta plans, but it was a forced smile that cost him a massive effort. This darned cold was taking a lot more out of him than he wanted to let on. If Rafael hadn't been sitting there, ready to mother him like a hen, he would have been tempted to find a spot for a small nap somewhere, or at least sit back and close his eyes for a minute. As it was…

He straightened and got out of his chair, forcing himself not to wince or rub his hands, even though he felt as if the furnace had been out all day. A little sideways glance at the thermostat confirmed what Rafael had told him earlier. The room was at a perfect comfort setting, so what in blazes?

"I do have a quick meeting with the fellows in marketing," he said to Rafael. "And I have to get used to the thought of hosting those Perfect Points shows Barry wants me to do."

"You'll get used to it."

"I don't doubt it. Check in with Kayla, why don't you—perhaps we can all go to dinner before you leave the country for several weeks."

Rafael gave him a thumbs up, already involved reading his emails.

Kayla Montecito, Rafael's fiancée and communications director of PerCan, didn't appear to be in the building today. She ran an extremely successful publishing house of her own and didn't need to maintain an in-house office.

Had she been around, Al was sure he would have noticed. The employees loved her and fawned over her to a degree that astonished him. You always knew when Kayla was in the building because everyone had an extra smile that day. *Oh, to be as popular with the staff as she is,* he thought, checking his pocket for his phone. *It would probably make it a lot easier to run PerCan.*

TWO

Rafael brought the dinner inquiry to Kayla later that night, as they shared a final glass of wine at home, and she nodded.

"Sure. If he's up to it. We'll have to order something, though. How did he seem today?"

"Seem?" Rafael asked with a blank look.

"Surely, Rafael, you noticed that Al has not been well in almost a week. I've been trying to get him to see someone about it, but he stubbornly insists it's nothing."

"Yeah, I noticed, but he said it was just a cold." Rafael shrugged and reached for his wineglass. "Got right tetchy with me when I suggested he get it checked out, so I dropped the subject."

"I think we know somebody else who acts like that," Kayla said with a headshake and eye roll, refilling his wineglass.

"What, me? I see doctors when I think it's necessary."

"When you think it's necessary, like when you have a finger dangling off your hand by a thread, yes. Go sew that back on please. Men!"

She took a sip of her wine and frowned at Rafael. "Aren't you concerned?"

Rafael shrugged and stared into his wine. "Yes, sure. But I'm really more concerned about Greg Turner coming around doing something stupid. That's what I'm thinking mostly."

"Turner." Kayla shook her head. "I had a chat with Barry about him today, and Barry seems to think he's long gone—taken off for parts unknown."

"That's what Barry would think because that's exactly what he did when he came under suspicion for the illegal grow op way back when. Best solution—run. And since when are you and Barry friendly again?"

Rafael picked up his glass and downed the remainder of the wine in one gulp. He frowned and put the glass down just a little too hard.

"You're not jealous by any chance, are you?"

Kayla grinned just a bit too broadly for his taste. The gossip mags had had their day when she and Barry were together, many, many years ago, until he disappeared and left her behind. Those had been dark days, until she and Rafael found one another. It had happened so quickly—it had surprised both of them.

Rafael still didn't know how to answer the question, 'What exactly does she see in you?' He was just happy there was something, and she kept him on the straight and narrow most days. Most days.

He rolled his eyes, shook his head, and picked up his glass, putting it back down immediately, realizing it was empty.

"Of Barry? Please. Give me a break, woman. Now would you take care of ordering dinner please? I have to go over my presentation for Malta for a few minutes, sorry."

"Wish I were coming along. Malta, this time of the year…" Kayla spread her arms and smiled wistfully. "It's said to be beautiful."

"I'm sure it's pretty, but I won't have time for sightseeing. Trust me. All I'm going to see are the insides of offices and extremely ugly warehouses while I show them how to put together a proper grow."

Kayla would be fine while he was gone, Rafael thought. Other than perhaps a bit sore about missing a trip she really wanted to go on. The fact that he was leaving Al gave him a bit more of a headache. Despite all of his bravado, Al did not look well, and, where he usually moved with a fluid grace and elegance, he walked cautiously, holding on casually to a table or a chair back for support, more often than not. Greg Turner's last words and message had to be going around his mind.

I won't rest until all of the Ivers family are gone.

Stupid idiot! And even more stupid of Barry to go teeing up a man who was so obviously mentally unstable.

Detective Sergeant Robertson, who had been handling Tadeo's murder from the very beginning, thought the note could be read either way. A direct threat or just the rambling of an unwell man with a lot of hatred and revenge inside him.

Rafael begged to disagree. How much more direct could you get? *I will now go out and find a gun and come 'round to shoot you*? Yes, that would have been more direct.

It worried Rafael, and he'd asked Al more than once to hire some discreet personal protection. Al had contacts, like that private investigator fellow Sandro who had worked with him to clear Rafael of any suspicions in Tadeo's death. And, if not him, any man on their security force would be happy to pick up extra hours to hang around Al while he was out—but, naturally, stubborn, thick-headed Al wouldn't hear any of it.

Rafael remembered the blistering grumbling and complaining, when he'd gone over to Al's house a few months ago and brought his toolkit to double-check Al's home alarm system. Nobody had checked the thing in ages, and the only reason there even was an alarm system was because the previous owner of the house had installed it.

"I don't want to get paranoid," Al had told Rafael. "That would mean Turner has already won. No, I am sure at this point he is doing anything to avoid getting caught. He wouldn't risk it. He has to know we are all on the lookout."

Maybe. Possibly. Hopefully.

Meanwhile, they were all reduced to keeping their fingers crossed, while waiting for Robertson to call with the news Greg Turner had been apprehended.

While I'm at it, Rafael thought. Pushing away his Malta paperwork and taking out his phone, he dialed Robertson's number.

"Rafael," the detective greeted him with a sigh. "What can I do for you? As if I didn't have a guess about that already."

"You could tell me you've apprehended Turner. That would kind of make my day."

"No doubt it would. I'm afraid, however…"

"You still haven't got him. Well, what are you waiting for?"

"Rafael, I told you before. Greg Turner has gone underground. He's found somewhere to hide. Maybe somebody is even helping him."

"And are you doing much to catch him?" Rafael asked, knowing before the words were out of his mouth that it was a dumb question.

"Yes, Rafael, of course we are, and you calling me every other day does not help this effort whatsoever. You also know this, as I have told you multiple times."

"Yeah, you told me." Rafael sank back into his chair and stared out the window at nothing. "It's just—I need to go out of town for a few weeks…"

"Your concern for the Ivers family truly honors you, but there is literally nothing we can do at the moment, until Turner either surfaces, or someone reports a sighting of him somewhere. And before you ask…"

"You don't have the manpower to monitor all of the security cameras, in the area," Rafael finished for him. "I know. You told me. I just…"

"Best I can do is inform the beat cops who are on duty in the area around the PerCan building and Al's home to keep an eye out, see if anything suspicious catches their attention and hope to catch Turner that way. That's our only chance right now. That or if he robs a bank. Besides, you and I both know that your security system at PerCan is superior to anything else out there. You'd likely smell Turner before he even thinks about coming into the area."

"I know," Rafael muttered again, tossing down the pen he'd been twirling in his fingers. "It's not the plant I'm worried about. Al stubbornly refuses to get a bodyguard. And I…"

"You want to help. I realize that. As much as I'd like to have better news, our hands are tied right now. Go on your trip, do business, have a good time, wherever it is you're going."

"Malta."

"Nice. Have a good time and ask Al to be careful. Personal protection would not at all be a bad idea, but it has to be his choice. That's all you can do right now."

'All you can do' was not enough by a long shot, but Rafael also knew when he was outvoted on all sides. He couldn't well stay behind and follow Al around like a puppy for the next few years, and he couldn't tell their clients overseas that he'd rather not leave the country because he was busy playing nursemaid and bodyguard.

Damn Al's stubbornness to all hell and back!

***

He avoided the subject of personal protection during their dinner, although Al would look at him with this searching look now and then, and he knew he'd been caught out. He opened his mouth to suggest that maybe a dog—then he closed it again and poked at his food listlessly. It would have been a non-starter.

Al still looked like he had risen from the dead just recently—pale, thin, and a little shaky. He'd always been lanky. Now his suit hung on him like a flour sack. He tried to tell both of them it was just an ongoing cold and basically already on its way out, which would have been far more believable if he hadn't had a violent coughing fit in the middle of his sentence.

He and Rafael shook hands as he left, Rafael forcing a gregarious smile and slap on the shoulder.

"You look after yourself while I'm gone, will you?"

"I always do, Rafael, nothing to worry about."

"And make sure to let me know if anything…"

"If anything at the company seems amiss and I believe you can help, I will definitely let you know. I've said that before."

"I'm only making sure."

"Are we going to have to have this conversation every time you are going out of town to work with one of our international clients? Because this is going to get very tiring if so."

Rafael closed his mouth and glared. *No,* he thought, *only occasionally, if there's a murderer out there to get you for example,* but he said nothing, clapped Al on the back one more time, and forced a smile.

"Oh, let me be a mother hen for once, if nobody else will do it. And try to listen to Kayla's advice. Go see a doctor as soon as you can."

Al waved over his shoulder and disappeared down the driveway, Rafael standing in the door, wishing he could shake the nagging feeling in his gut.

THREE

When he reached his car, Al had to fumble with the keys, dropping them twice before he finally fit them into the lock. He dropped into the driver's seat and took a massive breath, coughing so violently he had to steady himself against the steering wheel.

For God's sake, why wouldn't his hands stop shaking? He had not even had wine with dinner, pretending he still had to work that night. Walking away from Rafael without reaching for the solid support of the stair rail had been one of the hardest things in a long time. His legs wouldn't carry his weight, and every breath was a little harder than the one before.

As much as he wanted to dismiss them, his friends were right. This was no common cold, and the time had come to consult a medical professional.

Soon.

First, he had to get home safely, after he just sat here and rested for a minute. Thank God he'd parked around the corner from Rafael's, well out of view, or he and Kayla would have been right there, worrying. He just needed to catch his breath for a minute, that was all.

Then he had important investor's events tomorrow he needed to prepare for and a board meeting the day after that. Both of those were critical and required his full attention.

Then.

Then he would go make an appointment, he promised himself. He didn't like it, but something was seriously wrong. He could feel it.

He sat in his car and rested his head in his hands for a few minutes, worried that any time soon, someone would knock on the window and ask if he was all right. He had no use for another kind and thoughtful person telling him he should get himself checked out because he didn't look well.

When he felt he had himself sufficiently under control again, he sat up straight and looked around. Nobody had taken any notice of the man sitting in his car quietly. Why should they? Rafael had closed the door behind him before Al reached his car, and the street felt completely deserted.

Al started his car, opened all the windows wide, and drove home like a first-year student, counting on the cool night air to keep him awake and alert. Against his usual habit, he pulled straight into the garage and closed the property gates and garage door behind him. If he had another episode, he surely didn't need any spectators tonight.

He disarmed the alarm Rafael had checked and checked again and flung his keys, jacket and portfolio on the hall table. Silence surrounded him. Moments like these made him think of Greg Turner and his threats every time. The silence made him peer into the shadows and dark rooms of his house and listen to every creak and groan of the old walls. Come on now, did he really believe Greg was out to get him and his brothers?

Al shook himself mentally, turned on a lot more lights than he technically needed, and finally went to pour himself a stiff bourbon.

What were the probabilities of Turner creeping around out there in the shadows? Really? Statistically, probably very low. Most likely, Turner had done what Barry suggested—taken off the moment they figured out he shot Tadeo—and was already en route to Belize by now. Or some country where a foreign arrest warrant couldn't be served. Al wasn't really up on countries with no extradition agreements and wasn't interested either.

Barry would be, he thought bitterly while sipping his drink. Barry, who had gone straight to some deserted island somewhere and become their priest and guru, the first time he ran from a similar arrest warrant. What the heck was the place called? Valdez, Vardar—Vaomar?

Right, Vaomar, he remembered. A secluded, isolated playground for the super-rich and a handful of poor native workers, who had worshipped him.

Barry Wentworth, the preacher sent by God. The thought made him chuckle for the first time today. The reverend Barry Wentworth, with a gift to sell anything to anyone, and the knowledge that sometimes—in his case, frequently—the story he was selling was more important than the product itself. Oh, what he wouldn't give to hear only one of Barry's sermons. Only one.

Al drained the bourbon and, faced with the task of climbing the stairs to the second-floor bedroom, decided he'd rather camp out on the couch in his study for the night. He was merely exhausted from everything that had been going on, he told himself. Another belt of this fine liquor and a warm blanket on his couch, and he would be just fine tomorrow morning. Just perfect. Nothing at all to worry about.

FOUR

Rafael did not wait long to check on him again. Al checked his watch and figured he must just have landed in Malta.

"Your opinion of your fiancée's cooking must not be the greatest," Al joked, "if you feel the need to double-check on me already."

"Nothing to do with Kayla's cooking. We had takeout, remember? I was just trying to make sure everything is all right with you."

"Everything is perfect with me," Al replied with a confidence he didn't feel.

All morning, he'd been struggling with the effort to get up and grab a coffee from the machine in his office. By the time he finally carried it back to his desk, shuffling like an old man, he had to sit for five minutes to gather his strength. Something was slowly but surely draining him of every ounce of energy he had ever possessed, and it showed no signs of stopping any time soon.

"All good, don't worry about a thing," he said, marveling at how easily it came to him to lie to his best friend.

He'd have to hone that skill, if he wanted to make it through the board meeting, which Thomas Donnelly had foolishly postponed for an extra day. By all rights, he had wanted to take off the moment he made it through that meeting.

Several potential expansion plans were on the table, and he had to make sure the decisions went his way—their way. There was a skill to this whole expansion thing, and it was not 'do everything all at the same time,' as Barry, a major shareholder himself, was suggesting frequently.

Al felt he needed to be at that meeting, to slow down the pace just a little, to make sure their energies and attention were not spread too thin, too wide, and the store here at home caught on fire.

He needed to be there to make sure that didn't happen.

"How did the meeting go?" Rafael asked, clearly his mind being on the same subject.

"I wish I could tell you it went fine, but Donnelly had a conflict and postponed till tomorrow."

Rafael cursed softly.

"Barry is a capable fundraiser, and he has fantastic targets for this company and the investors to support them, but he gets too enthusiastic. I'm afraid he does not understand how much it takes out of our home base to have everyone's attention diverted to Malta or Spain, or Italy or Argentina, all at the same time."

"I know," Al said softly, wanting to reassure Rafael, failing to find the energy to string a paragraph together that sounded like it made any sense.

"I know," he finally repeated. "I will—endeavor to prevent that."

"Are you sure you're all right again? You still sound…"

"Annoyed," Al said and chuckled with an effort. "Massively annoyed at the delay, that's all." He closed his eyes for a moment before continuing. "Listen, I have to go. I have—another call coming in."

"OK, well, sorry to disturb you," Rafael said, clearly disappointed. "Never mind. I'll call back in a bit."

Al hung up the phone slowly and let out another massive breath. On his desk was the coffee he'd worked so hard to make, cold and disgusting by now. He pushed it away and flipped off his laptop. Chances of getting any meaningful work done today were at this point nearing zero, and he needed rest more than he needed to prepare.

He called the driver he had had the foresight to hire in the morning and had him take him home, claiming he needed quiet and privacy for a number of confidential calls.

***

Rafael tried calling again later and was told Al had gone home for the day.

Good, Rafael thought, *maybe the man is finally taking everyone's advice about getting some rest.* And, with that, he put the issue out of his mind.

Now that he had arrived in Malta, the excitement and joy of starting a new project had put their hooks into him. He wanted to talk to the business partners in Valletta and arranged for someone to take him to the site of the new greenhouses. Ideally, he wanted to fly over the area, to get an idea of the topography, but was told there was some bad weather in the forecast, and a ground visit would have to do for now. Never mind, he said. He'd be there for a couple of weeks anyway. There was time for a flyover later.

His translator arrived and gave him the brief rundown of the government contacts he would be dealing with and their peculiarities. He had to read through the brief intro on local suppliers, electrical supply issues, and labor laws. By the time the evening rolled around, jet lag caught up with him, and he sat through dinner with his chin in his hand.

Al, if he needed him at all, would know how to get a hold of him, he thought. And if Al forgot, the sky-high bill of Rafael's wireless roaming charges surely would remind him where to find his friend. This had everything he wanted right now—the spark and intensity of a new project, testing his knowledge and experience in a totally new environment, against challenges he had never seen, and he couldn't wait to put boots on the ground.

With that thought in mind, he fell asleep, sure in the knowledge that either Al or Kayla would let him know if something were amiss back home.

FIVE

Greg Turner was on the move again.

Always stay on the move. Never linger more than a day or two in the same area. Avoid repetition and notice. Blend into your surroundings. He'd never had a need to prepare for being on the run, but now, certain things came as naturally as breathing. *Stay on the move.*

From the forest worker's shed, he had moved on to an abandoned factory building that was slated to be demolished. Its lower floors were populated by homeless vagrants, and he had no desire for company just then. A few had come around seeking to talk to him, but the look in his eyes had driven them off in a hurry. After a day on the crumbling top floor, he moved on, looking for shelter, protection and ideally access to electricity, to recharge the old phone in his pocket.

He had pulled it from someone's garbage pile behind an office building. It was a ridiculous old thing, but it worked, and it kept him up to date, as long as he found a place to plug it in and an unprotected wireless network. Moving around with the homeless and teenagers on a limited data plan, he found plenty of those. Things he would never have needed to know in his old life now became vital to his survival.

The new place he had discovered would serve him well for a while to come. On the edge of a tiny little village, he had found a neatly kept campground, closed for the season, and partially hidden in the forest once again. It had been so easy to break into one of the trailers stored on the site and to make himself at home. He would be fine here for a little while, and there would be no reason for anyone to come by. The fewer trips into town he had to make, the better it was.

Slipping a hand out of a glove, he turned on the old phone and watched the latest installment of Perfect Points. When the final fanfare sounded, he cursed loudly and threw the phone against the side of the trailer.

"Damn you," he shouted and instantly regretted throwing the phone. He couldn't afford to be careless with it. It was the one link to his sworn enemies.

***

The next day, Al made sure to arrive in the boardroom before everyone else and installed himself at the head of the table. Usually, he would wait before all of the directors had arrived, leave them a few minutes to chat, and arrive last, his secretary in tow. Today, it would not do to have them watch him shuffle along the corridor and into the room slowly and methodically, using a cane to keep his balance, taking a break with every other step.

After this meeting, he promised himself, even as he hid the cane behind the door, right after this meeting, his driver would take him to the nearest clinic. Once and for all, he needed to find out what was wrong with him.

He flexed the fingers of his left hand again and again, recalling the horror when he had woken this morning to find he could no longer use his left hand. He had panicked and fought the impulse to call Rafael right then and there. Then he'd wanted to call 911, the police if necessary, anybody who could help him, but when he reached for the phone, he found he could not move. He'd lain in bed in a cold sweat, panicking, until slowly, far too slowly, the feeling had returned to his body and eventually his fingers, and the thought that Greg Turner had caused his malaise faded.

That technology did not exist. Nobody could use some sort of flu bug to knock out an enemy. He had simply read too many spy novels.

But it was eerie that this should happen right at the moment when someone had sworn to take revenge on him.

Again, he flexed his fingers. *There, all good again*, he thought, knowing he was not fooling anyone but himself. This was no ordinary flu bug. Damn Thomas Donnelly for postponing this meeting, or he would already know what was going on, probably sitting with a stack of medicines, complaining about having to take them.

Just get through this meeting, that's all, just this one meeting.

Kayla arrived and sat beside him, and he gave her what he hoped would pass for a reassuring smile.

"Hey, Al," she said, the concern in her eyes telling him it was not working. "How are you feeling?"

"Oh, all right, you know." He waved his hand, the right one. "Just under the weather. I have an appointment once this meeting is finally done, but please don't…"

"I won't gossip. No worries. It's nobody's business here if you are unwell. I'm merely concerned, as is Rafael. Nobody would have taken it the wrong way if you had cancelled this meeting, and…"

"No need."

"Hey, everyone—oh, hi, brother, you're here already."

His brother Dante sauntered in and dropped into a chair on Al's other side. "Everything all right?"

"Fine," he sighed, resting his hands in his lap this time. "Why does everyone insist on asking me that, unless I look utterly dreadful?"

"Well now that you mention it…"

"Don't go there." Al glowered at his younger brother. "I'm battling a terrible cold, and I have no desire to hold up this meeting because of it."

"If you say so."

Dante uncomfortably shuffled in the seat beside Al and, as if on second thought, scooted his chair away from him just a little. *Fine,* Al thought, *be that way. At least you won't try to keep a close eye on me.*

His secretary distributed the agenda he'd sent her, giving him a bright smile and pouring water for him, and one by one, the other directors came in.

Preceded by his loud voice and bold mannerisms, he heard Thomas Donnelly coming down the hall, explaining fluid-handling principles to Barry, who was audibly less than amused.

Barry stopped when he walked in, narrowed his eyes, and checked Al head to toe, the kind of scrutiny that would have made him uncomfortable without the added issue of a bad cold. He sat up a little straighter and folded his hands.

"Can we get started then?" he snapped. "If everyone is done chatting and finds a seat, please. We have material to get through, and some of us had to rearrange their schedule."

He glowered at Thomas. "I am actually under some scheduling constraints, so I would like to dispense with the usual formalities. Let Connie know if there are any issues, errors, or omissions with the minutes of our last meeting. They are part of your package, as always. Then let's get to the main discussion. There is only one item on the agenda today."

"What's the sudden rush?" Thomas asked, pulling his meeting package closer without looking at it. "This expansion business is important, so let's take all the time we need to discuss this—in detail—if you don't mind. I for one want to make sure we make the right decision, not just any decision. Just because you and Rafael are in favor of it."

"Of course. My apologies."

His heart beat a mile a minute all of a sudden, and he was glad for the distraction of people in the room finding their paperwork and flipping through it.

With an effort, he reached for the remote control and brought the projection system to life. "If you will check—will check—the minutes from the last—meeting, please."

The room dissolved, like a pixelated image, and rearranged itself again. The light from the projector strobed and pulsed in his eyes.

Somewhere, there was an odd sound. Where did it come from? This was not a good idea. Not a good idea at all.

"Al?"

Someone called out to him, from the other end of a long corridor. Wait—what corridor? He put his hands on the armrests of his chair, steadying himself. Of course. He was still in the main boardroom. He was seated at the head of the table. Perfect Cannabis Corporation. The expansion plans. International expansion. His presentation… His presentation was right there, in the projector. All he had to do…

The remote control for the projector fell from his hand and clattered to the floor. Al bit off a curse. Massive waves rushed in his ears.

"So—so sorry, my apologies."

"Al?"

He bent down to retrieve the remote and felt the floor dropping away beneath him. A tunnel opened, dark and cold. He heard his name called one more time, and the darkness swallowed him.

***

"Al?" Kayla screamed, jumping up from her chair as Al collapsed at the end of the table.

His chair upended, dumping him on the ground, his fingers still reaching for the dropped remote. Kayla knelt beside him, supporting his head, but his eyes wouldn't open.

"Thomas, call an ambulance, now," she called into the boardroom, hating the panic in her voice. "Quick, Dante, help me straighten him up."

Dante pushed chairs out of the way and knelt beside his brother.

"What can I do?"

"Ambulance," Kayla called again, even though she already heard someone talk to them. Probably Thomas.

"The nurse—you guys have a nurse working down in the grow rooms, don't you?"

"Stephanie, yes. I'll page her."

Stephanie showed up within minutes, and Kayla's dread grew watching her work. Al was not moving. His eyes were closed, and he had dropped from his chair as if…

Don't go there, she reminded herself, *just don't*. Behind her, Thomas and Barry cleared the conference room for more space, and she could hear speculations flying around the room. Heart attack? Stroke? Did he have some sort of illness? Poison? Turner? Al didn't look well and had not over the last week or so. Could he have caught that serious flu that was going around? Something more dangerous? Dear God, was it infectious? And what if Turner…

"No speculations," Kayla hollered over them. "This stays in this room."

And she turned back to Al, cradling his cheek in her hand. *Stay with me, Al*, she prayed. *Stay with me—help is on the way.*

"Pulse is there," Stephanie said, trying to reassure her as she put Al into a stabler position on his side. "It's weak, but it's there. We need to get him to the hospital as soon as we can."

"On the way," somebody said. "Couple of minutes out. Cleared it with the front gate—they know where to go."

"Thank you," Kayla said, suddenly aware she could barely catch her breath, even though she was snapping orders at people. Total helplessness overwhelmed her as it never had before. She made a fist and forced a deep breath.

"Thanks, everybody."

A hand on her shoulder. Barry helped her to her feet, guided her into a chair, and steadied her, reaching for a glass of water. She had to hold the glass with two hands, to keep it from dropping.

"Kayla, you've gone stark white. Are you OK? Don't you collapse on me as well."

"I'm fine." Kayla shook her head and forced herself to sip the water. "I'm fine. What is taking this damn ambulance so long?"

"He's breathing, Ms. Montecito," Stephanie said, still holding Al's wrist, checking her watch. "Try not to panic, OK?"

"Please don't tell me not to panic. That's Al on the floor there, our CEO and my personal friend. I am—where is that goddamned ambulance?"

She didn't swear. Never. No one had ever heard Kayla Montecito swear in public, and right then, she couldn't have cared less. Every fear she had ever had clenched her heart in an iron fist.

"Take it easy." Barry squeezed her shoulder and put the glass of water to her lips once again.

"God, I don't need any…"

Just then, the door flew open. The paramedics rushed in and immediately began checking on Al. They called out terms to one another Kayla didn't understand, but she understood one thing—this was not good.

"Is he—going to be OK?" she asked, voice trembling, and the younger paramedic focused on her for a minute.

"Are you family?"

"I am," Dante said and came to stand beside Kayla. "Al is my brother. It's OK. What's going on with him?"

"For the moment, we don't know, Mr…?"

"Ivers. Dante Ivers."

"Thanks—for the moment, we don't know. Your brother appears to be extremely weak. We're going to monitor his vitals for a moment, give him some oxygen, and take him to the hospital. Did he suffer from any conditions, complain about anything over the last few days?"

"I…" Dante shrugged, embarrassed suddenly that he had no idea. He looked at Kayla.

"He's been complaining about a cold for a few days," Kayla said. "Kayla Montecito, Montecito Publishing."

That last bit she just threw in, just so the guy knew who he was dealing with. Not that she was in a habit of asking, *Do you have any idea who I am?* That was more Barry's style, but just then, any straw she could grasp at would do.

"This is no ordinary cold, Ms. Montecito. This man had a complete systemic breakdown."

"Ready?" the second paramedic asked, and the young man speaking to them nodded at Dante.

"Can you ride with us to the hospital, sir? We're going to need your brother's details and a little more of what happened here."

"Sure."

"Keep me updated, Dante," Kayla called after them and watched helplessly as they put Al onto a stretcher and rolled him out of the conference room.

Security had cleared the corridor. She sent a silent thank you to whomever had arranged that and sagged into a chair again, suddenly drained of the last bit of her own strength.

Barry's glass of water still stood at the edge of the table, and for want of something to do, she took it.

"This meeting is officially finished. I'm going to organize a driver to take you home," Barry said. "Unless there is somewhere else you'd rather go?"

"Give me a minute. God—I can't think right now. I'm going to have to call Rafael. He needs to know what happened here. He will be…"

"He'll be fine, and there is nothing he can do just now while he is in Malta. Why don't you wait until you at least know a little more? You know how he gets."

"Yes, but…"

"Rafael and Al are friends. I understand." Barry pushed her gently back into the chair when she tried to get up again. "Take it easy. Al is in the best hands at the moment. They will take care of him. Trust me. Everything they can do is being done for him."

Everything they can do suddenly had a somewhat ominous ring, and Kayla shivered a little and brought a hand to her mouth.

Thomas Donnelly had been hanging around the fringes of the group and stepped a little closer. Idly, he bent down and picked up the remote control Al had dropped and placed it squarely at the edge of the conference table, nudging it with his finger until it lined up perfectly.

"While you are busy being chummy and comforting one another," he said a little flippantly, "somebody in this place has got to mind the store. I seem to remember we are involved in the business of growing medical marijuana around here."

"Not now, Donnelly!"

"Not now? Yes, now, Wentworth! Since when do you make decisions in a company where you are not even employed? While we don't know what exactly happened to Ivers and when or if he will be able to come back…"

Kayla winced at the 'if,' and Barry suddenly straightened to his full height, which was considerable at six-four. He had been known to use it to intimidate those who irritated or annoyed him.

"I said—later," he said, enunciating every word carefully.

Thomas, however, refused to be cowed.

"And I said forget about later, Wentworth. You are not even a director around here. You are a consultant."

"I am one of the majority shareholders, and if you had any common decency, Donnelly, you…"

"Gents." Kayla raised her hands, took a deep breath, and got up from her chair. She brushed imaginary specks of dust off the front of her impeccable Balenciaga blazer and made a show of straightening her shoulders.

"Barry, thank you kindly for your concern. I truly appreciate it." She gave a sideways glance at Thomas Donnelly. "As much as it seems a bit callous to see Al in such a grave situation and to go on with business as usual, the story of what happened half an hour ago is going to be flying around this place at the speed of light."

"You see," Donnelly said, and Barry glowered at him.

"And after that, it will be all over social media. We cannot allow this to happen without directing the narrative."

Donnelly visibly glowed as if he could see himself in charge already, and Barry shot more angry glances his way.

"Prepare to do some damage control, please," Kayla said and put her hand on his forearm. "I am going to go down to that hospital right now, and I would appreciate it if you don't try to stop me."

"All due respect, Kayla, I wanted to call a driver to take you home just now. I really think you should…"

"Thank you, but I will feel better when I know what happened to Al and how he is doing. Who knows? He may be back on his feet in a few days again."

Barry smiled. "Indeed he may. Let's not assume the worst right away—Al is tough as nails, Kayla."

That elicited a little smile from her.

"Will you please talk to the IR fellow?"

"He is incompetent!"

"Please go talk to him, Barry. Help him prepare something useful and have it have ready when the questions come pouring in. I don't want to leave things to chance and casual gossip."

"Hey, wait." Thomas Donnelly turned on his way to the door and was back between them in three giant steps. "He doesn't even work here."

He shook a fat index finger at Barry, and just like that, Barry turned instantly like a striking snake, took the extended finger into his hand, and bent it away from his chest.

"'He' is a consultant in charge of fundraising and image, 'he' is a major shareholder here, and don't you ever—do you hear me?—ever point your finger at me again, Donnelly."

There was enough of a threat in his voice to make Donnelly look down at his feet. He pulled his hand away and rubbed his fingers.

"Well, I…"

"Thomas, please, we are all trying to do what's best for the company just now." Kayla put her hand on Thomas Donnelly's arm and gave him the brightest, most charming smile she was capable of just then. "Let's all just pull on the same rope for the moment, and we'll figure out chain of command as soon as we have more concrete information."

"I'm just trying to avoid people issuing multiple commands and confusing our staff. I'm trying to protect my people, Kayla."

"Our people. As well as you should. We need to speak with one voice. So please, go down on the floor, quash any rumors, keep people calm, and our IR department will be issuing a statement shortly. And you…"

She turned to Barry. "Please go and meet Jim Kaiser, even if you don't like him. Draft that statement and send it to the directors. We'll approve it, soon as we can. Let's get out ahead of this thing, people."

Barry nodded and waited a moment as Thomas Donnelly left the room. Then he softly clapped.

"Wow," he said when the door had closed behind him. "There's a 180. And just like that, you have things under complete control here."

"Oh, please, Barry. You know how it works. You get one minute to grieve, or to panic—then you do what you have to do to get where you want to go. Panic is a luxury we don't have."

"No, it's just… I'm impressed."

"Don't get me wrong. I am terrified for Al and what happened to him, or is going to happen to him, but if you expected me to be a damsel in distress, fall apart in front of everyone, and have to be helped to the door…"

"Then I was wrong, noted. Don't mess with the lady. So go—see Al, find out what's going on with him. Let me know when you have news."

He gave her hand a quick squeeze and rushed off in search of Jim Kaiser.

When she was finally alone in the room, Kayla allowed herself to exhale and let her shoulders drop. She took the chair that had toppled when Al collapsed and sat in it heavily.

Taking out her phone, she cancelled the remainder of her

appointments for the day and had someone come over to pick up her car, not being sure how long she'd be at the hospital.

Her finger hovered over Rafael's profile picture on her phone, and she dropped it again. It would be evening where he was, and he had told her earlier the group wanted to head out for dinner after their meeting. For some reason, she found herself reluctant to call him and give him the news about Al. Rafael would panic. He would fly into control mode and insist on coming home that very day; she knew him. As if there were anything he could do here at the moment.

For God's sake, what had happened to Al?

His heart was strong, he was a lean, fit man, he exercised regularly, he didn't smoke or drink to excess—there was no indication whatsoever heart disease would ever be a factor. Besides, the EMT had said his heart was strong. Heart disease didn't usually manifest symptoms of a flu or cold either.

"Either way, no point in sitting here, Kay. Get a move on," she said to herself and put her phone away.

Just another minute—one more minute of peace and quiet of this boardroom—and she would have someone drive her to the hospital. She couldn't wait to get an update, and she was afraid of it at the same time. Kind of sitting in the doctor's waiting room to get the results of a screening test when you had dark, frightening suspicions to begin with.

"Get a move on, now, Montecito."

She rose from the chair again and asked the ladies at the front desk to call a car and driver for her and made her way down into the lobby.

Perfect Cannabis Consolidated was buzzing around her. The mood had changed quite suddenly. People were tense, worried and anxious. She could feel it just by walking down the hall. Here and there, people stood in small groups, gossiping. Normally, she would have stopped to talk to them, but not today. She nodded a quick greeting and moved on.

SIX

At the hospital she walked into the lobby and stood there for a moment, disoriented. As usual, no one would give her any information about a patient, or even if Al had been admitted.

Just as she was reaching for her phone, one of the elevators pinged, and Dante stepped off and toward her, as if her worried thoughts had summoned him.

"Dante." She enveloped him in a quick hug. "What is new—have they found anything—what are the doctors saying—can I see him—when…"

"One thing at a time, Kayla." He took both of her hands and steered her into one of the seating areas around a few potted palms. "First off, for the moment, he is stable."

"Oh, thank God."

"However, he still hasn't regained consciousness." Dante settled back and brought his hands to his face, exhaling. For a moment he closed his eyes.

"How can that be? What on earth would cause something like this?"

"They have no idea." Dante forked his hands through his disheveled hair, failing to keep the fear out of his voice. "Not even the slightest. I've just spent the last half-hour answering questions from his doctors. His heart is fine, his breathing is fine, he is just extremely exhausted—and unconscious."

"I'm so sorry, Dante."

"Nothing for you to be sorry about."

"I know, but…"

"You're worried. You're his friend, and I appreciate it. I can't—Kayla, I felt so helpless watching him lie there, pale and still…"

Kayla took his hand and squeezed.

"He'll be fine. Somebody just told me Al is tough as nails."

Dante managed a weak little smile. "I sure hope so."

"Can I see him?"

Dante shook his head and buried his face in his hands again.

"I don't believe so—for a couple of reasons."

"Dante, I am still a journalist as well as holding a seat on the hospital foundation board. I can make things happen!"

"I understand that, Kayla, but for one thing, Al is still in intensive care, and for another, while they have no idea what caused this, and if it could be something infectious, they have him under strict quarantine."

"Quarantine?"

That one took the fight out of her for a minute. It drove home the point that what happened to Al could be part of something much more sinister than she had ever suspected. Something far more dangerous than a collapse or a nervous breakdown.

"Yes." Dante sighed and closed his eyes again for a moment. "I was allowed to see him through a plate-glass window for a little while, and believe me. There is no point going up there right now."

"Still."

"Kayla, I'm so afraid he's not going to make it. It doesn't look good."

Dante's voice broke, and for a moment, he closed his eyes and brought his hands to his face again, taking deep, steadying breaths.

That sentence slammed into Kayla as if a giant fist had struck her. *I'm so afraid he's not going to make it.*

She remembered Al—mysterious, silent Al Ivers who came to the first investors meeting of Perfect Cannabis and listened quietly and attentively without chatting or touching the offered food and drink.

Al Ivers, who always carried large amounts of cash in his pockets wherever he went, who lived in his father's shadow and under his control.

Al Ivers, who had just inherited all of Tadeo's shares in PerCan and finally stepped into his own, assuming the role of CEO. Al, whom she and Rafael considered their closest friend, even if his secrecy and extremely private manner sometimes drove them crazy.

Al, who could respond to the worst situation with his dry, pointed humor and take the sting out of the moment. He and Rafael could go out on the lake on that boat of his and spend hours merely sitting in silence and call it a great time.

Al Ivers—that Al Ivers. Full of life, giving her one of his rare smiles, whispering, 'So happy for you,' when she told him she and Rafael were engaged. That Al Ivers.

"He has to," she said, forcing a certainty she didn't feel. "We only had dinner a few nights ago, and he said he felt better. He said this—this thing was on its way out already. He has to be all right. You hear me?"

Dante only shook his head and spread his hands helplessly.

The door flew open with a bang, and someone came rushing in with a gust of wind, looked through the crowd left and right for a moment, and finally steered in their direction. Nick Ambrose, their head of agriculture, gave Dante a tight hug and greeted Kayla.

"How is he?" he asked breathlessly, as Dante shook his head.

"We don't know," Kayla filled in. "Nick, I really appreciate that you're here to support Dante, but what is going on at PerCan? The rumor mill must be running on high speed."

"It is, and it isn't." Nick dropped into a chair and ran his fingers through his hair. "I managed to counteract the rumor, telling people it was a plain old breakdown, and Al had been working too hard."

"That will only keep for a while until we figure out what's really going on. If we are lucky. I have IR working on an official statement already and…"

"Kayla." Nick raised a hand, palm facing her, stopping whatever she might have said. "Sorry to dispense with formalities, Kayla, but the company is the last thing on my mind right now. I don't care. What did Rafael think?"

"I have not told him yet. No time."

"Well then, I suggest you do." Nick seemed to get a bit bigger in his protectiveness of Dante. "Please."

"I will, but I wanted to wait until we find out what is really going on. I don't want to have Rafael ending his trip and rushing back over here, just to stand in this lobby with all of us, waiting."

Nick folded his hands, closed his eyes for a moment, and looked around, as if he expected someone—anyone—in the cavernous hospital lobby to be listening in on them. He sighed and shook his head.

"Fine. Have it your way. Might I suggest you have a chat with that detective then?"

"Robertson?" Kayla froze in mid-headshake. "What does he have to do with Al collapsing?"

Nick paused again, narrowed his eyes, and stared at her. One long, hard stare until she finally had to look away.

"If nobody else is going to say this, then I will," he said softly. "What if this has something to do with Greg Turner and his threats?"

Greg Turner. How could he be involved? There was absolutely no proof—this couldn't be true—you couldn't make someone as sick as Al was artificially—as far as she knew—there was no proof—Greg was on the run—Barry thought he was… Greg? Greg Turner?

The thoughts chased each other round and round in her head while Nick held her eyes steadfastly without flinching. A strangled sound escaped her throat and broke the spell, and Kayla coughed to cover the moment.

"I've never heard…" she finally said. "You can't. You can't give something like this to someone—can you?"

"You forget that I have a degree in biology, Kayla, and I am not willing to make that statement. I saw Al—this was not normal."

Kayla got up and walked away a few steps, pacing the length of the hospital lobby and back again. *You couldn't, could you?*

Nick seemed pretty sure—and he did have a degree.

She needed to talk to Rafael urgently, but by now, she had lost track of time, and it would be the middle of the night over there. There was nothing he could do anyway, nothing at all, and still, he would be furious if he were the last to find out what happened to Al.

She returned to their little group, sat down again, and dialed Rafael's number. No answer. Whether the phone didn't manage to connect or nobody picked up the line was not immediately obvious to her and added another worry to her already long list.

Now what was going on over there in Malta? Rafael had never—never ever—been out of touch for her. It was a rule they had ever since they knew he'd have to travel a lot more frequently. And it was the middle of the night. He should be lying in bed in his hotel room.

Stop panicking, she told herself. *Just stop.*

She shook her head in answer to Nick's inquiring glance and settled in for a long wait.

***

A little while later, a nurse came to fetch Dante for another chat with Al's physicians, and she watched him go, exhaustion and worry leaching from him with every step. Nick still sat a few feet away from her. He'd put some distance between him and Dante and her. She could all but feel the waves of resentment rolling off him. They'd never really warmed up to another—she always suspected it was because Rafael had to clue her in to the relationship between him and Dante. But that was ancient history. Why now, she wondered? Just because she hadn't bought into his Turner theory?

"Do you know how to get in touch with Roberto?" she asked, but he only shook his head. "I think someone should tell him, no?"

"Yes, of course, but I've only seen him once or twice in the last while.

Dante would be the one who knows how to get a hold of him, but he's out of his mind with worry right now."

"I can see that, you know." She hadn't meant to sound this rude, but exhaustion and concern took their toll on her as well.

"Listen, if you need to go back to work, I'm going to stay here for Dante," he said now. "You can—you know—get stuff done, if you feel you need to."

"Do you really think I would get any work done now? Why do you believe Turner could have something to do with Al's issues?"

"I don't know. I hope I'm wrong." Nick shook his head. "I mean, you do have one point—actually giving somebody a dreadful disease is a lot harder than it looks in the spy movies. And even when it can be done, it is prohibitively expensive and difficult to get right if you want to avoid hitting innocent bystanders as well."

"Marvelous." She snapped a magazine she had been staring at without reading back onto the side table. The soothing green of this environment was starting to go on her nerves. "That leaves us reduced to hoping that Turner—if he is involved—is a decent human being who wouldn't want to hurt anyone he's not actually vowed to kill."

"Just telling it as it is, Kayla. I don't know if Turner could have done this. Did he want to? Yes. Is it possible? Yes. Did he actually do it? I don't know."

"Marvelous."

"Al was—is—a healthy, fit man. There was no indication he'd ever had any heart issues, nothing to suggest any other major diseases."

"I know all of that, Nick, all right? I know. I don't get it either."

Kayla was just about to get up to continue pacing around the lobby when her phone pealed, and Rafael's picture appeared on her display. Thank God, at least one mystery solved.

"Rafa? Listen, I have some…"

Instead of his voice, she heard a distant roaring and hissing, as if a giant wave wanted to break over her.

"Rafael, I can't hear you. What's going on?"

"OK—fine—worry…"

He sounded farther away than ever, and the rest of his words were drowned out in the strange roaring sound she had heard. A high-pitched whistle pierced her ears, and Kayla clenched her hand around the phone to rein in her temper.

"Rafael? What is happening there? Say again?"

"…no—way…"

No way. Then the connection collapsed, and Kayla was left holding a silent phone. She unlocked the display and stabbed the redial button several times in quick succession—all without success. *The requested number cannot be reached at the moment.* She swore softly and fired her phone back into her purse.

"What's going on?" Nick asked, and with an effort, she kept her voice even.

"Don't know—that was Rafael. Looks like they have some connection issues over there. I just wish he hadn't gone."

Nick put his hands together and sighed.

"Why don't we not panic, Kayla? The worst has likely not happened and won't. Likely, the doctors will have an answer shortly, and everything will be fine."

Kayla nodded and took deep, steadying breaths. Rafael and Nick were friends, and Dante and Nick—well, Dante and Nick, enough said. It was all the comfort she was going to get out of him just now.

Perhaps he thought she was too focused on business, and she thought he was too much of a hippie. For the moment—for the moment, in that huge lobby waiting for answers, they were as distant as ever.

***

Greg Turner, huddled in his camping trailer, let out a long hearty laugh when he scrolled through the newsreels and the latest investor news from PerCan. Almost more important than the daily city updates was the latest gossip on the investor blogs concerning PerCan. All the gossip relating to the cannabis manufacturer could be found here—a gold mine. Turner laughed long and hard and punched his fist in the air as if he had just scored a major victory.

"Al Ivers taken to the hospital with unspecified condition," he repeated and laughed. "You see, Mr. CEO Al Ivers, there is justice in this world after all. I hope you are deathly ill. There is justice."

He leaned back and got comfortable, enjoying the images on his little phone screen. When the newsclip had ended, he reloaded it and watched it again, and again and again and again…

He had downloaded the short and, to most people, almost meaningless newsclip on his latest trip into town, just so he could see it as many times as he wanted. It became his lullaby.

SEVEN

In the massive, old-style beach hotel in Malta, Rafael Covin appeared to be on the warpath. If it were not bad enough to watch the weather roll in over the ocean, he hadn't been able to reach Kayla, and there didn't appear to be any way in this godforsaken five-star hotel to make this happen.

Where, pray tell, had they sent him, when making a simple phone call turned into an operation of several hours? And how did they expect him to put a proper operation together when this kind of thing happened and nobody knew how to deal with it?

He stomped down the stairs to the lobby, since the elevator was out of service as well for some unspecified reason, and pushed through a small crowd of tourists to the front desk.

"Excuse me," he said, just a little harried, and not at all the usual, gregarious, friendly Rafael. "Excuse me—I need to make a phone call, and the phone line in my room appears to be nonfunctional. I already tried the business center, but that is…"

"We have a storm coming in," the desk clerk said, smiling, as if that explained everything.

"Well, I understand that. I can look out the window, you know. I see the weather rolling in. All I want to do is make a phone call."

"Yes, sir. A communications tower must be out near here."

"But that shouldn't impact your landline, good man."

"I don't know, sir. I am very, very sorry, but I cannot help you at the moment. I—can't."

There was just enough panic swinging in the young man's voice that Rafael stopped himself from getting angry and snapping at him.

It wouldn't do any good anyway. They were kids at the front desk, and utterly ill-equipped to deal with—whatever was happening. Rafael stepped back into the lobby and brought a fist to his mouth. More guests poured in from their rooms, complaining that the phones didn't work, complaining about the elevator, and complaining about the weather outside. Storm—weather—something was going on in this place. Maybe some unsuspecting worker somewhere had simply unplugged the wrong thing, he thought, and chuckled at his own joke. Probably. It wouldn't surprise him.

OK. Not being able to get a hold of Kayla was an annoyance for the moment—a big annoyance—but no more than that. He would catch up tomorrow and explain it to her when that same worker plugged the unknown cable back in.

Meanwhile, he had an empty evening to fill. Rafael was wondering what to get up to and was startled when someone touched his arm. He found Rick Galatia, his interpreter and guide assigned to him by the ministry. When he first met him, Rick had been an exuberant and sociable man, overflowing with energy and a warm personality. But now, despite his dark hair and eyes, he appeared unnaturally pale, his typically olive complexion looking damp and clammy, and his hands shook with tremors.

"Rick, good, you're here. What's going on in this country when a little storm will knock out the phone lines, huh? And the elevator and heaven know what else. If that happens a lot, we'll have to make some provisions for our greenhouse."

He wanted to invite his guide to have a drink in the lobby bar to shoot the breeze for a bit, but again, he met the same seeds of panic he had heard in the desk clerk's voice. Glass splintered somewhere, and

Rick startled and turned another shade of white. A door flew open, wind pushing in palm leaves and debris before a hotel employee hurriedly forced it shut again. His guide suddenly trembled with unseen terror.

"Hey—easy—you're making me nervous," Rafael said, fighting the uneasy feeling that was forming in his stomach. "What's going on out there? They told me this country does not have tornadoes and sh—stuff?"

"They're calling it a Medicane, Rafael," Rick said, his voice shaking, his fingers clawing into Rafael's arm.

"A what?"

"Medicane. A hybrid tropical storm." Rick Galatia looked fearfully toward the nearest window.

"So basically, a bigass storm in a country that doesn't get bigass storms, great. Now what? We just wait it out?"

"We're taking all precautions, Rafael. It should miss us."

"It should? It should, or it will?"

"Winds in the city are almost 70 miles an hour, Rafael, and at least one funnel cloud was spotted—you see the rain out there."

"Flood of sins is more like it. But that's just… Hey, it's just rain, isn't it?"

"It'll be bad, Rafael. I've come to take you to the Town Hall Office. We have a more secure structure there."

"You're evacuating me?"

"No, no, no. Nothing like that. I am just taking you to a more secure location. This hotel is charming and traditional, but old and—well, we really don't want anything to happen to you. You are a guest of our government. Come, hurry now, please."

Rick took his arm and hustled him along, past the gawping tourists in the lobby who stood by the giant glass walls, watching the torrential rain and massive waves rolling over the beach. They were getting taller with each one.

Rafael knew enough about construction that he didn't want to stand right there by the glass wall if this weather got any worse, and the knot of dread in his stomach became just a little righter.

"I need to—let my wife know," he said, slowing down just enough so Rick had to pull him along.

He usually called Kayla his wife nowadays and found himself unreasonably glad that she hadn't been able to come along on this trip. If she had been in any kind of danger, he would have been standing on that reception desk, screaming at someone, demanding her safety. Better not think about it. All the same, he knew she would be frantically trying to get in touch with him after their aborted call half an hour ago.

If she as much turned on the TV and saw this Medicane thing—this tropical storm over this place where he was—she'd be just as panicked for his safety. And if she still couldn't get a hold of him… that wouldn't be pretty either.

"We don't have time for that right now, Rafael, hurry."

"Look, I'm not going anywhere until…"

"We need to leave right now. Right this minute," Rick suddenly shouted, and in his wide, terrified eyes, Rafael finally saw the true extent of his panic.

"You have your phone with you, don't you?" he asked, and Rafael nodded, finally moving along.

"Yes."

"Then just come along—there may be reception in town. Keep trying, but we really have to leave right now, before…"

Before. A massive wave broke out at the barrier reef and rolled in with thundering, unstoppable force. Some of the people standing by the window screamed, and others laughed and snapped pictures, but the wave stopped just short of the glass front of the hotel, licking greedily at the foundations. And another one was building out there. Rafael shuddered. This time, he didn't linger and allowed Rick to pick up the pace.

"I wouldn't stand out there by that glass wall," he called out to a group of women who had a moment ago been videoing the spectacle for their social media feeds, and minutes later, Rick was gunning a massive Land Rover through the flooded streets toward town.

Phone reception continued to fade in and out just enough to make placing an actual call difficult, and Rafael kept thumbing the redial button on his phone. At some point, he thought, at some point the damned line had to connect—it had to—and he would finally be able to get a short message through to Kayla.

He looked up once, saw palm trees bending so deep their crowns touched the road before them, and chose to continue dialing. Rick had his hands clenched on the steering wheel, and his foot mashed on the accelerator, just as a wooden crate came bouncing down the road, struck the Rover, and rolled off into the dark. Rafael looked down at the screen again. *Come on, phone line.*

Back in town, his guide simply stopped the car in front of a massive, squat government building where they had sat through some meetings earlier that day and hopped out without bothering to take the keys or lock the doors.

"Come on," he shouted, and Rafael was just undoing his seatbelt when he saw the phone line finally connecting.

"Kayla, listen to me," he shouted. "We have a little storm situation here. I'll be out of touch for a bit but perfectly fine. I love you, OK?"

"Rafael—Al collapsed—hospital now, not sure—survive."

A gust of wind slammed into him, the phone dropped from his hand, and the call disconnected again. What—wait… Al had collapsed? Did she say she was not sure he would survive? Were those her words?

Rick pulled hard on his arm again, and Rafael stumbled along, downstairs to a designated safe area. Finally, a giant wooden door slammed shut behind them with a resounding boom. Almost at the same moment, the signal on his phone dropped to zero, and the screen went blank. No matter how much Al needed him, he wouldn't be able to be of any help to him right now.

***

Kayla paced her office and finally flung the quarterly sales report she'd been holding into a corner, where it landed flat against a credenza and split into disconnected loose pages.

Nick and Dante had finally convinced her that she was not doing anyone any favors by pacing up and down deserted hospital corridors all night, waiting for news. They were here to do that already. Dante was there because he was AL's brother, and Nick would not leave Dante's side no matter what. They did not need her there, maybe not even want her there.

She'd seen the two of them together, and maybe she should have figured it out much earlier that it was more than a shared love of cannabis plants that connected them. Rafael had. But she had felt like the third wheel at the hospital—Nick and Dante had each other, and no one had said a word to her for the last half-hour or so.

She needed Rafael to be here, to talk her out of her spiraling thoughts, to hold her hand and tell her to get real—but that was not going to happen either. When she finally reached him, it had been for a grand total of maybe 30 seconds.

Apparently, the country that didn't have tropical storms experienced a tropical storm right then. Mother Nature just had a fine sense of humor today.

In all her concern about Al, now she still worried about Rafael, too. Every time she thought about it, images of tropical storms she had seen on the news flitted through her mind, clenching her gut with an iron fist. What if something happened to Rafael while he was over there? What if something happened to both Rafael and Al?

Breathe, she ordered herself, made a determined fist, and blew out a breath. Her phone rang, and she answered with a sigh.

"Yes?"

"Hey! If I know you, you are pacing your office with incessant worry, spiraling down a long list of what-ifs," Barry said, and if she had had her way, she would have taken his chipper demeanor and shoved it…

"Naturally, I am concerned," she said coolly instead. "Was there something you needed?"

"I just want to talk you out of worrying—and I need to get your support to run PerCan for a while. Worrying is not going to do any good right now. Both Al and Rafael are in the very best…"

"Whoa, whoa, back up the truck here, Barry. What do you mean you want to get my support to run PerCan for a while?" Kayla sat down hard and rolled her shoulders. "What is this all about then?"

Alarm bells went off in her head, loud and clear. Barry J. Wentworth, master of the underhanded move! She could just see him, sitting there in the swanky hotel suite he called his home nowadays, working out a plan in his mind how he could make PerCan his own again. That he should try to get her support—that was just sheer chutzpah on steroids.

"No, it's Donnelly!" Barry said, trying in vain to hide his dislike of the man. "He took over running the company after they took Al away."

"He was taken to the hospital, Barry," she said mildly. "Not 'away.' And naturally, Thomas Donnelly should have taken over. He is VP of operations after all, and he used to own half of the company."

"Before the merger."

"Before the merger, that is correct. And is there a particular reason why you are trying to change this, now of all times?"

"Because nobody likes him, Kayla. He's been in charge less than a day, and already…"

Kayla shook her head and mentally counted to 10 slowly. Oil, water—Barry Wentworth, Thomas Donnelly. Some days, the rivalry could be amusing. Most of the time, it was merely annoying, like an irritating background noise. Right now, it bordered on disturbing.

"I understand that you don't like him, Barry," she corrected. "But by God, as a board, and as a company, we have other things to worry about right now than who doesn't like the CEO."

"It's not just me. Nobody likes him, the floor is in disarray, people are arguing, I can't get my job done…"

Here we go again, Kayla thought. Something about the current situation affected Barry and he didn't like it, so he started a war over it. *I can't get my job done.*

"Then grow up, Barry," she snapped. "And deal with the situation as best as you can. None of us are exactly dancing a jig with Al in the hospital, unconscious, and Rafael caught in a tropical storm out of contact, all right? It's just something we have to deal with."

"Well, you don't have to snap at me." He sounded downright insulted. "And I am thinking about the company. Who knows how long it's going to take before either Al or Rafa are back on their feet?"

"Don't go there, Barry. I am not in the mood to be sparring with you today," she said. "Meanwhile, have you been in touch with Roberto?"

"Me? Why would I talk to the man?"

"Because you and he were friends, at least a little while ago."

"Letting Roberto know something is wrong with his brother is Dante's job," Barry said. Oh yes, he definitely sounded insulted.

"Fine. Let him find out in the news, if that's what you prefer. Never mind that we are shorthanded in all areas, never even mind the rumors that Greg Turner potentially had something to do with Al's—problems."

For a moment, Barry said nothing. He usually skirted the issue if anyone asked him whether he felt any kind of remorse in having all but incited Greg Turner to murder Tadeo Ivers—with the help of Roberto, presumably.

I had nothing to do with it. How was I supposed to know the man would go insane over a story that's over 30 years in the past… And so on, and so on.

Kayla said nothing and waited him out.

"Fine," he finally snarled. "I'll talk to him. But he runs his own cannabis business by now, you know. If he thinks we are weak, he might just decide to come after PerCan."

"I'll keep that in mind. Now please."

She hung up the phone and squeezed her eyes shut for a moment. Thomas Donnelly was an engineer by trade and by heart. No doubt leading people had never been his first skill, and potentially, Barry had a minor point, and she did need to go and talk to him about giving their staff some slack.

Later. Later. When she knew what was going on.

Her private line rang almost instantly again, and she picked it up, ready to snap at Barry—when she read the number. The local hospital.

"Yes, hello," she said, heart hammering in her chest. "Is there any news about Al Ivers?"

Silently, she said thanks to Dante, who had left a message she was to be kept up to date about Al Ivers's condition at all times.

"Mrs. Montecito?"

"Yes. What is happening? Do you have an update?"

"Not yet. It is Terry Brooks from the hospital."

"I can see that. How is Al Ivers?" she asked, already impatient with the man's awkward manner and way of speaking. He paused for a long moment, and she could almost see him shaking his head.

"I'm afraid his condition is unchanged."

Unchanged. Meaning he still hadn't regained consciousness, still didn't breathe on his own, or speak, or…

"But you must know something, or you wouldn't have called me."

"I'm afraid we do."

Kayla's heart sank, even though the man did not elaborate. *I'm afraid we do*—nobody calling to give you good news led with a sentence like that. Nobody. She forced herself to keep breathing evenly and focused on a print on the wall, dropping her pen from her fingers.

"Go on."

EIGHT

"Rick, there has got to be a way to get me out of here," Rafael said for the hundredth time. "I know there's a storm out there and all."

"Government regulations. We are all supposed to stay put here until the situation is stabilized."

"I know you don't know this," Rafael said, undeterred. "But I've been through storms a lot worse than this, OK? I own a construction company—at least I used to—and I did a stint for a few years with a technical aid agency. We'd go into places like this and help. Anything and everything. War zones, floods, storms, that kind of thing. So, I actually know what I'm doing."

Technically, he had only been a consultant, and technically, he had only volunteered for a short stint, before the bureaucracy got to him and he left in a huff, but still…

"I didn't know that, Rafael, but we were told…"

"We were told to stay put—you said that." He could barely keep the irritation out of his voice, and only for the benefit of his one local guide. "You don't understand. I have got to get home."

Rick shook his head.

"My best friend and business partner collapsed. My wife can't get a hold of me. To say that the roof is on fire at home would be an understatement. Rick, please. Lives are at stake."

"I empathize with you, Rafael—but I cannot let you leave. Not until the all-clear has been given. Lives are at stake here as well. Please understand."

Rick sounded as desperate as Rafael felt, and with a flash of anger, he turned away and stalked down the hall of the cavernous, underground building he found himself in. Some sort of government bunker no doubt. Built who-knew-when as a safeguard against who-knew-what. As a representative of a foreign business interest, he was to be kept 'safe.' Safe and locked up. Damn it to hell and all back.

Still. He had not done anything wrong. He was not in jail, correct? If he chose to find a door accidentally to see what was behind it, who could keep him locked in somewhere he clearly didn't wish to be? Nobody!

Any way he could—he was getting out of there. No matter what.

Kayla had sounded desperate. And as much as he didn't have any of the exact details—except that Al had collapsed—he had to assume the worst. Greg Turner, that triple-damned criminal, had managed to do something horrible. It was the only thing it could be. Ergo, he had to get out of here.

He plunked down in a deep, comfortable club chair and folded his arms as if he were relaxing, while all the time checking the room with narrowed eyes. They appeared to be in some sort of library or clubroom, two exits, including the one they had come through.

Rick had gone off to get some food or drink, and everyone else under government protection appeared content to discuss the tropical storm, enjoy canapés, and wait it out. Everyone else did not have a friend at home who had just collapsed and a wife running in frantic circles.

Was he right to suspect Greg Turner, or was it a coincidence? What else could have made Al collapse all of a sudden? An illness? Some sort of accident? Al liked to call himself healthy as a horse.

They'd never spoken much about health—heck, guys just didn't do that—but he was not aware of any chronic illness Al might carry around. And would he even know? With a guilty pang Rafael realized that he knew many things about Al, but not if he were taking any medication on a regular basis, had a weak heart, or just high blood pressure.

Some friend he was.

Oh, get real, he scolded himself. Guys did not habitually sit down and talk about health issues the way women did. Unless you maybe had a knife sticking out of your body somewhere—that might cause some attention.

Heart attacks happened all the time, right? Wasn't Kayla always going on about that?

God, he was driving himself nuts. Rafael got up out of the chair, took a beer off a sideboard, and opened the bottle, popping it on the edge of the table. He took a healthy draft and wiped his mouth. Some lady in a starched uniform passed him and gave him the side eye because he hadn't bothered with a glass. Desperate times, right?

He ambled over to the wide double doors through which they had entered and opened one of them, peeking out into the hall. An attendant-slash-guard was all over him on the inside of 10 seconds, asking if he needed anything.

"Just—curious about the architecture." Rafael grinned. "Nothing serious, thanks."

The Maltese government apparently took their duties quite seriously, not letting foreign business contacts wander around outside in the middle of a tropical storm. Fine then. He'd find another way.

He ambled over to the other door, and the attendant kept a wary eye on him. He'd have to get a lot craftier if he were going to…

"Planning your escape?"

Rick appeared again beside him with a plate of food.

"Here, find a seat. Have something to eat. I promise we will make your time here enjoyable until it is safe to go outside again."

"Mmmm." Rafael chafed at being so transparent. "Should have known you and an army of goons would keep an eye on me."

"And what were you going to do outside, Rafael? Walk? On foot through what is going to turn into a full-blown tornado any time soon? I can guarantee you—you won't find a car out of the city or an airplane out of the country until this is over."

"I know." Rafael picked at his food. "Still—I can't just sit here while my wife and my best friend are struggling."

"I don't see how you can do anything else. We are cut off for the moment." Rick dug into his food—some sort of Mediterranean curry or stew—with great gusto. "This is really good, Rafael. Humor me. Try some."

Rafael took a few bites and had to agree.

"The company," he finally said. "The company is probably in disarray as well with our CEO ill."

"Surely you have a vice president?"

Rafael rolled his eyes. "Yeah. Nobody really likes him all that much. He's a bit of an—unbiddable fellow."

Rick frowned, struggling with the word.

"He can be a bit crude," Rafael explained. "And then there is Barry, likely working out some underhanded scheme… But that's all company internal, likely bore you half to tears anyway."

"Please do continue. It sounds like a fascinating story," Rick said, smiling, and Rafael dug into his curry again.

It really was good. But he was wasting his time. And he really did need to be more careful what he was telling this man, who might be involved in the future cannabis enterprise they intended to build here.

"How long do you think this storm will last?" he asked instead, looking around at the people who were still coming into the library. Foreign diplomats, businesspeople, all of them looking frightened and disheveled to some degree, and all of them considered important enough to find refuge here in this bunker. He would have preferred to be out there!

"Who can know Mother Nature?" Rick said, smiling, and bobbed his head, and Rafael bit off a pithy cussword.

"I was wondering if we were expected to spend the night here in the library," he said pointedly.

"We are hoping before nightfall it will be safe enough to assess your hotel and decide on further safety measures. But then again…"

"Who can know Mother Nature?" Rafael finished sarcastically. "You already said that. Any satellite uplink or other way to communicate in here?"

He had rarely felt any more helpless in his entire life, not even when Tadeo Ivers had blackmailed him into taking the CEO position at PerCan and tasked him with saving a company that hardly showed any life signs—or else. At least back then he had something to do.

NINE

Kayla all but ran into the office of the clinic director when they asked her to come in. There, in a small, out-of-the-way waiting room, she found Dante and Nick, sitting close together, talking in hushed voices. Nick had draped a protective arm around Dante's shoulder and glowered when she entered. On a functional basic couch sat two men in white doctor's scrubs and the clinic director who had called her.

"What's happening with Al?" she asked the moment the door closed behind her, without waiting for introductions, dispensing with a simple greeting.

The clinic director looked at Dante, who nodded softly.

"Mr. Ivers," he said slowly, "was diagnosed with a serious, system-wide infection."

"An infection," she said, a little confused. "All right, but that kind of thing is treatable nowadays. We have antibiotics, we have medications, we have all sorts of things—don't we? PerCan is a big name in the medical space. Infections are no longer…"

"This particular infection," one of the doctors interrupted, looking at her over the rims of his glasses, "is completely unknown to us. And so far, we have not found any of its markers in the usual medical databases."

"Unknown." Kayla sat down hard on a chair. "But where would he have… Doctor, where does something like this come from? Could somebody have deliberately given this to him—somehow?"

Both the doctors and the clinic director looked at her from narrowed eyes without speaking. Finally, one of them cocked his head.

"That is exactly the same thing Mr. Ivers here asked when we told him. Would somebody care to fill us in on what is going on here, or why this particular question is the first thing that comes to mind?"

Kayla looked at Dante and back to the medical professionals. Dante stared at his hands, and the doctors waited for her.

"Somebody swore revenge on Al," she finally said. "I am talking serious revenge. That person killed his father. So, you see, it is not all that farfetched. Now, could somebody have somehow contrived to infect him with this—unknown virus?"

"I know," one of the doctors sighed. "We've already been made aware of this theory about a revenge angle and a deliberate attack."

"And?"

"And—it would take some serious skills and resources to do so, Miss Montecito. I know they say you can find a tutorial for anything and everything on the internet nowadays, but this would take some extensive medical knowledge and experience in biology, virology, and a host of other specialties I won't get into." He shook his head and folded his hands gently. "No, unless the person you are suspecting is a professor at one of the highest-ranked universities in this country, I do not think this would be possible."

"I don't know if that makes me feel better or worse."

"We are here to find the source of this infection, Mrs. Montecito, and to eliminate it. What we need in order to accomplish this is for everyone to help us do so. Dante has already given us a lot of information. Perhaps you can fill in what happened at Perfect Cannabis in the days before Mr. Ivers fell ill and, after that, at your house, I understand."

"My fiancé, Rafael Covin, owns the house," she said, mechanically, shaking her head. "Al was a dinner guest. That's all. Wait just a moment. Are you telling me this—whatever it is—could be at PerCan or at our home?"

"It's possible the source is there, yes."

"Oh, dear God, that's the last thing we need. We are a publicly traded pharmaceutical company, Doctor. If even the slightest suspicion gets out that there is a dangerous infection on the loose in our growing areas…"

"It's not. No, no way. Al hardly ever comes down to the grow pods." Dante shook his head. "And if anything were going on in either Growing or Packaging, Nick and I would be affected. We've been tested already. Besides, we do comprehensive daily safety and spot checks. We run a clean facility. Nothing lives in our grow area we don't know about."

Kayla exhaled with sudden relief. God, she needed Rafael to help her figure this out more than ever.

"Good. That's good to hear," she said mechanically. "But that doesn't mean…"

"That doesn't mean your facility is in the clear. You are correct in assuming that viruses like this live and mutate in very specific environments," the doctor added. "It's not something you can just pick up from a box of stationery or a piece of equipment. Nevertheless, we will have to do a complete run of tests at PerCan to rule the company out as a source."

Kayla rested her forehead in her hands and sat for a moment. She'd have to inform the board and the employees, and they'd have to do a bang-up job stopping this news from getting out into the hands of the media, or the hedge funds would have a field day shorting their stock—again. Companies had been ruined by less than that. Her job had just become 10 times more difficult. And that was assuming there really was no source of infection at PerCan. If they found something…

"Wouldn't other people have caught this?" she asked. "I mean—why only Al?"

"We're going to be testing you, Mrs. Montecito, as well as everyone else who was in close contact with Al Ivers. That should help narrow things down."

"It's going to be a bit hard to get a hold of Rafael just now. He is in Malta, stuck in a tropical storm, completely out of reach."

The doctor didn't seem to like her answer.

"You can start with me, our board, Al's office, and the boardroom—that ought to keep you busy until we manage to get in touch with Rafa," she said, realizing that she was sounding somewhat snippy, not caring one bit.

"I assume Dante has given you permission to run tests in Al's home?"

One of the doctors nodded slowly, although his facial expression told Kayla he really didn't think it was any of her business.

"I am asking you to work with us here," Kayla said, flashing a bit of anger at him now. "We employ several hundred people at PerCan—as cruel as that may seem to you, don't you think if the infection originated within the company, more than the CEO would be sick?"

"Yes, but still…"

"Yes, but still. I understand you want to protect people. Trust me—so do I. They are my people and my employees. I know them, and I like them. I am not asking to cover up anything. I am only asking for your cooperation to avoid destroying a company and millions of dollars in shareholder value. Surely, you can see my point."

The clinic director knew exactly who Kayla Montecito was. He was quite familiar with Montecito Publishing through their stories, their magazines, and, not the least, through the regular donations the publishing house made to his hospital.

He folded his hands and nodded softly.

"We all have the same goal, Mrs. Montecito. For the moment—OK. Tell me. What do you suggest?"

"I am suggesting we let our agronomists here do the tests within our company." She held up a hand when one of the doctors wanted to interrupt her. "These are people holding the required degrees and the knowledge required. I can guarantee you they will do a thorough and qualified job. I stake my reputation on it."

"Not a chance…"

"Meanwhile, you concentrate on tracing Al's actual movements and contacts—the people and places we know of. If you need assistance, I can get you all of the help you need through the publishing house."

Nick looked at her, and for once, there was no anger in his eyes, and Dante reached over to give her hand a little squeeze.

"Thanks, Kayla," he said. "Thanks for everything—we knew we could count on you."

"From what I understand, you are not even the interim CEO of PerCan," one of the doctors said. "I am not even sure you are authorized to speak on behalf of the company right now."

"You let that be my problem, why don't you?" Kayla rolled her shoulders and straightened just a bit. "I will sort out competencies within our board. I am promising you right now there will not be a problem."

Finally, the remaining doctor who hadn't spoken until now rose. "I for one am not happy with this."

Kayla flashed a cool look at him, and the clinic director stepped between them before she could open her mouth.

"There have been no other infections, other than Mr. Ivers. If we get started right now and work as fast as we can, we can get a handle on this problem without causing widespread panic beyond PerCan. Mrs. Montecito…" He smiled at her carefully. "I am willing to work with you right now, for all of the reasons you mentioned, but you do realize if there is only one more infected person, only one more tiny trace of this virus anywhere, we will have to go to the public and roll out…"

"The whole program—as painful and ruinous as it will be. I understand," she said, exhaling deeply. "Thank you. Believe me. I am grateful for the cooperation you are giving me this far."

She pressed her palms together hard, raised an eyebrow, and cocked her head at Dante and Nick. "Nick, I think you should get all of the testing parameters and protocols from these gentlemen and get started the moment your feet hit the floor of the grow rooms. Dante, if you want to stay here with Al…"

"I would love to, but I think I need to do something useful, something that will actually help," Dante said and tried to sound positive, although he failed grandly. "I'm going to work with Nick. But I'd like to see Al one more time."

One of the doctors opened his mouth to speak, and Dante shook his head and waved him off. "I know, I know. He won't be able to respond. I'd just like to see him anyway."

"I was going to say he's been moved to an isolation ward until we figure out the manner and way of infection," the doctor said. "But yes, you can see him briefly."

Kayla clenched her hands together to keep from jumping up and down, screaming *me too, me too*. It wouldn't help anyone, but if she could—if she could, she would gather all of her strength right now and send some down to Al.

"Tell him I said hi," she said to Dante on a long exhale. "And he needs to straighten up and get out of here. I really need him to help me deal with this board."

Dante squeezed her hand again to say he understood, and she left to deal with a board and a set of directors who would be none too happy about all of the solo decisions she had made in the last half-hour and the assurances she had given.

I did what I thought was best. They will just have to deal, she reminded herself and straightened her shoulders.

When she had inherited Montecito Publishing after the death of her first husband, she had learned to be tough and, if she couldn't be tough, act like it until she made everyone else, including herself, believe.

Straight out of a club that might have belonged to Tadeo Ivers, into a fairy-tale life with a wealthy publishing magnate husband, nothing had prepared her for the opposition she faced every single day, seeking to break her spirit. And those had just been her husband's enemies. His friends had been worse—so much worse. But she had learned. And usually, those opposing her had figured out rather quickly how well.

Kayla left a message with her assistant at Montecito that she wouldn't be back for the rest of the day and drove back to PerCan. Thoughts, feelings, and emotions bounced around in her head like ping-pong balls—confusion, excitement, fear, concern, dread—all at the same time.

The doctors had thrown every test they could at her and finally given her the green light. She was clear; she wouldn't have to worry about the virus being inside her. That was one worry allayed—but what about Rafael? If this thing could travel, if he had picked up something before he left, he would now be somewhere in a foreign country in the middle of a storm, out of reach, not knowing what he was dealing with.

Don't think of that, she repeated to herself as a personal mantra. *Don't think of that right now.* One step at a time. She still had a massive bit of work ahead of her.

And the first step in this massive bit of work would be to convince the rest of the board of directors to fall in line with her. In her heart she knew that she had done the right thing, the best thing for the company, but what would Thomas Donnelly have to say about all of it? He would not appreciate her ad hoc decisions and actions—and what about the rest of the board? Who knew where their loyalties lay, who knew what they would decide? They might just vote to dump her, along with Rafael, altogether.

Ridiculous—don't think of it, she repeated. *Don't think of it.*

***

She had Al's assistant call the remaining members of the board together and now sat in the boardroom, her face even and unconcerned, breathing deeply and evenly, forcing the warring emotions and anxieties inside her to stay down.

The meeting is of utmost urgency, her message had said, and one by one, they came into the boardroom, some worried, others merely annoyed.

Thomas Donnelly swept in last, full of his usual swagger and bluster, making everyone aware that his time was precious and it was being wasted right here with a meeting he had not called or prepared.

"What's going on here, Kayla?" he asked, almost immediately rounding on her, then added a little afterthought. "Is there any news about Al?"

"Yes, there is, and it is not good. Please listen to what I have to say without interrupting. Then we can make some decisions together."

"Well, isn't that highly unusual and new—making decisions together," Thomas grumbled, but he couldn't really tell her off without looking like a massive jerk, so he settled for glowering and making plenty of disruptive noises and gestures.

"Thank you." Kayla rose, rubbing her chilled hands, and everyone in the boardroom realized that whatever was coming was bad—more than bad.

She told them what she had just heard in the hospital and what she had done about it, and, just as she had expected, Thomas Donnelly jumped to his feet the moment she finished and spread his hands.

"What? You did what? For God's sake, Kayla, what gave you the right to make assurances and take action on behalf of this entire board without so much as consulting us? Who the hell do you think…?"

"Thomas, please," Clint said. "I'm trying to get my head around what I just heard, but I really believe Kayla did the right thing."

"That doesn't mean she can fucking act on behalf of all of us, commit this company to a course of action without us, now does it?"

"Thomas, I am well aware this is highly unusual," Kayla said, "but perhaps you could pipe it down a bit. There is no reason for the employees walking by the boardroom hearing you swear."

"The hell with what they hear. Where are Nick and Dante anyway? This meeting is not good enough for them? They've already made you CEO of this company? You and Rafael? Did you grab them at the hospital, have a quick private meeting, and pull them on to your side? That would be like you—and Wentworth."

Back and forth it went, Thomas cursing at her and Kayla calmly giving him answers that laid out all of the reasons why she had done what she had done.

Clint agreed with her, Jim Kaiser, their Investor Relations director, agreed with her, Dante had sent word that he agreed with her, and, finally, even Thomas ran out of arguments.

"What did you expect me to do?" Kayla finally said, hanging on to the remaining shreds of her patience and composure. "I could have let them launch a giant virus testing program here, alerting the public health departments and the media, and our customers and investors, and just hope the fallout would not be detrimental. Hope the company would survive. Yes, I agree. I could have done that. And yes, I chose not to. My apologies. I felt the damage to the company might be irreversible."

She folded her hands in front of her and refused to take her eyes off Thomas. *Do it*, she challenged him with her eyes. *Do it—try and destroy me and my reasoning, and see who agrees with you. Just stand up and do it already.*

In the end they all voted to go along with the direction Kayla had already set out and committed to. She sat back in her chair and rested her forehead in her hands. Clint touched her shoulder on his way out, and she managed a little smile.

"Thanks for thinking on your feet," he said, winked, and gave her shoulder a little squeeze.

Finally, it was only Thomas and her left in the boardroom, and he sat there glowering at her for a while.

"Nice work, Montecito. How did you manage to get everybody to go along with you, making me look like a cold, callous idiot?"

Kayla shook her head and sighed. "I've said everything I had to say, Thomas. I would make the same decisions all over again every day. Right now, I am sorry—I don't care who looks bad and who looks good, whose feelings are hurt, and who should have been consulted in a perfect world on a perfect day. I don't have the energy to do so. My main concern is and always was Al, followed by this company and all of the people who work here."

"Oh, for God's sake."

The door to the boardroom suddenly opened, and Kayla looked up to see Barry. "Is it true?" he said without a greeting. "About Al—what I heard—is it true? Sorry I couldn't make the meeting. I was with a client and out of touch until 20 minutes ago."

Kayla tried to catch him up when Thomas interrupted with his usual bluster.

"She went over everyone's head and acted as if she were the god-damned CEO of this company is what she did, and don't give me any more excuses. It's as plain as that. And you're not even on the board, so I don't know why you bother."

"It's a good thing she did," Barry said when Kayla had filled in the broad strokes. "The one thing this company does not need is a massive media shitstorm. What were you going to do, Donnelly, sit here and twiddle your thumbs and tell people how you were not involved?"

"The hell with you, Wentworth—I do not..."

"Gentlemen, gentlemen." Kayla raised her hands, tamping down the flaring emotions. "Let's not do this again. Barry, I suggest you run down to Nick and Dante and see how far they have got testing this facility and everyone inside it for this horrible mysterious virus. Don't forget to have them run the tests on yourself at the same time. So far it looks like we are lucky—as of right now, there are no traces of this in here anywhere. Let's stay on it."

"Thank God." Barry put down a portfolio he was still holding and gave Kayla a quick hug. "Jesus, an unknown virus. Why Al and nobody else? Where would he have picked this thing up, and what on earth is it?"

"All unknown at the moment," she said, shaking her head. "Don't think I haven't asked myself those very questions over and over. There are no answers. That's the frightening part."

Donnelly grumbled an unintelligible answer, but a sharp look from Barry shut him right down.

"Tell me, have Nick and Dante tested you already, Thomas?" he said, fake sweetness and concern in his voice. "What did they find? Let me guess… They came up with 99 percent acid with a sprinkling of bullshit, no?"

"You and the horse you rode in on, Wentworth," Thomas snapped, but he did as asked and stalked off, presumably to see Nick and Dante.

Barry sat down beside Kayla and put a hand on her shoulder.

"You do needle him," Kayla said. "For the sake of everyone, turn it down a bit, will you? I don't need a war around here on top of everything else."

Barry folded his hands and glowered at her. "He deserves it. This is a nightmare, one end to the other. We need answers. We need to come up with a plan, or we might as well close up. There will be no tomorrow."

"What would you have me do, other than testing every person and every item in this facility?" Kayla asked and threw up her hands. "We are working on that. Nothing—nothing anywhere. I don't know what else…"

"I'm not only talking about that damned virus, although that is a massive disaster. I'm talking about Donnelly and his ideas about corporate leadership. He is—oh my God—he is filled with total bullshit. That can't have escaped you."

"He can be overbearing, true."

"Overbearing? Overbearing, Kayla? Overbearing would be calling Jim Kaiser a loser, which I have been accused of doing many a time, even though it is factually correct."

"Barry, please." She pushed her fingers into her temples, trying to stem the headache that was forming there with a vengeance.

"Donnelly's so-called leadership style consists of seeding rumors, causing discord and suspicion, which is divisive, ruins morale, and causes unrest among the employees. Do you need me to go further? It will eventually ruin the company."

"I understand."

"Do you really? Donnelly is enjoying his temporary role as CEO while running the company like his very own fiefdom and everyone in it as his underlings. I have no idea how things run in a publishing house, but this company produces medical-grade cannabis, and that can only be done safely and efficiently if everyone works together. Trust and understanding. Rafael used to pound that into me until I was sick of it."

"What do you want me to do, Barry?" Kayla slapped her hand on the table and flashed him one of her famous looks. "I can't very well fire Donnelly. The rest of the board is either too new or too inexperienced to run the company, and Rafael… I have no idea where Rafael is at the moment, if this virus affected him or if he has even received the message what is going on with Al. Forgive me if corporate restructuring is not at the top of my list right now."

"Then it needs to be," Barry shot back. "If Donnelly were just irritating, it would be one thing, but he is about to wreck everything we have built over the last few years, and we cannot let this happen. Do you know he's asked a few employees to check their coworkers' personal belongings for the virus? Do you know what that does within a company?"

Barry reached over, put his hand on her shoulder again, and gave it a little squeeze. "I know you're worried about Rafael, but he's a tough guy. He'll come back when that idiot storm is over and he can get out of the country. What's he going to say when he walks in here and finds the entire place has gone to seed meanwhile, and we didn't do anything about it? Just think about that for a minute."

Kayla leaned into the gentle squeeze for a moment, closed her eyes, and collected herself again.

"I don't see how I can do anything about it, Barry. Somebody needs to be at the helm to guide this company through this nightmare. God, I wish Rafael didn't pick this time to go to Malta of all places."

Barry leaned back and let out a long breath. He held her eyes with his longer than strictly comfortable, reminding her of everything they had been through together.

"You know what has to be done," he finally said. "Either you or I have to step up and take charge. Get a motion through at the board that relieves Donnelly of the position to concentrate on his other duties while Rafael is away and makes one of us CEO."

"Is that a wise idea, Barry? Now you're the one sowing distrust among the employees. You're confusing people with this jumping around. How are they supposed to follow if leadership bounces around like a ping-pong ball? And just how much confusion and panic in the markets is suddenly changing the CEO going to cause?"

"Anything is better than Donnelly—anything. Please believe me. We can do this if we do it carefully and if we are prepared. Rafael is gone, out of touch. That's our ace and our reasoning. Keeping the facility safe and in perfect condition is our top priority as a pharmaceutical manufacturer. Therefore, we need the VP of facilities to devote all of his energy and time to doing just that."

He wasn't all wrong. Kayla made a fist and rested her chin on it. Barry wasn't simply whining about the situation or Thomas Donnelly. The complaints about Donnelly and his abrasiveness had already reached her; she had just been too frantic and too busy worrying about Rafael to put much stock into them. Donnelly gloried in being CEO, without worrying about what was happening to the company.

And the facility—the facility needed someone strong and determined to ensure the safety of everyone, including their employees, their customers, and their shareholders. Perhaps there was a way.

"You've clearly thought this through from beginning to end," she said, buying time.

"Of course." Barry shrugged. He took both of her hands now and squeezed them. "You and I were there at the very beginning, when we founded this company, when we bought this building, when we had the grand opening…"

"Don't remind me of that! I still have nightmares of Mirko, that loan shark, showing up."

"You're not telling me you can just stand by and let Donnelly ruin PerCan the way he ruined his own company," Barry insisted, and his hands automatically curled into fists.

"Aside from the fact that his abrasive personality grates on your nerves and you hate his guts, you mean."

"Forget about that for a minute. This is not about what's going on between him and me. This is 100 percent about the company and what's best for it." Barry tapped the table with his fingers, emphasizing the last few words. "That is what we need to focus on here—nothing else."

There was a flash of fire in his eyes that belied his usual casual attitude of, 'it's just an investment, folks, nothing more, nothing less.' He did care about the company and its wellbeing—and still.

Still. All of the history he had with PerCan.

Kayla stood up quite abruptly and straightened her blazer.

"Go, down to the lab," she said. "Take that test. It is an unknown virus, and we still don't know where it came from or what it does."

"Then how do they even test for it?"

"I don't know, Barry, and I don't want to know. I don't have a degree in pharmacology—Nick does. Just take the damn test to ease all of our minds. The sooner we can say the PerCan facility and staff are completely free of any infection, the better it will be, OK? You gave me a lot to think about, so do not expect me to jump at the first mention of an issue, please."

Barry got to his feet, picked up his portfolio, and winked at her.

"Aye, aye, ma'am. Consider me down at the labs and tested already. Just think about what I told you—it needs to be done, and it needs to be done soon."

"Go."

She pointed at the door, and only when Barry had gone and the door had closed behind him did she allow herself to drop into a chair and sag back to be supported by it soft upholstery. Against her better judgment, she took out her phone and dialed Rafael's number for the hundredth time that day. Still the call did not connect. The news outlets were vague, and the local embassy either wouldn't or couldn't get her any answers either.

Rafael's hotel had been virtually destroyed by a giant rogue wave, but they were sure he'd been evacuated and moved to a secure government building before the wave hit.

They were sure. And as soon as communications were restored over there, she would be too.

That was all she had to cling to for the moment.

TEN

Rafael was still pacing the building he'd been taken to like a caged tiger. They were in one of the embassies; he'd found out that much. And the beach hotel, along with everything he hadn't taken with him when they left, had been destroyed or scattered all over the bottom of the ocean.

His phone had been in his hands when they ran, and Rick had set him up with temporary chargers and cables. Probably to make them feel safer. None of it would do any good while cell service and wireless were still out.

What a country. He suspected someone somewhere in this embassy still had to have contact with the rest of the world, however they managed it. But he had another suspicion that having to call his wife would not be considered enough of an emergency to be allowed access. Everybody crammed into this building wanted to call home, to let their loved ones know they were safe and unharmed.

At least he had been able to get that message through to Kayla. If she were watching the news, she was likely frantic for his safety. He had to keep hoping she wouldn't panic.

They were going to get out of here soon, he knew that, but his irritation still got the better of him. Rick had already told him the storm was showing signs of finally letting up. After that, it was a question of what shape the island was in. Rafael was a builder. This was something he knew how to do, and it didn't scare him in the slightest.

A little chuckle escaped him, thinking about the cannabis project and all of his plans, now in tatters in what had been his room. That project was going to be on ice for a few months now, if not years. At the same time, having gone through a storm like this one opened up a number of questions and ideas surrounding the safety of greenhouse grows.

Always look on the bright side, he thought. *We have a lot of usable material now, once we get around to applying it!*

"I'm glad somebody is having a good time," a stranger who had dropped onto the couch beside him said.

"Hm?"

"You were laughing at something just now—even though personally, I don't think there's much to laugh at, at the moment. I'm Jonas, by the way."

Like the others in the building, Jonas appeared fatigued and disheveled, his once-immaculate slim suit now stained and sweat-drenched. Despite his appearance, his steel-blue eyes, however, still shone with determination and shrewdness.

"Rafael." He leaned over to shake Jonas's hand. "I was here to help this country build a first-rate cannabis grow facility. From the way it looks out there, that project is going to be on a back burner for a while, but at least I take home a lot of excellent info on tornadoes. That was my chuckle."

"I'm an investment banker." Jonas smiled and straightened his once-perfect suit. "In another life, I might actually want to look at your business. Cannabis projects are something everybody wants right now."

Rafael raised his hands and leaned back a little. "I just build the things. That's what I do—finance is something I leave to the people who didn't fail math in 10th grade."

"Why am I absolutely convinced there is more of a story here than you are letting on?" Jonas said and winked. "Right now, I just want to get out of here. Hopefully, my company's jet is still in one piece and can take me back home."

"Private jet, huh?" Rafael played with a loose string on his jacket and looked up over the rim of his reading glasses at Jonas. "Now you have my full attention because I have to get back home just as badly to avoid a full-scale disaster at our facility. So, if there are any extra seats on that plane of yours, Jonas…"

"Still trying to run away, are you, Rafael?" Rick joined them with a plate of sandwiches and water for everyone and sat between them. "We have managed to get a message to your fiancée. She knows you are unharmed and doing well. Does this convince you at all to take it easy for a little bit and enjoy our hospitality until things are absolutely safe?"

"No." Rafael grabbed a sandwich and took an enormous bite. "Hey, this is not half bad."

"We try." Rick smiled gamely. "I must tell you again—we cannot take a chance on anything happening to you while you are an official guest of the government. There would be no end of trouble."

Jonas leaned over, took one of the sandwiches for himself, and grinned at Rafael. "Now the story is getting juicy. Let me hear it and we can talk about that seat you were inquiring about."

ELEVEN

Thomas Donnelly wandered through the halls at Perfect Cannabis Corp and soaked in the silence and peace and quiet of his empty facility. It was late at night, and he was the last person in the building. His building. His steps echoed, and he let the sheer size of the growing area settle in on him. All his to command right now.

How often had he left at the end of the day and turned around in the parking lot to see the light in Al's office, or Rafael's, sometimes even both? Now he understood the appeal of the facility when it was empty, the lights dimmed and the environmental controls turned down low. There was something about it that felt—primal and powerful. You could breathe that feeling, and it felt comforting and empowering at the same time. He was in control here now. He called the shots, and he decided what was happening and what was not.

Oh, he'd made a few mistakes along the way—did not everybody? People said he was stubborn and pigheaded and difficult to get along with. He didn't listen and didn't have any respect for anyone. What now, they thought he couldn't hear it when they whispered about him behind his back? They really thought he missed the scowling faces and one-word answers?

He was neither blind nor deaf. Deal with it. With Thomas Donnelly, you got what you saw. That was just who he was, end of story.

He was neither aloof and distant like Al, nor chummy and approachable like Rafael. They would just have to get used to it. He was the

CEO now, and he liked it. He liked being in charge of this huge facility where everything was in place and everything running almost on its own. His own cannabis facility before the merger had been much smaller, and everything had been a struggle. Then, already, he'd battled staff issues and turnover on a regular basis, always been told his people skills were lacking.

Never mind, he'd figure it out in time. He had all the time in the world because the last updates on good old Al still showed no change in status. It would be a while before the old crow finally waltzed back into his office to start throwing his weight around.

Thomas grinned. With his tall thin frame, usually wearing a dark suit of some type, Al really did look like a crow wandering through the halls. A crow picking his decisions apart. Pick—pick—pick. His style was different, and he wasn't Rafael.

Yes, it looked to be quite a while before Al would be back, and, in the meantime, he was CEO. If they didn't like him, well, so be it.

Who else was going to do the job if not him? Barry Wentworth, that crazy nutter who had founded the company? Not likely. Investors would be leaving in droves, screaming if that happened. Rafael? Good, basic choice, but also gone for an undetermined time. That left Kayla Montecito. Ah, the former Playboy Bunny-type, turned trophy wife, turned executive of a publishing house? Ah yes, he found so much information on her on the internet. Information she had desperately tried to erase, but it was there, and he was prepared to show it to anyone who wanted to see it.

And that gossip rag she published, calling it a newspaper—please. He'd have a field day if she tried to step up, and the board would stand behind him, one and all. Even if they resented him, he was the best choice for a CEO right now, and he was going to ride that train until they pulled him off by force if it became necessary.

Thomas Donnelly used his swipe card to enter the growing space and slowly made his way through the gangways between the grow pods. It really was amazing what Rafael had built here—isolated rooms, or pods, for every stage of the cannabis growth that never had to be accessed by anyone, except the agronomists who had to work with the plants directly.

Everything else, from irrigation, fertilizing, testing and environmental control, was done from the access ways between the pods. "Keep humans out of the grow pods," was one of Rafael's favorite sayings, and it worked.

Their yields and purity were among the highest out there and would soon be the new industry standards. They had only had one infection in a grow, and it had been dealt with immediately.

Rafael's pride and joy, the integrated monitoring system, kept tabs on everything, at all times. There was simply no way they could have introduced a virus in here for Al Ivers to infect himself on, no way. Rafael's monitoring systems would have gone insane if the slightest out-of-spec deviation were found, and he would have been down here personally, digging around until he found it.

That silly Montecito airhead had never thought about that, had she? No, she'd rather waste everyone's time and energy running tests, instead of trusting the processes that her own fiancé had designed. Thomas's fingers ran along the side of a monitoring panel. Yes, he'd have finance run an analysis of all of the funds she'd wasted, running tests instead of trusting this monitoring system—and he'd present them at the next meeting, maybe even put them in the quarterly report. Why not let people know how she was assigning company finances without rhyme or reason?

Donnelly walked up to a monitoring pad and looked at the rows of status lights—green or dark amber, all of them. Everything OK in Cannabis Land. Montecito would look like a fool when he was done with her, and that was just the way he liked it.

He slid the observation hatch on a pod aside and looked through the glass window into the grow room. Rows and rows of cannabis plants, with guide wires and fertigation lines above and below, nothing out of the ordinary.

Just as he slid the hatch closed again, he heard a noise in the grow area. A sharp report of some kind, as if someone had accidentally dropped something or banged a piece of equipment. He stood perfectly still and listened. He could almost hear his own heartbeat in the silence.

Nobody was supposed to be in here after hours, save for the security guys. There it was again, followed by a rustle. Somebody was definitely in the building, and most likely not someone who had proper business here.

Thomas stepped out into the main hall, trying to remember where the lighting main switches were located, but just then, everything on the main panel ran together. Which one of these? Damn Rafael and his irritating automation in here anyway. If you needed to look for somebody who didn't belong here, low light and power-saving mode were shit. Did he not know that?

"Anybody there?" he called out into the dim manufacturing hall and felt a finger of fear crawl down his back. He was, after all, alone in this building. What if somebody had broken in? Could that happen—had that ever happened?

Broken in, for God's sake, he scolded himself. *Damn, Donnelly, you are letting your imagination run wild. You look at our security features lately? It would take somebody smarter than the average rocket scientist to break into this facility.* He'd seen the specs.

"Anybody there?" he called out again, but this time, the sound did not return.

Could he have imagined it? No, he was sure he had heard something. Perhaps a piece of equipment was loose somewhere and banged against another? Or something had finally fallen after teetering precariously for hours? That wouldn't surprise him. Having to test every piece of equipment for a nonexistent virus certainly had disrupted everything and made a mess of their routines.

He straightened up, looked and listened around for another moment, and finally shook his head.

Whatever it was, he would likely discover it was completely harmless when he searched the securities logs tomorrow. He would do that first thing, he promised himself, just to have a laugh. Evidence of yet another problem Montecito's solo decision-making had caused.

He made his way back to the administration side, locked the door into the grow areas, and sighed with relief when he set the final lock and armed the security system again. Out of habit, he patted the side pocket of his cargo pants, satisfied when he felt the solid rectangle of his executive keycard there. For a panicked day, he had mislaid the thing a few days ago and been horrified at the thought of having to confess to Rafael. Rafael would have given him a lecture of gargantuan proportions, for sure, but then the card showed up again, right where it was supposed to be, on his desk, in a tray. Go figure. Building locked tight, he sighed with relief.

So much for enjoying an empty building. They were nuts, both of them, Rafael and Al, if this was what they did for fun.

He saw the security guard wandering by out by the main gates, doing his regular patrols, and briefly considered telling him he had heard something. Almost instantly, he dismissed the thought again. If he did, he would have to hang around while they investigated the noise and wrote protocols about it and his own presence in the grow areas. Rafael didn't like it when people wandered around the grow areas without any good reason, including directors and executives. No good reason—stay out of the grow areas… Christ, here he was, thinking about Covin again.

"Rafael is not here," he said out loud, pleased with the way it sounded. "And he's just going to have to put up with it because I am CEO now."

That made him smile again, and by the time he had reached his office, he had convinced himself that it was likely just a piece of loose equipment, and he was going to rag on Kayla Montecito about the

confusion and disruption all of this testing had caused in their manufacturing areas.

TWELVE

Kayla sat in her living room with her feet up, twirling a glass of wine in her hands. She missed Rafael's advice and his no-nonsense way of speaking. She missed him always apologizing when he used a bit of crude language, and she worried about Al and about Dante. Heck, she even worried about their brother Roberto, even though she hadn't seen or spoken to the man in over a month and barely knew him. She had not seen him around since that time when they found out what Greg Turner had done to Tadeo, she realized…

Had anybody heard from Roberto or spoken to him? It suddenly occurred to her that she had not run into him at the hospital, nor heard Dante mention he had been there. Why? He would have gone to check on Al, wouldn't he?

Roberto and Al had their differences, but just recently, after Roberto had bought a small marijuana producer of his own, they had settled those issues. At least, that's what Al had told her. Yes, only in passing, and only quite casually. That was just Al, and she had never seen any need to find out more.

Kayla put her glass down and rubbed her chilled hands. Every single one of those scientists had told her there was no way Greg Turner could have had anything to do with the virus that attacked Al. And yet she couldn't help but wonder.

Greg Turner had sworn revenge on all of the Ivers men, including

Roberto, who had been the very person to give him the background story between Tadeo Ivers and his father.

The story that caused Tadeo's death and Turner's revenge.

So why had nobody heard from Roberto?

Perhaps she could make a few inquiries the next day, call up Roberto, get his input on things. It surely couldn't do any harm. If nothing else, it would give her an excuse to get to know him. Her phone's insistent peal startled her out of her reverie.

Unknown Number.

She could just see Rafael's face and hear his grousing when the phone interrupted his dinner or a game he was watching, only to find out it was an unknown number.

Now, who in their right minds answers an unknown number after hours? he would say. *It's guaranteed to be some idiot marketing ploy. Sorry for the language.*

Kayla stared at the phone for a minute, then picked it up.

"Montecito."

At first, she didn't hear anything but a far-off roar and hiss that sounded like a white noise machine. Kayla held the phone away from her ear. Could it be Rafael? For a second, a voice broke through, just a few words and phrases, and then the rushing was back.

"Hello, anybody there?"

And then he was there, clear as a bell. "Kayla, thank God you picked up."

"Rafael, oh my God, it really is you. I'm so happy to hear your voice. How—what—speak…"

"I don't have much time, Kayla. This is the only phone in the building that works, and I'm sneaking around to use it as is. So, we're good. I'm good. The hotel is trashed. The storm is slowly going down."

"Thank God."

"Communication is coming back bit by bit. It will be a while. I'm sorry I have no idea when or how I'm going to be able to come back home. Tell me—what's going on with Al?"

"He collapsed. They say it's an unknown virus. No change so far."

Rafael swore softly. "The company?"

"No trace of the virus so far." Almost automatically, she matched Rafael's staccato way of speaking.

"Who is running things, with me and Al gone?"

"Donnelly."

"Donnelly." Rafael swore again. "That won't end well. Staff hates him. He's clueless and rude. Make sure…"

The roaring white noise drowned out anything he might have said next.

"Rafael?"

"Don't let it go on—do something—for the best of the company fast…"

Then the connection cut out, her screen went blank, and Rafael was gone. Kayla let her phone sink into her lap and wanted to cry. He was OK, she told herself. Rafael was OK, and everything would be fine. Soon. Soon. But right at that moment, she felt more alone than ever.

"It's OK," she said and made a fist to steady herself. "Everything is fine."

Rafael was OK. He had survived the storm without injury, and he would be coming back to her as soon as possible. Everything was OK.

***

Kayla went to bed early, still intending to follow up the next morning with Dante and, potentially, Barry to see why Roberto had not been around, but her phone started at the crack of dawn and simply refused to shut up.

She hadn't even had her first cup of coffee yet when several PerCan department heads had called her for help.

"Why has Donnelly fired four of my cultivation technicians? I need those people, or we are sunk."

"Donnelly promoted three of his own people who are totally inexperienced and fired good, capable workers while he was at it. What the heck?"

"Does he not know you can't fire people without notice and without cause…?"

"Donnelly absolutely has no idea what he is doing, or he would not…"

Obviously, Thomas Donnelly had arrived early and gone to work with a vengeance.

"Dante, wait…" Kayla pinched the skin between her eyes, forcing back the headache that threatened to explode, even though it was not even nine o'clock.

"Listen to me, Kayla. He's cut down my personnel with a hatchet. I have half the people I need today to do the work we need to accomplish, let alone safely or properly. We can't function like this."

"I'll talk to him."

"Not enough. You need to do more than talk, Kayla. I cannot do my job here without the proper staff. Nobody can. And that's not even counting the two that quit on their own because of his behavior and remarks…"

Dante hesitated, and Kayla reached for her coffee cup. She'd need a refill before the call was over.

"Remarks about…" she probed, and Dante sighed.

"They're—girlfriends. Well, more than girlfriends, if you get my drift."

"None of our business what employees do at home, as long as it doesn't harm the company in any way. You know that, Dante, better than anyone. Consenting adults can do as they wish, so what's the issue here? Why bring it up?"

"Oh, you don't have to give me the lecture, Kayla. I get it, and I don't have an issue. These two are fantastic cultivation technicians and entertaining to boot. But they booked it, and when I found Dana's and Jenn's resignations this morning, there was a personal note with them."

"And?"

"And apparently Donnelly made a number of insensitive comments about them and told my scheduler to keep the 'two dykes' on separate time schedules so they wouldn't get up to anything inappropriate on their breaks. Out loud, and within earshot of both of them. And he didn't phrase it as delicately as that either."

"Jesus." Kayla put her coffee down hard. "What is he trying to do, create a massive labor lawsuit before lunchtime hits? When has he even had time to make this kind of a mess? Dear God." She made a fist and swore quietly to herself. "Do you have contact information for these ladies? I need to do damage control—apologize to them personally for starters—before I do anything else. Maybe there is even a way to see if they will consent to come back."

"I doubt it, but please do," Dante said dryly.

"Meanwhile, tell the people in personnel to assign you as many people to you as you need to get the job done today. I'm taking full responsibility for this if anyone gives you any flak about it."

"Good." Dante still didn't sound any better. "And see that you do something about Donnelly. I really don't need all of this crap. It's tough enough to get the job done."

"I will, Dante. Thanks for understanding."

She hung up and checked her calendar for the day. Ideally, she would have spent the day at Montecito Publishing, doing things she enjoyed: planning the next issue of the magazine, assigning editorial staff, checking over the layouts, meeting with her journalists. None of it would happen while she dealt with Donnelly and his management style.

She let her own staff know that she wouldn't be in—again—and speed-scrolled through her messages.

Donnelly had a massive head start on her. Jesus, how much damage could one person do in the span of 24 hours? Unfair promotions, unfair firings, racial slurs, discrimination, arbitrary decisions, and no end to the list that she could see.

She blew out a breath and started to consider that Barry might be right. Donnelly had no business on the executive roster. None of this had ever become an issue while he was running facilities, where Rafael, by some miracle, appeared to have kept a lid on his man up to now, but he was a disaster in the CEO seat.

Kayla rolled her shoulders and called for a driver to take her to PerCan. With her mind skipping between 10 different subjects, she had no patience for driving.

THIRTEEN

"**I**'m so glad you're here," she heard at Reception, and the greeting took on an entirely different meaning, knowing what she did.

Connie, Rafael and Al's personal assistant, whom Kayla had in fact hired years ago, came straight up to her, thought about it for only a second, and finally gave her a massive hug.

"I told them all to hang tight. Once you were here, you were the only one who could do something about that—that—that man."

Connie brushed her hair back with shaking hands, and Kayla returned the hug.

"Connie, hi," she said with a wry smile. "I don't even have to ask who you mean by 'that man,' now do I?"

"If it were not for Rafael and you…"

"Not you too, Connie." Kayla raised her hands, stopping her. "I'll deal with him, just a bit of patience."

"Just a little, and only because it's you," Connie said and stalked away. "And while you are at it, will you please tell Mr. Donnelly I don't care how many things he drops at my feet—I will not bend down in front of him ever again. Ever, are we clear?"

Kayla smiled weakly and raised a thumb.

She stalked into Thomas Donnelly's office without knocking and dropped into his visitor's chair.

"Well good morning, Kayla. If I had heard you knocking, I would have said just a minute."

"And if I thought you had any kind of manners, I would have knocked."

She flashed angry eyes at him and shook her head.

"Thus far, I've received complaints about, amongst others, racism, sexism, and gender discrimination involving you, and it's only 10 o'clock in the morning. This is not your finest day, is it?"

"You let me worry about those people," Thomas said, closing a file in front of him and throwing it carelessly onto a pile on the floor. "I don't coddle them the way Rafael or Al do, so they go complaining to you behind my back, is that it? Typical. Change is part of this business, and if they don't like it… Why are you here anyway? We don't have a meeting scheduled. You've got nothing to do at Montecito? Gossip spreading itself now?"

He leered at her, and Kayla made a fist with her left hand, hard enough to feel her manicured nails digging into her palm. Then she took a breath, smiled as sweetly as she could, and shook her head.

"No, I actually have tons of work over at the publishing house. None of it, however, involves threats of lawsuits in labor court, or discrimination, so I thought why not come over and help out a bit."

"Rubbish."

Thomas got out from behind his desk and walked over to his coffeemaker, pushing the button on a cup for himself.

"Those people need to get real about a few things. We are a production facility here, not a kindergarten. We work, and we work hard. If the tone gets a bit rough now and then, that's part of the job. Get used to it or move out. Don't think Rafael doesn't use the F-word now and then."

He took his cup and returned to his desk. For a moment, he seemed to be considering offering Kayla something, then changed his mind. With a minute shrug, he sat back down. Kayla chose to ignore it and folded her hands before her.

"You leave Rafael out of this. And those people? Those people? You mean the employees who have been loyal to PerCan for several years now, despite the rough patches we had to overcome? The people who are all part of a welcoming and diverse working environment where everyone has rights and duties and is heard and listened to? Are those the people you mean?"

"Sentimental bullcrap," Thomas said again, taking a noisy slurp of his coffee. "You see, that's what's wrong with this country. The staff think they can just run the place with their demands, but it doesn't work that way. Discipline, rules, order—that is what they need, nothing else. I never had those problems over at Mariposa, I tell you that, never. Maybe you can run a gossip rag like that, but not a marijuana plant."

"No kidding," Kayla said and rolled her eyes. "And I don't know about Mariposa, but without looking it up, I can tell you that 90 percent of your employees were probably white, straight, and male."

"So?"

"You don't get away with misogynistic behavior any longer. Sorry to be the one to give you bad news. There are rules and regulations, and the government made them, not me. And as far as getting used to it goes, we have labor laws, we have discrimination laws, and, as a public company, we cannot simply pick and choose which ones we want to ignore today."

"Rubbish."

Kayla sat a little straighter and slowly counted to 10 in her mind. Then she put her hands together and smiled.

"Sorry, Thomas, it's not rubbish. It's the law. And you have a board to answer to. As a member of said board, I am requesting your cooperation."

"Oh, you're requesting, are you?" Donnelly rose and stood behind his desk, waggling his head, mimicking her speech. "And I'm requesting that you get the fuck out of my office, and don't bother me with this sissy stuff again, just because a few people don't like the way I speak. I am the CEO of this company, and I make the decisions and the rules. Do I make myself clear? Now piss off."

"As you wish."

Kayla stood, nodded a brief greeting, and didn't allow herself to exhale until the door had closed behind her.

"He's like that on a regular basis."

Connie stood behind the door, not even bothering to hide the fact that she had been listening in on their conversation. Kayla decided not to mention it. She still felt shell shocked from the conversation she'd just had.

"Seriously?" She put a hand out against the wall to steady herself for a moment, blew out a massive breath, and shook her head.

If Rafael had been around to hear that exchange… If Rafael had heard it, there would have been hell to pay. No, more like a small nuclear explosion. And it still might happen once the story got back to him and the fact that she herself had been on the receiving end of that tirade.

"I am so sorry, Connie," she said and put her hand on the other woman's arm. "I didn't know how bad it was. I promise you I will deal with this—with him."

Connie shrugged. "Didn't want to tattle, or I would have told you."

"You're not. I'm the one who should apologize."

She turned on her heel, opened Donnelly's office door again, and took only one step inside, leaving the door so Connie could hear every word.

"And just so we are clear, if I hear one more incident about you asking Connie to bend down in front of you so you can ogle her from behind, I will personally drag you in front of the labor court, and it will be my pleasure. Is that understood?"

She turned and slammed the door before he could answer. "That was a little petty," she said, grinning at Connie.

"But fun."

Kayla smiled again and sighed. "Look, I'm sorry I have not done anything about this earlier. I did not realize how bad it had become. But rest assured I am doing something about it right now."

"That makes me feel better, Kayla, thank you."

"While you are at it, please find out for me if Barry is in the building today. If not, would you mind locating him for me please? I need to speak to him urgently."

Anything she had meant to ask Dante about Roberto went straight out of her mind, while she walked as fast as she could down to the production areas to smooth out a few more feathers ruffled by Donnelly. People were not as happy to see her as they usually were, she noticed. A lot of employees barely acknowledged her walking by, their heads lowered and their hands busy with whatever task was on their list for today.

Without double-checking, she knew there were a lot fewer people on the floor than any other day. People were rushing, hustling through their tasks. They snapped at one another and fired back angry remarks, and none had a smile to spare or a kind word. This was not the kind of working environment that lasted long. She would bet money on it.

FOURTEEN

Barry Wentworth, it turned out, spent the day at his own office, straightening out a few things, while being filched by his own staff for paperwork, notes, and receipts. It was all done in good spirits and humor. He knew better than anyone that he couldn't keep any kind of order himself, so he invited his assistants to turn him, his car, and his portfolio upside down and inside out on a regular basis for information they needed.

There was a lot of laughter and joking involved, though for once, Kayla couldn't even think about joining in when she arrived there a few hours later, disheveled, exhausted, and reeling from a conversation with Dana and Jenn.

"Anything wrong with Rafael?" Barry asked, the moment they had sequestered themselves in his private office and closed the door.

"No. He's in fact fine, just stuck in Malta for the time being."

"Oh." Barry dropped into his chair and forked his hands through his hair. "I see what happened. Let me guess. You had a run-in with Donnelly."

"Why did nobody tell me he was a misogynistic pig and that he's running the company like a barnyard? His barnyard?"

"I told you he was ineffective."

"Yes, Barry. You said he is not effective. You said people don't like him. Those are things that are an irritation, not a disaster. As far as I remember, there was no mention of gender discrimination, racial discrimination, or asking Rafael's assistant to bend down repeatedly so he could ogle her from behind."

"Ouch."

"Ouch? Ouch, Barry? This is a disaster on so many levels. I can't even… Good people have been fired. Mediocre people have been promoted into positions they are not qualified for. The morale is lower than it was when Tadeo owned the place, and that's saying something. Try it. Go down on the production floor and see if anybody will even look at you."

"I heard—some of it. I didn't know it had gotten this bad this quickly. I was tied up with a client for the last day or so. In my defense, I did tell you he was unsuited to the position."

"Oh, Barry, he has to go. Now."

Barry shrugged. "My words exactly."

"How did he even manage to hide his true colors for that long? I never heard anything about him. No complaints, no issues. He was fine at the board meetings when I met him. And now this comes up?"

Barry moved a pen back and forth on his desk idly. "I couldn't tell you either. I have my suspicions, but my guess is Rafael kept a pretty tight leash on him on a day-to-day basis, keeping him in areas where he couldn't cause problems. And even he wouldn't dare step out of line with Rafael."

"Well, he's stepping out now," she confirmed. "He's wiped the line out completely. He all but told me he had no intentions of cleaning up his behavior or his language, and what the bleep was I going to do about it? Except he didn't bother using the word *bleep*."

"And that brings us right back to where we left off yesterday. What are we going to do about him?" Barry threw up his hands and raised his eyes to the ceiling. "Hallelujah, you finally understand what I was trying to tell you all along. Now what?"

"God."

She got to her feet and began pacing the length of Barry's office.

"I told…"

"I remember what you told me," she snapped at him. "I didn't listen, and I'm sorry. Can we move on, please? The more important issue is what are we going to do about it, and how?"

"I could step in as CEO again."

"Barry…" She let out a deep sigh and continued to pace. "I know—I know you have the talent and the drive to do an excellent job…"

"But?"

"But you have a history, remember? We don't really want to go there. Do you remember the shitstorm that came down on the company the first time you were at the helm and things went sideways? Whatever we do, it needs to be right for the company and for all the people who work there. Before Donnelly manages to fire any more, that is. No trying things out, no hoping it will work."

She thought of their anniversary celebration then, when all of the employees had greeted her with big smiles and hugs and told her how happy they were to work there. Right there, she vowed to personally hire back each and every person Thomas Donnelly had fired.

"I am just not sure if it is going to send the right message if we put you back into the CEO seat. People have not forgotten about the hoopla with the illegal grow out back, and then Tadeo's murder…"

"And I hope you have not forgotten that I was found not guilty of all charges in both of these cases."

"I know, I know." Kayla sighed. "I was there, remember? But you're a fundraiser now. You talk to investors and shareholders every day. You know how volatile markets can be. You know how much foreign investor money is in this company. Money that can be withdrawn at a moment's notice. Al is unconscious with an uncertain future, Rafael is unavailable—Donnelly just made sense in that situation. What is going to happen if we change our mind again after such a short time?"

"People will wonder. They might even panic, and there's nothing you can do about it. It's all in the spin. Word things in the proper way and have Donnelly sign that wording, and things will be fine. Stuff happens—we deal. That's life."

"And what about the inevitable rumors and conspiracy theories, that you did something to get the CEO seat back while Al is incapacitated and Rafael away? All of the old stories are going to be dug out again and served up as news. Do you want to do that to yourself?"

"You care?" Barry grinned broadly, and she wanted to smack him.

"I care about PerCan. That's it, that's all, that's everything," she fired back, and Barry held his cheek as if she had in fact slapped him.

"That hurt."

"Will you stop?" Kayla jumped up and spread her hands. "Work with me here. Stay serious. This is not the time to joke around."

"I had forgotten how intense and passionate you get about things when you're into it."

"This is your five-second warning. Keep up this nonsense and I will walk out of here for good, and with that, you will lose one of your most lucrative clients. Don't think I haven't noticed that you advertise, 'I am the guy who saved PerCan.'"

"I didn't know you followed me on social media," Barry said, but the smirk was gone, and it was said in a much kinder tone.

"I don't follow you." She sat back in her chair and folded her hands. "But I do read the financial pages, you know. You and I have a history."

Barry sighed and arranged the items on his desk in precise order. He nodded with a weak smile.

"Yes. And it wasn't always a good one."

"No, Barry, it was not. When you left town after the illegal grow op was discovered…"

"I didn't exactly leave town," he said, eyes lowered. "I panicked, and I ran away. And, in doing so, I left you and Rafael holding the bag."

"Well, here is a man seeing the light. Insight and humility. Hallelujah, I didn't think it was possible." Kayla turned her eyes up to the ceiling.

"I was innocent. I didn't think I could make that case and win, so I ran to save my own skin. I am sorry."

Kayla only nodded, not daring to look at him. The grandeur, the swagger, and sheer hubris of Barry Wentworth all of a sudden were gone, and if she made one false move, the moment might shatter, and she'd get the old bluster back. She waited and finally heard him exhale.

"I am sorry I left you hanging with everything."

"It's not OK, but it's ancient history, Barry. It turned out OK. We made it work."

"You and Rafael."

"Rafael and me." She looked up and found him smiling.

"You and I were not something that would have worked in the long run, although we did kick big-time ass in our day. Not in a million years would I have thought you and Rafael…"

"Nobody would have, including me. Can we get back to the subject at hand, please? It is a little urgent."

"Yes." Barry leaned back in his chair and steepled his hands before his face. "I've been wanting to make peace with you for the longest time, and this seems as good a reason as any."

Kayla only nodded. In truth, she'd probably forgiven him just as long a time ago, but clearing the air between them had been overdue, and it felt good.

"Fine, Donnelly…" Barry said, breaking the spell, his face all business once again. "He's far too happy to be interim CEO to care about anything else, and he's making a hash of it. I'm afraid fixing this will take the nuclear option, though."

"I don't like the phrasing 'the nuclear option.'"

"One of us—you or I—will have to gather enough support on the board beforehand. Then we force a vote, remove him as a director, and do the job ourselves."

Kayla sighed and nodded. That was the very definition of nuclear. The company might be merged, but the merger was still fresh and uncomfortable. Many of the employees defined themselves as either Mariposa, or PerCan staff. She'd heard Rafael complain about it. He had started to work on that amalgamation and unity. Rafael…

"I wish Rafael were here," she said.

"Well, he's not. And if you ask my humble opinion, I'm changing my mind here. I think you are the far superior choice."

"What?" Kayla's head snapped up, and she blinked rapidly, to make sure she was not dreaming. "You want to say that again after I recover from that heart attack I just suffered?"

"You heard me. Either one of us is capable of doing the job and doing it well."

"My sentiments exactly, but for a minute there, I thought you would insist…"

"Because I founded the company? Because I bought most of the Mariposa shares to get back what I considered my company? Believe me, Kayla, everything inside me is screaming right now—get your company back. Screaming so loud I'm almost going deaf here, as a matter of fact."

"And yet…?"

She still couldn't fathom the thought. Since the day she had met him, Barry Wentworth had had only one goal: to run Perfect Cannabis. He had done everything, risked everything, and given every dollar he owned to do so. And now…?

"You're going to have to explain this to me, Barry, because right now, I feel like I fell through a wormhole or something. Surely I'm in another dimension."

"You're not. I can vouch for that."

"Then you really just suggested that I should be running PerCan? That I am the better choice to replace Thomas Donnelly, more so than the man who'd do anything for the job and actually has—that is what you just said? Did I hear that right?"

"You don't have to enjoy it so much."

Barry rose and stood before the tall floor-to-ceiling windows that afforded a sweeping view of the entire city below.

"It's killing me to even say the words, but I wouldn't be an effective CEO," he said, his back still to her. "Number one, you're right. I have a lot of baggage, I committed a few critical errors in judgment, and it will take people a little longer to forget."

"It'll happen."

"That's kind, but we can't wait."

"Number two?"

"Number two, the people love you."

"I wouldn't exactly say…"

"Don't talk it down, Kayla." He turned around, his hands still folded behind his back, and smiled at her. "The hell if I know how you do it, but every single one of the employees at PerCan absolutely adores you."

"I listen to them. That's all," she said, looking down at her hands again. "But…"

"No *but*. In this situation, what the company needs is a unifying force. Somebody who brings everybody together, somebody they can agree on, somebody they love, trust, and respect."

"Me?"

"You." Barry nodded and stretched his arms toward her, palms up as if he were offering something. "So? You up for the challenge? You did say you cared about PerCan about half an hour ago."

"That's not fair."

"I know."

"I have my own company to run."

"And Montecito Publishing is solid and well run and will continue for a little while without its iconic and beautiful owner."

"Not disagreeing with you, but watch yourself. Why did we have to have this entire discussion then? Why not cut to the chase half an hour ago?"

Barry shrugged and grinned again—that boyish, charming grin she remembered so well from their time together. The one that allowed him to get away with everything.

"I just wanted to see if you could even think about me running PerCan again."

Kayla leaned back and ran her hands through her hair, something she rarely did. Of all the ways she had expected this meeting to go, this was not one of them. Blindsided 100 percent. Where did all this insight come from all of a sudden?

"Are you sure you're OK? Did you hit your head when you crashed Irv Moody's plane there while fleeing?"

"I did not. But if Irv Moody has forgiven me, he would be a good man to have on our side. He owns a lot of shares, and his opinion carries a lot of weight."

"He's never participated in running the company, though. We tried."

"Doesn't mean he won't. Surprises happen all the time."

"I'll say." She forked her hands though her hair again and shook her head. "Right—right, I'm going to have to think about this for a little while."

"Don't think too long. This is of the absolute essence. You know that better than anyone."

"I am not going to make a decision like this one on a 'right here, right now' basis, Barry. I need a few days."

"You don't have a few days."

Suddenly, the jovial, smiling Barry was gone, and his face had become all hard edges and his voice sharp enough to cut steel.

"What do you mean I don't have a few days? Of course I do. Maybe Rafael will even be back by then. He sure is working on it. Maybe we can hang on. It would make me feel better in any case. What difference does it make anyway?"

"Kayla." Barry came and took both of her wrists just hard enough to make her want to draw back. "Kayla, Nick Armstrong called me this morning."

"Nick? All right. Do you two know each other? I can't see why he would be calling you, but fine. What does this have to do with our discussion?"

"Nick knew I would be in a position to do something about Donnelly and to talk you into it if I couldn't."

"I will not be talked into anything," she said, bristling. "And Nick should know better than going around behind my back. I am going to talk to him too. When did he decide backroom deals and talking me 'into something' were a good idea? What is the matter with people?"

"No, Kayla, listen to me for one minute. Listen. After I let him speak, I realized Nick is right and how urgent this matter really is. He has three grow pods ready to be harvested in just a couple of days."

"Three?"

"That's right." Barry nodded. "It's one of the biggest harvests we've ever done at PerCan. Millions of dollars in cannabis."

He used the word *we* as naturally as if he were still a part of the active life of the company, she noticed. He still thought of PerCan in that way.

"You know what that means."

"Yes." She nodded slowly. "All hands on deck. Everybody's got to pitch in. I've been through it with Rafael."

"Not on this scale you haven't. And with everything going on, there is no 'all hands' any longer. If everybody's pitching in, expect to put on an environmental suit and to go into the cannabis plants."

"But…"

"But Donnelly fired way too many of Nick's cultivation technicians to get this harvest done properly, and Dante and Nick have been begging and pleading with them, but while Donnelly is in charge, they have no intentions of coming back. It's their final 'fuck you' to him."

"But the harvest…"

"Is going to spoil. Millions of dollars if we don't do something about it. Did I mention that? Now do you see why this is urgent?"

"How come you didn't tell me this when I walked in?"

"Because I needed to square things between you and me first, so we would be on the same page. And I needed to do that before you knew why it was so urgent. If I saw even the slightest hint that you would be on Donnelly's side, I would have had to work around both of you."

"Slow down for just a second, Barry. I can't follow you at this speed." Kayla covered her eyes with her hands and pulled in her shoulders, wanting to shut out everything for one moment. "You are telling me that in the space of just a few days that Donnelly's been in charge, we've gone from one of the most successful marijuana growers in the country to the brink of losing everything, just because of that man? Is that what I am hearing? How is that even possible?"

"That's the long and the short of it." He nodded. "Cannabis is pretty fickle, but nothing is as volatile as people if you treat them like crap. Don't be surprised to find a few more resignations on your desk when you get back. And the people who are staying? They are doing it because of the money." He rubbed thumb and forefinger together. "And they're going to hit you where it really hurts—in the wallet."

"That can't be. I've always been on great terms with all of the workers."

"Go ahead and try then. Donnelly has broken that trust. And just like that, 'we're going to get back at Donnelly' has turned into 'we're getting even with PerCan.'"

"This is a nightmare."

Kayla still had her hands pushed into her temples. What had Rafael told her? *Don't let him go on, for the best of the company—do something?* He would be… Oh, yes, Rafael would be more than livid if she let things go and the company were in tatters by the time he got back—again.

How often do I have to pull this thing out of a pile of manure? She could almost hear him. The thought made her smile, but only for a moment. Rafael had invested his life in this company. He would do anything to save it, no matter what.

"Rafael would give anything to save this company," she finally said very, very softly. "He's done it before."

"He's a standup guy all right," Barry said impatiently. "But, Kayla, he's not here. This one is on you and me, kid, and a lot of new people on the board with no idea what is going on right now and who we're going to have to pull over on to our side."

"I don't like the way that sounds, our side and their side."

"Would you rather have us all pull on the same rope? Right into bankruptcy if it comes to that?"

"No, of course not. And it is not going to come that far."

"You willing to guarantee that? Because I'm not. And I'm only the guy who founded the company and came up with the very first idea. Together with Rafael. Who I am sure would want you to do anything to save this company."

"All right, Barry, stop beating me over the head with it already. I am in." Decision made, Kayla stood again and began pacing Barry Wentworth's office. "So, we take over, you and I."

"Wrong. You take over. I'm going to give you as much cover as I can, but for many reasons, I have to stay in the background."

This part still didn't make any sense. This man had fought for the company almost as much as Rafael, and the fact that he wanted to 'stay in the background' was nothing if not suspicious.

"Why?" she asked slowly. "It might not be any of my business, but every word I've heard out of your mouth for a very long time was how you wanted to be CEO again. This entire mess with Turner only happened because you wanted to be CEO of PerCan Consolidated again. So what gives?"

"Well." Barry looked down at his hands, visibly struggling with something. "Well…"

"Well what, Barry? Spit it out. As you yourself mentioned, we don't have all day."

"Well, it might be that the SEC had a few minor issues with the way things were handled back when we started PerCan. Nothing serious, nothing earth-shattering. All the same…"

"You were suspended? You were fined? For God's sake, Barry, this is a fine time to find out that you can't be of any help at all."

"Relax, it's just temporary." Barry raised his hands in front of him, backing up from the flash in her eyes. "It's not a big deal."

"For how long?"

"I can't be a director of a publicly traded company for a couple of months yet. Up till now, I've been keeping it under wraps."

"For God's sake."

"You said that already, Kayla, and if you remember, I told you that this was your time to step up."

"I thought you meant I was a good CEO, not a replacement because you've been suspended by the SEC for—for what exactly?"

"Nothing big."

"Out with it, out."

"Of all the things we did back then…"

"Barry, you're going to tell me right now, or I swear to God—"

"No need. Remember when we were going through the name change and reverse takeover with the original PerCan?"

"Vaguely."

"Well, I needed signatures from all the shareholders on a document, and there was this one guy, this one little investor. All he owned was 5000 shares kind of guy."

"Let me guess—he wouldn't sign."

"Not unless I explained it to him personally. As in come down to his house and tell him why he should sign this."

"And?"

Barry looked down at the floor as if he'd lost something and shuffled a bit. "Let's just say I didn't go to his house."

"You made it up!"

"It was a done deal, Kayla. And we needed the reverse merger in order to go on the stock exchange. You know this. I explained it to you."

"Me, yes. This fellow, apparently not."

"He complained. And it became a big thing, and of all the crap that happened back then, every single issue was dismissed. Every single one. Except…"

"Except faking somebody's signature on a shareholder agreement."

"If you say it like that, Kayla, it sounds obscene."

"And if you say it real fast, it doesn't go away either, and it doesn't become the right thing to do either," she snapped at him. "It still means only one thing. I am on my own saving PerCan at the moment because the gentleman to my right has got himself suspended."

"And fined, don't forget fined." Barry groaned. "You wouldn't believe how much they…"

"Right at the moment, Barry, I fail to feel any sympathy for you whatsoever, OK, so please don't go there because all that's going to happen is I will tell you—you deserved it."

Barry put his hand over his heart, but said nothing, confronted with another flash from her dark eyes.

"Back to the issue at hand." She stopped pacing and squared off to him. "You could have saved me an hour and just said, 'Things are mucked up; you need to be CEO right now.'"

"I tried."

"Not hard enough, you did not. No, you had to take the long way around before you dropped this bombshell into my lap. Now, we'll start with a list of the board members, what you know about them. We need to contact all of them, and we need to know who is on our side. If we're not sure, we need to know who can get them on our side. I will talk to Dante. His brother in the ICU with an uncertain future. It pains me to say this, but it gives him credibility."

"Good idea."

"Start writing, Barry."

"Why me?"

"Because I am not your flipping secretary, and because I will have enough to do running PerCan and Montecito if we actually manage to pull this off. So, start writing. We need to get Dante on our side and Nick. After that, as many board members as we possibly can. I'd like for it to be unanimous."

"Not a chance." Barry shook his head. "Too many original Mariposa people. They will never go along with it."

"Fine, as many as we can convince. I will have to speak to the employees, I will have to try and get some of our fired staff back to save this harvest, and we will have to do all of this without Donnelly noticing and ruining our plan."

"Total blindside?"

"I don't like it either, Barry. But if we give him time to prepare, it will just be that much harder to get him out of office and to move on."

"No, I was going to say I like the way you think. You know, in spite all of the time we were together, I never once knew how capable you were as a CEO. How weird is that?"

"Well, thank you, Barry, but it's a little late now. For a lot of things."

"Sorry, I…"

"I know." She made a throwaway gesture with her hand. "All water under the bridge now. For now, let's just focus on saving PerCan—again—and when all this is over…"

"Well get drunk together and hash it all out." He grinned.

"Oh no, Mister." She raised a forefinger between them. "The day you get this lady drunk is like never. Believe it."

But she was already grinning again. They had a lot of work to do, but it was work she was good at and enjoyed.

***

Getting Dante on their side proved to be the easiest part of her mission. 10 minutes into the story about their fired employees, he paled and said, "Oh God, Kayla, you can't let him keep going on."

The thought of having his brother wake up to a financially damaged, if not bankrupt, PerCan was too much to even think about, and while he didn't plan on leaving the hospital any time soon, he told Kayla to prepare a proxy for him. He'd sign anything she needed any time, any day, as long as she kept the company safe for Al when he returned. Because he would return—he had to.

Kayla watched Dante's pale face and the way he said, "He has to," over and over, and her heart wanted to break for him. Dante had lost his mother before he was old enough to know her and his father to the revenge fantasies of Greg Turner, and he had handled the murder and the suspicions around it with surprising grace. But his brother's mysterious illness all but did him in.

Kayla asked Nick for a private conference back at PerCan, and, to no surprise, he would go along with anything Dante decided and continue to encourage the employees to support her.

"Be careful," Kayla said. "There are a lot of staff members who were original Mariposa staff before the merger. They may feel some loyalty toward Donnelly."

"That ass." Nick made a dismissive noise.

"Ass or not, Nick. I don't want you to put yourself into a position where he ousts you as a traitor."

"I'll be careful."

"What about the testing? Anything new on that front?"

"Nothing, Kayla. Think about it this way—this is fantastic news. It means that whatever this virus is and wherever it came from, this grow operation and these greenhouses are not it."

Kayla smiled weakly. "Don't you let Rafael hear you call his indoor grow a greenhouse. He will personally…"

"Plant me in a pot somewhere and put a grow light on me. I know. You must miss him something awful. Any news?"

Kayla shook her head. "I do—miss him, that is. But we have a job to do here. We have got to make sure this company is OK and in good shape for him and Al to return to. You got me?"

Nick raised his hand for a high five.

"Gotcha. And personally speaking, I can't wait for you to run this show. You are going to kick ass."

Kayla looked down and raised a foot clad in a black-and-white Louboutin high heel. She raised an eyebrow and nodded.

"Thomas Donnelly's. Can't wait."

Nick had already reached the door when Kayla remembered something and called him back.

"Hey, Nick, just a sec."

"Something else?"

"Have either you or Dante heard from Roberto recently? At all?"

"Dante's brother Roberto? Not that I know of. Why?"

"You don't think that's strange?"

"Don't really know." Nick shrugged and looked out through the half-opened door into the hallway. "I guess he and Al were not that close."

"Maybe. Still… I just wanted to know. Thanks, Nick."

The door closed behind him, and Kayla settled into a chair of the tiny office she had commandeered for the day. It was still odd. Both brothers were acting odd. Dante for never leaving Al's side, and Roberto for not showing up in the first place. She would have loved to figure out why, but right then and there, she had bigger problems to solve.

FIFTEEN

Kayla started phoning employees who had been fired and begged and pleaded for them to come back for the harvest. Just when she thought they had barely enough of them convinced to pull off the impossible, Thomas Donnelly found out what she had done and stormed into the office she occupied with a head full of steam. His face had turned bright red, his eyes were bulging, and his hands flew through the air as if he wanted to both beat up and strangle her at the same time.

"Who gave you the fucking right to override my decisions?" he screamed at her, loud enough for them to hear him down the hall and in the elevator if needed.

Kayla was prepared. She knew this moment had been coming, and she had gathered support enough on the board to be hopeful about a vote. She casually reached into the pocket of her blazer, ostensibly to pull out a handkerchief. Her finger pushed a small button on a recording device in her pocket. Now every word Thomas Donnelly said to her would be captured forever. Nasty? For sure. Illegal? Probably. Admissible in court? No chance at all—but if anyone on the board still remained unconvinced, this would do.

"I made a decision to save the company, to retain staff critical to the upcoming harvest and the investment it represents," she said calmly.

"And you had no fucking right. I make the decisions, all of the decisions. I am CEO, do you hear me? Leave your manicured fingers off my orders and go down on the floor and tell all of those idiots they can turn right around and take their asses back home."

"I will do no such thing, Thomas. If you would listen for a minute…"

"I have no intentions of listening to you. You are nothing but Rafael's latest girlfriend. I gave an order. I expect it to be followed. I run this company. Do you hear me? I do. You have no right."

"Are you finished?" Kayla asked, still barely raising her voice. "Because there is a harvest down there, three grow pods full, representing around $2.5 million of potential profits—profits, Thomas. Which are going to spoil if we fire those workers again. Aside from the fact…"

"Aside from the fact that you had no right to fuck up my personnel decisions. Hire new people if you need them, not those bleeding-heart dykes and welfare cases you stuck me with."

"What did you just say?"

"I said hire new people."

His neck and face had turned so red as to be almost purple. For a moment, Kayla felt sorry for him, but, just as quickly as the thought had come, it passed again.

"I would like to see you try," she said. "Because the way you dealt with those you call welfare cases earned us a big fat zero score on every major job search board in the vicinity. Nobody wants to work for us any longer. And believe me—I checked. Do you understand that?"

"It isn't my fault if the personnel department can't make better choices and keep their people in line, Kayla. By God, I can't do everything. Now are you going to go down there and fire them again, or do I have to do that personally?"

"They are staying."

"The hell they are."

Thomas Donnelly pushed aside Kayla and opened his door. "Connie," he called out into the hall. *Screamed* might have been a better term because faces suddenly appeared in many of the doors. "Connie, fire those fucking losers again that Montecito here brought back. She had no authority."

He didn't receive an answer. Kayla had wisely sent Connie home for the afternoon. When he realized that he was on his own, Thomas let out a string of foul-mouthed curses that would have turned the air blue on any construction site in the world. He stormed back into the room and slammed the door.

"Fine, I'll do it myself."

"Feel free to do that," she said, proud of the fact that her voice didn't shake even a bit. "But I've already paid them for the day, so you might as well get work out of them for that money."

"You did what?"

"I paid them." Kayla shrugged. "I knew this would happen, and I wanted to get work done. At least until after the board meeting at three. After that, you can do whatever you wish, Thomas."

"There is no board meeting at three." Thomas stopped for a moment and rounded on her. "You," he snarled, shaking a finger at her. "You went behind my back and called a board meeting for today?"

"I did. We need to deal with this situation because if we lose this entire harvest, I do not want to be the responsible person who let it happen. So, we'll talk about it, and if we all agree, I will happily step down."

"You goddamned meddling… Fuck. You will leave if we all agree? Your word on this right now?"

Kayla crossed her fingers in her pockets. She still had work to do before this meeting, and the outcome was by no means certain. Not everybody was enthusiastic on voting with her; not everybody understood why things had to be done. Not everybody, not the majority she needed. Bet everything on red, then.

"Frankly, Thomas, if the board as an entity agrees that you have acted ethically and in the best interest of the company, then I can see no way to continue as a board member in good conscience. One way or another, I will be gone."

"Good riddance. I'm looking forward to it. I will personally kick your ass out of those front doors, and your boyfriend can stay in fucking Malta for all I care. I am taking my company back."

His eyes glittered. He was actually enjoying the thought of everyone on the board agreeing with him and of getting rid of Kayla once and for all. How he thought he could face Rafael after this, she couldn't fathom, but Thomas seemed to think that the good old boys would stick together.

"As you wish, Thomas. Try not to be late. Three p.m. in the boardroom."

She stalked out of the office and straight into the nearest ladies' room, where she had to put her forehead against the cool mirror for several minutes before her heartbeat felt anything approaching normal again. *Now or never*, she told herself. She had several hours in which to make it happen. Now or never.

***

True to their promises, Dante and Barry had been calling board members, preparing them as best as they could. When Kayla dropped in on them to prepare them for the meeting, she had no illusions that, right then and there, Thomas Donnelly would be doing the same thing—getting as many board members as he could on his side. But she had something they didn't: a recording of Thomas acting like a bull in a china shop, expressing no concern about the company's financial wellbeing and all the more about having his orders followed to the letter.

Kayla spoke until the words wouldn't come any longer. The fact that she seemed to be working with Barry J. Wentworth did not endear her to many of the longtime board members, such as Simon Graff, who'd been one of the founding members. They had seen and heard too much about Barry to be comfortable with any decision that originated at his end of the table.

One thing they had to agree on was that Kayla had always been honest with them. In the end she walked away with several proxies and enough promises to keep an open mind to be cautiously optimistic.

"I've done my best," she said to Barry on the phone when the clock was just inching up to two-thirty in the afternoon. "It is up to the board now to make the right decision, and if they don't…"

"They will."

"Well, if they don't, then I still have the publishing house to come back to," she said with a confidence she didn't feel. "When Donnelly kicks me out of the front door, as he promised. He would enjoy that. I have no idea how I am going to explain that to Rafael, though, if the worst happens."

"They will make the right decision," Barry said. "Don't you worry about that. They will."

SIXTEEN

The storm had finally blown itself out, but the devastation it left behind struck Rafael and his new friend as enormous when they finally emerged out of the government building, into a sunny, humid environment they no longer recognized.

"Je-sus," Rafael said to Jonas. "I'm not sure your jet survived all of this, but I don't think it's going to take to the skies anytime soon."

The building where they had found shelter had survived mostly intact, but many around them had not fared so well. Toppled trees, crumbled structures, damaged cars, and miscellaneous debris blown in by the ocean blocked every inch of roadway they might have used to get out of there.

They had stepped outside in an unguarded moment and looked around, unsure if they should believe their eyes. The Mediterranean paradise they had arrived to was gone, leaving a mangled, broken, and filthy mess.

The storm had left a cloud of damp heat over the city, and Rafael already wiped his forehead with a sleeve, killing one of many bugs that had obviously survived, now looking for a meal, swarming the two men.

"You're right on that one. I am told the airport looks just exactly like this. Massive destruction, not much else," Jonas said, kicking at a palm tree in their way, then pulling his toes back, wincing. "The plane was hangered, and I think it's fine, but—no tower, no runways, and no clearance."

"So, we're getting out of here another way."

"Geez, Rafael. Do you know anybody who is in construction and halfway talented? He's bound to earn a small fortune just now."

"I used to be in construction," Rafael corrected. "Now I just grow marijuana."

Jonas shook his head and swatted away more bugs.

"You know, most of the time I don't know if you are for real or just having me on. You are one weird dude, Rafael Covin. But forget it. There's not going to be any getting out of here going on for a while."

"I try." Rafael shrugged and kicked at the same palm tree. Fortunately, he'd been wearing his steel-toed boots when they left the hotel, and he didn't come away with a sore toe, as Jonas had.

"First, we gotta get all of this crap out of the way to open the road. If they have any heavy equipment around here, we can get started right now."

Rafael looked around as if he expected a backhoe to materialize behind him.

"I doubt it."

More out of habit, Jonas checked his cell phone and slipped it back into his pocket.

"They said that was going to be tomorrow," Rafael reminded him. "Which gives us all day to tackle this."

"You just don't give up, do you?"

"Nope. I've been told that's a bit of a character flaw."

"Depends on which way you look at it." Jonas looked around him, desperation clouding his face. "Shit, this is going to take…"

"A while, but it's doable. All we need…"

"What's so important back home anyway, if I might ask? Important enough for you to risk life and limb for? Now that the storm's over, I think the government was planning to put us up in any surviving luxury hotels until they can get the airport back up and running. Kick back, take it easy, have a vacation. We deserve it. We've been through a kickass storm."

"I left my fiancée with a perfectly working manufacturing setup. Meanwhile, the CEO caught some mysterious ailment or something and is completely out of commission. The guy who took over for him is a total dickhead who's going to wreck the company, and there's a harvest coming up that's going to lose millions of dollars if they don't manage it. So, you go on ahead to that hotel and your vacation. I need to be getting back yesterday, if not sooner."

"Jesus." Jonas shook his head and climbed over the next pile of fallen trees alongside Rafael. "I can see why you're pushing so hard, but if you want to get back to that fiancée of yours, I would be…"

"I'm being careful—always," Rafael said, just as he cut himself on a sharp piece of metal caught in the debris. He shook his hand and sucked on the cut.

"I can see that. Seriously, Rafael? You have no idea what's in that. You want to lay down alongside that CEO of yours?"

Rafael stubbornly pulled and kicked at another metal container in his way until Jonas put a hand on his shoulder.

"It's just another day or so, Rafael."

"It's not just another day. It's everything I built over the last few years. Everything. I left my fiancée with this lunatic."

"She sounds like a smart lady, Rafael. If she is with you, she would have to be."

"She is." Rafael kicked a rock and winced when it wouldn't budge. "The best. And if I had known Al would kick it, and this—this Donnelly would take over, I wouldn't have gone anywhere."

"Obviously. But we'll get back home." Jonas grabbed his arm a little harder. "I got two little kids at home I want to get back to. You think I'm taking any chances here? I suggest you ask our handler there, Rick, if you can help with anything—safely. Heck, looking at you and with your construction background, you probably know how to drive all of this equipment stuff and make it… do something."

Rafael shook his head and shoved his hands into his pockets, fingers curled into fists with frustration. "No," he said.

"No what?"

"I don't know how to drive all of that shit," he said, grinning broadly. "I know how to make it dance."

"Jesus Christ." Jonas reached for his forehead and smothered a grin. "Now, let's get back inside and find Rick. He might be happy to have you lend a hand—safely."

"Probably not. He has issues with my—attitude."

Despite the devastation around them, Jonas laughed and slapped Rafael's shoulder. "Hell, I can't imagine anyone who wouldn't."

"What? I'm a likeable fellow," Rafael said. "Most of the time. I just have opinions."

"I bet. Tell you what—when we finally get out of this place, I want to meet that fiancée of yours. She must be one heck of a remarkable woman to put up with your stubborn head all day long."

"She is, and she tells me that on a regular basis," Rafael said, scratching said stubborn head. He stared at the devastation around them, trying to reconcile it with the beautiful paradise he had arrived in days ago. Someone called out to them, and he saw Rick leaving the building, waving his arms wildly. He elbowed Jonas in the side and grinned.

"Oh, look, there's our official handler now, getting ready to chastise us for coming out here. Think he'll faint if I ask him for a 'dozer and a boom crane?"

Rick joined them, and, to his credit, he only paled a little when Rafael made his request. Despite his disheveled appearance, he was probably grateful as could be to hand off this crazy man and make him someone else's responsibility very, very soon.

"No need to drive one of those machines, Rafael, although I am sure you could show us a thing or two. I have excellent news."

"Do tell."

"Tomorrow morning, first light, there will be a military transport coming in. They have supplies to drop off, and they are in a hurry, but they'd be happy to take you to the nearest functioning airbase, unless you'd like to be our guest for a while."

"Aw." Rafael pushed out his lower lip. "I was kinda getting all excited about driving construction equipment again. That's one of those skills you never lose, you know. That pile of uprooted trees over there, give me a crane—gone. Poof. You ought to try it someday."

"I am sure," Rick said, trying his best to smile. "You too, Mr. Hurst, if you would like."

"I would like," Jonas said. "And I would keep an eye on this one. If there's a piece of equipment around here somewhere, I'd make sure the keys aren't in the ignition."

Rick herded them back inside, away from the suddenly oppressive heat and multitude of bugs that had come out, realizing there were real live humans to be had here. Rick swatted at the swarm around his head and steered them inside toward the bar. If this wasn't cause for celebration, he didn't know what was.

SEVENTEEN

Dante. Dante Ivers, youngest of the three Ivers sons, had long ago traded in his father's chauffeured limos and bought himself a motorcycle. He used it regularly to escape the snarled downtown traffic on his way out to the PerCan building. It wasn't one of those super-fast machines, nothing made for racing or, God forbid, off-roading, but cherry-red, tricked out, and big and heavy enough to be potentially dangerous in so many ways. Motorcycles could be like that—dangerous. Very, very dangerous and sometimes deadly.

Greg Turner flipped through the images on his cellphone and went quite still for a moment, narrowing his eyes and cocking his head. Was that a noise outside? After a minute of holding his breath, listening for anything that might be coming at him, he relaxed and turned back to the pictures on his phone.

He'd have to find a new spot soon. As the weather improved, people would start coming out here again. The dedicated campers would swarm the place the moment the ground was no longer frozen solid. Hiding would become a lot more difficult. Essentially, he thought, he had two choices. Either get done what he needed to before that happened or find a new hideout.

Each option had its own beauty. The pull of just getting it done was strong, but then again, so was the enjoyment of the process.

Turner grinned as he remembered sneaking around the interior of PerCan at night. It had been so ridiculously easy to sneak in, for someone who knew how cannabis growers worked, anyway. And that idiot, that CEO wandering around at all hours of the day, he'd nearly peed his pants when he heard him! He'd even called out for God's sake. *Anybody there…?* Turner chuckled to himself. Oh, if that fool knew what he, the mastermind, had been able to do, while he blundered about the grow area.

He was tempted to savor this triumph just a little longer. There had to be a way. There had to be a way to avoid detection and stretch out this delicious feeling of revenge.

He looked back at the image of Dante and tapped the head of the man on the motorcycle. Obediently, the image zoomed in, on the black, brand-new motorcycle helmet. There was not a mark on it—yet. Helmets were good. Helmets were nice and safe, but now and then, things happened to motorcycles. Mechanical things, things that might make that safe driver lose all control and go flying! He'd never go near one of those machines himself, and he could list all of the reasons why.

Turner zoomed out of the picture again and ran his thumb along the side of his phone, thinking.

A plan began to take shape in his mind, and it was a great plan. It started as an idea and grew into something with real substance. Yes. This was good—this was perfect. This would finally put some zing into his revenge, rather than wandering around merely frightening the Ivers boys. Yes.

EIGHTEEN

All of the board members had filed into the conference room with the briefest of hellos to one another, found their places, and sat, pens and papers in front of them. No one dared move or chat with the person beside him or her. The gravity of the situation was all but written on their faces.

It almost felt as if a spell had been cast over the conference room, Kayla thought, and if anybody moved, it would be broken and leave them in confusion. She glanced around the room surreptitiously, trying to gauge individual moods, but no one would meet her eyes directly. Was that a bad sign?

Her hands clenched in her lap, and she forced herself to breathe deeply and evenly. In and out. She was doing the right thing, doing the right thing, doing…

Then without warning, the door to the conference room flew open and hit the wall hard enough to leave a mark in the drywall. Bang, the spell broke. Thomas Donnelly stood, backlit by the fluorescents of the hallway, arms out by his side, like the proverbial avenging angel. He ignored all of them in the room and zeroed in on Kayla.

"You," he thundered, taking two steps to stand beside her. "You. You dare to try to get rid of me? What the fuck."

"Please take a seat, Thomas."

"You don't give any orders around here. I will do no such thing. You—all of you." He swept his arm around the room. "All of you.

There will be no meeting today. You can all just go back to your little offices or your little cars and split. I am CEO here. I am! And nobody gets rid of me. Do you hear me?"

Everybody could probably hear him, down to the last person in the farthest corner of the building.

"This is a properly called meeting," Kayla began, all but ignoring him, while she hoped to God her voice wouldn't shake.

"Enough."

Thomas grabbed her shoulder hard enough to hurt. Without thinking, she cried out, and that sound brought all the male board members to their feet.

"Thomas."

"Enough already."

"Calm down."

Thomas drew his hand back and stared at it for a moment, as if it were a thing separate from him. He took a step back and shoved his hands into his pockets. One by one, the men sat again.

Kayla drew in another deep breath and continued. She looked at her meeting agenda in front of her and put it back down.

"Why am I bothering with the formalities anyway? It is exactly this type of behavior that has caused me to call this meeting today."

Thomas flippantly grabbed a chair and dropped into it. If she'd been hoping for contrition, she was getting none.

"I can be a bit rough. So what?" he said. "My people understand. They're used to me using the occasional cussword. And before you open your mouth again, let me just remind you that Rafael is no choirboy either."

"We are not talking about Rafael today."

"Might as well, Montecito. If you're going to have somebody follow me around all day and count how often I say 'fuck this shit,' they're going to be pretty busy, lady."

Someone at the table gasped. Kayla did not look up to check who it was. *Just keep digging,* she thought and finally smiled sweetly at Thomas.

"It is also not your language we are talking about, Thomas. Bad as it is, it is not at the heart of the issue."

"This is a colossal fucking waste of time." Thomas's eyes darted around the room and finally came to rest on the face of Clint, his former CFO and staunch Donnelly supporter. "Clint. You've known me for years. Through Mariposa and before that. Back me up here. I get rough sometimes, and there are times I have to—it's our business. But it works. I always get top performances out of my people. Always."

Clint reached down and pulled a thick folder out of his portfolio. He carefully positioned it in front of him and put his hands flat on the cover.

"This is from the personnel department," he said softly. "All complaints, Thomas. Every single one of them. And I followed up with all of them, to ensure they are aboveboard. Surely you understand that as a publicly traded company…"

"Fuck it, Clint. I fired a few Nancies who were not doing their jobs. So what? We need hands that work, able bodies. We've got a harvest coming up. A big one. I don't need anybody who won't pull their weight. Fuck."

"And this harvest would never even happen if Kayla had not managed to hire back these people."

"Bullshit. They were useless in the first place! Are you going to be the judge of what works down on the production floor, or am I?"

"Thomas." Clint spoke up a little and straightened his shoulders. "You know I am your friend. I've known you for a very long time, and I know you mean well. You are a very capable man, but this is an issue you need to work on. It is a serious issue."

"Clint—I…" Thomas sighed and started again. "I'm disappointed to see all of you ganging up on me like this. I assume this thing is unanimous, then?"

He looked up, but closed faces met him. No one dared to speak, and for a long moment, the conference room was steeped in heavy silence.

"I see." He pressed his lips together and looked at the members of the board, one after the other. "You might have had the fucking guts and courtesy to come to me first instead of conspiring with her."

"Thomas, the timing of this harvest…"

"The timing, the timing, fuck the timing, OK? The least you could do before you ruin a guy is look him in the goddamn face and say what you have to say."

He brought a fist to his mouth and refused to look at Kayla, who had done just that. "Congratulations, looks like you won. So now what? Who gets to do the honors and kick me out of here? You, I assume?" His eyes blazed fire at Kayla.

"Nobody is kicking you out, Thomas. You're still a shareholder, you're still vice president, and you can even take an active role."

"Who is it? You or that douchebag Wentworth?"

"In light of everything that happened…"

"Fuck it, Montecito! Just answer the question already. You or Wentworth?"

"I will be taking the CEO role in the interim until Al is well enough to return."

"Jesus fucking Christ." Thomas gathered his papers haphazardly into the portfolio he had brought and stared around. "Good luck following her, all of you sheep. Good luck. You'll be hearing from my lawyer."

He violently pushed back from the table, jumped to his feet hard enough to make the chair slam into the wall behind him, and turned his back on all of them without another word, storming out the room with the same fury as when he had entered it. When the door slammed shut behind him, Kayla exhaled in one long breath.

She covered her face with both hands for a moment, leaning forward, before she straightened up again and looked around.

"My apologies," she said quickly. "That did not go well. Thank you all for your support today. I know this was extremely difficult. Especially for you, Clint. Thank you."

Clint, earnest and quiet, slowly took off his glasses, folded them, and nodded his head ever so slightly.

"The only reason I went against him was because I felt it was for the best of the company. Right now, PerCan and the impending harvest need to come first. This harvest will make or break our budget for the coming year, if not more. That's all."

"Of course. Thank you all. For the sake of propriety, let us have and record a formal vote to relieve Tom Donnelly of the role of CEO and furthermore to install me as the CEO of PerCan Consolidated effective immediately. Clint, would you second please?"

Clint nodded.

"Any objections?"

No one raised a hand, and Kayla nodded. "On record then as passed. Again, thank you all. I will cause the minutes and resolutions to be prepared this afternoon. Our Investor Relations department will produce the required news releases."

She finally managed a thin smile and looked around the room at her fellow board members. They looked all but shell shocked. "I believe we are adjourned, unless there is anything else?"

She heard someone say, "Time for a drink, for God's sake," and felt the stress of the moment leave her body.

A general shuffling and murmuring ensued, as her fellow board members gathered their paperwork and belongings and filed out of the room. Every single one of them stopped by her chair and gently touched her shoulder or shook her hand, along with a few encouraging and supportive words, and, by the time the last person had left, she was close to tears. Her hands trembled hard enough to hide them under the table.

No time for that now. There was far too much to do.

Reluctantly, she left the boardroom and installed herself in Al's office.

She didn't want to hang her blazer on the coat rack he had personally brought in, didn't want to put her laptop onto his desk or go through the files in his drawers.

It felt all wrong—and still right at the same time. Al was still here, in this room, evident in the neatness of the pens and pencils and other items on his desk, in the precise layout of his calendar and file system, as if he had just stepped away for a moment and would be back any second.

Thomas Donnelly had never set foot in here and simply used his own office in the building. Even the last entry on Al's desk calendar was still the board meeting, the horrible meeting where he had collapsed.

Kayla made herself sit in his chair and ran her fingers along the edge of the desk. *I'll take care of things for you,* she thought and immediately called Dante at the hospital to give him the update.

Al's condition had improved slightly, Dante told her, and they expected him to wake up any time now. That was all the news she needed to put aside the last few days and push ahead with everything that needed to be done.

NINETEEN

Kayla sat down to draft a memo to all current employees, starting again and again, until she had the tone just right. She carefully described Thomas's 'departure from the board' as something that was happening due to 'other opportunities in his career' and sent it down to IR and the personnel department. She wanted to run the company properly, not do a hatchet job on the guy.

Next came the endless list of people who needed to be hired back and numerous rumors circulating within the company which needed to be squashed.

Eventually, she thought, eventually, someone needed to put their butt into a chair and begin drafting a useful code of conduct and ethics policy, but it was not going to be Kayla Montecito, and it wasn't going to happen right now. For now, the most important item on the agenda had to be the harvest.

Kayla had no idea how a cannabis harvest happened or what was involved. All she knew was that Rafael came home dead tired when a harvest was on and usually said something like, "Thank God that's done."

It was a frightening thought that this upcoming harvest was to be one of the most significant in company history—and on her shoulders. More than ever, they needed to be a team, and, more than ever, that spirit was entirely missing from the ranks. *Great, just great. Do the impossible without knowing how and without getting any help.*

In a perfect world, where everything went to plan, Rafael would have been back by now, full of energy and enthusiasm, and he would have handled everything. He would have said go, and people would have gone there. Where was Rafael when she needed him? *Hopefully safe*, she thought and sent a little prayer to whichever entity was in charge of protecting him just now.

No, she'd have to figure this out on her own. And there was only one person she could think of right now, who would have all of the information she needed—Dante Ivers. Dante and Nick knew every moment, every minute step of the process, and she needed them. As much as she hated pulling Dante away from Al's bedside, she needed Nick to work his magic with the staff while Dante brought her up to speed.

And surprisingly, Dante agreed without the slightest bit of hesitation.

"I understand," he said. "Harvest time is tricky, and one of this size is… well, I don't want to frighten you. When you know what you're doing, it's easy. Don't worry about it. I'll come to PerCan and get you up to speed."

"Thanks, Dante, I hate to pull you away from Al…"

"He's looking much better, Kayla. They've taken him away for another round of tests just now anyway, most likely for the rest of the afternoon. Your timing is excellent. I'll pop in to see you right now, probably be back before he is. I should probably shower and change first, but…"

"I am grateful for any time you are willing to spend away from your brother, to get me up to speed," Kayla said quickly. "I can send a car for you if you like."

"No need. My motorcycle is still down in the hospital parking garage. Probably cost a small fortune to get it out."

"God, I hate that thing." Kayla shook her head, although Dante sounded more hopeful and energized than he had in days. It was hard to argue with him. "It has got to be a male thing I don't understand. Rafa thinks the thing is exceptionally cool too."

"Yep. That's because the man knows what he is talking about. Nick, on the other hand, is with you, gives me a lecture every time."

"Just please drive carefully."

"Always do, Kay. I can't tell you how good it is to see Al doing better. I'll see you in half an hour."

Finally, Kayla allowed herself to exhale.

***

"I have things in hand," she said to Barry a few minutes later when he called for an update. "Donnelly left, the appropriate news releases have gone out, and Nick is unofficially updating the staff here."

"Wonder what he's telling them," Barry laughed. "Ding dong, the a-hole is gone?"

"I don't want to know, Barry," she said a little more sharply than intended. "Our official news release states that Thomas left to pursue other opportunities in his career."

"The usual BS."

"Exactly. And officially, that is what we are sticking to. Nick is free to tell fellow staffers anything he needs to in order to restore morale and teamwork. Meantime, Dante is on his way here to give me a rundown on the harvest."

"I could have done that. I still know a few things. But if Dante is coming to see you, Al must be feeling better. That's good news."

"Slight improvement," she confirmed. "I didn't want to pull Dante off, but he's the best person to clue me in on harvests. No offense to your purportedly vast knowledge."

"None taken. There were those who thought I knew enough to run an illegal grow op in a hidden part of the building, so don't knock it."

"Oh, I remember all too well, Barry."

And, she thought, *I remember how you ran off to avoid explaining yourself, leaving Rafael and me with a pile of broken pieces.*

"Speaking of which, you still have not heard from Roberto?"

"I have not," Barry confirmed, and Kayla's unease grew a bit again.

"I don't like it. Soon as Dante and I are finished here, I think I will take a drive out to Roberto's operation and see him in person. Something is going on here."

"Let's try not to overthink everything, OK?" Barry said. "He's probably steamed at Al for one thing or another."

"I beg to differ. This is more than a tiff between brothers. There is a man out there who swore revenge on the Ivers family, and Al is in a hospital with an unknown virus. This is not the time to carry a grudge because of some little thing. I'll figure it out. Dante and the harvest come first."

"Well, girl boss, if you need my help, I'm here, OK?"

Barry sounded his usual cheerful and charming self, and he made Kayla smile again, despite everything that was going on around her.

"I will be sure to let you know, Barry. Dante should be almost here, so I'll talk to you later."

Reluctantly, she fired up Al's laptop and pulled up previous harvest records to get marginally up to speed before Dante arrived and immersed herself in the data.

***

Kayla looked up a little while later, feeling as if she couldn't cram another byte's worth of data into her head. Who knew there was that much to a harvest? Who knew this much could go wrong, be neglected, or just plain go undetected—and how many of those little things could spoil the entire harvest? There were mountains of questions, warnings, and checklists, and Al had studied, annotated, and bookmarked them all. He probably knew them by heart. If she didn't already, Kayla developed a newfound admiration for the tall, quiet man so many thought of as aloof.

Dante would have his job cut out to help her make sense of it all. Dante...

Dante had not arrived yet. *Odd*, she thought. Traffic apparently was worse than either one of them had anticipated. Hopefully, it wouldn't cut too far into the time Dante would be able to spare for her.

Kayla thought nothing of it and pulled up another document on harvests. This one was written by Al himself, listing numerous issues and problems, and how he thought they could be avoided. She bookmarked that one as well to ask Dante's opinion about it when he finally got there.

Fighting a mild sense of irritation, she realized that she had spoken to him over an hour ago, when he wanted to see her in 30 minutes. The hospital was a good half-hour's drive from PerCan. Allowing for traffic and some time to get from his brother's room down to the parking garage…?

She pulled up his phone number on her phone and realized that if he were driving just then, he wouldn't answer the phone anyway. *Fine*, she thought. Another 20 minutes of patience before she would get irritated about having been stood up.

She picked up her phone when it rang, hoping for Dante, only to find Barry on the other end of the line.

"It's you again."

"Don't sound so enthusiastic. I was wondering if I could interrupt you and Dante for two minutes."

"Interrupt away—still waiting on Dante."

"I thought he was there."

"I know. He's late. Either something came up or traffic is particularly horrid. Nothing going on with Al, I hope."

"Probably just traffic."

Barry didn't sound so sure. His hesitation echoed her own worries, and she reacted a little more harshly than she had wanted to.

"So, what? Why were you interrupting then? We only spoke 20 minutes ago."

"No big deal," Barry said slowly. "You were asking about Roberto earlier, so I thought I'd take one thing off your plate and call him. Get the lay of the land, see what's happening in his world."

"And?"

"And nothing. That's what's weird. Nobody answered the phone."

"Well, why didn't you call the company then? Pride, I think it's called."

"No, Kayla, you don't understand—I did call Pride Cannabis Products. Nobody picked up the phone."

That one gave her pause for a moment. A business not answering its main line during the day—that was usually a very bad sign. Al's brother Roberto had put a nice little operation together: small-batch cannabis growing, specialty and unusual strains for the most part. They were a small but robust operation, and there was talk about specializing in private grows, something for customers who were happy for a specially tailored product.

Al didn't speak of Roberto often, but usually with pride. His erstwhile criminal brother had finally found something he enjoyed and put all of his heart and soul into. So why wouldn't they…

"Checked their online store," Barry continued. "Just has a note that they're not accepting any orders at the moment, due to delivery issues."

"A harvest gone badly potentially," she said with a sideways glance at all the reading she'd been doing over the last hour. "There are issues…"

"I know there are issues," Barry said, a little impatient now. "I was in the business, remember? And Roberto is strictly small batch—one at a time. If one harvest goes wrong, it's one product you lose. All others are fine."

"I know that. Will you not rag on me?" Kayla found herself nibbling on a thumbnail, something she'd quit years ago. Quickly, she tucked the thumb into a fist. "Can you do me a favor and check into it? I'm still waiting for Dante, wherever he has gone to before seeing me, and I'm hoping Rafael will try to get in touch again."

"You got it, sweetheart."

"Barry!"

"Just joking. I was planning on driving out there anyway in about

20 minutes, when my last appointment of the day leaves, OK? Let you know what I find."

Kayla hung up the phone and went over to the picture window down into the manufacturing area to watch the hustle and bustle below. Rafael tended to pace when he was thinking or nervous, which drove her insane. She preferred to stand still and let her thoughts do the wandering.

Three Ivers men, all out of touch in one way or another.

The same three Ivers men who had been threatened by a revenge-crazy criminal. Coincidence?

Kayla didn't believe in coincidences. *Dammit, Rafael, where are you? I need your help,* she thought, and just as if she had summoned him, her phone rang.

The connection was terrible, but her heart leapt at hearing his voice and hearing him be cheerful and boisterous as ever.

"Hey, sweetheart, they had to get the army out here to get me back to you. About to fly out in one of those massive military transport planes. What do you say about that?"

"I'd say it's just about time. I really need you here, right now."

"What's wrong?" Rafael asked, all cheering and joking forgotten just like that. "Is it Al? Is he worse?"

"No change in Al, but Roberto has been completely out of touch. Even his business phone isn't being answered. I have this massive harvest to deal with, and Dante, who is supposed to talk me through it, somehow found something better to do."

"What do you mean, 'something better to do?'" Rafael cussed softly. "How could he find 'something better to do' with this harvest on the calendar?"

"I don't know. He was supposed to be here," Kayla checked her watch, "an hour ago, to brief me on the harvest, and he hasn't shown up."

"That's not Dante. Those plants are his life. He will literally go without food and drink to make sure those plants are treated right."

Kayla fought the rising panic. The background noise on that call grated on her nerves. Yelling, commands, engine noises. There was too much she needed to explain and not enough time. Rafael sounded like he was in a car somewhere, likely a military vehicle, hopefully being brought somewhere safe. It would be several days yet before he could even think about getting back. If she worried him now, he'd just panic and do something ill-advised to get back here faster. This one was on her. She would have to do it without his help.

"Kay?"

"Still here, sorry. Just irritated that he stood me up, that's all. What's the plan for you guys, then?"

Somebody yelled woo-hoo, and Rafael laughed and called back. It was so good to hear him and to know he was all right.

"If you hadn't guessed yet, right now, we are sitting in the back of a military pickup truck, damn uncomfortably too. They'll drive us to the nearest city to be checked over, which is a waste of time if you ask me."

"Please don't skip it. I know you. You think everything is just fine, and then…"

"I know—my new friend Jonas says the same thing.

"All our stuff went down along with the beach hotel, so I'm assuming they'll outfit us with new passports and things and fly us back into the country ASAP."

"Good. It'll be so good to have you back."

"Aw, shucks, I wasn't even sure you'd miss me. What about Donnelly? Is he behaving himself?"

"Donnelly? No, no chance. We voted him out with a meeting. 'Tis I who has to run this show now."

That gave Rafael a bit of pause.

"Wow," was all he said. "I mean—wow. But how on earth did you…"

"I'll tell you when you get back. Hurry."

"I will, my love—I have to go now. There are other guys on this truck who want to use the phone. I love you."

"Love you too, Rafael."

But the connection was already broken. Kayla held her phone tight in both hands and turned back to the window and the production floor. That was one of them safe.

Now all she had to do was figure out this harvest.

And find a way to bring peace back to this company.

And figure out where Al had picked up this infection and how to get him better.

And finally get hold of Dante.

Her irritation with him suddenly grew into a large, smoldering thing. If Dante had wanted to stay at the hospital with Al, he should have just said so, perhaps pointed her in the right direction to read up on what she needed.

She raised her phone again and punched out his number with angry stabs.

"Dante, what is going on?" she asked when the line was answered.

But an entirely unfamiliar voice said, "Hello, are you there?"

Not Dante.

"I'm sorry," she said, looking down at her phone. "I must have dialed a wrong number..."

How could that happen?

"Wait—don't hang up. Are you family? There's been an accident. They're heading to the hospital."

"Hey, you! Put that phone down right now."

Somebody laughed hysterically; then the connection was dropped. Kayla wanted to scream. Dante! He was on his way to her from the hospital. What on earth had happened here?

There's been an accident—they are going to the hospital...

In an instant she knew why Dante had been so late. That damned motorcycle. She dropped her phone and pounded her hand with her fist. Too many things in her hands, in her life just then. Rafael in a tornado. Al at the hospital, fighting for his life. A mega harvest due at PerCan. Roberto completely out of contact. Dante—Dante?

She needed help.

Nick—Nick could likely handle the harvest until they figured out what had happened, what was going on, but if he up and left now…

Compartmentalize, Kayla, she told herself. *Nick needs to handle the staff and this harvest.*

She had no idea what to do in a harvest. He needed to take the lead for the moment, but if she told him about Dante… She couldn't. Nick would drop everything and be in his car five minutes from now if she told him—harvest be damned.

I can't let that happen, she thought. *Dear God, I cannot let that happen.*

She tried Barry, but didn't get an answer on his phone. He was probably already on his way to Roberto's. She was entirely on her own to figure out what was going on with Dante.

Pull yourself together.

With shaking hands, she dialed Nick's phone number and prayed once again that she could keep her voice steady.

"Nick, I hate to do this to you."

"Never a good thing when you start like that. What's up? Isn't Dante teaching you all about the harvest just now?"

"Something came up, Nick, and I'm going to have to deal with it. I'm sorry, but I have to leave you alone with the preparations for this harvest for a bit. Please tell me you can handle it and the staff."

A long pause ensued, and for a moment, she crossed her fingers he wouldn't say, *No, you need to be here.* If that happened—if that happened…

"It would be better if the new CEO would put in some face time after all this mess we've been through, rather than take off at the first drop of a hat," Nick said slowly. "It doesn't look good, but, if you think it's vitally important…"

"Please trust me, Nick—it is really, really important."

"Something going on?" he asked suspiciously. "Something with Rafael?"

"No, God, no. He's making his way back slowly but surely. I just have to take care of this. You're going to be OK?"

"Well, yeah, but I don't like it."

He didn't sound happy, and he would be even less happy when she came back with news. God. Why did everything have to come together when she was alone here to take care of things?

Because you can handle it, a voice in her head said, and she forced a bit of levity into her voice.

"Thanks. You're a gem. I'll be back before you know it."

"See ya."

This time, she didn't bother waiting for a car and driver, but grabbed Rafael's car and got to the hospital as fast as she could. A part of the main road was blocked off—the accident she was worried about, perhaps—and she had to take a massive detour.

By the time she arrived at the hospital, she was angry enough to spit nails, and she should have suspected that information was not available to anyone but family members.

"But I'm his fiancée," she lied, crossing her fingers behind her back. "His brother is in this hospital in another wing, and his parents are deceased, so I suggest you hurry."

They put her into a waiting room, and Kayla waited. One of the things she was worst at in life—waiting.

Other patients' family members were in the same position, sitting in uncomfortable plastic chairs, staring at outdated magazines without reading or at the posters on the walls espousing healthy living.

Don't ever drive. She thought that should be one of those posters. *Don't drive—no cars, no motorcycles. Just walk everywhere.*

She checked in on Al's condition in the meantime, and at least he showed some encouraging signs of recovery. Just as Dante had said, they expected him to wake up, any time now.

Dante…

Kayla almost ran down an orderly with a tray of water bottles when the door at the end of the hall opened and a tall man in doctor's scrubs came in, looking around.

"Sorry," she murmured to the orderly who gave her a dirty look, but Kayla had already reached the doctor.

"Sorry—I'm Kayla Montecito. Are you the doctor who is treating Dante Ivers?"

He looked her up and down, and Kayla thought she must look a fright. She still wore the severe suit she had put on to manage the directors' meeting this morning. Somewhere along the line, she had ditched the high heels and put on a pair of ill-fitting running shoes from the promo department. They were neon green and said "PerCan Cannabis" on them. Her hair felt like a bird's nest from running her hands through it all day, and she had left her purse behind, carrying a phone and a wallet only. Besides, as Dante's fiancée, she was just a bit too old…

"Sorry—it's been a day," she said. "What about Dante?"

"No doubt," the doctor quipped. "Perhaps both of you need to slow down a little."

Kayla nodded and kept the angry retort inside. "Dante?"

"Your fiancée," the doctor said and put just enough sarcasm on the word, "is lucky he was wearing a lot of high-end safety equipment, or he would not be alive any longer."

"What happened? Tell me—how is he?"

"As to what happened, I can't tell you, other than he flew out of a curve at a very, very high speed. As to his condition, he is lucky. Several broken bones, a concussion, and assorted lacerations. He's being moved into a regular room. You should be able to see him soon."

"Oh thank God." Kayla felt her legs go weak and reached for a nearby chair to steady herself.

"As I said, ma'am, the protective suit, airbag vest, and helmet he was wearing saved his life. I suggest you encourage him to keep wearing them if he ever gets onto another motorcycle."

"Most definitely," she said, feeling her hands shake.

There were airbags for motorcycles? Dante owned one of those? *Dear God, thank you. Nick is with you on that. He hates the thing.*

"And I suggest both of you slow down. And you should eat something. You look like your blood sugar is in the basement."

"Yes, yes, of course."

The doctor walked away, and Kayla still clung to the back of the chair beside her.

Dante—was—alive. He was going to be OK; that was all that mattered right now. At the same time, a little nagging voice in the back of her head reminded her: two of the Ivers men in hospital, and one of them disappeared. It did not take a detective to start thinking about the man who had sworn revenge on the Ivers family.

Who was it who had answered the phone when she called Dante earlier? An innocent bystander or someone more sinister? The laugh, that manic laugh just as the call ended, still haunted her.

Kayla wanted to walk away, but her feet refused to move, her hands couldn't let go of the chair, and finally, she allowed herself to sit in it and take a few breaths.

TWENTY

Kayla put her palm against her forehead and just—rested. Rested for a few minutes, letting the hospital world with its hushed voices, beeps, and clicks and soft footfalls on linoleum floors ebb around her.

Greg Turner—Al—Dante. More than ever, it seemed to her she needed to speak to Roberto, to ensure that he was safe, and to get his take on all of this. But first… first, she would have to speak to Nick and admit that she had kept the information about Dante's accident from him.

She took a deep breath and blew it out again, rolled her shoulders, and started to get to her feet. This was not a conversation to look forward to. Nick would be understandably furious with her. If anyone had information about Rafael and intentionally kept it from her in order to advance business interests, then…

"Miss? You can see your fiancé for a few minutes now. He said to get you."

Kayla blinked and shook her head before she realized the nurse was speaking to her. "Err…?"

"You can come in and see him. A few minutes only, and please don't upset him, but he is alert again."

The nurse, who was just about Kayla's age, mustered her head to toe, but to her credit did not even blink as she led her to Dante's room. Another thing to apologize for, Kayla thought, at least to Dante, if not to Nick.

Dante was just being wheeled into a room, obviously from the emergency department, and he looked white and tiny in the hospital bed, an arm and a leg in solid braces and his head swathed in bandages. A cut on his cheek and another one along his neck told their own story.

"Hey there, Kay," he said weakly and managed a little wink. "Knew it had to be you."

"Sorry," she mouthed and looked around the room for a chair. All that was available was an uncomfortable stool, but she took it.

"How do you feel? Dumb question, I know."

"Ask me again when all of those fine drugs they gave me wear off," he said, smiling crookedly. "I seem to be in one piece."

"Trust me, I am giving thanks for that."

She took in all of his braces, bandages, stitches, and IV equipment in one long look and shook her head.

"I knew I didn't like motorcycles."

"It's safe if you do it right."

"Oh yeah?" She put her hand on an un-bandaged spot on his shoulder. "Airbags? For motorcycles? I had no idea they had such a thing."

"Yup. It's like a collar with a bunch of sensors and compressed air cartridge. Inflates when you fall. Expensive as shit, but Nick insisted when they came out. Seems to be worth it." He waggled his injured leg briefly. "You think?"

"But what on earth happened, Dante? Did somebody clip you?"

It seemed like an obvious thing, if you were trying to get rid of someone—clip him on the road, watch him crash, and take off as if nothing had happened.

"That's the thing. I don't know." His voice became quite hard, and something cold came into his eyes. "All of a sudden, I lost control of the steering."

"Horrible." Kayla shuddered. "But I guess that can happen, right?"

"On a long stretch of road? In midtown traffic, at a normal speed? There was not another driver even close to me. I know. I checked."

"But… You think?"

They looked at one another, and, without speaking, they understood.
You think it could be Turner?

Maybe.

Kayla pressed her lips together and took a few deep breaths. "I'll ask them to examine your bike," she said softly. "With a magnifying glass. I want the best technician there is to tell us what happened."

"What's left of the bike, you mean?" Dante tried a weak attempt at a smile. "We ran into a concrete overpass abutment together—I ditched before we hit."

Kayla closed her eyes and wished she could un-see the image that suddenly forced itself on her. Hitting a solid wall at high speed—downtown. The real miracle here was Dante there in bed, alive, joking about it.

"We'll find out," she croaked. "But first I have to apologize to Nick."

"Nick? Why him?"

"I came here before telling him what happened," she admitted and took her hand away. "I didn't… He has so much on the go with that damned harvest."

"He'll understand, Kayla."

"I don't know. I wouldn't be so quick if it were me. But I have no idea what needs to be done with the harvest. I couldn't even begin to speak to the staff, and if he left…"

"Kayla, look at me. Nick will understand."

Kayla did, and he held her eyes with his for a long moment. "Nick will come around—it might take him a day or two."

"That's what I'm worried about."

"But he will understand. I'll make sure he does. Now, go tell him I'm not dead."

"Don't even talk like that."

The nurse came to fetch Kayla again. Apparently, this visit had gone on long enough, and she was not impressed with Kayla's insistent inquiries into hospital security.

"We are an institution of healing, not a prison," she said stiffly. "I assure you, your fiancé will be just fine."

TWENTY-ONE

Kayla felt everything but fine on the way home. Consciously, she avoided the overpass where the accident had happened, as if by not looking she could un-see and unhear—and, most of all, stop being frightened.

The one thing she needed most was nowhere to be found—answers. Someone needed to figure out how the cases of Al and Dante were connected, if they indeed were. Someone needed to find Roberto and make sure he was safe, and, first and foremost, someone needed to find and apprehend Greg Turner.

She called Detective Robertson's line and left an extended, rambling message for him, probably more like a tirade, but she was beyond caring.

And then there was Nick.

Nick knew the moment she walked into the PerCan building and asked to see him privately in the conference room that something was wrong.

He dropped what he was doing and came running into the conference room armed with at least a dozen questions. Kayla asked him to sit, took a deep breath, and just let the entire story out in one long monologue.

When she was done, Nick stared at her, mouth hanging open for a moment, his hand in midair as if he were grasping for something. He tried to form words that wouldn't come out, he stood and immediately sat again, and, finally, he exploded. Kayla stood still in the conference room, her hands locked into one another, and endured the relentless storm of accusations, curses, and angry shouts he unleashed on her. She'd known this wouldn't be as easy as Dante had thought, and she simply let Nick vent every last bit of his anger.

After a few moments, he finally ran out of words and stood square to her, holding her eyes.

"My partner could have died while I took care of that goddamned harvest for you. Are you aware of that?"

Kayla only nodded.

"I am leaving right now, to go see Dante, and so help me God, if anyone tries to stop me…"

"We won't."

"And tonight, I am drafting a letter of resignation for both Dante and myself. Do you understand? Do you hear me, Kayla Montecito? I don't care about our contracts or the terms or the harvest or you, understand? Fine me—fine me anything. Dante and I are gone. Gone for good."

Kayla nodded yes.

In the door he turned around one last time and shook his head.

"I don't know what's gotten into you, Kayla. Is this what the CEO job does to you? First, you fire Donnelly for acting like a jerk. Then you turn around and do the same thing. In the same 12 hours. Tell Rafael I feel sorry for him."

The door fell shut behind him, and Kayla dropped into a chair.

Compartmentalize, she told herself. *You're in charge of this company now and of the multimillion-dollar harvest.*

Get that harvest done, get the people under control, do the best you can. That is all you can do and hope it is enough.

She went back to Al's office and his laptop, opened the files on harvesting cannabis, and read them through for the hundredth time.

Anything that was not found or not mentioned in here just would not get done, and if that ruined the harvest… She'd seen the figures, knew well what was at stake, and that thought frightened her more than anything else.

TWENTY-TWO

Barry Wentworth stopped his sleek little Mercedes sports car in the lot in front of Roberto's Pride Cannabis Products, pushed the sunglasses back onto his forehead, and looked around for a moment. Roberto's facility wasn't what he had expected. Not even close.

Perhaps he had thought he would find a neglected, dirty little greenhouse with a few ailing plants and a lot of shady characters running around. That would have matched his image of Roberto as he had met him in Singapore, long ago. Instead, he stood and stared at a tidy two-story building, relatively new and well taken care of by the looks of it. A security fence extended around the perimeter, and cameras angled down at him from at least four places he could see. Everything appeared to be neat, clean, and organized. And yet everything was also eerily quiet. Where were the delivery trucks, the suppliers, and where were the employees' vehicles?

He approached the guard house and showed his ID to an alert, uniformed young man who'd been eyeing him since he arrived. "Barry Wentworth," he said rather snappily. "I'm here to see Roberto Ivers."

"Sorry, Mr. Wentworth," the guard said. "There must be a misunderstanding of some type. My deepest apologies, but we are closed at the moment."

"Closed? Right now? Midweek during the day? How can you be closed?"

"My apologies, sir. We are doing some maintenance that requires us to close the building completely to all visitors."

"Well, young man, I am in the cannabis business, and I have never heard of that kind of maintenance before. But be that as it may. I can wait for Roberto out here if necessary. You just tell him Barry is here waiting for him, OK?"

He leaned against the side of the building and took out his phone, scrolling through messages as if to indicate that he had all day to waste if necessary. Something was going on in that building, a couple of hundred yards from the gatehouse, and he was not about to leave until he found out.

The guard began to sweat and tried a few other tactics to ask him to leave, without success. If he hadn't invented them, Barry had certainly perfected numerous stalling tactics, and he merely smiled politely, kindly repeated he would wait for Roberto, and proceeded to do just that.

It didn't take more than five minutes, and his cell phone rang. Grinning at the guard, he answered.

"Oh, hi there, Roberto. Fancy that..."

"Mike told me you are out at the gate, hoping for a quick meeting."

"Just dropping in to see how things are going. You can spare a few minutes for me, right?"

"Well, the thing is, Barry..." Did Roberto sound a bit frantic just then?

Surely, that couldn't be the case. Look up the word *cool* in the dictionary, and there was a picture of Roberto Ivers. The cannabis space was still a close-knit community, and amongst all of the dreamers and simple nutcases, Barry had heard somebody say, *Roberto Ivers probably pees ice cubes.* He had put an illegal grow operation into the backrooms of a legal one. Roberto did not panic.

"The thing is—we are in the middle of something right now."

"Something big, no doubt, seeing as how the place is closed up hermetically, the people who would be coming and going or just having a break out here have either been told to stay home or locked inside, and your Mike is keeping every living being out with some sort of lame excuse. Yes, I'd say it sounds like you're in the middle of something."

"Well, you see, we are…"

"Maintenance, Roberto, I got it," Barry finished sarcastically. "No worries. I can come back another time. I was going to tell you about Dante's accident—but it will keep. Some other time then."

"What happened to Dante? What accident?"

"Nothing life-threatening, I'm sure." Barry flung the words out there with deliberate carelessness.

"Barry, what's happened?"

Barry didn't speak. He waited, and counted silently in his head. 17, 18, 19…

"Fine. Stay where you are. I'll get somebody to come down and get you."

Barry hung up and gave Mike, the gatekeeper, his most shit-eating grin.

"He's coming down," he said, but most of his bravado was getting out of there in a hurry, leaving a nagging feeling of concern in its place.

Ding, ding, ding—alarm bells, he thought. *Whatever on earth is going on in there? It is not normal.*

A worker in a teal-blue Pride Cannabis Uniform indeed stepped out of the building to get him and led him inside and up to Roberto's office without stopping anywhere or making any kind of conversation with Barry. They shook hands, and Barry dropped into a modern, spindly-looking chair.

Roberto looks old, he thought when he sat. Pale, worried, tired, and old, and none of it fit with his memories of the man.

"What happened to Dante?" Roberto asked the moment Barry had leaned back and opened his mouth to make small talk. "You mentioned an accident?"

"Lost control of his motorcycle," Barry said and shrugged. "Hit the bridge abutment at a pretty damn high speed."

Roberto muttered an expletive and sagged into his own chair, resting his elbow on the table, forking his hands through his hair.

"How bad?"

"Luckily, your brother is pretty smart. He invested. Not in the motorcycle itself but in safety gear. And he had a big fat guardian angel riding with him that day."

"He's safe then?"

"Banged up from here to Christmas, and he'll likely spend some time in the hospital and in physical rehab, but given enough time and dedication, he'll be just fine. Unlike you."

Roberto looked up at him and opened his mouth to contradict, but Barry shook his head and brought his hands up, palms out.

"Oh, no, you don't. Look at you. Look at this place."

"We are…"

"You are not doing any damned maintenance, Roberto. A blind man without his cane can see that. What it looks like to me is you are mitigating some type of disaster, but what do I know? I only built a cannabis facility. I know something is going on when doorways are hung with plastic drapes, and there are buckets of sterilization liquids in the hallways."

"Rafael built a cannabis factory, not you," Roberto muttered, and Barry said nothing. He merely waited him out.

"OK. I'll tell you. But this cannot leave this room—ever. Do you hear me? I need your assurances on this."

Barry said nothing, letting his gaze wander around Roberto's office, from the awards on the wall to a picture of Roberto holding their grow license aloft, a broad grin on his face.

"Barry!"

"Fine. Unless I see an absolute massive necessity for someone in an official capacity to know what you are about to tell me, and I feel that I make myself complicit and or guilty in any way…"

"Jesus H. Christ," Roberto interrupted him, reached for a bottle of water under his table, and drank most of it in one gulp. He grabbed for another, tossed it to Barry, and put his hands together as if in prayer.

"Grow medium is fucking expensive," he finally said, referring to the enriched gel that held and nourished the young plants until they were ready to be transplanted into proper soil. It had to be the exact right consistency, contain the exact perfect amount of nutrients, and, most of all, be free of any contaminants. Barry shrugged.

"I heard that."

"It was ruining us. Our main supplier went bankrupt, everybody else had endless delivery times and supply-chain issues, and big outfits like yours bought up everything available. Available at a decent price anyway."

"Supply and demand. That kind of thing happens. It's called economics." Barry nodded, waiting him out.

"We're a small outfit. We can't keep up the price wars like you can at PerCan." Barry nodded again and said nothing.

"It was ruining us. Didn't know what to do any more. I even laid off a bunch of staff. People who trusted me and had nothing else. Then, one day, I get an offer."

"Go on."

"Grow medium. From the Middle East—at a fantastic price."

"You do know you're not supposed to use anything that hasn't…"

"That has not been cleared by the Department of Health and checked and double-checked and labelled in this country. I fucking know, Barry. But my back was against the wall, do you understand that? I had nowhere to turn."

"So, you thought what's the harm?"

"I was going to try a small batch, just to see what happened," Roberto defended himself. "Just one small batch. We were going to test the thing every step of the way, just to make sure. I had one delivery deadline to make—one. After that, I could have gone to shop around."

"And it didn't go well?"

It still doesn't make any sense, Barry thought. Yes, everything that touched the actual marijuana plants had to be vetted by the Ministry of Health, but a small batch of grow medium? Heck, he might have been tempted had he been in the same boat as Roberto. You had to cut some corners now and then; it happened. But, in this case, somewhere, something had to have gone wrong on a grand scale.

"It smelled funny when it got here, like something had gone off. I even asked Al to look at it, and he told me the same thing—don't risk your license."

"Al? You asked Al to check the stuff?"

That pesky alarm bell started to go off in Barry's head once again, dinging louder and harder this time than before. Al, who was at that moment in the hospital, just a few rooms down from Dante? Al… His hands grew icy cold, and he rubbed them subconsciously down the sides of his pant legs.

"And?"

"He gave me a hard time, and we got into a massive argument. Then two of my workers started getting sick."

The alarm bells were not just ringing now. They were making enough noise to rival the trumpets of Jericho.

"The virus," Barry said tonelessly.

"I don't know, Barry. Something about that medium was infected or something. I had them burn the damn shit in the boiler furnace the moment I realized it, but it wasn't enough. It was going around my greenhouse."

"Good God."

Barry automatically jumped up and spread his hands away from his body as if he wanted to avoid touching anything—except it was too late. He was in Roberto's office, had been in this building for the last 20 minutes.

What if Roberto—what if he…? Unbidden, the picture of Al came to his mind, Al, who right now was lying in a hospital bed, unconscious, fighting for his very life. Good God, what if that was the fate all of them were in for?

It couldn't be. It couldn't end this way. He didn't have survived a goddamned plane crash just to die from Roberto's mistake.

"Relax," Roberto said. "I've fogged the entire building with antibacterial, antiviral stuff every night. I'm using UV-C LEDs. There's not a shred of any living bacterium, virus, or other compound left in here. Probably the cleanest place in the city right now."

Barry sat down again, gingerly this time.

"What—what did you do with the sick workers?" he asked, needing to know the answer and being afraid of it at the same time. He didn't want to hear that all of these men were dead, but if they had gone to the hospital, he would know, wouldn't he?

"Private clinic," Roberto said. "There's this—doctor—I know from… well, from before. Usually, they specialize in cosmetic surgeries and treatments that—aren't exactly cleared for use in this country."

"I thought you were finally going straight," Barry said, shaking his head.

He had a million questions that needed answers, and at the same time, he wanted nothing as much as to kick Roberto Ivers's butt from here all the way—well—all the way to Vaomar if necessary.

"I tried, man. What did you want me to do? First, Al blocked me from buying any but the most expensive equipment. Then we had a couple of crop failures while we were still learning, then the shit with the grow medium…"

"You could have come to me, Roberto. When the shit hits the fan, you go see the people who can make stuff happen, for fuck's sake. You don't just go rogue and try some unknown shortcut without thinking,

'Hmm—what could possibly go wrong here?' I could have organized financing, could have found people to help. Investors even. But no, you buy cheap shit on the black market hoping it will solve all your problems. What the hell is wrong with you?"

He blew out a breath and forked his fingers through his hair.

"You need to fix this. You need to report what happened and why to the proper authorities."

"Not happening, Wentworth. I will lose my license and everything I have built if I do that. That's not happening."

"And if you don't do that, Al might die. Has that ever occurred to you? Does that go into that criminal birdbrain of yours? He's your brother, man. If there's anything that can help save him, who cares if you lose this place? You build again. We've done it before. I've done it before. It sucks, but it can be done."

"Don't threaten me, Wentworth." Roberto jumped up and began pacing the length of his office. "Do not threaten me, you hear? You are on my turf here. You came to my door, not the other way around. I was trying to keep you out there. I was going to handle it my way until you insisted on wandering in here."

"And the hell with your brother? If he dies, so be it? Is that what I'm hearing? How did he get involved in this sordid thing anyway?"

"I told you. I asked him to look at the grow medium when it came in," Roberto said, straightening a picture of a large, healthy cannabis plant on the wall. "Told him I had some concerns about the quality, and could he have a look at it? So he came in, opened the package, and started to put his hands into it. He immediately knew something was off with it."

Barry shuddered. Al had always regretted making things harder for Roberto at the beginning, back when he had found out that Barry and Roberto had played a role in setting Greg Turner up. Greg Turner, who had shot their father Tadeo as revenge. And Roberto put a cherry on the sundae trying to frame Rafael for it. Al's revenge had been quick and cruel. He'd struck like a viper, regretting it later, when he'd cooled down, when everything was running well again at PerCan.

Hotheads, all of the Ivers, Barry thought.

Al had tried to make it up to Roberto, helped him wherever he could. He'd even offered him funding—funding Roberto was reluctant to accept, and only in the direst circumstances.

If Roberto asked for help, Al would have dropped anything he'd been holding at the time and come out to give his opinion on a new grow medium or a new way of handling fertigation. Didn't matter. He would have been there.

"And you?"

"I didn't touch the stuff. Always hated the way it feels on my hands." Roberto rolled his shoulders inward and shuddered, and Barry shook his head. Trust this big lug of a man to be grossed out by gel medium.

"He immediately knew it was off, said it smelled weird. And that's exactly what my workers were complaining about."

That's how Al had infected himself then—touching the grow medium, smelling it, rubbing it between his fingers…

"Where'd you get that crap anyway?"

"Middle East. It was a one-time only bargain."

"Oh, I just bet. And it never occurred to you that somebody might be trying to set you up?"

"Who would want to set me up, Wentworth? And why grow medium?"

"Use your brain, Rob!" Barry rolled his eyes and slapped his hand on the desk, hard. "Maybe if you introduced a virus in here, it would wipe out your entire operation? Could that be a reason? Maybe a man called Greg Turner who vowed revenge on everyone with the last name of Ivers?"

"Turner is just blowing hot air," Roberto blustered, but suddenly, he didn't seem so sure anymore. "Isn't he?"

"I don't know. Is he? I just…"

I just don't know how you could be that stupid, he wanted to say, but cut himself off. He'd done enough stupid stuff in his own lifetime to recognize desperation when he saw it. Would he have been tempted to take a similar shortcut if he had his back to the wall, the way Roberto had? Of course he would have. The SEC had suspended him for taking just those shortcuts. Administrative shortcuts, but they had been just as wrong, and just as dangerous. There by the grace of God, all of the stupid things he had done in his life had never injured another person, only himself.

Subconsciously, he rubbed a scar on his temple, a reminder of the plane crash he had caused trying to run from the police. If anyone understood stupid, crazy, and desperate, it was the man he looked at in the mirror every day. That man had invented it.

"I don't see it." Roberto shook his head. "I bought the stuff from a shady fellow I met at the track and got talking to. He said he had a connection. I don't think Turner would be smart enough to set up that many coincidences."

"A shady fellow at the track." Barry covered his face with his hands and sighed. "If we get out of this in one piece, I am going to kick your ass until you sleep standing up for a week, and then I'm going to sign you up for business lessons. Do you hear that? If you want to run an honest, straight business, this is not what it looks like."

Roberto walked away and kicked the wall behind him with the heel of his shoe. He glared at Barry for a moment.

"Listen to you talk about an honest, straight business. I heard something about faking signatures on consent documents, you know. Does that sound familiar at all?"

"I know," Barry sighed. "That's how I know stupid from really idiotic. I've done both."

"Look, if you came in here to beat up on me and trash my business, you can turn right around and leave. I'll handle things."

"Wait, wait." Barry raised his hands again, pushing back the invisible tirade of abuse from Roberto's side of the table. "Let's not argue which one of us made more mistakes than the other. We're probably even. The big question here is how are you going to get out of this? When the media gets hold of it…"

"Well, why do you think we're closed, Barry? They're not going to get hold of it."

"You can't hide something of this magnitude. At least not for long."

"Says who? You telling me you're leaving here and calling the press? Watch yourself. You're on my territory here if you've forgotten already, and before I lose everything…"

Roberto looked downright crazy just then, Barry thought. His stance wide and powerful, challenging Barry, his eyes glassy and wide, and his hands balled into tight, hard fists raised up to his waist.

"Roberto, you will definitely lose everything if you try to hide what happened. This kind of thing always comes out in the end—always."

"Not if you do it right."

"Do I look like the guy who doesn't know how to do it right? What about the guys who got sick? Their families? Their friends? Somebody is going to talk at some point. You want to pay off all of them? And if they don't talk today, they will next month, next year, when they need money. There are too many people who are in on this. You can't control it any longer."

Roberto's arms dropped, and he struck his forehead with a fist. He sighed, and all of a sudden, he didn't look angry any longer, Barry thought. He didn't look fierce or aggressive, only sad, like a man who was staring down the possibility of losing his life's work. Greg Turner maybe? *Don't go there. Don't think that way,* he reminded himself, and put his hand on Roberto's shoulder.

"I have an idea," he continued. "It will be difficult, it will bruise you, but it won't wreck you."

He had Roberto's full attention now. "Say."

"You're going to report you had a contamination. You don't know where it came from, but you took care of it. You panicked, shut down for a few weeks to protect the public health, eradicated everything. You'll have inspectors from the health department crawling up your ass for a little while, but that's no problem. Everything has been cleaned, right?"

"You can perform heart surgery in my grow rooms."

"Let's not. They'll want to know where it came from. Make sure all of your accounting, all shipping, receiving—everything—is up to date and clean. But we don't know where it originated."

Roberto only nodded.

"Then we will drop Turner's name, all casual like. 'Jeez, what if Greg Turner actually did have something to do with it?'"

"Turner? Why him?"

"You know of a better scapegoat? He must have broken in sometime, contaminated something. We're not chemists. We don't know how he did it. But there's an infection in our facility, right after he threatened the life of all Ivers men. Nobody knows how it got here. Coincidence?"

Barry let the sentence hang, and slowly, the weariness disappeared from Roberto's face, to be replaced by wily cunning.

"Damn bastard tried to kill all of us in here," he said slowly. "Al just happened to be in here for a friendly chat and some advice. And now he's got Dante too."

"You're catching on." Barry nodded. "Just enough of the truth to keep everyone happy, not enough to bury you."

"Besides," Roberto said, rising to his full height, "we were not really hiding anything. We were all so afraid of Turner and his threats. We were keeping a low profile."

"Go easy on that one," Barry said. "That one's a bit over the top. But if somebody asks why you didn't go to the authorities…"

"We might just insinuate it a bit."

Roberto came out from behind his massive desk and clapped Barry on the shoulder. He was grinning broadly now.

"I wanted to wring your neck when you hung me out to dry at the directors' meeting, Barry, but you came through when I needed it."

Barry shrugged.

"On to the real deal. What about that little fuck Turner and my brother? What's he done to him, and do you have any clue where he is hanging out just now? When I get my hands on him…"

"I don't know—I really don't. And I have no idea if Turner is involved in Dante's accident. Nobody has mentioned sabotage or any third-party involvement, but that's not to say it's impossible. You're lucky your brother spends big-time on protective gear."

Roberto kneaded his massive hands, and Barry could see the thought processes unfolding on his face and in his angry narrowed eyes. He really would not have wanted to be in Greg Turner's shoes right now, but then again, Turner had no one but himself to blame.

"If you're going to follow your logic," he said dryly, "it really plays into your hands if Turner stays under the radar for a while longer."

"So he can come after… Oh."

"Yeah, *oh*, Roberto. Unofficially, I would worry if I were you." Barry's phone pinged in his pocket, and he looked down at it.

"This day just keeps getting better and better. On to my next assignment, people. I gather Al just regained consciousness. I better go see him."

"You do that, Barry, while I…"

"You get your butt into a chair and get started on your reports to the health authorities, Roberto. Now. Before the delay looks any stranger. And remember, you don't know where the contamination came from. But you have a suspicion. Can't prove anything, but still…"

"Gotcha."

TWENTY-THREE

Rafael dove straight into reading all of the messages that had arrived on his phone, once he finally found a wireless signal again. He knew he was filthy, ragged, and he probably smelled too, but what had been going on at home slowly turned into more of a horror story with every message he read.

How anything going on back there could ever be worse than being caught in a tropical storm devastation here, he couldn't have imagined, but there it was.

He met up with Jonas in the communal area of the medical center they had been transported to, and his new friend frowned, handing him a bottle of water.

"I don't know, Rafael. Maybe I should get you something stronger. You're a little pale there. Everything all right?"

Rafael thumb-scrolled through the lengthy message Kayla had sent him.

"Yes—no, maybe everything at once."

"Do I have to understand that?"

Rafael didn't answer for a long moment as he read through Kayla's missive until he felt Jonas at his shoulder.

"Anything I could help you with?"

"Wish I could tell you. Best I can say, things completely and thoroughly fell apart back home the moment I left."

Jonas only laughed. "You're kidding, right? Like, we made it through this wicked storm in one piece, man. How could anything fall apart worse than that?"

"Wish I knew. Last count, I have two company directors in hospital. The vice president became CEO, but he's a horse's ass, so my fiancée had to step in and kick him out. Now her best agronomist just quit because—well, we'll still be here tonight if I tell you the whole story, but it's sordid all right. I have got to get out of here and back home, like right this minute. Things are a mess."

"You're not alone in that. We all want to get back home ASAP. I really don't like the look of these guys either."

Rafael looked around at the military presence in the common area. He presumed they were there for their protection rather than preventing them from breaking out, but they were all armed to the teeth. Large, dangerous-looking weapons he couldn't name, but would rather not get to know better.

"Word is they're finally going to fly all of us back home, courtesy of the Maltese government, just as soon as they check us through and take care of us."

"Check us through? Please, Jonas. What the hell does that even mean? Who knows how long they're planning to hold us here, or why?"

"They want to get rid of us just as much as we want to get out of here, Rafael. I listened in on a few of the nurses, but, at the very minimum, they want to make sure we don't carry any viruses back home."

For some reason, that statement made Rafael break out in raucous, uncontrolled laughter, and Jonas moved away from him a bit.

"What? Why is that funny?"

"Nothing. Nothing at all, forget my manic laughter. You wouldn't believe me if I told you."

One of their heavily armed guards came over and looked over both men head to toe without cracking a smile.

"Is there a problem?"

Yeah, there's a problem, Rafael thought. *I need to get the company through this, and Kayla through this, and you all want to poke and prod me for another week. I'd call that a problem.*

Instead, he shook his head and tried for a winning grin.

"Just happy we got through the storm, and happy we're getting out of here pretty soon. That's all."

The guard nodded and walked off, and Rafael dropped into a chair and popped the top off the bottle of water Jonas had handed him.

"You want to tell me about it," Jonas asked, and Rafael considered it. Finally, he shook his head.

"It's insane at best. I have to work through this in my own head first," he said. "Meanwhile, let's push these guys a little bit. The sooner we get out of here, the better."

TWENTY-FOUR

Kayla thought of the personnel department of Perfect Cannabis Consolidated, somewhere down on the ground floor, and shuddered a bit. She didn't dare go down there personally. Somewhere on one of the walls, she was sure they probably had a dartboard with her picture on it, taking turns throwing, coming up with new cusswords as they did. And the worst part—she couldn't even blame them. She'd fire herself if she could.

What have I gotten myself into, she thought, for the hundredth time. *What have I done, and how did I manage to lose both of our main growers and Responsible Persons all in the same day?*

They would have to find and assign a new Responsible Person immediately if not sooner. Their license to grow depended on a knowledgeable, educated individual being assigned that status, thus being responsible for the quality of the product, the adherence to safety and security standards, and a whole lot of other issues she couldn't even name at the moment.

And yet she should be able to.

No Responsible Person—no license. They were in deep trouble the moment Nick walked out.

Scratch me as RP, she thought. *And what does that say about my performance as CEO, I wonder? People threatened to leave while Thomas was in charge. The moment I was, they actually did leave.*

She answered a knock at the door and admitted Pamela, their rather disheveled-looking head of HR. On any other day, Pamela would have been short, bouncy, and full of bubbly cheer. Today, her smart suit was missing its jacket, and her blonde bob might have been a bird's nest.

"Pamela, I'm so sorry. Things appear to have kind of—gotten away from me."

"I'll say."

Pamela dropped into a chair and kicked off her high heels.

"First things first, how is Dante?"

"Awake—injured—recovering. Thank God his safety equipment prevented the worst. Did you know there's an airbag…? Never mind."

"How did it even happen?"

Kayla shook her head. "No information yet. Couple of eyewitnesses say he suddenly lost control of the motorcycle. That's all I heard."

"Weird."

Pamela crossed one leg over the other and opened a file folder she had brought.

"And then you managed to piss off Nick Ambrose—big time."

"Well, I couldn't—I didn't…" Kayla let her head drop back and closed her eyes. "I tried my best," she finally said after a deep sigh. "I thought it would be best if I looked into what was going on with Dante, since I was on the phone with someone just after it happened, while Nick looked after the harvest. Turns out I was wrong."

"Who were you on the phone with? Dante? What? While this accident happened?"

"No." Kayla shook her head. "I called him because I thought he'd blown off our meeting. Some—one, answered the phone, said he'd been taken to the hospital."

"I just got goose skin." Pamela crinkled her nose. "That's beyond creepy. Who the heck answers an accident victim's phone? Isn't that, like, illegal or something?"

"None of the witnesses knew who he was." Kayla shook her head again. By the end of the day, she'd be headshaking in her sleep. "No information who this person was. They just—took off, taking Dante's phone along no less."

"Scary!"

"My sentiments exactly. Thank God he is conscious. I asked him to remote wipe his phone."

"I never heard of that. That's just…"

"Frightening," Kayla finished and clamped her hands around a cup of coffee.

Something about that brief exchange would always haunt her, she thought. It felt like something only an extremely disturbed person would do. A person mad with revenge, perhaps? And could it be Greg Turner? That would mean she had spoken to him. For now, there were no answers, which made it all the more frightening, but she still had a business to run—somehow.

"None of it changes the fact that we now need two new master growers," she said with a sigh. "Nick did not take it well that I left him in charge of the harvest without telling him why."

"I can't say I really blame him…"

Kayla patted both of her shoulders with her hands. "Pile it on. Nothing I haven't told myself yet, I assure you. It was a knee-jerk reaction gone wrong."

"Well, the good news is—if you want to call it good news…"

"Call it good news," Kayla said. "I need every bit of it you have got on offer. Even if it is not much."

"The good news is Nick has not officially resigned."

"Oh."

"Well, he sent me a furious text saying he was done, but there are official steps he has to go through terminating his contract. That will take him a few days at least. He can't just up and disappear. It doesn't work that way."

"Not sure he agrees with you."

"Tough." Pamela screwed up her face. "Until we find a new

Responsible Person, he will be that—on paper anyway. Meaning our license is intact until he files said required paperwork."

Kayla exhaled a sigh of relief and nodded. No need to close up shop just yet. But they still needed a new RP, immediately.

"Anybody on the roster ready for promotion to RP? I mean, if we do have to go outside to hire, I'm sure it will be a lengthy process."

"My thoughts exactly. And if I had a master grower on staff, I would right now talk to them and ask him or her for a recommendation instead of sitting in your office. Fact is…"

"You don't," Kayla said. "Wow. When I make a mess, I make a good one, don't I? I am…"

"Never mind. It's done." Pamela waved a hand. "No sense beating yourself up. Nick did us one favor in all of his hurry to leave, which is good news number two."

"Oh?"

"He seems to be in touch with most of the employees via text. He is texting them detailed instructions on what they need to be doing."

"Not sure I like that with him leaving," Kayla said, and it was Pamela's turn to shrug.

"Don't ask how I feel about it either, but until he's officially terminated, we really can't move on without his input. Here's the million-dollar question…"

"Shoot."

"Do you want me to terminate Nick Ambrose's contract? He's not an employee. He's an independent contractor."

"And a friend," Kayla threw in before she could stop herself, and Pamela put out her hands, palms up.

"So, give me some direction here. What do I do? Are we terminating him for good from our end? He left us in a lurch in the middle of the harvest. He told you to—erm—bugger off, I'm sure."

"Quite eloquently, yes."

"And what about Dante? If we terminate Nick, or he quits, then what?"

"Dante owns just as many shares as Al and Rafael do. There's no way he'll leave." Even as she said it, Kayla doubted her own words. Dante would go exactly where Nick was going, no matter how many shares were at stake.

"God, what a mess," she said, blowing out a breath. "Short answer, I don't know. I am going to have to leave Dante to decide on his own. I've caused enough mayhem deciding for others today. Although it will be quite a while before Dante is ready to come back to work."

"Meaning I advertise for growers outside. It's not going to be easy while people know we're desperate. All I can do is offer huge salaries, massive incentives, the whole package, and hope somebody bites."

"We had better. I'll sign off on it."

"Kayla, you don't need somebody from HR to tell you this," Pamela said, gathering her things back into her folder. "But this massive harvest, it was in danger when Thomas was around making everyone uncomfortable and firing people, but now? I don't think we have a fighting chance in hell getting through it."

"Thanks," Kayla said dryly and looked at a spreadsheet open on her laptop.

Clint had laid it all out for her: the financial implications of a ruined mega-harvest, the impact on reputation and relationships, the projected loss of revenues and customers, fines for broken delivery schedules… She flipped the screen down with an impatient sound. All on her watch. All while the board, not to forget Rafael and Barry, had trusted her with PerCan. Way to go.

Running a tabloid magazine was a cakewalk compared to this.

And when Rafael got home—she didn't even want to think about that. When Rafael got home, she would have to explain in exact detail just how she had managed to mire the company in a pile of manure while he was gone only a couple of weeks.

Could he—would he have done anything different? Who knew, but Rafael certainly would think so, and what it would do to their relationship was not anything she wanted to think about right then.

"What a mess," she said, but Pamela had already left her office.

Kayla sat for another five minutes. Then she took a deep breath and let it all out again.

Yes, it was a mess, but it was her mess to fix. By God, she'd been through worse. She stood, straightened her blazer and skirt, and walked out of the office. In the washroom, she fixed her hair and face as well as she could. This time, nobody would really care how she looked.

She inhaled deeply to steady her nerves and walked down the hall into the production area of PerCan.

People were coming and going, darting past her with a quick 'hi' or a nodded greeting. Times used to be she couldn't come in here without being stopped and regaled with the latest tale of children and grand-children, or given big hugs. Suddenly, no one could meet her eyes.

She carried on and found the group of people who would have worked closest with Nick and Dante—their assistants and a group of grow technicians. All conversation stopped when Kayla drew near, and almost everyone looked down at their work.

Pamela had been right. Most of them had their cell phones by their sides, glancing down at the screen frequently. Nick apparently still kept in touch with them over his missives on what to do. Bless him for caring enough to give this harvest a chance.

Kayla cleared her throat.

"For those of you who haven't heard," she said, and cleared her throat when she realized how weak and tinny her voice sounded, "Dante Ivers was involved in a motorcycle crash today."

Still, no one spoke. A few people nodded; a few looked away point-edly. That's where it all went off the rails, they probably thought.

Kayla cleared her throat again, realized she was looking down at her shoes, and straightened up. *Never cower. Never look down, ever.*

"I was with him until a short while ago," she said. "And I am happy to tell you all that, while his injuries are serious, they are not life-threatening, and he is expected to make a full recovery."

"How did this even happen?" someone called out, and Kayla wanted to hug that person.

"We don't know as of yet. Officially, he lost control of the motorcycle."

"No way. Not D. Dante's a good driver."

"Yeah—he can ride, and he doesn't do stunts."

"I bet some dickhead in a sports car cut him off."

"We don't know that yet," Kayla said, taking heart in how much they cared about Dante. Perhaps… No—it was too much of a stretch to ask them to understand.

"I—made a decision when I found out about the accident," she said. "I went to the hospital to check on what had happened, when I should have let Nick do so on his own."

Suddenly, no one spoke any more. Save for the far-off hum of the machinery and environmental fans, the production floor had become silent.

"Nick Ambrose left PerCan once he found out," she finished softly. "And I am not sure he will be returning."

Her hand shot out to find a steadying I-beam beside her, and she looked over the workmen and women—her people. Most looked down at their feet. A few shook their heads.

"They're together, man, and you knew that," someone muttered. "Of course he's pissed. How would you feel?"

"Family first."

"I thought—with everything going on, I was the one person that could be spared," she said. "But as it turns out, I was wrong. I know this has made your jobs immeasurably harder, and I want you to know we're doing everything to hire a capable—capable head of the growing department as soon as we can. In the meantime, you've all done harvests before. All I can do is ask you to do the best you can to get this accomplished."

It was all out. Kayla let her words sink in and let go of the I-beam. *Say what you want,* she thought. *I made a decision, and I stuck to it. Right or wrong.*

"That's all." She nodded curtly and turned to leave.

"Well, if he had left in the middle of the day to go to the hospital, we would have been totally lost, wouldn't we have…"

Kayla looked around who had said that and gave a glance of gratitude to a silver-haired, plain-faced grow technician. Eva, she thought her name was, and they had spoken before.

"Great, Eva, so instead we are totally lost now."

"We are not lost. Just read your messages. His instructions are pretty clear."

"Why don't you stop talking, Eva, and give me a hand with this?"

As suddenly as they had stopped, her workers started talking again and returned to the tasks in front of them.

Except no one spoke to Kayla. She felt dismissed—by her own people. It hurt, like a physical slap, but she wouldn't let them see it. She walked out of the grow area, head high, and brushed off the protective booties in the outside hallway.

Pamela stood right there inside the door and gave her a weak, encouraging smile.

"Nice," she said. "At least you went in there personally and spoke to them instead of sending a memo. That was a good start."

"Thanks." Kayla shrugged. "Alas, I don't know how much good it will do. They are all angry with me, and I don't blame them. And I still don't know how we're going to be able to pull off this harvest."

"We do the best we can, no more, no less," Pamela said and pulled a folder out from under her arm. "I've pulled a few possible applicants out for you to choose from, should you wish to be part of the interview process, and there's a new app out there, Joyce AI, that helps folks find their life's work, or so it advertises. It's not cheap, but I've put a massive ad on to that and another couple of boards, so we should have some applications come in soon."

Kayla looked over the applications she'd been handed and realized she had neither the knowledge or the experience to tell if any of these applicants were even halfway suited for the positions that needed to be filled. She handed the back to Pam and shook her head.

"Perhaps I'll be part of the final interviews," she said. "For the moment, I wouldn't even know what I am looking at."

"And that gets us to another problem." Pamela paced her right back to Kayla's new office. "Who is then going to do these interviews, if not you? Suggestions?"

"Both of our department heads are out of commission or gone. I don't know, Pamela. Don't we have someone—else—to do this?"

"Do you see somebody else? You're the CEO now, Kayla. I take my direction from you. Meaning you tell me how we are going to handle this, not the other way round."

I don't bloody well have any answers, Kayla wanted to say. *I am adrift at sea just like the rest of us. Don't you get that? I cannot give you any answers. Deal with it.* Instead, she smiled what she hoped would be serenely and put her hands together as if in prayer. Heck with "as if." She was praying all right.

"Fine then. Who is our most senior worker in the grow department?"

"Kayla—that person has zero experience with leadership whatsoever. None."

"Beggars, choosers, and all that, Pam. Who is the most senior?"

"If you go by who has been here the longest, that would be Eva."

Eva. For the first time today, Kayla smiled honestly. Eva was the person who had just spoken up for her. She got along with Eva rather well. She knew about her family, her kids. She could work with that.

"Fine," she said. "I want to see her in my office. No promises. I just need her input and her opinion. She can give me that, and we will take it from there."

"People won't really like it. There are some who have more education, some have experience in other operations, and…"

"Didn't you just get through telling me I am the CEO now? We're not talking about other operations here—we are talking about PerCan. If Eva is the one who knows the PerCan operation better and longer than the others, then I need to talk to her. Regardless of what people think. Can you make that happen?"

"Suppose I can," Pamela said and walked away rather stiffly.

Nice work, Kayla thought. And for a bonus, add another person to the roster of people she had teed off today. What's one more? *Give me printing gossip any darn day of the week.* This manufacturing gig really was kicking her rear end in ways she hadn't thought possible.

Rafael was coming back soon, she reminded herself. Rafael was right now making his way back here, and he'd be able to make sense of all of this.

Every strong, independent, capable businesswoman she had ever known was probably going to burn her in effigy for even thinking of a man coming to save things, but they hadn't tried to run a cannabis manufacturer with half a roster of staff.

If a man could make sense of the royal mess she had made, then all the more power to him.

***

Eva knocked at her door and came in on her invitation, tiny, unassuming, and almost afraid of the acting CEO of the company, Miss Kayla, as most of the cultivation technicians called her.

She sat across from Kayla, clasped her hands hard, and kept her eyes somewhere in the area of her shoes. Kayla took in the simple patterned blouse and jeans she wore and the handkerchief knotted around Eva's grey curly hair. She sat stiff and unmoving, as if she were afraid of touching anything here, in this fancy, stylish office.

"You've been here longer than anyone, I understand," Kayla began, and Eva nodded, still looking down at the floor.

"Yes—but I—I don't have the education or schooling many of the other technicians do. I am just…"

"Never mind schooling for the moment, Eva. I need information, and I believe you can help me out a lot if you are willing."

"Me? Help you?" Eva's eyes came up cautiously.

"Yes. You've been here from the very beginning, I hear?"

"Yes, Miss Kayla. First-ever cultivation team. Mister Rafael hired me, when Mister Tadeo was still in charge. He said I could make something of myself if I worked hard here."

"That sounds like Rafael." Kayla smiled. "And you've worked with Nick and Dante a lot, yes?"

Again, Eva nodded and smiled. "Yes. Mister Nick and Dante. They are really smart. They are good people."

"Good," Kayla said, wishing she could get the other woman to relax just a bit. "You know the work, and you know the people, so, if you are willing, I'd like you to help me out, telling me everything we still need to do regarding this harvest."

Eva's eyes became large and round, and for the first time, she looked directly at Kayla.

Tell me everything we need to know about the harvest was a tall order, but Kayla felt this tiny, unassuming woman was up to the job. She had a harvest to save, end of story. She needed to make sure, even with Nick and Dante both gone, they had a chance. Kayla brought out Al's spreadsheets, and Eva giggled softly.

"That looks mighty impressive on paper, Miss Kayla, but down on the floor, it is all different, you see…" And she started to tell a story about the work she did every day.

At some point during the conversation, her phone rang, but Kayla didn't even glance at it. She let the call go to voicemail and the one immediately after as well. Right now, Eva and the harvest were the most important thing in her life.

When they were done, Kayla felt she had at least a decent understanding of the process and the requirements. She had made enough notes to fill a yellow legal pad and finally understood how cannabis was harvested and processed.

Not on her list of important things to know up to then. She also had a half-decent list of things to look for in a new candidate of head of the growing department. At last, she was armed with knowledge. Rafael would still want to rip her head off when he came back and found out what had happened to the company—but they would deal with all of that later.

They would deal if their relationship survived the dumpster fire she had made out of his company.

***

Evening had rolled around while she learned how to deal with a cannabis harvest and the elusive personality of master grower when she remembered her cell phone and the messages that had come in during her meeting. She picked the phone out of her bag and checked, and all at once, her priorities shifted 360 degrees once again.

"Call the hospital," one of the messages read. "Al Ivers just woke up."

Kayla didn't care how she looked or that in her exhaustion she had not eaten or drunk anything all day. She swiped her purse off the sideboard, told the people at the front desk she was gone for today, and headed out to the hospital.

TWENTY-FIVE

It was a sad state of affairs when you went to the hospital often enough to know all the best shortcuts around the nightmare of downtown traffic, Kayla thought, as she threaded her way through secondary streets and back alleys.

Al had been moved out of the ICU and into a private room, and he greeted her, sitting up in bed when she arrived.

"Good God, Al," she said, afraid to hug him, "you have no idea how happy I am to see you awake."

"I appreciate the heartfelt greeting, Kayla," Al said with a weak smile. "Albeit you are not generally as exuberant as all this. Do I take this to mean things have been difficult while I was—incapacitated?"

"You can't even imagine." She pulled out a chair and sat beside him. "Don't ask. I don't want to dump on you all at once. How are you feeling? What have they told you? When can you get out of here, for crying out loud?"

Al smiled again. Weakness still showed around his eyes and in the tiny, careful movements he made.

"One thing at a time. They tell me I picked up an unknown viral infection from somewhere, and I've been in isolation for some weeks. I assume you and everyone have been tested?"

"Yes, of course. Everyone, including everyone, at PerCan. Thank God it was all negative. But how…"

Al stopped her with a small raise of his hand. "What about Roberto?"

"Roberto?" Kayla furrowed her brow. "Roberto? Well, no—I haven't seen him in weeks, come to think of it. He was nowhere near PerCan, and I had my hands full. I believe Barry went and had a talk with him. Why do you ask?"

"Never mind, Kayla. This is very important. I need to speak to Roberto as soon as I can. It's vital."

Al took a heavy breath and settled back into his pillows. His ashen skin and sunken features gave him the appearance of a ghost. No wonder—he'd been unconscious for weeks. And yet, Kayla thought with a bit of irritation, he had never asked about Rafael or anyone else, just Roberto. Roberto Ivers, the one person who hadn't bothered to show up at the hospital for him.

"I believe what you need first is a lot of rest," she said, a little more sharply than she had intended to. "Roberto has not been around since you fell ill—at all. I will let him know if I see him. We still don't know where this virus came from, but I have some ideas."

All at once, Al's eyes snapped open and fixed on her. "You do?"

"We have suspicions, Al." She sat back and little and shook her head. "Nothing I really want to bother you with right now, especially…"

"Tell me. Now."

Rarely had she seen him so intense, so angry, especially with her. What was going on with Al all of a sudden? Kayla cocked her head and regarded him for a moment.

"Look…"

"Tell me, Kayla." He sat up again and made a move to flip back his blankets and get out of the bed.

"No, you stay right there." Gently, she pushed him back. "You're being silly. We thought at one point—well, Dante suspected it, and I spoke to Barry. We thought maybe Turner may be behind all of this. But there is no solid proof, nothing to…"

"It wasn't Turner," Al said, dropping back into his pillows and closing his eyes. "I can see why you think it might be, but I assure you—Greg Turner had nothing to do with this virus."

He settled back and refused to say any more about the subject. Kayla folder her arms and glowered at him, more than a little irritated just then.

"I should probably leave you to recover," she said a little stiffly and reached for her bag.

She scooted her chair back, and Al opened his eyes again and raised a hand.

"Oh, don't be cross, Kayla. Never mind me and my babbling. I can tell there is more you are burning to tell me, so please, don't go. From what I hear, I've been out of commission for several weeks, and from the way you look, they must have been harrowing ones at that, So please, do tell me what's been going on. Where is Rafael anyway? Should he not be here keeping an eye on you?"

"You have no idea."

Kayla sat back and folded her arms, knitting her fingers into one another. Really, Al was right. She was cross with him. Cross? No—more like furious. While he lay there, pale, weak, but otherwise outwardly unharmed, she had just dealt with the worst two weeks of her life. Period.

And what did Al Ivers do? He asked about a brother he hadn't really spoken to in months, a brother he had once tried to ruin—before they made up again.

Al sighed again, settling a little deeper into his pillow, and smiled at her. And, just like that, she couldn't be mad at him any longer. Darn him for that usually well-hidden charm!

Before she could change her mind and leave, it all spilled out of her. Rafael's ill-fated trip, the Mediterranean tornado that wasn't one, Thomas Donnelly's bad behavior, Dante's accident, and, finally, Nick leaving PerCan.

"Is Dante all right?" Al asked when she reached that part of the story. His eyes snapped open, and he wanted to sit up straight and would have climbed out of the bed if he'd had the strength to do so. Frustrated, he sank back.

"Dante is banged up," Kayla said quickly and adjusted his blankets. "Cuts, bruises, and a few broken bones, but nothing that won't heal again, given time and a good physical therapist. Nothing life-threatening."

She handed Al a glass of water and a straw and watched him drink greedily.

"I gather he invested rather heavily in safety equipment."

"Our father made him do so as a condition of buying that cursed motorcycle," Al said weakly and closed his eyes again. "As it turns out, he was right to be concerned."

As he closed his eyes again, he handed her the water with a weak gesture. Kayla couldn't help but notice how impossibly small and frail he looked in the sterile white hospital linens, as if he could vanish into the sea of white that engulfed him. His skin was so pale, it seemed as though all the color had been drained from his body, leaving him barely visible amidst the stark surroundings.

"I should leave," she finally said. "All of this will keep until you are well again."

"Will you just tell me the rest?" Al's hand snaked out from beneath the covers and clamped around her wrist with surprising determination for a sick man. "You've been dealing with far too much on your own over the last few weeks."

"And you shouldn't have to listen to me go on about it, moments after you wake up."

"I'll be fine," he said and smiled weakly. "The virus that can kill an Ivers has to be a lot meaner than this little bug I caught."

This little bug? This little bug almost cost you your life, she wanted to say, and held back with an effort. At the same time, she thought, why was Al not asking any more questions about it? If it had been her, she would have wanted to know every single detail about that little bug, and yet he took it awfully lightly. Almost as if he knew what it was, where it came from, and what it could do.

"It was bad enough, Al," she finally said. "Although the doctors have not told me a lot by any means. You seem far better informed than I am. Have they figured out where on earth this thing came from?"

Al waved his hand feebly, trying to wipe her arguments away. "Anywhere, really. I probably just have a sensitivity. Now what about Dante?" he asked. "You are sure he will recover completely?"

"Yes, as far as I am told," she confirmed. "I don't know if he will want to return to PerCan, though, considering Nick and this horrible argument we had."

"You did the right thing," Al said, eyes closed. "You put the company first. Eventually, Dante will understand that, and so will Nick."

"Everybody keeps telling me that, but it may not be soon enough for this harvest," she said and bravely tried to keep her voice from shaking. "I just don't know how we are going to get it done."

"You will." Al opened his eyes again, and Kayla thought it was strange to see the dark intensity of his eyes set against the stark whiteness of the hospital room, like a sharp contrast of light and dark. "You are the strongest person in this three-ring circus. You'll find a way, and you will get it done. Trust me."

"From your mouth straight to God's ear." Kayla took his hand and gave it a careful squeeze. Al coughed a few times and pointed, and she handed him water again. He drank deeply, and his hand holding the cup dropped by his side. Kayla barely caught it.

"You will figure it out," he said, a little stronger now. "And the moment they let me out of this place, I'll help you do so, but..."

"You will do no such thing, Al Ivers. You will recuperate and do exactly what your doctors tell you, which, at the moment, I believe is getting a lot of rest. And I would assume they also need to find out everything about that virus you caught. Like where it came from, for starters, just so nobody else catches it. Last I heard, it was all still a great mystery, and I am not sure 'I might have a sensitivity' is a good enough explanation. There's a lot more work to be done."

Again, he waved his hand as if it were nothing.

"Don't worry about that just now. That virus is not going to cause any more issues."

"Exactly why, Al?" She held his eyes with hers now and didn't allow him to look away or feign exhaustion. "Do you know something I don't? What if Greg Turner really did have a hand in this incident? What if he found a way to infect you with this whatever-it-is? Does that not scare you?"

"I don't believe that, and neither should you."

Al settled back into the pillow and closed his eyes. Nothing more, just *I don't believe that.* Kayla felt the familiar surge of anger bubbling up inside her, threatening to boil over. She took a deep breath, trying to calm herself before she said something she might regret.

"Oh, you don't believe it? Great. Just great, Al. Meanwhile, you are ill, Dante is in the hospital with numerous broken bones, and Roberto is missing in action. At least as far as we know. That sounds like an awful lot like somebody has it in for the three Ivers boys, you think?"

Al chuckled, which did nothing to soothe Kayla's temper. "The last time somebody called us the three Ivers boys, I believe I was 17," he said. "But seriously, put it out of your mind. It's not Turner."

"Turner is the only thing that makes any sense," Kayla insisted. "And it is the one theory I can believe. You are the most stubborn, pigheaded…"

Anything she might have said to him then was interrupted by the nurse with a tray of food and medications for Al. Kayla rose and took a few steps aside, but Al's nurse left no doubt that Kayla was in the way just then, and Al needed one thing—rest.

His nurse was here to make sure he would get it, and after a few more pointed hints, Kayla finally said her goodbyes and left.

She walked down the hospital corridors, past rooms of patients and visiting families, past doctors and nurses, and past a few empty rooms. She felt as if she just wanted to sneak into one of them, pull the blankets over her face, and fall asleep until this was all over.

You are the strongest person in this whole three-ring circus. You will find a way, and you will get it done. Trust me.

What did he know that she didn't, and why would he not tell her the whole story? Sure, he was tired, exhausted even, but Al had a piece to this puzzle nobody else had seen. She was almost sure of it, but he refused to tell her what it was.

***

Kayla stumbled towards her car, her body feeling heavy and unwilling. She drove herself home, each turn of the wheel feeling like a monumental effort. When she finally stumbled through the door of their house, she collapsed into Rafael's old chair, feeling completely drained of energy. The events of this cursed day had taken their toll, leaving her feeling raw and exposed, with too many thoughts and emotions swirling around in her head to process.

Al—Dante—Rafael—Nick. Her mind raced in circles, even when she closed her eyes.

When her phone rang, she picked up without thinking, hoping against all odds it might be Rafael.

"Hey, darling," Barry drawled, and Kayla wanted to hang up on him.

"It's been a horrible day," she said. "Worse in fact than any I can remember in recent memory. Scratch that, any bad day I've ever had. So, keep it short."

"Well," Barry hesitated, "I was actually going to drop by."

"God, Barry, not now. I am definitely not up for visitors. Can you not tell me whatever it is you want to tell me on the phone and be done with it? And if it is another catastrophe, I for sure don't want to know anything about it."

"No—I believe it is better if I drop by." Something in his voice made her head snap up.

"Rafael?" she asked quickly. "Did something happen to Rafael? Did somebody call you? Did you hear something?"

"No, no, relax. Rafael is perfectly fine, at least as far as I know. I've located Roberto."

"Roberto—well, whoop-dee-doo. That makes two of you. I went to see Al when he woke up, and you know what the first thing was he wanted to do? Talk to Roberto. Not Rafa, not you or me, nor Dante—no. Roberto. That's who he wants to talk to when he finally wakes up after being unconscious for weeks. Jesus Christ."

Barry was silent for a long moment, long enough for Kayla to look at the phone in her hand, to check if the connection had dropped.

"Barry? Are you still there?"

"I'll be there in 10."

"Wait, I am not really up for…"

But he had hung up the phone already. Kayla cursed softly and slipped her feet back into her shoes. She had a good mind to turn off the lights and leave him knocking at the door when he came around, but Barry was not the kind of man who would take no for an answer, and he had sounded a little off.

"You look beat," he said as he walked in, and Kayla took a step back.

"Well, thank you, Barry. That's just what a woman wants to hear when you walk into her home, late at night, after a harrowing day. 'You look beat.' Now before I show you how this door works from the other side, why don't you tell me what was so all important you couldn't tell me over the phone? And make it quick."

"We know where Al's virus came from," Barry said, looking behind him as if to make sure there was no one there. "It had nothing to do with Turner. Although—in the press, Roberto will likely make it look like that. And all of us need to be on the same page. Is that quick enough?"

Kayla sat hard in Rafael's chair again and tried to process what he'd said. Surely, a trapdoor had opened beneath her feet, and she'd been dropped into an alternate reality. Slowly, she shook her head.

"What? Where? Maybe you better say that again—and this time give me the entire story."

Barry grabbed a chair, straddled it, and told her the entire story then. He told her about Roberto's financial issues and his attempt at saving some money by purchasing cut-rate growing medium from some guy he had met at the track. He told her how he had asked Al for a second opinion because something looked off, and he didn't want to risk an entire harvest on it if the product were inferior, and how Al had opened the container, put his hands into it, touched and smelled the suspect growing medium.

"So," Barry finally said. "That's how Al got it. Roberto never touched the stuff himself, so he got lucky. He is also an idiot because he tried to hide the whole incident, and I already reamed him out over it. In great detail. Expect to see the report about that contamination cross your desk tomorrow."

Kayla still said nothing, brought her hands to her chin, and let her eyes rest on Barry, thinking.

"Has he gone completely crazy?" she finally said. "You do not buy supplies for what in essence is a naturally growing pharmaceutical product from some random guy. How the heck does something like that even come up in casual conversation?"

Barry only shrugged.

"Hey, have you got some cheap growing medium?" Kayla mimed and shook her head again. "I agree it needs to be reported, and it might cost Roberto his company—but I am still thinking Greg Turner might be behind all of it, aren't you?"

Barry finally got up, went to her kitchen, opened her fridge, and returned with two rather full glasses of wine. He handed her one, took a long draft of the other, and finally put it down beside him.

"How do you figure?" he finally asked. "Unless Turner flat-out walked up to him and offered him the contaminated medium with the outright intent to poison him."

"Unless I misunderstood you, that is exactly how Roberto wants to play this to the media and the health officials, is it not? Grow medium is not something that is commonly traded on some underground black market somewhere. You have to go looking for it. You have to research approved places to buy it or, in Roberto's case, unapproved places. I don't see this to be a very common thing. Personally, I am rather inclined to think someone noticed he was in trouble, decided to take advantage of his issues, and made him a dangerous offer."

"Could be." Barry stroked his chin slowly. "I don't know—it is a little farfetched."

"That's because the notion of cutting corners with supplies not approved by the ministry makes perfect sense to you and Roberto," Kayla snapped. "The rest of us would—well, it's just not something most of us would do."

"Look at you considering yourself a grower." Barry grinned, and Kayla got to her feet.

"I'm glad we finally know where this thing came from," she snapped. "I'm glad Al is going to be OK, and I'm hoping Roberto will have learned a very valuable lesson. What I am not is ready to let Turner off the hook just like that."

Barry stared at a spot on the floor by his feet, rolling the stem of his wine glass between his fingers.

"If you put it like that."

"I think Roberto should go and speak to the police to initiate a full investigation. But that's entirely his business, and neither you nor I are going to have a say in it. Especially not tonight. So, if you would please," she took a few steps toward the door, "I need to process this day, and tomorrow is not going to be any easier. See yourself out please, Barry. We will talk tomorrow."

Barry left, but the anger that had taken hold of Kayla when he revealed Roberto's illicit little deal continued to simmer beneath the surface. She walked around the house, opening and closing closet doors with a bang, checking things that didn't need checking, and generally wearing a track into the wood flooring of Rafael's house.

What utter nonsense to be trying—what utter, idiotic carelessness—to buy growing medium from an unknown source. There were rules in place, and reasons why these rules were there, and this, this was exactly one of many of those reasons.

Finally, Kayla fell into a restless, agitated sleep on the couch. Cannabis plants haunted her in her dreams, and viruses with little arms and legs. The past day might have been the worst in long memory, but the new one was not promising to be any better.

TWENTY-SIX

Kayla rose only a few hours later, groggy and sore from sleeping on the couch, and grouchy from being groggy and sore. But she straightened and forced herself into the shower. This day was not going to handle itself, not even to do a favor to Kayla Montecito, so she had better get on with tackling it.

She found a brief message from Rafael on her email. They were still checking him out for injuries, illnesses, and diseases, and providing all of them with temporary papers, and as soon as that was done, they were headed home. He sounded none too happy over all of the pokes and prods he was receiving, and none too patient with the process, but he would be home soon.

Not soon enough for some. She brought her fingers to her lips, touched his picture, and steeled herself to tackle another day at PerCan.

***

The very air in the PerCan building felt electrically charged. Staff members gave her a quick smile, a brief greeting, and carried on what they were doing.

Pamela was sitting in Kayla's office, waiting, when Kayla stepped into it.

"Tell me you've hired 15 qualified cultivation technicians overnight," Kayla said by way of greeting, and Pamela shook her head.

"Not even one—it is a great wasteland out there."

"Well, then, it's up to us. You ever been part of a harvest?"

"Me?" Pamela spread her hands in front of her. "No, no, no. Don't get me wrong, Kayla, I am all for taking one for the team, but I am not going down there and…"

"Didn't suggest it." Kayla smiled thinly. "I, however, don't have a choice."

"You can't be serious." Pamela sounded truly horrified.

"Can't I?" Kayla dropped into her chair and looked down on herself. Jeans, sneakers, and a plain white sweatshirt. Admittedly, they were Balmain jeans, and the white sneakers had just the tiniest pattern of rhinestones, but so be it.

"If I'm asking the staff to go the extra mile and make the effort, I am going to have to get right in there and lead with a good example."

"I don't think that's the best idea you ever had," Pamela said, shaking her head. "For one, forgive me, but you don't really know what you're doing, and for the other, it will be way too easy to blame you when things go sideways."

"As they will," Kayla said and tied her blonde locks into a ponytail. "At least I am going to go down swinging. I've read all of Al's research. I've watched the videos. I am doing this."

"You can't possibly conduct a harvest of this size and this value after watching a YouTube tutorial on how to do it. No."

"Pamela, I already said I would. End of discussion. I am going to go down there into Production and offer to do anything they need a hand with. And if that is holding a flashlight or carrying buckets of whatsit or something-or-other from here to there, then so be it."

"I admire the spirit, Kayla, but, for the record, I advise against it."

"Noted and appreciated, Pamela. But I am out of options. I have a lot of product that needs to be harvested, and I have no people to do it."

Kayla sat again and folded her arms in front of her chest.

"I know this might be the worst idea I've ever had, but it is all I've got at the moment, and I have to do something. I can't just sit up there in an office and wait for either Rafael to come back, or that harvest down there to spoil. I can't. Doing nothing is the worst thing in my opinion."

"And if anything goes wrong with that harvest, do you know how many lawsuits that will open you up to? I'm no expert, but what I do know is that something going wrong with a harvest that's—well, that's almost a given. Please."

"I know. And I still have to do it. There's no guarantee that Rafael will get here in time to avoid disaster. From his email this morning, he likely won't."

"I hear you." Pamela looked down at her hands. "I get it, and I admire your courage. It is not what I would do, and I am advising against it—but I am here for you if you need any help, except…"

"You don't have to head down into Production with me, Pam," Kayla said and smiled at the HR manager. "Just keep things on an even keel up here, try and keep peace amongst the staff, and let me know if there is anything you can't handle."

Just then, someone knocked at her office door hard and fast, and, before she could even raise her head to say something, Connie opened the door and stuck her head in. Her eyes were wide, and a steep line of concern ran between her eyes.

"Ms. Montecito? There are eight people from Pride Cannabis down in Reception? They say it's extremely urgent, they are here for the harvest, and you would know what it was all about? They refuse to go away. What do you want me to do?"

"Say what?"

Kayla looked from Connie to Pamela and back. For a moment, neither of them spoke, and an idea started to take hold in her mind.

"I'm sorry. I have no idea why they are here or what this is all about, but do not send those men away. Do not. Matter of fact—get them right now and bring them up into the boardroom for a minute. Now, hurry."

"Ms. Montecito?"

Connie still hesitated, looking at Pam, and Kayla forced a smile.

"Probably just crossed wires, Connie, a message I didn't get. But please do not let them leave. These men could be just what we need." She turned to Pamela and gave her a little double thumbs up. "One of us has got this prayer thing down pat because that right there is the answer to a heartfelt prayer."

"Kayla? I can see what you're thinking, and be careful. Pride Cannabis is Roberto Ivers's company. There is some bad blood between Roberto and Al as far as I know. For all we know… Well, I'm not sure I like the look of this."

"If these men can help us with that harvest, then that's all I need to know," Kayla said, already standing and on her way to the boardroom. "Make them employees then, or consultants. Somebody with liability—write up agreements. I don't care. We just got handed a chance, and I am going to find out right now what's happening and how this came to be."

Dear God, thank you, thank you, she thought on her way to the boardroom, although, in all likelihood, Al had spoken to Roberto. Al, who had just regained consciousness, just mentioned urgently talking to Roberto. How the heck this entire thing hung together, she had no idea, didn't even want to know.

If you're in a deep pickle, Rafael would say, *use your survival training. You look at what is in front of you, deal with it, and take one more step. Then you see what is in front of you again and repeat.*

What was in front of her was a harvest just then. One step at a time.

***

"Kayla, Detective Sergeant Robertson is on the phone and would like to speak to you," another staff member called after her, and she waved the lady off.

"Later. I have some important business with some staff members I have to take care of right now. Tell Robertson I will call him back later."

As she reached the boardroom door, she paused, placing her hand on the cool metal handle. With a deep inhale, she drew in a cleansing breath, allowing the fresh air to fill her lungs and calm her nerves before stepping inside.

Whatever you do, whatever the reason they are here, you need to hire these guys on for the harvest, she told herself. Then she put on her most brilliant smile and opened the door.

There they were, sitting in her boardroom. Eight men, all youngish, clean-shaven, dressed in light teal uniforms with a Pride Cannabis logo on the left chest pocket.

Stitched below were their names, and Kayla took the time to read all of them.

"Gentlemen," she finally said, "I don't know who is responsible for sending you here this morning, but you are the most welcome sight I could wish for today."

"Ms. Montecito." The oldest of the men rose out of his chair a little and offered a hand. His uniform read *George,* and he just blushed a little when she took his hand and shook it enthusiastically. "Roberto said there was a need at his brother's company, a need for workers who had completed a harvest before, so he told us to check in with you."

"We are delighted to have you on board," she said with a bright smile, even though she wanted to shout, *Thank God and whatever angel sent you to me today because you are saving my life and this company just now.*

"You look like you were about to help out personally." George smiled, and Kayla looked down at herself.

"The thought had occurred to me, George. Thank heavens it won't come to that. But won't you all be missed over at Pride? Don't you have a harvest of your own coming up?"

All the men looked down at their feet, and none wanted to speak. A few of the workers looked at George, who put his hands in his pocket and chewed on his lower lip for a long moment before speaking.

"Well, the thing is," he finally said, drawing it out as long as possible, "I mean—there is going to be a news release coming out today anyway. So it's not like I'm giving away company secrets or anything, you know…"

Kayla waited and crossed her hands behind her back so she wouldn't grab this man by the shoulders and shake answers out of him.

"Of course not," she finally said.

"Well, we had an infection go through our manufacturing area. So, it's kind of like—everything has to be destroyed."

Kayla fought for composure. The word *infection* put her on edge. It was that looming issue in the back of her mind, knowing where that infection likely came from, knowing what was going on in the back, and still not being able to say anything.

Infections happened in cannabis operations. Rafael had told her about fungal and bacterial infections in the plants, and he insisted on an environment as close to sterile as possible. That was his one reason for keeping the plants in individual grow pods, for keeping the pods independent from one another and for locating all of the mechanical and environmental controls outside, in the access corridors between the pods.

Rafael was paranoid about infections among the plants. No one came near the plants, truly no one, unless they were actively working with the plants in one way or another, and only after they had taken extensive special showers, changed their clothes, and disinfected their hands, put on environmental covers and booties.

Cultivation technicians walked through the pods looking like they were about to perform open-heart surgery—and in a way they were. *Damn finicky plants*, she could hear Rafael grousing, and it made her smile.

"I'm sorry," she said to George. "I'm so, so sorry. I'm not laughing at you, and an infection in your harvest is one of the most heartbreaking things for a cannabis manufacturer. I was just thinking about our head engineer always giving us a hard time about cleanliness protocols."

"Rafael." George smiled. "Yes, he has his ways, and he's not shy about telling you."

"You know him?"

"He visited our operation once. And he just would not stop talking about cleaning protocols. I think Roberto was having a hard time keeping his temper in check."

"I'm so very sorry about your harvest," Kayla said again. "Truly. Although of course I am delighted to see you here, ready to work, so shall we see the operation?"

"Of course, yes."

What would Rafael say if he were here right now and saw her walk the workers from a rival operation right into his grow areas? And Al? Did it even matter any longer? She needed to get this harvest done, and whether she hired outside workers or brought in these folks, she would let strangers into their grow areas, and of course Rafael wouldn't like it. *Look at what's in front of you and deal with it.* This was her way of dealing.

Just in time, Pamela showed up with agreements for all of the men and with a handful of uniforms for them. Kayla waited to be called upon to tell them what to do, but there was no need. They knew exactly what needed to be done, and officially, they could get started immediately. Kayla exhaled, and for the first time in days, she felt as if a pinprick of light had appeared at the end of a long tunnel.

She left Pamela with the new people and went down to the staff rooms, where she found Eva and a few of the regular staff to explain what was going to happen. Nobody liked the idea of having strangers in the grow pods, rivals even, but if she had said it once today, she had said it a dozen times: this had to be done. If they wanted their company to survive and to thrive, it had to be done, and they went on to do it.

TWENTY-SEVEN

Rafael had never seen a military supply plane from the inside before that day. As a matter of fact, he had skipped the entire military experience completely. But the sheer size of the plane that was to pick them up to take them home almost made him drop the meager plastic bag he was holding, containing his remaining belongings and temporary papers.

"Holy cannoli," he said to Jonas, who walked beside him, eagerly stabbing at his phone. "This thing looks big enough to transport the entire city."

"That? We're going to fly home in that?" Jonas's eyes widened. "This is…"

"Immense," Rafael confirmed. "I think you can drive a tank into this thing, when the back hatch opens. I always wanted to see the inside of one of those bad boys."

"What's wrong with a common, old-fashioned Boeing 747?" Jonas said, craning his neck to check out the massive transport plane. The closer they got, the more they had to tilt their heads backwards to take in all of it. "I for one would not have had an issue with an old Boeing."

A conveyor belt unrolled from the back of the supply plane, and massive crates of supplies started appearing from its belly. Rafael stared in fascination.

"I'm sure you wouldn't," he said. "But this monster is going home today after dropping those emergency supplies and getting a spot of gas. I bet you it's faster and way more fun."

Rafael dropped his bag and waited on the tarmac as they had been instructed to do. Ground workers bustled around them, and forklifts picked up the crates of supplies from the plane and drove them off, one after the other after the other…

A few more people joined them on the tarmac, vacationers and other businessmen who had been caught out by the tropical storm and who needed to get out ASAP. Rafael recognized a few people from their temporary government refuge and chatted.

He tried to act cool, but failed miserably. At this point, he just wanted to get home, to see Kayla, and Al, and PerCan. Now that the immediate danger to them had passed, the need to get home to PerCan became more urgent with every minute that passed.

An urgent need to make sure that everything there was all right was gnawing at his insides and driving him on. He wanted to be sure that the harvest was proceeding and that these strangers Kayla had hired out of nowhere were not wreaking havoc in 'his' grow spaces.

Who were they, and where had they come from? Yes, he'd been told Roberto had recommended them, actually sent them, but Rafael didn't trust Roberto if he couldn't actually see him. Kayla had mentioned Al was involved, and that made him feel a little better.

But hadn't Al been unconscious until a day or so ago? How did this all happen then? How did all of these pieces fit together? There was no logical explanation to be had. At the end of the day, he wasn't going to be a happy man until he could put eyes on the people working on the harvest and in his facility. Impatiently, he bounced on the balls of his feet as the last of the supply trucks lined up to the plane.

"When are we leaving?" he asked one of the crew who busied himself with something mechanical at an open hatch.

"Not long now," the man said. "In a few minutes, you can go in, and I'll show you how to secure yourself. Once we get final clearance, we'll be off. Stand by. It'll be a rocky ride, but fast."

Securing himself involved sitting on a hard, fold-down seat built into the side of the plane and pulling down a three-point security belt, latching it in, and hoping your butt would survive several hours of a rough ride on an unpadded seat. It would be hell all throughout the flight, he knew that, but that's what he got for insisting to be on the 'first flight out.'

Jonas paled just a bit when they showed him the seating arrangement and swallowed hard. Fortunately, with the hatch open and the engines warming up already, there was no way to speak and be heard.

They communicated via hand signals. All around them, people buckled themselves into the side of the plane. Rafael thought he even recognized a few of the government officials he'd spoken to. Go figure. They were on the first plane heading out of here, together with the bigwigs! He elbowed Jonas in the side and nodded in their direction.

Maybe Barry had pulled a few strings to get them home, could have been Al too. It would be the kind of thing Al would quietly do and then pretend he hadn't done anything.

Rafael leaned back against the vibrating metal body of the aircraft and closed his eyes. *Almost there, baby*, he thought with Kayla in mind. *Just hold on for a little longer.*

TWENTY-EIGHT

Kayla ended up suiting up anyway and getting right into the harvest, along with the men from Pride Cannabis and her own staff.

Curious glances followed her everywhere she went, and she heard more than a few whispers. Likely, none of them were kind, but Kayla didn't care. She held her head high, gave people a thumbs-up sign wherever she could, and bravely did anything she was told to do.

Eva, with a clipboard in hand, assigned tasks, and more often than not, Kayla found herself pushing away large carts of waste product, carrying buckets of supplies from here to there, or holding things for another, infinitely more accomplished worker. Didn't matter. She wasn't here to show how talented she was, or what a big shot she could be, but rather that she wasn't afraid to get down and dirty for 'her' company, 'her' harvest, and 'her' staff.

Finally, she understood what Rafael was always going on about.

Some of the hostility thawed bit by bit, until she could chat with people and not be faced with an angry glare. By late morning, her coworkers even told her what to watch out for and actively prevented her from making huge mistakes, and a bigger fool of herself than absolutely necessary.

The lunch hour came and went, and she ordered pizza for everyone and shared it with them in the breakroom.

"I have a new appreciation for the things you do every single day," she said to Eva, putting her hands in her lower back, stretching. "This is super hard work."

"You get used to it." Eva smiled. "It's just because you are… Well, you know…"

"Sitting in an office all day?" Kayla suggested. "No worries—I get it now."

A young man from the executive offices came running in with a note in his hand. Confused momentarily, he looked around until his eyes stopped where Kayla sat, eating a piece of pizza off a brown paper napkin.

"There you are."

"There I am indeed, if it is me you're looking for."

"Yes, Ms. Montecito, of course—all over the building as a matter of fact. I didn't think I would find you, well—here."

"There's a harvest to be done, and it's not going to wait for anyone. So what do you need?"

"There is a…" The young intern consulted the note in his hand. "A Detective Robertson upstairs in the boardroom, and he needs to speak to you."

"Now? I have my hands full right now."

Probably just an update, she thought. They were after all still searching for Greg Turner, even if she herself hadn't even thought of the man in a long time.

"As you can see," she swept a hand around the room, "I'm a little busy, and I really can't just leave my post at a moment's notice."

"Um…" the young intern shuffled and looked down at his note again. "He kind of did say it was a matter of extreme importance and…" Another glance at the note. "No matter what she says, tell her to drop what she is doing and get her rear end up here."

Kayla didn't really want to leave, but Eva shook her head and waved her way with her hand.

"Go on. It sounds important. We'll be fine down here, thanks to the wonderful workers from Pride."

"Are you sure?"

"Very sure. Go. It does sound important."

"I'm so sorry to leave you hanging." Kayla snatched another piece of pizza out of the carton and nodded to the remaining staff, chewing. "If you need anything—anything at all—just ring through to the boardroom. I will deal with it."

Nods and murmurs of assent followed her out, and she thought she heard a few people clapping. They loved Rafael, because he was so 'hands-on' and direct, whereas Al seemed often distant and reserved. Perhaps she had broken that barrier today, at least a tiny little bit, but if she never had to harvest cannabis again for the rest of her life, she would not complain either.

She walked into the boardroom as she was, sweaty, her hair in a ponytail and chewing a piece of pizza out of her hand.

"Detective, what brings you here?"

Robertson stopped short and took her in head to toe.

"I—well, I daresay it looks like I am interrupting something."

"Harvest." She waved her hand and wiped them with a napkin before she offered him a handshake. "Now then, it sounded urgent."

"Extremely. Have a seat."

He pointed to the chairs around the boardroom table, and Kayla complied, if only because her entire body felt sore, and his face had the somber look of someone being the bearer of some bad news.

"I don't like the sound of that."

"I don't imagine you will like this, no. First off, how is Al? I heard he came out of his coma?"

"He woke up, yes. Considering the circumstances, he is stable at the moment, even though they still don't have an idea what that virus is or where he may have picked it up."

"I'll get to that in a minute."

He had made the connection then? Kayla stopped fidgeting and dropped her hands into her lap. The only reason this detective would ever get involved with this particular virus…

"Are you telling me you have an answer?"

"One thing at a time. What about Dante?"

"Dante is bashed up and owes his life to safety equipment. Same hospital, a few floors down and in a different wing. But he is on the mend. What's this all about, Detective? You are really starting to frighten me a bit here."

"As well as I should." Robertson took her chair beside her and spun it around so his arms rested on the back of the chair and he was facing her.

"Anything new from Greg Turner?"

"Here—at PerCan? No, of course not. Why would he…?"

"Now listen to me. I don't want to panic you, but we've inspected Dante's motorcycle. What was left of it anyway. First glance, the whole thing appeared to be an accident, maybe even driver error, but then one of my techs got curious."

"How curious, exactly?"

"Seems his nephew owns the same brand of motorcycle—just a concerned uncle, wanted to know what exactly caused this accident, since no other vehicles were involved. How could this happen and why? Was there a flaw within the machine itself?"

"Sounds like more than a concerned uncle."

"Got that in one." Robertson paused for a moment and sighed. "That tech started to search with the idea in mind that there had to have been some tampering. And do you know what he found?"

Kayla held her breath and fixed the detective with her eyes.

"From what I have been told," the detective continued, "the steering linkage of Dante's motorcycle was definitely tampered with. Unless you went looking for something in that area, you would miss it. Making it worse, that steering was tampered with in a manner that would allow

Dante to drive for quite a distance, without an inkling something might be wrong before it gave out—all at once.”

“He said he just suddenly lost control,” Kayla breathed, remembering Dante’s words. “That means…”

“That means somebody wanted him dead, Kayla. Theoretically, if Dante were coming here to the plant, his most natural route from the hospital would have been via the highway.”

“Which was closed due to a spill that afternoon.”

“Yes, it was. But just imagine for a second if, instead of crawling through midtown traffic, the accident would have happened at full speed on the highway?”

“Dear loving God.”

They would be planning a memorial right now, and brutally speaking, there would not be enough left of Dante to have a memorial with. Kayla shuddered.

“You’re thinking…”

“Yes. Aren’t you?” Robertson asked.

“Greg Turner.”

“Well, unless the Ivers men have another criminal on hold who wants them all dead, yes, my bet would be on Turner,” Robertson said, a little irritated. “And this also puts a whole new spin on Al’s sudden mysterious illness.” He put air quotes around the phrase. “And that coverup out at Roberto’s place.”

“What coverup?” Kayla’s head snapped up instantly, and she squared her shoulders. The word *coverup* never really went down easy around a magazine publisher. “I don’t know of any coverup, Detective, so you’re going to have to get a little more specific here.”

“Get off it.”

Robertson walked away from her. For a moment, he looked like he wanted to strike the far wall of the conference room. Then he turned around and came back to her, his eyes blazing with an angry fire.

“You should have told me. No matter what went on, no matter what somebody was doing that might not have been totally aboveboard, if there was any chance Turner and some criminal activity were involved, you should have told me."

Kayla became quite still and folded her hands in her lap as her mind clicked away a dozen miles an hour. What had Barry and Roberto told the detective? How much did he know? What had they put into the incident report to the Ministry of Health?

She felt Robertson's eyes on her and licked her suddenly dry lips.

She hoped to God the detective was not here to arrest any of Roberto Ivers's men because she was not going to give up so easily.

"Dearest Detective," she said as calmly as she could and gave him her most convincing fake smile, "I hate to be rude, truly, but I have no idea what you are talking about. Whatever coverup you are investigating, I assure you I'm not in on the game. I've been trying to harvest three grow pods' worth of cannabis without having enough people for half the job." She looked down at herself and pointed at her stained jeans and sneakers. "Do you think I would walk into a meeting looking like this if I hadn't been involved in a task so important it could mean the difference between profit and bankruptcy for our company? Do me the courtesy of filling me in, will you?"

Robertson stopped short and worried his lower lip with his teeth for a moment.

"You really don't know?" he asked after a long moment. "You've got Roberto Ivers's men working down there in your plant. Are you asking me to believe you don't know where they came from or why they are out of a job all of a sudden?"

"I've had men walk off the job here," she snapped. "Difference of opinion. Roberto, at Al's behest, asked them to help me out."

"I'm having a hard time…"

"Believe it or not, that's bloody well your choice," Kayla snapped and glared at him for a moment. "Two brothers helping each other out. Now either tell me what this is all about or leave. You are kind of pissing me off here, Detective."

"God, you sound like Rafael when you say that."

"I take that as a compliment, Detective. Now. If Dante's motorcycle has been tampered with, I suggest you double your efforts at finding Greg Turner and arresting him, before anybody else in the Ivers clan gets hurt."

The detective pulled out a chair and sat in it, folding his hands under his chin. "I guess I can see that with harvest and everything…"

"Detective!"

"Perhaps you haven't seen the news releases."

"I have not really had the time and leisure to sit down and read, no."

"Pride Cannabis announced just a few hours ago that, due to an unspecified viral infection, they have had to destroy the entire cannabis harvest in their greenhouses. If and when they will bring another harvest to market is as of yet unclear."

"Every…"

Automatically, her hand went to her mouth as she thought of the plants in the grow rooms below—the work and the effort that had gone into raising them from a clone, into ensuring their health and viability, the endless job of feeding, watering, and checking them—and, though she had cursed him a few hours ago, her heart broke all over again for Roberto.

"God, that is—devastating," she said and felt the blood drain from her face. Robertson was still watching her like a hawk. "That is horrible. How did this happen?"

"It gets worse, Kayla."

"How could it get any worse than that?"

"That very same infection also made some of the workers sick. Extremely sick, Kayla."

A rushing and drumming sound built in her ears. No. it could not be. It simply could not be! She hadn't known that. Barry had somehow neglected to tell her other workers had fallen ill. But how could the hospital have failed to make that connection? Wouldn't they have realized they suddenly had several patients with the same symptoms? People who also happened to work in a cannabis greenhouse? The rushing sound became so loud she could hardly hear Detective Robertson.

"Kayla, are you all right? Kayla!"

Her hand gripped the edge of the table, and she forced herself to take deep and even breaths. She didn't need to fake it any longer, hearing the news for the first time. *My dear Barry,* she thought, clenching her jaw, *I will have to have a word with you later.*

"What happened to those workers?" she managed to ask, and Robertson shook his head.

"Recovering in a private clinic. Don't ask me why Roberto made that particular choice."

Kayla exhaled fully and rubbed her tired eyes, not wanting Robertson to see her face while she tried to get a handle on the warring emotions inside. Dante's accident—not an accident. An unknown virus at Roberto Ivers's place of business that happened to infect Al as well. Three incidents, three men of the same family, three men who had one common enemy. Greg Turner.

Even if he had tried, Barry couldn't have spun the story in a more elegant way. It made sense—terrifying, logical sense. The question was still there, though, despite all of their media spins: could he have done it? Could Greg Turner be responsible for all three of the incidents?

"And you're thinking Greg Turner," she finally said, raising her head and daring to meet his gaze at last.

"I don't think anything right now, Kayla. I want to know why I wasn't informed of the incident at Roberto's, why they let so much time pass before releasing the news and informing the police. If I'd known about it earlier, Dante's accident might never have happened. Do you understand? I want to know…"

"You've come to the wrong place looking for answers, Detective,"

Kayla said and straightened her posture again. "I have just as many questions as you do, and, if your suspicions and hypotheses are correct, then I will have to add an additional layer of security to protect this company from a chemical or viral attack, although how in blazes I am going to accomplish that, God only knows."

"So, you have not heard anything? You have not received any threats, any comments, any communication at all?"

"No, Detective, I have not." Kayla rose again and straightened her filthy sweatshirt as best as possible. "I have not heard from anyone claiming responsibility or wanting to comment in connection with these incidents. Now, if you don't mind. I have to finish our harvest, work on beefing up our security, and hope Rafael gets back here in time to help me with all of it. Please do keep me updated. Specifically on the virus issue. I might be overstepping, and I really don't mean to tell you how to do your job, but catching Greg Turner would be a really good thing just about now. He's killed once and attempted to do so again. He needs to be apprehended!"

With that, she left Robertson sitting in the boardroom, his mouth agape, and went back down to the production area, back to her workers and her harvest despite the turmoil in her mind.

She still couldn't make up her mind whether all of those incidents could really have been Greg Turner's work. Could one man on the run have the resources to do all of this? And how on earth was she going to protect Perfect Cannabis from an attack until he was apprehended?

TWENTY-NINE

Greg Turner let out an angry roar and threw a piece of wood against the wall. He'd almost been caught last week at the trailer park, after someone had spotted him coming and going. As a result, they had doubled security in that place. No doubt, by now, they had reported a vagrant on the premises to the police. It would be easy to figure out he had spent time in the trailers stored there, and the police would put two and two together and come up with his number.

So, he had hightailed it out of there and found an abandoned house on the outskirts of town. He'd been safe there, until some urban explorers came upon him one night. Young people who lived for the thrill of breaking into and photographing abandoned places. What an oddball hobby. He'd been in a murderous rage when they discovered him in the middle of the night, and he had…

Greg closed his eyes and took a calming breath. That explorer wouldn't be found anytime soon. Meanwhile, he had had to crawl back to the forest worker's hut in the woods. As a safe spot, it was ideal. As a campsite, it was a lot more problematic.

Charging his phone and getting news updates meant a hike into town and hiding around areas where he could find free wireless access and power. Getting supplies meant a series of small break-ins that wouldn't be noticed, and all of it meant he was taking risks and wasting time.

Wasting precious time and distractions from his final goal: revenge on the Ivers clan. And now this. Now this. Not only had Dante Ivers survived that motorcycle accident, someone had struck against Roberto Ivers before he himself could.

How was all of this even possible? Could he have a competitor, someone else out for revenge against them? It was possible. They were, after all, despicable human beings. It was possible. But it was not very likely.

He paced up and down in the little forest worker's hut and pulled up the news report again—an unknown viral infection, possibly an attack.

A viral infection. He kicked at the pallet he used for a bed. An infection—that had to be the most stupid way to get revenge on anyone. Yes, it would lay waste to their precious plants and their crops and their harvest. Sure, it would probably bankrupt the company, but it was almost impossible to target a person with any kind of accuracy. It was like blowing up a city block hoping to kill one single person. Stupid risk.

And look at what happened at Pride Cannabis. Several workmen fell ill, of course. Had Roberto Ivers been affected? Of course not. He wouldn't have been working down there on the floor with the common people. It was idiotic. And somehow or other, Al Ivers had become involved. There was the real mystery in that sordid tale. A confounding, stupid mystery. Unless he could make it play into his plans—somehow. Was there a way?

Greg paced back and forth, chewing on his thumbnail. No one would plan something like this. It was too farfetched. The whole thing could have been an accident, of course, or maybe they were trying to hide something—something much bigger.

And who made the most convenient scapegoat for something like this? He did, of course. Too bad he had jumped the gun with Dante and his triple-damned motorcycle. He should have taken more time, should have been more thorough. Could have, should have, would have… Too late now. They were running scared now, and on the lookout, and they'd be more careful.

At least they were scared. The man grinned and kicked the wall. Scared was good, but it didn't give him the kind of satisfaction he craved.

He'd have to lie low for a bit, but he was working on an idea. If he could get all three of them at once—that would be the ideal scenario. One last explosive showdown, and be done with it. Yes, explosive, why not? And throw in that idiot construction man who did their bidding. Just for a bonus ticket, take him too. Yes, it would work. It would be spectacular. He just needed a few supplies, and he needed to disappear for bit.

Maybe hole up in another town for a week or so and perfect his plan.

The outlines of that plan began to form in his mind, and it was a thing of beauty. A no-fail guaranteed massive statement. Yes. Now he knew what to do. He'd disappear for a bit now. Lie low where nobody would think to look for him, and once they felt safe again, once they got careless again—he would strike from an area where nobody expected him and where they felt safe. Their own house.

THIRTY

Rafael didn't bother dropping his bag at home. He was the epitome of travelling light. He'd scored a beat-up old duffle bag from one of the soldiers at the military outpost where they'd spent the last few days, shoved his little plastic baggie of supplies into it, and called it done. Most of what he had brought along originally had been lost in the collapse of the beachfront hotel. He said goodbye to Jonas at the airport, promised to stay in touch, and called home. No answer. His fingers knotted into a fist. Maybe it would have been a good idea to call ahead, let them know he was arriving, but he hadn't wanted to take that time.

He called at Montecito Publishing and was told Kayla wasn't there. Hadn't been there in several days, matter of fact. She was simply too busy at PerCan.

This was not good. At this hour of the day, she should be at home, relaxing with her feet up. If she was still at work, this meant nothing good. He shifted his bag to the other shoulder, called an Uber, and was on his way to PerCan in the time it took to say *welcome home*.

Connie, his former secretary, now Al's assistant, happened to be looking for some stray paperwork at the reception desk. When she looked up and saw Rafael wandering in like a vagrant, disheveled, dirty, and sweaty, her face split into the broadest grin he had ever seen.

"Rafael, oh, thank the lord you are back!" She darted out from behind the reception desk and threw her arms around him. "Thank God you're here, thank God."

"Um, well…" Rafael stiffened a little with the unexpected embrace. He'd shaken hands with Connie—once, that was it.

None of this was any good, and his dread grew by the moment.

"Where's Kayla, in my office?"

"Yes—of course… Jeez, you must think me a lunatic. She left the harvest, and she's now in the conference room with—well, you'll see."

Rafael straightened up a little, his casual aw-shucks demeanor all but gone now, while the nagging feeling that absolutely nothing was all right around here grew by the second. His bag slipped off his shoulder to thump to the floor behind Reception, and he was already reaching for the door to the office when Connie stopped him.

"Wait. Wait, Rafael, you forgot your badge." She waved hers at him.

"I didn't forget it. It drowned in a hotel in Malta," he muttered and took Connie's badge off the ribbon around her neck. "Get me a new one, will you? Meanwhile this is going to get me anywhere I need to go in the next hour or so."

He didn't wait for her to protest and didn't give the security guard at the door more than a glaring look. By all rights, they should have stopped him, but… He was Rafael Covin after all.

Taking the stairs two at a time, he ignored the 'welcome back' calls from a few employees and opened the door to the conference room without knocking.

"Somebody care to fill me in—and do it quickly?"

The room was empty, save for Detective Sean Robertson, sitting in Al's chair, scrolling through messages on his phone.

"Rafael, you're…"

"Yes, I'm back. Obviously. Now where is Kayla, why are you sitting here, and what's going on with Al and my harvest—in that order?"

He let the door fall shut behind him and planted himself before

Robertson, military style, shoulders and feet squared, without taking his eyes off the man.

"Well?"

"I—I think Kayla went back down to production to help with the harvest."

"Nonsense."

Robertson swallowed. "Some sort of staffing issue here, I think. I'm here to investigate a link between Greg Turner and the recent attacks on Al, Roberto, and Dante Ivers. From what I hear, Al is recovering and… Well, how are you, Rafael?"

"Lousy. Thanks. But back home. Now I have to find Kayla. What the fuck would she be doing down there with the harvest, pardon my French? I'll talk to you later."

He turned on his heels and stalked out of the room, only to change his mind at the door. His hand on the door handle, he turned again and gave another withering look to Robertson.

"Hang around, Robertson. I want to hear the rest about those 'recent attacks' you just mentioned. Don't go anywhere."

"Rafael Covin, I am most certainly not here to do your bidding…"

Rafael never heard the rest of it. He'd let the door swing shut behind him and stalked down the hallway toward the production hall access doors.

The fuck? Kayla doing the harvest? Where the hell was Nick in all of this mess, and why did Dante not… Wait, recent attacks on Al, Roberto—and Dante? His steps became faster as he neared the heavy metal doors. Rafael hated running, always had, but this called for an exception.

He rushed through changing into a sterile gown and booties and putting on the required facemask, and finally, he saw her.

Kayla was pushing a massive wheeled hopper of freshly harvested cannabis leaves toward the processing hall.

Two more steps and he was by her side, putting his hands onto the handle beside hers. "Why'nt you let me do that," he said. "You look just about done in."

Kayla looked up at him and gave him the most beautiful smile he had ever seen. Her eyes filled with tears, and she blinked hard to fight them.

"Rafael. Of all the people I wanted to see here today."

Cleaning and sanitation protocols probably had a rule against it somewhere, but he put his arms around her, hard.

"I'm home, sweetheart," he said softly. "I'm home."

Kayla leaned into him, and he thought he could feel her sobbing softly.

"God, it's been…"

"I know," he said, "I know," painfully aware that all the work had stopped in the room and all eyes were on the two of them. Finally, Kayla straightened again and wiped her hands over her eyes.

"God, look at me. Bawling when we have a harvest to finish around here. We have a job to do, people—let's go."

"No," Rafael said and physically turned her around in the direction he had come from. "You, go upstairs, have a shower, get changed, and pour whatever drink you can find in Al's office. The good stuff is in the cupboard. I'll be riding herd on these guys."

He spun his finger around the room, indicating all of them, and landed on George.

"You. I don't know you, do I?"

"Well…"

"No, I haven't seen you. Didn't you use to work for Roberto?"

"Yessir, still do. I am on—loan to PerCan."

"The fuck?" Rafael looked around, but suddenly, everyone seemed to find something interesting on the floor down by their shoes some- where. "Well, I'm sure I'll catch up with the narrative here. And stop the *yessir*—we don't hold on things like that around here."

"Yes—um, sure."

"Great, now where is Nick in this whole lame-brained mess? Nick," he called into the farthest reaches of the production hall. "Get your ass out here so I can give you a hard time about making Kayla here help with the harvest. Jesus!"

He waited, but the buzz of chatter amongst the workers had suddenly died away to nothing. More people found more interesting stuff on the ground by their shoes and shuffled, checking paperwork that didn't need checking, adjusting their booties and hairnets.

Rafael fought the knot of dread in his stomach. Something around here was not only going sideways—it was bad. Very, very bad.

"Look," Kayla said, visibly struggling, "there was a lot of stuff that was going on and…"

"And apparently, I have a few gaps in my knowledge," he said loudly enough for everyone else's benefit. "No worries. Like I said, I'll catch up eventually. Now let's get all of this weed harvested, people. It's not going to get done all by itself."

He worried. Even as he checked the progress of the work, which was alarmingly slow but steady, assigned workers to tasks, and fell naturally into the rhythm of his old workdays, he dreaded finding out what had happened, why everyone was looking at him askance when he asked about Nick and why Roberto's workers were here in his production hall. If Kayla had hired them, he assumed they were OK, but still…

And what was up with her down here in production, putting her hands on the harvest?

That had to be the weirdest of them all. Number one, she didn't know anything about harvesting cannabis…

"It will be OK," someone said beside him, and he looked up into Eva's face. "Everything…"

"Of course it will be, Eva. Good to see you." He said and gave her a quick smile. "I've just been away for a bit, it seems."

"I know. It is—not all her fault."

"Of course not," he answered more harshly than he had intended, and Eva took a quick step backward.

"Sorry, Eva," he said and forked his hand through his hair. "Still a little tired from my trip, you know. We'll sort it all out later. Don't you worry. Now let's get all of this cannabis harvested, shall we?"

But still he worried. They shouldn't be behind like this with the harvest. If they didn't pick up the pace and get it done today… Well, if they didn't get it done today, there would be hell to pay, put it this way. And even if he worked all day and all night, and called in every favor he knew how to call in, he figured it would be a little miracle.

Take that, nature, he thought, and gave a box in his way a savage little shove. *Rafael Covin is one hell of a lot more stubborn than you are, and he didn't come all the way through a goddamned tropical storm that never should have happened in the first place, in order to find his harvest ruined. No way, no sir.*

He worked. His exhaustion and worry of the past week fell away all at once as he fell into his old tasks and rhythms. His hands moved at double speed, it seemed to him sometimes. He moved product, made space on the drying screens, reorganized the drying rooms every 20 minutes, it seemed, called out orders, and just kept going, refusing to stop.

He was going to kick this thing's butt, never mind anything else.

Finally, when he allowed himself to grab a stale piece of pizza and some water in the lunchroom, someone filled him in. Nick had quit.

Quit!

Nick Ambrose of all people. Rafael made a fist to stop himself from saying something that shouldn't be said in front of employees and surprised even himself when he didn't shove that fist into the nearest object.

"Is that so," he answered instead, dropping his hand, shrugged, and disposed of his paper plate in a trash bin. "Huh. Go figure."

And the person who had told him walked away, disappointed because he had robbed them of a great scoop. *You wouldn't believe how mad Covin got when I told him about Nick.*

Rafael wouldn't give him the satisfaction. Inside, however, his temper was slowly shifting up into overdrive and beyond. Naturally, the man had a right to quit, but whatever he had been quitting over couldn't be half as bad as leaving Kayla on her own, without any help, with a triple harvest on the go.

Common decency would have demanded to give some sort of notice and make the transition orderly and—well, decent, without creating utter chaos. Dante was out of commission because of his accident. He carried no blame, but Nick? Nick had zero excuse to leave them hanging, and he would hear about it.

***

It was either late night or early morning when he arrived back home, dirty, tired, and at least halfway convinced they would manage this triple-darned harvest. And if not, there was a small possibility he didn't even care any longer.

He found Kayla waiting up for him, wringing her hands, pacing the length of the living room.

"Look, I know I should have sent you a message. But everything happened so fast, and then I had to figure out this harvest…"

"Never mind." Rafael dropped into his old beloved recliner, let his head fall back, and closed his eyes.

"I have no idea what possessed you to think you could handle this by yourself, hands-on in production, but my hat is off to you."

He groped around the crown of his head, and his face darkened. "If I had one, that is. My favorite hat drowned in that bloody hotel."

"I know, I know. But Nick and Dante… And I knew I had to get this harvest in, so I didn't tell him anything. I figured I would fix whatever had happened and then come to him, and he really didn't see it that way."

"And you're not making any sense right now, sweetheart," he said and rubbed his tired, gritty eyes. "And that is the half that I can actually hear and understand right now. Tomorrow. Tell me what the heck went all on here tomorrow. If I live that long."

After coming through a tropical storm, hanging around government facilities and a military hospital for weeks, and a harvest he had jumped into without thinking, he amazed himself just keeping his eyes open.

One step at a time. And he would deal with all of this another…

THIRTY-ONE

Rafael woke up lying in his recliner with a blanket snuggled around him, and his first thought was, *Where have they shuffled me off to now?* Then he recognized the recliner, the blanket he had given Kayla for Christmas, and the smell of coffee from the kitchen.

At the same time, he realized that he was still wearing the clothes as when he had stepped onto a military transport plane in Malta, so he went upstairs and broke his rule about short showers being just as good as long ones.

When he came back down to the kitchen, Kayla was waiting with coffee and all of his favorites for breakfast.

"Is that all I had to do?" he asked and kissed her cheek. "Get caught in a tropical storm and you make all of my favorites for me?"

"No." Kayla rested her cheek in her hand. "Rafael, I made a mess of your company."

"Doubt it. Number one, it's not mine, and, number two, that damned harvest is almost all in. I'd say you did pretty OK, considering the lousy hand you were holding."

He slathered a piece of toast with enough butter to drown in and ate half of it in one massive bite. "Why the hell would Nick quit?" he asked, his mouth full, butter dripping down the side of his face. "That's the one question I have."

"Well, it's a bit of a complicated story. And it's ugly. Pour another coffee. Ready?"

And she told him. She told him about Dante wanting to teach her about the harvest, about him taking that triple-darned motorcycle—Rafael had called it that—and the accident that almost claimed his life. She told him about leaving Nick with the harvest preparations while she saw to Dante, and about an unspecified incident at Roberto's place, and how Detective Robertson needed to think Greg Turner was behind all of it.

When she was done, she sat there, hands around her coffee mug, head lowered, staring into the dark liquid, and she waited for Rafael to say something—anything, really.

Rafael blinked once, twice, dumped an entire packet of sugar into his coffee, and stirred a little more vigorously than strictly necessary.

"Go figure," he said. "That is so unfair. The one time I get caught in a real-life natural disaster, everything I own drowns, I get evacuated by the military, and meanwhile, everybody at home plays out a story that tops even that one. That's just not fair."

"Rafael, be serious. If you hadn't come back when you did, there was a good chance that harvest…"

"I am serious, and there still is a good chance that harvest will be—" He threw out his hands and shrugged. "It happens. Nothing we can do about it now any longer. What I can't figure out—how in blazes did you not go insane with all of this going on and manage to push, pull, drag, and box this company as far as it has come through this, without any kind of capable help?"

"Barry was there, and I had help." She smiled weakly. "Connie, Eva, Pamela, they've all been fantastic."

"Two admin ladies and a young, enthusiastic girl, but one whose first language is not English. Trust me. I would have gone insane." He drained his cup. "Not only did you not, but you managed to make good progress. Any time you want to give up that publishing gig of yours, I have a job as COO for you around here."

"Oh, no, no thank you, I have had all of that I can possibly handle."

She spread her fingers in front of her. "Never again. But Nick—it didn't have to… If I had handled it better."

"Nick totally overreacted because of the stress and what happened to Dante." Rafael made a throwaway motion and shook his head. "I'll straighten out Nick when I get my hands on him, and I'm sure by now he's feeling lousy anyway. It wasn't malice, just a desire to protect the company. He'll see that."

"I sure hope so."

"No worries. And Robertson still thinks Turner was behind all of it."

"Robertson thinks so, but we know better. And I can't tell him without really getting Roberto into hot water and… Let's just say I've had enough of pissing people off for the moment."

She told him what Barry had found out at Pride Cannabis, and Rafael whistled.

"Jesus. Roberto, that dumb fool. That had to go wrong 100 percent. Jesus." He shook his head. "I really cannot leave any of you alone for even a few weeks, can I? Tell me again how it is you're still walking upright?"

"It's not really funny, Rafael."

"It kind of is." He got up and poured himself another coffee—his third in the last 40 minutes if he counted right. "Do we know Turner was the one who messed with Dante's bike?"

"I don't think there's any concrete proof, no, but the bike was definitely tampered with, and who else has a beef with Dante or Nick?"

"I now do, but that's beside the point. You're right. We can't tell Robertson about the whole 'contaminated grow medium thing' or we ruin Roberto and his chances at a grow license for life. And now Robertson is wasting his time looking for Turner in places where he may not exist."

"That's just about it."

"Well." Rafael spread his hands. "All right. There is only one thing that will help here then."

"Oh, please do tell."

"We do our job best as we can do it," Rafael said, shrugging. "Ignore whatever else is going on, keep our eyes peeled around us, and—we wait."

"Wait?"

"Wait," Rafael confirmed. "There is no way Turner can get into PerCan. Read my lips, no bloody way. It's just not possible. We're safe while we're in there, and Al, Roberto, and Dante will have to look into hanging out together for a while, maybe even hire a strong, hefty fellow to keep them safe."

"A bodyguard?"

Rafael raised an eyebrow. "Don't make it sound so terrible. I've had to wander around with a guard for the last few weeks now. Trust me, I know what I'm talking about. And my bodyguards carried nasty guns. If it is any consolation, at least they will have a fourth man to play cards. Look on the bright side."

***

"An actual bodyguard?"

Al looked about as incredulous as Kayla when Rafael suggested it to him. "Are you insane?"

"Nope." Rafael rubbed his hands. "Look, I know you don't want to ruin your brother and his business, so that means we're going to have to wait it out until the police finally do locate and incarcerate Turner."

"Which won't take all that long, I hope."

"You hope."

Al struggled to sit up in his hospital bed and fought off Rafael, who wanted to push a pillow into his back.

"The weeks going through the aftermath of a tropical storm has given a snippy new side to your personality, Rafael, and I'm not fond of it. I have no interest in ruining Roberto. I just don't understand why that automatically means I have to have a—a—guard dog following my every move. No. Never."

"People will say it is so vintage Ivers," Rafael said and steepled his hands on his chin. "Like father, like son. Tadeo was usually surrounded by bodyguards. There'll be rumors that the old Ivers habits are back, and then—then we…"

"Enough, Rafael." Al briefly closed his eyes. "I'm told I'm getting out of here tomorrow, and once I settle in at home, I promise you I will think about it. Right now, I'm not in favor."

"Or Roberto could just admit that he tried to buy substandard contaminated grow medium on the black market and get it over with," Rafael quipped, earning another glare from Al.

"Stop it, Rafael. Do you know how much money I loaned him just to get as far as he is and get his production up and running? I wanted to make peace in the family, after my foolish attempt to get revenge. If he were shut down now, that would ruin all of us. While I do not relish the thought, I could survive it—unlike Roberto. And that's always considering I don't strangle him for trying to take stupid shortcuts on something this important."

"I was wondering how he had managed to finance such a nice facility." Rafael scooted a bit closer in his chair and sighed. "Realistically, Al, I don't think it's going to take all that long. Turner can't get into PerCan. At all. Period. You're safe while you're at work. But everywhere else, you will need someone. And Roberto will just have to hang out with us for a bit while Pride is being scrubbed down and go home with you at night."

He grinned at the look of horror in Al's face.

"Dante, he's in the grow rooms most of the time anyway. Just stick together for a little while. Sooner or later, they'll nab Turner."

"Sooner, I hope," Al said, and Rafael thought he had paled a bit more.

"He can't hold out that long," Rafael said and made a face. "Winter is coming!"

He grinned broadly, and Al shook his head. "Not funny, Covin. Not funny at all."

"I thought it was." Rafael grinned at his own joke. "I'm going to talk to your old pal Sandro. Maybe he has a few support staff he could lend us, just for the time being."

Al closed his eyes for a moment, his face visibly pained.

"I hate being around people 24-7," he muttered. "You of all people know that. It exhausts me beyond belief."

"I have a cot in the engineering monitoring room you could use."

"Don't tempt me."

The brief exchange had exhausted Al, and he closed his eyes and let out a long breath, fighting for the next one. His skin still looked pale and papery against the white hospital linens.

It was frightening how quickly he became tired, Rafael thought. How fragile they all were, no matter how much they liked to pretend otherwise. All the more, he was convinced that the inside of Perfect Cannabis Consolidated was the safest place on earth for Al Ivers and his brothers to be right now. Count it as a bonus that he, Rafael, could keep an eye on everything and everyone there.

"Enough about me," Al said softly, keeping his eyes closed. "You came through a hurricane in a country where there are no hurricanes. I'm sure that experience is not one you want to repeat any time soon."

"Not really." Giving Al some space, Rafael rose and walked to the window of Al's private hospital room, looking down into a lovely garden below. "I mean, they dragged us to a safe location before I knew what was even happening. And after that, it was just waiting for things to be completely safe before they let us back out."

"Ah yes, one of your favorite pastimes, waiting for something. I would have expected you to ask for a crane and help with the cleanup efforts."

Rafael chuckled. "Oh, you know me too well, my old friend. But you're wrong, I asked for a backhoe."

Al chuckled and coughed painfully. "Sorry—breathing tube down my throat for a few weeks."

"Hey…"

Before Rafael could even answer, a doctor stepped into the room and mustered Al and Rafael.

"Let me give you some privacy," Rafael said, but Al raised a hand.

"Stay—please. I'm sure the good doctor is here to tell me I can go home tomorrow."

"I don't really want to," the doctor said and looked from Al to Rafael and back again. "This infection is still pretty baffling, and, while you've fought it off, we would prefer to monitor you for a few more days."

"But?"

"But I know you will insist, and I can't really make you stay against your will."

"Yeah, no. I wouldn't recommend trying that with Al," Rafael quipped, and Al glowered at him.

"I really would prefer to go home, Doctor."

"They tell me your brother Dante is acting the exact same way." The doctor smiled, making Rafael chuckle again.

"Doctor, if it makes you feel better, we can hire a daily nurse for those two, until they are cleared for active duty again."

Al glowered at him even more, but finally nodded.

"If it gets me out of here, a nurse it will be, Doctor."

"Do that. I cannot emphasize enough how important it is to keep an eye on potential long-term side effects. This—thing—appears to be out of your body at this point, but, again, it's the unknown quantity in the room, and the question as to where it might have come from, or who may have wanted to use it against you."

A quick look of alarm passed between Al and Rafael, and the doctor couldn't help but notice it.

"I know, I know. That police detective alerted me to a few—a very few—suspicions as to what may be going on with that. As a doctor, that scenario horrifies me beyond belief, gentlemen, which makes it twice as important that we keep an eye on your recuperation progress."

Al squirmed uncomfortably under his blankets.

"Relax, Mr. Ivers. All I know is that there is a suspicion as to some wrongdoing and that there is a police officer outside of your, as well as outside of Dante's, door."

"There is?" Al snapped to attention immediately and looked at Rafael with alarm in his eyes. "And you failed to tell me anything about this?"

"Relax. He's just keeping an eye on people coming and going from this end of the corridor. I actually know the fellow from back when…" From back when he himself had been under suspicion of killing Al's father Tadeo. Rafael stumbled and made a face. "From before," he finished weakly.

"Fine, fine. I do not appear to have a choice, if all of you insist I require a guard." Al sighed. "But I need somebody to get me my laptop and my phone, please. Until I actually get to go home, I want to get at least a small bit of work done."

The doctor opened his mouth to argue and closed it again just as quickly because Al raised an index finger.

"And I need my laptop to arrange for this nurse everyone feels I require as well."

Rafael walked out of the room and greeted the police officer at the end of the corridor. Too many police officers, too many hospitals, too many revenge plans and shootings, he thought. Just too much…

***

Rafael stopped by to visit with Dante and found the same quarrelsome spirit, wanting to get out of the hospital and back to work. Dante had dozens of questions about the harvest at PerCan and Rafael's experience with a hurricane. And, as if by mutual agreement, neither of them spoke of Greg Turner or revenge.

For a few minutes, it felt good and wholesome to joke around with a colleague, and too soon, Rafael had to leave to get back to the harvest again.

He hurried out of the hospital, and, just as he turned the corner of a corridor, he ran into Nick Ambrose.

Nick froze in his tracks, looking left and right as if he were trying to make his escape, but Rafa took three giant steps, squaring up to the shorter, slender Nick.

"Hey, Nick," he said pleasantly, smiling so hard his mouth hurt. "How are things going with you? Everything all right at work?"

"I'm sure you heard—Dante…" Nick said, nodding toward the hospital room down the hall.

"Yes, of course. I am so sorry. He's lucky nothing worse happened. This is why I'm no fan of motorcycles. Walk with me for a minute, will you? I have something to ask you."

"Um—I really would rather not."

"It's not going to take long, Nick, promise. Come on. We'll grab a coffee in what passes for a cafeteria in this lousy hotel. My treat."

His hand gently took Nick's upper arm, and they walked along in the direction of the cafeteria.

THIRTY-TWO

A tiny bit of normalcy had finally returned to PerCan, Rafael thought. The dreaded triple harvest was finished. Now everyone groaned under the triple burdens of drying, packing, and storing.

Roberto Ivers's men were well trained and skilled, and fit into the existing work groups as if they had never done anything else. Indeed, they confessed to their fellow employees to be glad for the experience and the chance to work here with Rafael, while Pride Cannabis was being dismantled, scrubbed, and disinfected before being put back together.

Rumors were rampant as to what might have caused the strange viral outbreak, which news releases only described as *unknown*. Roberto's men stayed silent and shrugged. No clue.

Barry Wentworth had suddenly taken up residence inside PerCan again, doing his work from one of the available temporary offices, and, if people wondered what he was doing there all day every day, they kept their mouths shut and greeted him politely every time they passed him in a hall.

Rafael had felt the relief among the staff when he'd come back, straight off the rescue plane into the plant to help with the harvest. A collective sigh had been heard amongst the staff that day when they saw him, the man they most trusted to keep them and their jobs secure.

***

A few days later, Al Ivers walked back into the building too, gaunt and pale, carrying his portfolio under his arm and smiling a little weakly, all while leaning on an old wooden cane. All the employees who were not needed desperately at their stations had lined up in the front lobby to welcome him back, and Al waved with an embarrassed little smile and hurried into the elevator and up to his office.

Kayla, who had been sitting at his desk, all but jumped to her feet, darted out from behind the desk, and came to hug him.

"Thank you," he said and actually blushed a little. "Was it you who organized that little welcoming committee down in the lobby?"

"It was Eva," Kayla said and gave him another quick hug. "I do believe she felt that between you and Rafael, the company was finally in safe hands again. I have it on good authority—they will never trust either Thomas Donnelly, or me, to lead this company anywhere."

"Nonsense. You did what had to be done, and I appreciate it."

"Well, I…"

"Nonsense, Kayla." Al put down his portfolio and awkwardly took a seat behind his desk. His hands ran appreciatively over the armrests of his chair and along the edge of his desk, and he managed a smile. "That fool Donnelly risked the company, and you took care of it. And Dante's accident put the harvest at risk, and again, you took care of it. That was exactly what needed to be done."

"Nick did not see it that way."

"Judgment." Al waved her argument away with a swish of his hand. "I'm going to go through his contract and see what we can do about it. Worse comes to worst, we'll go looking for a new agronomist. They are not numerous right at the moment, but not impossible to find either."

"What about Dante?"

"Dante will have to learn to deal with things as they are and make his choices from there. At the moment, my youngest brother is running a bit scared since hearing a dangerous lunatic may in fact have tried to kill him. That does tend to bring you face-to-face with reality."

Kayla looked down at her hands and finally busied herself at the coffee machine in Al's office, bringing two cups to his desk.

"And yes," he said softly, touching the top of her hand with soft, papery fingers. "I also know how Barry and you turned Roberto's serious error in judgment around and—prevented worse harm."

"Mostly Barry," she said, looking down into her cup. "Master of the spin."

"It did have all the hallmarks of a Barry Wentworth operation, yes. I suspected as much. Now then, the main question remains—how do we move on here?"

"What do you mean, Al?" Suddenly, her head snapped up. "You are back and are taking over again, and I will go back to doing what I know, which is publishing magazines."

"Well, thank you, and I appreciate knowing that you have no intentions to fire me, but that is not what I was speaking of. While it is wonderful the police are finally hunting Greg Turner with renewed energy, since they believe him guilty of three attacks, it also means that Turner, if he is still in the area, will have to ramp up his efforts to do away with the three remaining Ivers men."

Kayla shuddered and rubbed suddenly chilled hands together. "Don't even talk like that, Al."

"I will admit I did not take the threat as seriously as I should have when I read his confession about killing my father." Al brought his palms together and frowned. "Losing his company appears to have put him over the edge, and he has lost touch with reality. More attacks are to be expected, I'm told. Your Rafael seems to think the safest place for me—for all three of us Ivers men—will be in here in this very facility. What's your opinion on all of this then?"

Kayla cupped her hands around her coffee and leached the warmth out of the white porcelain. She rose and walked to Rafael's favorite spot, the glass wall looking down into the production floor.

"I'm not keen on seeing you in protective custody anywhere, Al," she said. "You should come and go as you please. I imagine being locked in here for however long it takes could get pretty oppressive. A prison, no matter how pretty, is still a prison."

"My thoughts precisely. One might, of course, look at the police department case-solving rate and hope the entire spook will be over soon."

"Still. I'd have to say Rafael is right," Kayla said, turning to face him. "Look at what happened to Dante. His motorcycle, of all things, parked in the hospital's underground garage while he was there visiting you. If Turner has gone over the edge, lost touch with reality, he could strike anywhere. This place," Kayla spun a finger in a large circle, "Rafael tells me not even a mouse can get in here without him knowing about it."

"Fine then." Al put his hands on the desk, palms flat. "That settles it. We'll just have to try to get comfortable around here without stepping on one another. It will give me a chance to give Roberto a hard time about his—ill-advised purchase."

"He's not going to like it."

"Neither will Dante when he is finally released from the hospital. But he sounded rather shocked last time I spoke to him and ready to be convinced of any workable solution to our little Turner problem. I will leave you in charge then to find suitable accommodations in here for us. Without quoting Thomas Donnelly, it sounds like a task more suited to a woman's talents than mine."

***

And so Kayla ended up recruiting a few workers to help out and set to creating a living space for Al, Dante, and Roberto within PerCan. The logistics around the security systems access zones, and the supply of water, power, and enough space for everyone, soon turned into a nightmare, not aided by Rafael storming up to their little group on a regular basis, proclaiming they were turning his plant into a fugitive B&B.

In the end, they managed to create sleeping quarters in a zone that could be separated from the manufacturing space, showers that were a bit of a walk from the quarters but adequate, and a large-screen TV from the boardroom thrown in for entertainment. The Ivers men would have to carry their executive key fobs with them at all times, and, against his better judgment, Rafael exempted all executive keys from all security measures. Just temporarily.

"Just until Turner is in the big house." He glowered at them. "I really don't like punching exemption-holes into my security setup."

"It was your idea that we should stay here in the first place, and there's only us five who have executive-level key fobs. I'm sure you can trust us for a little while, right?"

"Yeah, well, I still don't like it." Rafael paced away for a bit and came back. "Day is not an issue. Let's try to limit movements at night as much as possible, shall we? I'll have to come up with some adjustments to that setup, but I need time."

"I'm sure everything will be more than adequate," Al said, smiling at his brother Roberto. "It's in our interest to see Turner caught. Think of it as camping without the tent, Rob."

"It's called glamping," Roberto said stiffly. "And I'd be just as safe in my house or my own company." He flexed his fist and finally struck one of his palms. "I don't know why you insist I have to hang out here, unless you are trying to smoke out Turner."

"Not a bad idea," Rafael said, tapping his leg. They were sitting in the conference room to make a proper plan, as Rafael called it, and Roberto still needed quite a bit of convincing.

"Your company, at this point, is being disinfected, fumigated, and God knows what, using unspeakable, likely unhealthy chemicals," Al reminded him and raised a single eyebrow. "For reasons which we shall never go into again—ever."

"I know, I know. I just don't get…"

"Keeping you safe." Barry had wandered into this impromptu meeting a little while ago, and while he had, technically speaking, no business here, nobody had told him to leave.

"I can handle the little turd if he comes at me." Roberto's eyes flashed with a dangerous fire. He struck the fist of his right hand into the palm of his left one a few times.

"If he comes at straight at you, you mean. He might just decide to manipulate your car, or the HVAC system at PrideCan. Next thing you know, you're breathing something entirely unhealthy. And then there are the elevators…"

"Are we not giving him a bit too much credit?" Roberto asked, looking at Rafael. "Maybe Dante's cycle was just a fluke."

"I wouldn't count on it." Rafael shook his head. "I studied the guy's bio way back when we were still considering a merger, and he knows his stuff. He took a series of engineering courses. Never graduated as far as I could find out—but enough to know how to manipulate things you really don't want manipulated."

Roberto let his head fall back and pulled back the hair from his face. "I don't want to do this at all," he all but yelled. "Hide out in here, while this—this asshole is out there to get us."

Al sat up a little straighter and pushed his hands into the armrests on his chair. He took a deep breath, and the knuckles on his fingers turned white with the anger he was holding in just then, but Barry shook his head just the tiniest bit.

Of all the people in the room, Barry was likely the one person Roberto might listen to just then. Barry, Rafael thought—Barry, who had cut plenty of corners and looked away when things were going down, in the name of moving a deal forward or making something happen.

Those two had cooked up trouble together in the past, more than anybody, and, some might argue, this was why everyone was in this predicament to this day.

"You're not hiding, Rob," Barry said now. "You're flushing him out for the cops. The way I see it, they've been dragging their feet on catching this guy since he shot your father for some idiot reason."

"Revenge," Al muttered, but neither Barry nor Roberto were listening.

"He almost got to Dante, but he is not going to get to all of you. You are safe in here. But while he is trying to get to you—boom." He struck his table with the palm of his hand. "The police are going to get him, right there."

"You're making it sound like we are sitting ducks."

"Sitting ducks inside the world's securest facility." Rafael raised his hand. The security of this facility, his pride and joy, was all he'd been talking about for the last two hours.

"We know," Al sighed. "And I wish you would do a full audit of said security systems while you are at it. Donnelly left some very cryptic notes that leave a bit to be desired."

"Donnelly didn't know what he was talking about," Rafael said, making a fist.

"And what happens if we, God forbid, have an emergency in here?" Al asked, and Rafael threw up his hands.

"Then we deal with it. Your executive-level badge can bring down the system, and you deal with whatever is happening. I told you that. Not a problem. And as long as you keep your hands off all of my automated processes, everything will be fine."

"Guys, I propose we don't argue about this any longer." Barry smoothly got to his feet and looked around the little group. "I'll pick up Dante from the hospital shortly, and I'll fill him in. You two get comfortable in here." He looked at Al and Roberto and shrugged. "And try to make the best of it you can. If it turns out this doesn't work, we'll come up with something else. In the meantime, it is a lot more comfortable than protective security, or some HoJos somewhere with a bunch of rent-a-cops standing at the doors, while you're crawling up the walls with boredom. At least you can work in here. And during the day, life will be almost normal."

"Almost…" Roberto muttered and slouched back into his chair. "If being locked up with your brothers is considered normal. And why is it you are going to go get Dante? I could just as easily…"

"Stay," Rafael and Al said simultaneously. "And get used to the accommodations. It won't be long."

***

It won't be long.

It became a mantra for all of them over the next few days. *It won't be long.* There might have been some rumors circulating among the staff, but none of the confined Ivers brothers would talk about it publicly.

It was obvious enough that they seemed to be there at all hours of the day, wandering the hallways, disappearing into the unused wing of the company. And then there was Roberto.

Most of them knew who Roberto was, or had heard of him, but suddenly, he decided he would 'help out' wherever he could. And at the same time learn about Rafael's concepts for the perfect cannabis operation.

He asked dozens of questions, poked his nose into everything, and, more than once, the unsuspecting employee being questioned ran off to check with Rafael before giving him a definite answer.

"What do you do to these people, threaten them with daily beatings if they don't obey?" Roberto asked Rafael one day, while they worked to clean up the packing bay. "I've never seen a bunch of more well-trained, obedient puppies in my life."

"They know I always have a reason when I make a request." Rafael shrugged. "And they also know I expect them to make good decisions on their own and follow through, even when I'm not breathing down their necks."

"Right. Yeah, I bet you put something in their coffee," Roberto muttered.

Rafael chuckled and picked up a broom. 'His' people and 'his' facility were a topic he could spend all day discussing. All the more, he felt bad for Roberto and the amazing facility he had built at Pride, before losing it all.

"Any news about your place?" he asked cautiously, and Roberto looked away.

"Not sure, man. The ministry may decide to pull my license after all, since they can't figure out how anybody could have introduced a virus into a cannabis manufacturing plant as a revenge plot."

"That's a tough break. I'm really sorry to hear that. I know how much work you put into it." Rafael clapped Roberto's shoulder. "If you think it will help, I can try to get in touch with them to speak on your behalf."

Roberto shrugged again. "We'll see what they decide when they decide. I might take you up on that. Why are you being nice about it anyway? I thought you'd be the first one to say, 'Hey, it's your own fault for cutting corners, Rob. Live with it.'"

Rafael stopped and leaned on the handle of his broom. "Look, don't make a big deal of it. We've all been there, made that one decision we wish we hadn't and then hoped somebody would help pull our asses out of the resulting fire. Maybe I just feel like being that guy. Besides, your people saved our asses when the harvest was on the line, and Kayla all alone trying to bring it in single-handedly. You have great people over at Pride. All you have to do is focus a little more. On the main thing."

"Says you. The person everybody in here—hell, in the entire industry—seems to worship."

"Aw, shucks." Rafael chuckled and turned an imaginary hat in his hands. "And that's not quite the way it is. Look at Nick Ambrose." He became a little bitter when he said the name and sighed. "Guy just packed up and left, one day to the next, because he didn't quite agree with a decision."

"And you haven't heard the rest of the rumors floating around down on the production floor. Dante is pretty beat up about it."

Rafael sighed, shrugged, and picked up his broom again, swiping at the floor harder than strictly necessary in order to collect a few dust particles.

Roberto watched for a few moments and finally took a dustpan off the wall to help Rafael.

"You know, I spoke to Dante," he said, without looking at Rafael, just bending over the sweeping task at hand. "I did ask him if there was anything he could do to fix it."

"Yeah?" Rafael kept sweeping and said no more.

"He's kind of in no-man's land here, Rafael. This is the business his brother runs."

"So is yours, just a different brother."

"Yeah, but he's been running this with Al and you ever since—well, ever since our father was still alive. He found something he really wanted to do here at PerCan. And at the same time…"

"At the same time, he doesn't want to lose what he has with Nick."

"That's a nice way of putting it."

Roberto dumped the contents of the dustpan into the nearest garbage pail.

"So you see, Dante either loses the business he's worked so long at, or he loses his relationship with Nick. He's going in circles up there—or would if he were allowed to do anything but sit in a chair all day."

Roberto nodded in the direction of the rooms that had been set aside for the Ivers brothers.

"Damned Turner just mucked it up for everybody," Rafael muttered, firing his broom into a corner. He shoved his hands into his pockets and gave the garbage pail an angry shove with his foot.

"I don't know if it's the industry or just this particular company, but every single goddamned time we finally get everything running the way we want to, somebody comes around to muck it all up again, and now we're in this predicament." He sighed.

"Might as well make the best of it. Know any good agronomists who are wanting for a job?"

"Depending on what happens to Pride."

"Don't go there. You'll get your company back, Roberto."

"Maybe, Rafael, maybe. But I'm also a realist. What happens when they catch Turner, and he confesses going after Dante—but not the virus at Pride? You think that will cause issues? You think maybe they'll come down on me worse? Sometimes I wonder if I should just call it."

He shook his head and leaned against the wall beside Rafael, mimicking his pose, hands shoved into pockets, eyes focused on nothing on the floor by his feet.

"One crisis at a time," Rafael finally said. "We'll start with getting an agronomist in here and follow up by catching Turner. Then we'll deal with everything else. After all, it was Barry's harebrained idea to blame the whole incident on him. He doesn't always think things all the way through. That's the problem with lying."

"Lies have short legs," Roberto chuckled.

"What?"

"When we were kids," he explained. "We used to have this nanny, came from Europe somewhere. She always berated us for lying. Said she'd find out anyways—because lies have short legs."

"Guess they do."

Rafael pulled up a foot and was just about to push off the wall behind him, when the door to the packaging rooms opened once again. Rafael stood there, frozen, mouth agape, and said nothing.

"This what happens in here now," the man who had entered asked. "You stand around leaning against the wall, chitchatting all day?"

"Nick Ambrose," Roberto said, not moving. "As I live and breathe. Of all the cannabis joints in this country, you had to walk into ours?"

"Um…"

Nick didn't laugh. He looked a little uncertainly from Rafael to Roberto and back again. "Guess this is where I have to come to see Dante now. I'd… I'd like to see you, Rafael, if I might."

"You're looking at me now," Rafael said gruffly, pushed off the wall, and grabbed his broom again. "That enough for you?"

"What I mean is—I'd like to talk to you."

"All of a sudden? After you chewed me out at the hospital up one side and down the other? Why? So you can tell me for the seventh time that Kayla made a mistake not informing you when she went to check on Dante first—before she pulled you out of one of the most important harvests in this company's history?"

"Rafael…"

"You know, I've checked your contract, Nick, and apparently, yes, you can just up and walk away without so much as 'by your leave.' I guess we didn't do contracts very well back then. What was that—oh, five or six years ago?"

"Rafael, listen." Nick came to take Rafael's shoulder, but Rafael shook him off.

"No, you listen to me, Nick. I've said all I was going to say, and you told me to go and stuff it. In so many words. Stay here, Roberto. You might as well…"

Out of the corner of his eye, he'd seen Roberto's hand on the door handle, and he shook his head.

"You might as well stay around. Learn another thing about running a company." He tore his glasses off his head and used them to point at Nick. "Yes, OK, I will admit that Kayla may have mishandled this and you by putting the company first. But she came to you to apologize, and I came to you to apologize, hat in hand, saying it was a call in favor of PerCan and all of the shareholders out there." Now the glasses swept around to encompass the entire room and company. "And the delay in telling you about Dante's accident, or what they thought of as an accident at the time, was no more than an hour or two."

"And if he had passed in that hour?"

"And if he had passed in that hour, Nick Ambrose, then even you, running out of here, leaving everything behind, would not have changed that fact. You were identified in his things as the person to call in case of an accident, and nobody at the hospital had done that. Nobody had called you—why? Because they knew they had time, that's why, and then Kayla showed up."

The words stood in the room for a while, and Rafael rolled his shoulders.

"I explained all of that to you when I found you, to speak to you. When Dante was still in the hospital, and you insisted on throwing it into my face. What was that you called us? Self-centered maniacs who thought about profits first and let their people go to shit because of it?"

Nick picked on a piece of skin on his thumb and didn't dare to look at Rafael. Roberto tried and failed to blend into the shadows.

"I think I might also have called Kayla a ruthless bitch," Nick finally said, still not meeting Rafael's eyes.

"I know that," Rafael said gruffly. "No need to drag it out again. So, if you're here to see Dante, take that visitor's pass around your neck, check in, and go see him. Round the back way please. If you're here to rub it in—don't. I have enough on my hands keeping a deranged maniac out of the building who wants to kill two of my executives and a good friend. I think I am busy for a while yet."

Roberto blinked a couple of times at the word 'friend,' but he still didn't say anything. The anger coming off Rafael in great big waves was apparently enough to make a wise man keep his mouth shut for the moment.

Nick stood there and looked at Rafael as the minutes ticked by. Rafael had picked up his broom once again and swept at the ground, collecting nothing in his dustpan, dumping nothing into the garbage bin, only to repeat the process with stubborn insistence.

"Well," Nick finally said slowly. "You think you—you think you could use an extra pair of hands? Keeping that maniac out of here, I mean?"

"What the fuck are you talking about? And don't start off with work-place etiquette. With you in the room, I'll talk any damn way I please."

He threw the broom and dustpan away, where they clattered against the far wall, making far more noise that they should have.

"I thought, well, seeing as how that maniac there is still after Dante. And—and his brothers—and—well, since you're still short-staffed—"

"Talk in complete sentences, man," Rafael said.

"I thought—maybe—I could come back," Nick finally said. "If you would still… I mean… work with me, that is."

He couldn't look Rafael in the eyes, and if he had hoped Rafael would drop everything and draw him into a man-hug, saying, "Oh, thank God, you're back," he was wrong.

"And why would I want to do that, pray tell?" Rafael asked gruffly, his hands still on his waist.

"I—I overreacted," Nick said softly. "When I heard Dante was injured, and Kayla had gone to the hospital without telling me. I… I thought she shouldn't have."

Long minutes ticked by again. Rafael didn't speak. Roberto stood by, still trying to keep to the shadows, watching the energy between the two men. Finally, Rafael softened just a little.

"It—might have been," he said. "I would have been angry at her too. For a bit."

"But—Dante really let me have it," Nick finally said. "Told me how frantic Kayla was when she got here, how she didn't want to give me the bad news. And how the hospital folks didn't think it was a life-or-death situation either, or they would have called next of kin right away."

"Aah," Rafael said, nodding. "I see. Like some folks might have been suggesting earlier."

"You need me to say I was too fool-headed to see it, or listen back then?"

"That might be nice." Rafael nodded.

"Fine, I was." Nick shrugged. "But this is Dante. If it were Kayla lying there…"

"I would be going stark-raving insane." Rafael nodded. "Like she was at the time, knowing I was in the eye of a hurricane, so to speak."

Nick nodded, and again, the conversation stalled.

"So?" Nick finally asked.

"So what, Nick?"

"Can I come back?"

"I don't know—can you, do you think? After leaving everything and everybody high and dry when we needed you the most, can you?"

"Did Kayla really try to…?"

"Did she try to do the harvest, all by herself, down here in rubber boots and work clothes watching YouTube videos on how to harvest cannabis? One word—yes."

"Dear God."

"Leave him out of it," Rafael said. "He had nothing to do with it. The man who did save everybody's ass, this harvest, and this company is standing right over there."

He nodded at Roberto. "If it hadn't been for Dante's brother Roberto, we'd be filling out bankruptcy protection forms by now."

"Surely it can't…"

"Don't split hairs here, Nick. This is not the time. When I left for bloody Malta, I told you—this is the most important harvest to date in the company's history. Right?"

"Yes."

"And… wait. Did I say something else? Yes, I think so." Rafael touched his chin with his index finger. "Yeah, I said if I didn't know you were down here and in charge, I wouldn't go in the first place, especially since I knew Al was feeling out of sorts and didn't know what was wrong. I said, save for knowing you and Dante would hold things together, I would blow off this whole Malta contract until after the harvest."

Nick looked down at his shoes again.

"Just go, you said. Don't worry, you said. We'll be fine, Rafa. Just think of how important this will be for PerCan in the end. Go. Have a great time. We have everything in hand."

"And we did. Who knew there'd be a tornado? And Donnelly."

"Everybody knew Donnelly was useless. His own people knew Donnelly was useless. He had run his company almost into the ground. You know. That very fact is why I left instructions for people to look to you for decisions."

Nick took a step closer, but Rafael, not quite ready to close the distance, took the same step backward.

"Rafael, I can't tell you…"

"How sorry you are? Oh, I believe that. I believe that you are sorry, I believe that you wish you could do it all over, but that doesn't help me now, does it?"

Roberto finally stepped in and put his hand on Rafael's elbow. Rafael glared down and back up at Roberto but wouldn't speak.

"A wise man said something to me a little while ago, Rafael."

"I'm sure he did, and I am equally sure it was probably bullshit, Rob."

"Don't know about that. He said we've all been there, made that one decision we wish we didn't and then hoped somebody would be around to help pull our asses out of the resulting fire."

Rafael let out an exasperated breath and worked his tongue around his mouth for a moment.

He walked over to the barrel of garbage, gave it a satisfying kick with his steel-toed boot, and walked back again.

"That was an awfully big mistake," he said to both of them, refusing to look at either one.

"One you might have made yourself if it had been Kayla lying there in the hospital," Roberto said, and Rafael glared at him.

"Don't you bring Kayla into this one, Rob."

He walked away again, muttering things under his breath, moving things that didn't need moving with more force than they required, and finally walked back again, stopping directly in front of Nick.

"I can tell you one thing," he said. "One thing. Even if I did let you work here again—even if—and that's not decided yet. Last word is up to Al. But there is absolutely no way Al will ever let you walk into the executive suite again. Mark my words."

"I understand that."

"And the people who were down here, Nick, the people who were fighting with Kayla to save a harvest they knew they couldn't save. Those people have questions, and they are going to need an explanation from you, and it had better be a good one."

"I understand that too, Rafael."

"Don't think I'm going to help you out there either. You gambled away their trust and mine, and you're going to have to earn it back again, and there's nobody going to help you with that."

Nick only nodded and stood completely still as if every movement could change Rafael's mind for the worse. Finally, after a few minutes of watching Rafael pace, he looked up and chanced a smile.

"Rafael? Does that mean…? Am I—part of PerCan again?"

"Goddammit."

Rafael cursed, walked away again, turned at the wall, and came back.

"Look at the mess in here. Do I teach these people to clean up after themselves, no matter what department they are in? Does anybody down here ever listen to me—ever? What are you standing there flapping your gums, Nick Ambrose? Do you need an invitation, engraved maybe? If you want to work at PerCan again, I suggest you go get a proper uniform, not this nonsense you're wearing, and some proper boots and get to work. And you can start by cleaning up this pigsty down here."

He gave the barrel of garbage another kick with his boot, this time making it slide away a few feet, and that's when he saw it. Right behind where the barrel had been, in the dust that shouldn't have been there if people would listen to him, there was a shoeprint. There shouldn't have been any dust down here in the first place—even if they were in Packaging, not in the growing areas—but the shoe print was that of a running shoe.

None of the employees were allowed to wear running shoes down here. Kayla had, for her short stint on the production floor, but everyone else knew better and had strict orders to show up in steel-toed work boots. Besides, Kayla's feet were tiny. These were large prints, almost as large as Rafael's own.

Rafael glanced at Nick and Roberto's feet, satisfied that his orders were at least followed to that extent, and glowered.

"And while you are cleaning up, find the person who wears running shoes down here, against health and safety rules, and my strict orders, so I can chew out his ass. That's just what I need to do today."

He stalked away, muttering again how nobody cared to listen to him or to follow his orders, leaving Roberto and Nick alone.

***

"Thanks," Nick said and offered his hand to Roberto.

"Don't mention it. Rafael is all right. You know that. Seeing Kayla trying to finish that harvest all on her own—well, that just kind of did him in."

"Yes, but it was an unusual..."

"Hey, I know, I know..." Roberto raised his hands and shook his head. "Don't try to convince me. I know all about it, and Rafael will get back to normal again. He wanted you back..."

"He came to me just after he was back in the country," Nick admitted and picked up the discarded broom. "I was just too angry to say yes."

"He'll get there." Roberto began organizing packing tools and supplies. "You know him better than I do. Just at the moment when you think he's going to rip your head clean off, he'll say—oh, that could have happened to anybody, and he helps you fix it. But that guy......"

Roberto nodded at the footprint of the tennis shoe and finally swept it away with his foot. "That guy is really getting his ass chewed when he finds him."

***

Rafael walked around the production floor for another hour, checking on the progress of plants in the grow pods and clones in the labs, but mostly looking at people's feet. So much so that someone asked him if he had a crick in his neck and was told to mind his own goddamn business.

Rafael wanted to find the man with the tennis shoes, and when he couldn't, that bothered him more than an employee who wasn't following the rules.

Who had been in there in the packing area and why?

By the time he got back there to check on the footprint, Roberto and Nick had cleaned the area up beautifully, and it was gone of course. Hopeless! Now he would never figure it out. Just before he spiraled down the rabbit hole of people getting into his plant, a messenger came down to tell him Detective Sergeant Robertson wanted to see him in the conference room, and the footprint was forgotten. After all, there were far more important things to worry about.

THIRTY-THREE

Detective Robertson sat in the conference room, having moved his chair so he could look out over the production area down below, although he would never admit to anyone how much the view fascinated him.

"Detective," Rafael said, offering a quick handshake. "I got work to do."

"No doubt. So do I."

"Found Turner yet?"

"No, but I'm worried. Now that you have convinced the Ivers men to stay here in the plant, you might meet him before I do. I wish you had consulted me. I'm not in favor of this plan."

Rafael shrugged. "They were not either—at first."

"You do know that you cannot guarantee their safety in a manufacturing plant of this size, right?"

"My plant is the safest place in this town right now."

"I beg to differ."

"Oh, do you now, Detective?" Everything that had happened over the last few days—from finding Kayla in manufacturing, and Dante in the hospital, Nick gone, and Al barely hanging in there, chaos on the production floor and no one following his instructions—all came bubbling up and sat just at the tip of his tongue. He wanted to, oh, he wanted to tell this slick little detective there just how he felt and what he thought of his damned stupid comments, when Robertson lifted his hands.

"Hold on there, Rafael. You look like you're about to tear me into six pieces and bury me out under your plants."

"Eight," Rafael said and sat roughly in a chair. "And I would never put you with the plants—nothing would grow there."

"Ouch."

Robertson splayed his fingers on the tabletop for a minute and stared at them. "Look, I'm merely concerned about the safety of the Ivers men."

"So am I. I have…"

"Hear me out, Rafael. There's a madman out there." Rafael snorted.

"Turner has lost touch with reality to at least a certain extent. I'm wondering about the wisdom of the idea of keeping all of his targets in one spot. Right here."

"You leave that up to me, Detective," Rafael said, flashing dark eyes at him. "I've said it once and will say it again—this is the safest spot in town right now. Do you know the kind of controls and safety protocols we have to comply with to be certified by the health department? How often these are inspected and checked to keep our license active and up to date? The only persons who can go everywhere in this building are the five people with an executive-level badge."

"Things slip in, Rafael."

"Things slip in—things!" Rafael pushed back and jumped to his feet again. "Not in my plant, Detective. Uh-uh, not here. Things do not 'slip in' under my watch, OK? I am going to keep Al safe. And Dante and Roberto. You just go out there and worry about getting your hands on Turner. ASAP, if it's not too much bother."

"Calm down." Robertson waved his hands and finally shook his head. "I needed to say this—although in all honesty, I figured you would react like this. Even though," he shrugged and looked Rafael straight in the eye, "Turner must have broken in at Pride Cannabis to spread that mysterious virus, right? What makes you think he won't be able to do the same here?"

"Because we are better equipped than Pride," Rafael said, but most of the bluster had suddenly gone from his voice.

If he wanted to keep lying to the detective, he would have to get his act together and stop being an angry bull in a china shop.

"Maybe." Robertson tapped his fingers on the desk. "Help me out here if you can. Why a virus? Why this virus, how would he have gotten into the building in the first place, and where would he have placed that virus to get Roberto infected? Much of this doesn't make any sort of sense."

"You said it yourself: Turner is unhinged. Your words, just about five minutes ago. So how should I know why he does anything?"

"But a virus, Rafael? Is there anything within the cannabis-producing space that makes this a logical choice?"

Not at all, Rafael thought, *unless you're making the whole thing up to cover up something tremendously stupider in the first place.*

"I don't know," he said, shrugging. "And to tell you the truth, I've had my hands a bit too full to worry about what happened over at Pride. He got in, spread a foreign compound or something. That's all I know or care to know. Turner was not the sharpest tack in the toolbox in the first place."

"Why do you say that?"

"Why? Because he cooked up his foolish revenge plan. And why did he do that? Because of something Al's daddy did to his daddy 100 years ago. Yes, his father offed himself, and he had a tough life thereafter, but that's not Al's fault—or Dante's."

"Roberto?"

"Of course not. I just don't know him that well."

"He collaborated with Barry there, to bring down that merger," Robertson probed. "Maybe there's something in what those two did?"

Alarm bells started to go off in Rafael's head. He'd spent enough time under suspicion for the murder of Tadeo Ivers that more than 10 minutes in a room with this detective made him feel claustrophobic. Enough of this now.

"Well, why don't you ask Turner when you finally catch him?" he said, dusting off his pants and heading toward the door. "I really don't know how I can help you," he tossed over his shoulder, "or how any of this might contribute to putting this madman behind bars. Where he belongs. Good day, Detective."

He walked out of the room without looking back and stalked down the hall, promptly bumping into Al coming around a corner.

"Sorry, man."

"You look decidedly out of sorts, Rafael. What's the matter? I thought I heard a rumor that Nick Ambrose was looking to come back."

"He is—or he wants to," Rafael said, forcing himself not to grab Al's shoulder to steady him. It still shocked him every time he saw how weak and thin Al had become, and the cane his friend carried to get around served as a steady reminder.

"The folks in HR will have to work that one out. He's always been an independent contractor, not an employee. Whatever—they'll work through it. And make it good this time. I did tell him it was your final call, and not to even think about being a part of the board."

Al nodded. "Thank you. Let's let the man get on an even footing again first before we entrust him with the decision-making process of this company."

"Isn't that what I said?"

"Apologies. Of course. Might I presume that the presence of Detective Robertson in the boardroom is the reason for your ill humor?"

"I don't have any…" Rafael's head snapped up, and he stopped, seeing Al's wry smile, and he sighed. "Yes and no. He's asking me a lot of questions that make perfect sense, but I don't have any answers for him." Quickly, he looked up and down the hallway.

"And the answers I do have, I can't give him if I don't want to make a big mess any bigger, if you know what I mean?"

"I understand completely. If it troubles you to lie on Roberto's behalf, please—tell the truth and let me worry about everything else."

"Thanks, but I got it," Rafael muttered and looked away.

"Our friendship is more valuable than protecting my brother from the consequences of his own foolish actions."

"I said I got it."

He was being gruffer than he needed to, and the probing, unwavering look from Al's eyes was not making things any easier. Rafael rubbed his forehead and squeezed his eyes shut for a moment.

"I can deal, Al. I'm not happy, but I can deal. I'm just worried about you. And Dante and Roberto yes, but mostly you. Look at you. This—this thing already half killed you. If Turner walked in now, and I got my hands on him…"

Rafael's hands formed menacing claws between them, illustrating just what he might be given to do if he got his hands on Turner.

"Your concern is touching. For what it's worth, Kayla shares the sentiment and keeps checking in on me to see if I need food or drink, or any other personal ministrations."

"Sounds like her," Rafael muttered and looked down.

"However." Al lightly tapped his steadying cane on the ground. "I will rely on you to make sure Turner does not walk in right now, regardless of what you might wish to do to him."

"Oh, he'd better not even think about sticking his nose past the site gates out front," Rafael said, eyes flashing. "I'm thinking I might even get some dogs to patrol the grounds at night. Big ones." A dreamy look came into his eyes and a malicious little sneer.

"Please don't." Al lightly tapped Rafael's shoulder. "Kayla would be on the phone 10 minutes later, worrying about the fate of said dogs when the crisis is over."

"Well, maybe we could rent some…" Rafael wondered, knitting his brows.

"I trust you to come up with a solution," Al said with a smile. "And

I'm off to concern myself with this company's future once again. Let's hope this Turner saga will be over quite soon."

He walked off down the hall, his cane tapping lightly as he went, and Rafael sighed. The safety of this building had always been one of his first and foremost concerns. Now it included the safety of his friend.

Like everyone else, he hoped Greg Turner would be apprehended shortly, and he worried about it at the same time. What would happen if Turner confessed to hurting Dante, but not the virus attack on Pride Cannabis? Or what happened if they were all wrong about Greg Turner, and there was another person out there after Dante?

"Goddammit," he muttered and made his way down the production floor. If nothing else, at least he could manage a clean, efficient, and safe cannabis manufacturing facility. That was one thing he could do.

THIRTY-FOUR

Staff became used to Al and his two brothers basically living in the back section of the plant. They wandered the halls during the day, Roberto quite often cussing about the fact that he was being held prisoner at Perfect Cannabis, followed by a stern look from Al and an invitation to get himself a personal bodyguard just to walk down the street.

Rafael started a clampdown on best practices in security and working environment, and never found anyone as much as violating the dress code—good. He needed everyone's buy-in to get this done.

Detective Robertson came and went on a regular basis too, a fact that nagged Rafael rather than bothered him, and he chose to avoid the man as much as he could. He was busy after all.

But with every day that passed, it became clear that this was not a situation that could endure. Stress levels rose another notch every day. Staff members snapped at one another and had to apologize. Rafael snapped at staff and had to apologize. Al, Dante, and Roberto had stopped snapping at staff and one another, merely looking exhausted and tired of the status quo and their confinement. Then they stopped speaking to one another altogether.

Less than a week later, Rafael realized that things would likely completely unravel within a few days. It was just a matter of who would be the first yelling, 'I can't take this any longer.' If he had had to guess, he would have thought Roberto, and it didn't take longer than 24 hours, before he heard a commotion in the boardroom.

"I'm done," Roberto yelled, as Rafael stepped into the room. "I'm done being locked up in here, done living like a prisoner. If Robertson and his men can't catch Turner, I'm just going to have to take my chances out there!"

He got out of his chair, walked over to the wall, and punched it hard enough to make a picture of Tadeo tremble.

Al, who had started to recover to a certain extent, leaned back in his own chair and steepled his fingers to his face.

"Be reasonable, Roberto," he said a little weakly and looked up when Rafael wandered in.

"What's going on here?" Rafael asked, as if he didn't know.

"I'm getting out of here. Is that OK with you?"

"Technically, sure." Rafael shrugged. "Practically—like your brother says, maybe not the smartest idea ever."

"Shut the fuck up, Covin," Roberto snapped and wheeled on him, making Al jump out of his chair.

"Roberto! I will not have you speak like this to…"

"It's all right, Al—it's all right." Rafael raised his hands. "I can deal. Rob is a grown man. He can do whatever he pleases. Go then. Take a chance with a messed-up psycho who blames your family for his equally messed-up life, or stay in here and endure a little bit of inconvenience. It literally makes zero difference to me."

He pantomimed a great big zero with thumb and forefinger and shook his head in the direction of the door.

"Really, whatever suits you, Roberto. Just remember when you're out there looking over your shoulder that every single person in here is going to great lengths—including possibly lying to the police—to keep your rear out of the fire. Other than that, I'm not standing in your way."

He stepped aside, opened the door again, and held it for Roberto. From out in the hallway, the usual daytime noises of people walking and talking and the far-off hum of the environmental controls trickled into the room. No one spoke. All of the bravado left Roberto, and he dropped back into his chair, nodding at Rafael.

"Close that damn door again," he muttered and picked on something nonexistent on his fingernail.

"It's just…"

"Cabin fever," Al said softly. "Perfectly normal. Let's everyone just calm down now."

"No." Roberto shook his head. "Rafael is actually right, much as I hate it. You—all of you—are working to keep a lid on my mistake with the grow medium."

"Well, it's not…" Nick started, but Roberto cut him off.

"It was my mistake. Costs were getting out of hand, and I tried to cut corners. I knew it was a risk, and I took it anyway. I didn't care. Then…" He looked at Al and shook his head again. "Then you got sick, and I realized people could have actually died out there. This is medicine we're making, not just—growing pot on a grand scale."

Rafael bit back the 'just about time you realized that' that sat on the tip of his tongue. No need. Roberto did a fantastic job beating up on himself without any help at all.

"It's a mistake, Roberto," Dante said and awkwardly moved his leg, still encased in a plastic support shell. "We've all… well, you know."

Rafael saw Nick opening his mouth and closing it again, coming to the same conclusion he had.

Roberto shoved his hands into his pockets and sat hunched for a long moment before he continued.

"I'm gonna go talk to Robertson," he finally said. "Nothing illegal about what I've done, at least."

"It might cost you your license."

"Yep, little brother, it might." Having made a decision, Roberto looked up and grinned. "Along with everything I own for the—oh, next 10 years or so. But it's going to come out anyway, the moment they apprehend Turner, and, right now, the chances of me keeping my license are pretty small, and likely getting smaller by the minute."

The room fell silent then, with the four men looking down at the table or at their hands. For once, even Rafael didn't have a smart answer or a snappy comeback.

"My offer still stands," he finally said. "I'll go speak to the licensing board on your behalf if it will help anything."

Roberto raised his hands and shrugged. "Don't see how it could, but I appreciate the offer and the man who's making it. I mean it, Rafael. Sorry for going off on you earlier."

"No worries."

Again, silence fell over the room. Al brought his palms together, resting them against his face, a sure sign that he was trying desperately to work out a solution to something. Nick and Dante whispered something, and Nick shook his head. Finally, Roberto got to his feet and knocked on the boardroom table a few times.

"Well then. It's been a scream, guys."

He looked around for his phone, which for some reason had fallen to the floor, and just as he bent down to retrieve it, someone knocked at the boardroom door with a fair amount of desperation and urgency.

"Come in," Al called, admitting a junior staffer in the uniform of the PerCan security department.

"Mr. Ivers, sorry for interrupting. I need Mr. Covin… Rafael—there you are. Thank God I found you. You need to come with me. You need to have a look at this right now. This is urgent—right now!"

Hand still on the door handle, the man turned right around as if he wanted to run back down the hall, before Rafael stopped him.

"Hold on there, Stan, before you trip all over yourself in your hurry. You found me. What's this all about?"

"It's Turner. Turner, the one who wants all of you—you know—all of you…"

"We know," Al snapped. "What about him?"

"He's—we got him on video. He was here. Right here."

As one, they all got to their feet and rushed the door, headed by Rafael.

"Where?" Rafael yelled, almost running down poor Stan. "Where? Hurry, for God's sake, man, where is he?"

"No, it's, like—on video," Stan called out, and somehow he had ended up behind everyone in the boardroom. "The security office."

Rafael automatically headed down the next hallway to the left, all but running in the direction of the security office. They had him; they finally had the mean little bastard who was trying to kill Al and his brothers. Rafael knew exactly what he wanted to do to Greg Turner when he finally got his hands on him. His fingers flexed into claws again, and he already regretted that he would never be allowed to follow through on his plans.

THIRTY-FIVE

The forest worker's hut was just as he had left it—was it days ago, weeks ago? He could hardly remember. The place was still small, remote, and desolate. There were some comforts he had to do without—reliable internet access and indoor plumbing for a couple, but he knew it would all be worth it in the end. It would be worth it, and he would finally be able to rest again.

He had stolen some blankets and pillows from the campground before he left it and made himself comfortable. Every time he closed his eyes, he imagined the Ivers brothers running in fear from him, their faces contorted with fright, arms wildly gesticulating. That vision gave him comfort; that vision was what he lived for.

Those fools thought he didn't know they had moved into PerCan! Did they think he was blind? He'd been shadowing them for weeks, after they brought the youngest one, Dante, out of the hospital. He still cursed when he thought that Dante had survived. How? How could anyone survive this? He could not fail again—he would not fail again. They were fools, and the biggest fool of them all was Rafael Covin, who thought he could keep them safe.

Turner chuckled and closed his eyes again, to see his fantasy.

Oh, yes, they would be running scared now. So scared! They would know he was coming, just not from where and not when.

By now, they would watch him on their camera system, and they would know he was coming.

Again, he imagined their faces when they saw him—and the fear he knew must be in their eyes sustained him through a long night.

Nowhere was safe.

***

Rafael stubbornly reached for the video console and stepped back the recording the same three minutes he had been recapping for the last little while. One by one, he let the frames crawl over the screen, searching every inch of a grainy, dark image.

"Rafael." Al gently put his hand on his shoulder. "Rafael, leave it be. It is Greg Turner. We all can see that."

"There," Rafael said, stabbing at the screen with his forefinger. "There he is, inches from the back door. And that—that bastard is grinning at the camera. Dammit!"

Rafael struck the desktop with his flat hand and rewound the last frames of the video again. Al squeezed lightly. Rafael was taking this one personally. Greg Turner had violated his personal space, his inner sanctum.

"When I get my hands on him…"

"We are going to call Detective Robertson and let him deal with it," Al said quietly as more people crowded into the tiny security office behind them.

"Is it true…?"

"Did Turner really try to get in here?"

"Where—how did he get in?"

"Oh my God—is everything all right?"

Rafael sat back, folded his hands behind his head, and squeezed his eyes shut for a moment.

"Folks, let's not get all excited about this incident, all right? We still have a job to do here."

"We heard Greg Turner had broken in here," one of the workers said, and Rafael could see a crowd gathering outside the security office in the hall.

Word was spreading, and at the speed of light at that. As if it were not enough that the shooting of their former CEO and major shareholder Tadeo Ivers had dragged PerCan through the news for weeks, as if it were not enough that Rafael had been under suspicion and in fact had discovered the shooter—now that man had broken into their plant. This was personal. Their people had been attacked, their building invaded. Everybody wanted to help all of a sudden, and they all wanted the same thing: to get Turner.

Al let go of Rafael's shoulder and turned to face the mob.

"I am touched to see how personally you are all taking this," he said, speaking in a very low voice, so the shouts and murmurs stopped. "And I see how concerned you are about my safety and that of my brothers. Thank you, but let me assure you—Greg Turner has not broken into PerCan."

"And he won't," Rafael muttered, earning a stern glare from Al.

"We do have security footage of the man sneaking around the outside of the building, correct, but that is how far he got."

"Damn straight he won't get in," somebody called out, and Al smiled.

"He will not. Our security systems are amongst the best in the world, and he will not break in here. I truly appreciate your concern, but Rafael is right. We have a job to do."

A few people still muttered comments; one or two walked away. Others came closer, as if they planned to form a barrier of bodies around Al, Dante, and Roberto.

"Thank you, very much, but I must ask you to return to your jobs, please. I assure you—we are perfectly all right."

They left at that, in small groups, and one by one, the people who had been standing closest to him slapped Rafael on the shoulder, as if to let him know, 'we've got this.' Finally, Rafael, Al, and his brothers were the last people left in the security office, and Rafael dug his hands into his eye sockets.

"It seems young Stan caused a wee bit of panic amongst the staff before he came to see us to tell us about that…" He nodded toward the bank of monitors on the wall. "I will have a talk with him."

Al nodded agreement. "And just like that, every staff member at PerCan is suddenly in hunting mode. I had underestimated how much they care and want to see Turner stopped."

"Many of them have been with us for years, Al." Rafael shrugged. "They know of the history between Turner and PerCan. They may not have liked Tadeo all that much—sorry—but shooting him? That they took personally."

Al smiled. "It appears I'm surrounded by personal bodyguards. What could go wrong? Now let's get Robertson here and show him. I doubt he will be happy about this."

***

Al had hit the nail on the head with that. The detective watched the segment of security video as often as Rafael had—zooming in on details, stepping back to get an overview, zooming in again. And he was not happy about seeing Turner.

"This," he said, pointing at the screen that had been set up in the boardroom. "This means he knows you are hiding out here. I'm going to say it again, just so we are clear on official record, I don't think it's a good idea, the three of you in here, together."

"On the contrary." Rafael bristled. "He obviously tried and failed to get in."

"Unless he meant to taunt you, unless he meant for you to see him so you would run scared. And he might succeed the next time."

"Then it will be your job to make sure there is no next time by catching the bas—the man, isn't it, Detective?"

"Rafael—Detective." Al raised both hands and stepped between them. "Let's not argue about this. I am perfectly content to stay here, rather than running from place to place to be one step ahead of this man. This video here clarifies three things for me. One," he ticked items off on his fingers. "Greg Turner is in fact actively trying to harm me, Dante, and Roberto. If there was any doubt before, there is none now. He's stalking this building. Two, I feel this location is a safe place until he's caught. I can't speak for my brothers, but I'm staying here."

"So am I," Dante said, adjusting awkwardly in his chair. "I have months of physical therapy ahead of me before I'll be back to a semblance of normal. I can't be running around, away from Turner."

Roberto stayed silent, leaning against a wall, glowering in the direction of Detective Robertson.

"Three," Al finally said, ticking off his middle finger, "we can't sustain this in the long-term. It has become imperative that you locate and apprehend this man, Detective. I don't mean to tell you how to do your job, but whatever manpower and PR you need to make sure he is found…"

"I have all of the available resources on him," Detective Robertson snapped. "You're right about not telling me to do my job, but this is a big city. Maybe you haven't noticed, but Greg Turner is not the only criminal out there."

"He's the only one who wants to harm me and my brothers," Al said gently. "And knowing that Kayla of Montecito Publishing is on our board of directors."

"You're threatening me with the press now?" Robertson's head snapped up, and he challenged Al with a look. "I am the one out there trying to apprehend Turner, I am the one keeping you safe and protecting you, and you're threatening me with the press?"

"I'm glad to hear that you're keeping us safe," Al said. His face smiled, but the dark eyes fixed on Robertson were pure, hard steel. "Might I suggest, then, that you get back out there and back on with your job? I will be expecting your updates quite anxiously."

He turned and walked away, leaving Robertson sputtering.

Al sat in a chair at the opposite end of the conference room and opened his laptop, checking email as if nothing had happened.

"Rafael, look at this. Did you see that quote from our packaging company?" he called out. "I think his pricing is a bit out of line. Your comments on that if you would please."

"Ah, yes, I did—and he is dreaming." Rafael said, looking at Robertson, then Roberto, and, finally, Al. He rose and came to stand beside Al. "I was planning to have a call with him later. None of his prices make any sense."

No one paid any more mind to the detective, who finally glared at all of them, packed the video into his portfolio, and stalked out of the room without another word.

Rafael broke off his sentence about the packaging supplier.

"Now there goes a guy who is mighty pissed off," he said and turned to Roberto. "I thought you were going to confess?"

Roberto only shrugged.

"Nobody is confessing around here," Al said firmly and focused on Rafael. "And you will please not mention this again."

"Yes, sir." Rafael mock-saluted.

"Rafael! I'm not joking. I don't have to tell you, of all people, that this would be the moment to have your security measures in top shape and all of our employees at their peak."

"Hey, if you don't trust me…"

"Did I say that? Relax, Rafael. But this situation has just become critical. Turner is actually and in fact stalking us at this very moment. There is a man out there with a gun, and he means us harm. So, forgive me if tiptoeing around the issues is not at the top of my list at the moment."

"I'll make sure everyone is on top of their game," Rafael mumbled and looked down.

"Dante, I know you're going out of your mind with boredom, but if you would perhaps restrict your movements for a bit? You are quite right that, because of your injuries, you are most at risk of the three of us."

Dante only nodded. A chill had crept into Al's expression and speech that had not been there before. *This is not serious; it's dead serious.* He didn't have to say it. It was right there in the quick, economical movements of his body and the way his eyes darted around him, checking corners and shadows.

"Roberto, I cannot advise you whether you should or should not come clean to Robertson. That is solely at your discretion. I might hesitate diluting his efforts at the moment, for what it's worth."

"Diluting?" Roberto asked and cocked his head.

"He may not be searching for Turner as eagerly as he is now if he believes we were lying to him about the virus," Rafael said and raised his hands. "I know, I know—that's your personal business. I'm off to make sure none of my security guards are loafing around."

He was halfway toward the door when one word from Al stopped him. "Rafael."

A look passed between them—a silent apology and a reassurance—and Rafael put his hand on the door handle.

"No worries," he said softly. "You know I always do my best for you. Today is no different. Except I'm going to kick everybody's ass from here into next week if I catch the slightest break in security protocols."

A hint of a smile stole over Al's face. "You do that," he said softly. "And if you need more men, tell HR I said you have carte blanche."

Rafael smiled, bit off a funny retort, and opened the door, only to find Barry explaining something to Jim Kaiser, a tall, greying, older man who had been their Investor Relations manager for the past few months. Jim had a hand raised to knock.

"Gents," Rafael said and slipped out. "No time to chat. I have asses to kick."

***

"Al," Barry said jovially, as he entered the room. "So great to have you back. How are you feeling?"

His words sounded too loud and too boisterous, even in the large conference room, and Al straightened with a sigh.

"Just fine, Barry, but if you are this enthusiastic, and dragging Jim along with you, something tells me you're about to give me some news I probably don't want to hear."

"On the contrary," Barry said, putting that day's copy of a national newspaper onto the conference room table. "Are you familiar with this?"

"The publication or today's edition? But, no, I have not seen today's paper. I have, unfortunately, been just a tad preoccupied." He hesitated for just moment, looking at Jim.

Barry looked at Dante and Roberto whispering at the far end of the conference table and sat heavily in a chair, nodding for Jim to do the same.

"Turner?" he asked, and Al nodded. "They didn't get him yet?"

Al shook his head.

"No," he said. "Although Detective Robertson assures me his capture is—imminent."

"Meantime," Barry said. "Rafael has things in hand, I'm sure, and you are going to like this."

He tapped his finger on the newspaper.

"So tell me what I'm going to like."

"These guys," again Barry tapped the paper, "have a massive readership, analog and online. Their online news channel is obscenely successful, and we have caught their eye."

"I'm assuming *obscene* is a good thing in this case?" Al asked, one eyebrow raised.

"Extremely so. They want to do a video feature documentary on us."

"Barry." Al wiped his eyes with one hand and dragged it down his face. "Your efforts are all much appreciated, but are you sure this is the time? Might I suggest when all of this is over, when Turner is safely behind bars, might be a better time to do a video feature with a national newspaper in here?"

"Au contraire, mon Capitan." Barry jumped to his feet, bounding with energy. "This is the perfect time." His arms spread wide, and he almost clocked Jim in the process. "We may be hit, but we are not going down. We do not give up."

"Barry…"

"No, no, no—no news is bad news. People love this kind of stuff. Our expertise was wanted all the way in Malta, and our facilities director almost bought it during their Medicane. Some guy is after our owners, but we don't back down."

"Perhaps not the kind of story I want to go through the press, or the image I wish to portray," Al said, but nothing would stop Barry now.

"What, so Turner doesn't find out? Well, he already knows you're in here. That secret's been out for a while."

"That doesn't mean I wish to post it to the news media," Al countered. He looked tired, and pale and weak all of a sudden, compared to Barry's boundless energy and drive.

"It may not be such a bad idea," Jim said in his quiet, unassuming way. "There are a lot of speculations out there. Pretty much every day, we get requests to clarify if there is indeed a hit out on the Ivers men and why."

"Dear God," Al muttered and shook his head.

"And it might help to portray it as the desperate act of revenge of one man—one man who can't let the past go and potentially has mental issues," Barry said, moving his hands, as if he were already setting a stage and sharpening the focus. "Besides, we keep going on about how our security and our processes are the best. We have confidence in them, so time to put our money where our mouth is."

"Jim?" Al asked, quite obviously desperate to get an *it's up to you*.

"I think it's not the worst idea he's ever had," Jim said. "I told you. People think there's a hitman out there, stalking us. Kind of makes everyone in the industry look like a bunch of crooks who are after one another. It's not bad to show them it is just one incident, one man—and we are running a safe, solid, and extremely profitable business here."

Al closed his eyes for a moment and brought his fingertips to the bridge of his nose. He sighed and finally opened his eyes again.

"I can't even go there. Fine. News instead of rumors, facts instead of speculation—I understand. We keep this as small as possible. Clear it with Rafael first. If Rafael feels it can be done safely, we are a go."

"But…"

Al raised a hand, stopping any argument Barry might have made.

"Clear it with Rafael, Barry. That is my last word. He's in charge of security, and, for the moment at least, responsible for the safety of my brothers and me. If he can't see a safe way of doing this—this documentary film—then we don't do it."

"Fine."

Barry swiped his newspaper off the conference room desk again and pinned it under his elbow.

"It really is a massive opportunity, you know," their Investor Relations director said, squirming as he looked at Barry. "There are too many wild rumors floating around about PerCan, once again. And this would give us a perfect chance to set the record straight. Show that we're not gun-toting criminals running a drug operation here."

"Talk to Rafael," Al repeated stubbornly.

"Are you the CEO, or is he?" Barry snapped, and Al slowly got to his feet.

He stood at his full height in front of Barry and looked him straight in the eye for a long moment before he spoke again.

"I am the CEO of this company, Barry Wentworth, and, while you are a major shareholder, you are in here as a consultant. So hear this, because I'm only going to say this one more time. I trust Rafael Covin with my life right now. Yes, I do want to put out some good news, and a well-done profile on what we are doing. It sounds like the company image is in desperate need of it. If Rafael can see a way that we can do this safely, I'm going to be the first one who is on camera telling our story. Is that understood?"

"Understood," Barry said tightly.

"Perhaps we could hire additional security personnel," Jim suggested, and Al nodded but didn't speak again. The two men finally left, and Al sat down hard, digging the heels of his hands into his eye sockets.

"You look like you should rest," Dante suggested, and Al shook his head, opening his eyes again.

"I'm fine, thank you. Some days, it just feels like I'm surrounded by people who mean well but fail to think fully through the consequences of their actions."

"Idiots," Roberto said.

"Pardon me?"

"You could have saved yourself a lot of time if you just said *idiots* instead."

Al closed his eyes, a hint of a smile playing around his mouth.

"They try, Roberto," he finally said. "They do try. Meanwhile it might be good for you to sit down to figure out your own future and that of PrideCan. Is there going to be a company? Are you going to try to repair your relationship with the ministry? What are your options and next steps?"

Roberto looked down at his hands, silent.

"Nobody will know the contamination didn't come from Turner," Dante threw in. "All you have to do is keep your mouth shut. You got a contamination—who knows from where? End of story."

"I was not aware that was the way we run things here at PerCan."

"Al…"

"Dante, a heretofore unknown virus was introduced into the manufacturing at PrideCan. The only logical way that is possible is by it being shipped in."

"Or introduced intentionally. Doesn't have to be Turner. Could have been any of our competitors."

"Guys, guys…" Roberto raised his hands. "Don't argue on my behalf. I know I will have to confess. I know I will have to tell the police what

I did, and after that the ministry. It'll be the end of my license, which I only received with a lot of help from you in the first place, Al. I know all of this. It's just—difficult—to watch it all go down the drain. Especially since PrideCan…"

He swallowed hard and looked down at his hands again.

"Was the first thing you really enjoyed doing?" Al asked, and Roberto nodded silently.

"That's why you should keep your mouth shut," Dante repeated stubbornly, but neither Al nor Roberto paid him any mind.

"It will be hard," Al said softly. "But whatever you need, wherever I can help you, know that I'm going to be there."

Roberto only nodded. He turned his face away from both of them and finally punched the wall again, but there wasn't really any power behind the punch.

THIRTY-SIX

He had enjoyed it—it had been the performance of his life. Strolling by the corner where he knew the security camera focused in on him, walking with purpose, letting the hood of his sweater fall back. In another life, maybe he would have been an actor. It could have worked.

He'd had to stop himself from going back and sauntering past the camera for a second time. After all, he was supposed to look furtive. He was supposed to be hiding, not staring up into their security cameras, all but holding a sign, 'Here I am—come and get me.'

He wanted to be there. He burned to watch them when they discovered those few frames he was walking through, analyzed the figure, and finally realized who was moving through the dark.

And there would be that fool, Rafael, who always thought he was better than everybody and did everything the Ivers asked him to do. There he would be—pointing his stubby little fingers at the screen.

Look, there he is, he would say. *The wind is pulling his hood back. You can see his face. It is him—it is him.*

And they'd be frightened, wondering how he had gotten in, wondering when he was coming for them.

Oh, how he loved to mess with their minds. It was almost better than doing any actual harm, he discovered. Messing with their minds lasted longer—and it wore them down.

They had been hiding out at PerCan for weeks now. Tempers had to be flaring on a daily basis, the three brothers at each other's throats.

If he walked away now—if he just packed the few things he had managed to salvage or steal—they would likely destroy each other in a matter of months.

Already, the middle brother's firm was closed down because of some unspecified infection, he had found out. It was either an excuse or a cover, which meant they were afraid of him. Just as he had planned. He could just walk away now and leave them to finish off each other. He never even had to get his hands dirty with those filthy Ivers men. They would do it for him.

It was tempting.

So tempting. Except he wouldn't see the thing play out if he walked away. He wouldn't see the fear on their faces or hear it in their voices. He wouldn't be there. And that wasn't enough.

"Ivers brothers, I will read your obituaries," he said, his voice rough. The only person he'd been speaking to for weeks had been himself.

He got to his feet and took the three steps to the wall of his hut. Wind was whistling through the gaps in the boards, and he shivered lightly.

But it wasn't the cold that made him tremble—it was the anticipation of seeing his revenge through.

He was almost there now, the debt was almost paid, and then—then he could walk away, steal another identity, and start over in a different place where nobody knew him. He'd become a capable criminal during the last few months.

In the first few days, after they figured out he'd shot Tadeo, he had worried that he would be caught immediately and locked up without a chance to see his plan through, but then he had adapted. He had learned, like a wild animal, where danger lurked, when to strike and when to pull back and lie in wait. All in preparation for the day to finally come and fulfill the promise.

The promise a little boy had made by his father's graveside—*I will find the man who destroyed my family, and I will destroy his family.*

That's why Tadeo Ivers hadn't been enough. That's why he had to eliminate his sons as well. His family was destroyed, and now it was the rest of the Ivers brothers' turn. Who knew what he could have been if he had grown up in a happy family like those three brothers? Who knew what he could have achieved, what he might have done, if Tadeo had not destroyed his father, and, with that, all of his dreams?

The man punched the wall and let loose a wild roar that echoed through the forest, where other wild animals perked up their heads and burrowed deeper in their dens. He would not give up and leave, never. He had to see it through.

THIRTY-SEVEN

Detective Robertson looked through the photos his young assistant, Brian Winston, had brought to him just a few minutes ago. The campground out at the edge of town, a few camping trailers that had been broken into, the interior of a trailer.

"You think this could be Turner-related?" he asked, and Brian nodded.

"Don't you?"

"Could be just an unfortunate unhoused person living there. Not every vagrant is automatically Greg Turner just because we're looking for him."

"Yes," Brian said, "but the internet was accessed through the campgrounds network. Ordinary vagrants usually don't use the web, I would imagine."

Detective Robertson raised an eyebrow and shuffled through the pages in front of him.

"I don't know. Maybe you're really reaching. I don't know about ordinary vagrants as opposed to not-ordinary ones, but they all probably carry a phone. They may want to look up help wanted ads, for crissakes."

He dropped the glossy 8-by-10s back into the folder and closed it, shaking his head.

"I don't think this is necessarily Turner-related. Give it to the guys from the neighborhood watch if you like, but I think it's a waste of time."

He turned back and studied the still from the PerCan security feed.

This, in fact, was definitely Greg Turner-related. There was something about the way the hood of that sweatshirt fell back—maybe the wind, maybe something else. He couldn't put his finger on why it looked off and just a bit unnatural. Reminded him of a terrible actor he had known. In any case, this was the lucky break he had been waiting for because the face had been identified clearly. This man was unmistakably Greg Turner. They had him. He was staking out Perfect Cannabis Consolidated, and all he had to do now was watch and wait for him to come back. Turner would run right into their waiting task force.

And none too soon. He was getting tired of daily calls, inquiring into the whereabouts of the criminal Turner—the Ivers men, the media, and, lately, his own boss for crying out loud.

He spread out the plans for PerCan and ran his forefinger over the marked area where the cameras had captured Greg Turner. If they were to assume this was close to where he intended to break the perimeter, he could make certain assumptions. The office and administrative area was right in the vicinity. Presumably, security measures were less tight there than in the growing areas. Was that the case? He made a note to ask Rafael.

The loading docks were situated on the other side of the building, and he could potentially hide his command vehicle where the access road to the docks entered the property. One more white nondescript van with a made-up delivery company name would hardly matter.

He hoped they would only need a few days. Resources were tight and getting more so. Given more funds, he could have cast a wider net for Turner, but there were no extra funds. As he had told Al, Greg Turner was not the only criminal in town. He was the only one, however, threatening a person or persons close to Kayla Montecito of Montecito Publishing, and she was making a lot of noise.

Detective Robertson made a face and circled the observation area with a lot more intensity than strictly necessary.

He didn't exactly hate the press, but every random person who had a beef with the police department felt entitled to spout off, 'I will go to the press.'

Surveillance then.

One team in the van, opposite side of the road. There was a wide perimeter fence and far too much open ground around the entire building. Rafael had planned this well. He couldn't very well have a surveillance team hanging out by the fence, which was, according to his information and the notes on this map, equipped with security microphones. Every time someone as much as touched that fence or spoke in the vicinity, that sound was transmitted and caused the security cameras to zero in on that spot. How Turner had gone past this fence, he didn't know, but there on the printout from the monitor was the evidence—he had.

THIRTY-EIGHT

Kayla Montecito looked over the proposal from the TV station and shook her head. "This is amazing. The fact that Barry landed that particular station—in prime time, no less. Let's just say it's a once-in-a-lifetime chance."

Rafael paced their living room at home and rolled his eyes at her.

"You media types. All about the hype."

"Us media types, Rafael? Please don't generalize. You need good PR, end of story. This will give you that. Just because you don't like it doesn't mean it's rubbish."

"I know. I am sorry…"

He raked his fingers through his hair and sighed.

"It's just that Al made this entire thing contingent on my being OK with it and on me giving the green light that it's safe."

"It's a moderator and a few cameramen. What's the big deal?"

"I don't know—you tell me. People? Cameras? Equipment? How do I contain this thing? How do I make sure nobody comes in with them? Ever since I've spotted Turner on the security feed, I'm creeped out."

Kayla wagged her head left and right for a minute. "That's a completely different thing."

"I don't see it that way!"

"You can prepare to your heart's content for a TV crew." Again, she picked up the media proposal and flipped through it. "This right here tells you exactly what is expected and what is required—when, where, who, how many. Everything."

She flipped through the pages and, finally finding what she was looking for, followed a printed paragraph with a red-polished nail.

"Here. A 30-minute tour through the facilities with a qualified person explaining the equipment and processes. That would be you. Entirely up to you how long you want to talk."

Rafael only rolled his eyes and kept his mouth shut.

"Interviews with the CEO, the head agronomist and head of the marketing team, the story of Perfect Cannabis, and finally a brief explanation on what makes you different, and why countries as far away as Spain and Malta are interested in your setup."

She looked up and took the glasses off her nose.

"You've got this. You are in control every step of the way. Besides, you've done tours a hundred times. You can do them in your sleep."

"Not on TV I haven't," he muttered.

"What about Al's TV news minute?"

"That was filmed in the boardroom. One guy, one camera."

"Then film part of this thing in the boardroom. And you're going to know exactly who is in the building—at all times."

Rafael still stroked his chin, running through every possible scenario.

"Jesus, Rafael. You do this every single time somebody wants a tour of the place. Why is this different? You ask them ahead of time who is coming so you can have visitor badges made up. Same here. You can even quote extensive health ministry regulations."

"True."

"And they will comply, in a minute. They're used to it. Then you give the list of attending people to me. Our media department at Montecito is going to vet each and every one of these people and get you a current picture. And if you really want to be sure, you can even ask Tessa to help research these people. How often have you told me..."

"If there's anything to be found, Tessa will spot it." Rafael finished the sentence. The former assistant to him and Connor had a reputation for being a computer hacker. And if not that, she was at least more adept than anyone else in his IT department. Though she had betrayed Connor, she had found the evidence that cleared Rafael in Tadeo Ivers's murder.

"Exactly," Kayla said and spread her arms. "Now you know you have verified media personnel only on site."

"And their pictures could be fed into the security cameras," Rafael mused. "Yes, that could work. Matter of fact, I know our software guys can do that. As these people come into the building, the camera can scan them and tell me if they are who they say they are."

"You see?" Kayla threw her hands up. "It is really no different than any other tour, except for a few TV cameras. But the exposure, and the bonus to the credibility of the company—that's priceless."

"I still don't love it," Rafael said, chewing his lower lip. "Can they not wait until after the Turner mess is over? I haven't figured out yet how he gets past perimeter security and close to the building—but he obviously does."

"News doesn't wait, Rafael. PerCan is a hot topic because of what you call this Turner mess. You can tell them they have to wait, sure, but I can guarantee you they won't come back."

Rafael sighed. Every time he found something that spoke in favor of this documentary, he thought of something else that spoke against it. *Do it or don't. Damned if you do and damned…* He sat in his favorite chair and rested his chin on his fist.

"I'm still tempted to tell them to forget it," he said. "But you, Barry, and our IR guy all apparently think this is a massive, big deal."

"It is."

"I even tried to talk Barry out of it, but you know how he gets. Anything for a good story."

"I'm not surprised. Prime time, Rafael. Worth every minute of it." She picked up the proposal and let it drop on the table again. "Of course, it helps that everyone, including everyone, has heard of Tadeo Ivers's murder and the threats against his sons. People want to see more."

"Morbid curiosity?" Rafael asked and closed his eyes for a moment. "That's why they're doing it? So, everyone can see the company where the main shareholder got killed?"

"Morbid curiosity, whatever." Kayla shrugged. "It was front-page news when Tadeo was shot, remember? Why do you think all those true crime shows and podcasts are number one on the trending charts? People want to see the blood. They want to watch somebody else's tragedy. Makes them feel better about their own lives."

"That's it." Rafael slammed his hands on the armrests of his chair. "If that's what this is about, I am not playing into it."

"Relax, Rafael. I know you are trying to protect everybody, but I would strongly advise against turning the reporter down. Honest opinion, you will never get another shot at a show like this one again—ever."

Rafael buried his face in his hands and said nothing for a very long time, thoughts tumbling all over themselves until Kayla gently massaged his neck.

"Fine," he finally said, raising his head again, taking her hand. "Fine. But they had better agree to every single one of my security stipulations."

***

In the boardroom, Al rested his chin on his fingers, listening quietly to everything Rafael had to say, and finally nodded.

"All right," he said quietly. "If you say we can do this safely, I trust you. I'll tell them we're doing it. Being on TV is not my favorite, but Barry tells me it's necessary."

If anything, the words 'I trust you completely' made it worse for Rafael.

"You could still change your mind, you know? You do know that they are secretly hoping something dreadful will happen, don't you?" he asked, forking his hands through his hair for the tenth time.

"Yes," Al said, smiling quietly. "People do have the capacity to derive pleasure from watching someone else's misfortune. I have never quite understood the appeal of this. What joy is there to be had in watching a deadly accident or exceedingly bloody crime for entertainment?"

Rafael groaned. "Would you please not use words like *deadly*, Al? My blood pressure just shot up 20 points."

"My apologies." Al grinned and leaned back in his chair, folding his hands behind his head.

He looked better and better every day, Rafael thought, as his body finally fought off the remnants of this dreadful infection. He had a long way to go before he was the same old Al again, but he never complained even once. He rose and went to the coffeemaker, and Rafael did a little double take.

"Your cane—I mean, no cane. Look at you! You're walking without a cane again!"

"I was wondering how long it would take you to notice. I've been practicing on the sly in the hallways every night and finally decided I was strong enough to walk unaided. Things are looking up."

He turned and brought a coffee to where Rafael sat.

"Wandering the hallways? At night? Al Ivers, I thought I told you it would be safer if you stayed…"

"If we stayed in the small space you set up for us, yes. You did tell me it was safer. But it was far healthier for both my brain and body, and the relationship with my brothers, if I pushed myself a bit harder every night, walking the corridors and hallways."

"I forgot I was talking to an Ivers." Rafael took a sip of coffee and rolled his eyes. "None of you will ever do as you are told anyway—ever. Why do I even bother?"

"Because you care."

"Kayla said the same thing. And still, nobody is listening. Wait…"

Rafael stopped grousing, put down his cup, and furrowed his brow.

"Wait—wait. You just wandered around the halls without worrying you would set off alarms every which way?"

"Dear Rafael." Al dug in his pocket, pulled out his security access card, the one with a colored stripe denoting it to be an executive one, and put it on the table in front of him. "See—you need to stop believing that we are all luddites or dunces when it comes to technical issues."

"I was not…"

"Did you not tell me when we set all of this up that the executive keycards are the only ones with the ability to disable the motion sensors in the halls as you're moving through them?"

"I might have told you. I just didn't think you were listening." Rafael looked down at his hands, fumbled with a skin tag on his thumb, and finally picked at a nonexistent sliver on the boardroom table. "Plus, there was a huge amount of other stuff to explain to you when we set up the system, and I didn't really relish the thought of you wandering around the plant at all hours of the night. Stay put."

"No offense taken, Rafael. I could have asked. Our security system is quite complex and very sophisticated. I studied all of the manuals, but…"

Rafael blinked as if he hadn't heard quite right. "Sorry," he finally said and forced a smile. "Did you say every manual? I'm—I'm dumbfounded."

"Every manual. This is a top-rated security system—the best, in fact."

"German engineering," Rafael said with a little smile, trying in vain for a German accent.

"I understand that. It's worth every penny to me at the moment. And I also understand that the only people who can manipulate the system in any way—have to carry one of these." He picked up his executive keycard and turned it over in his hands. "So, God forbid, even if Turner managed to get in here somehow…"

"Which he won't—ever."

Rafael knocked on the wooden conference room table.

"I said if, Rafael, if. I don't think even a mouse could."

"We don't need mice in here. Not while I'm in charge."

"Even if Turner made it past the perimeter section, the first motion sensor would grab him. And he can't turn those off from the outside. He can't. We're perfectly fine. So please, Rafael, don't go worrying about scenarios that will never take place."

"From your mouth to God's ear," Rafael muttered and picked up his coffee cup again. "And you really read the entire set of manuals? Like…"

"Like all of it, yes," Al said with a grin. "Before I ever even considered that news segment of Barry's. If this CEO thing doesn't work out for me, I think I can always hire on with them as an advisor."

"You'd have to learn German," Rafael said, and the grin was back on his face, too.

"There is that, Rafa. There is that."

***

Detective Robertson, on the other hand, took the news with a lot less cool.

"Have all of you gone completely out of your mind?" he asked Al, when he heard a TV crew would be at PerCan, filming a documentary about the medical marijuana producer.

Robertson paced the length of their boardroom, stopped briefly where Rafael and Al sat to glare at them, then turned to pace back the other way.

"Is this your idea of staying low, not presenting a huge, wide-open target to a man who has basically announced he means to kill you?"

"I appreciate your concern, Detective," Al said, smiling pleasantly. "But Rafael assures me he has security issues in hand."

"Oh, well, why didn't you tell me that in the first place?" Robertson threw his hands in the air. "Do you know that we have made little to no progress on tracing the virus Turner introduced at Roberto's company? Do you? Minute amounts have been confirmed in China, at some random manufacturing plant, but that's it. We have no idea. And suddenly, you want to open the doors to anyone…"

"Not anyone, Detective."

"To do what? Come in here, wander around, get a tour, speak to you—one on one even? That's insane."

"Detective." Al raised both hands. "Only a limited number of station personnel will be allowed in the building. They'll be identified visually. Our security system will know who is in the building at all times."

"That's supposed to make me feel better?" Robertson stood in front of them again, glared, and turned on his heel.

"Not to criticize your security system, Rafael."

"Gee. Thanks."

"But I would like to introduce the possibility that Greg Turner is not acting alone. He quite possibly has some outside help."

"How so?" Al asked, folding his hands in his lap. "The attack on Dante appears to be the work of one man."

"And the virus, Al? I think it's a miracle that you survived. Somebody must have helped Turner to obtain it, to smuggle it into PrideCan, and onto—something—that would infect you. Have you had any more luck recalling what it might have been that you touched when you were there?"

"Much of my visit there is a blur," Al said, keeping his face as carefully neutral as he could. "And I wouldn't worry about the virus just now. We are mainly concerned with keeping suspect persons out of our own building, and to that end…"

"And I believe that's not enough," Robertson snapped. "Something infected might already be here, in this building as we speak."

"Now wait just one minute." Rafael jumped to his feet. "We have done security sweeps and testing on every material in here and everything that comes in. We are clean. Whatever happened at Roberto's…"

He looked at Al and sat again.

"Please concentrate on outside observation, Detective," Al said pleasantly. "Rafael is quite capable of keeping the TV crew monitored when they get here. The only thing I need from your group is to continue keeping an eye on the outside."

"I still think you're wrong. It's on your head." Robertson said sourly and swiped his portfolio off the boardroom table. "I will deploy my men as I see fit."

He stalked out again, and Al put his palms together flat and stared at the door for a long time.

"There is never going to be a virus coming in here," Rafael said, and Al nodded.

"Yes, of course there is not. But Robertson can't understand how we are so sure about it, that all he needs to do is keep an eye on one man. Greg Turner. He probably thinks we're insane even considering this documentary."

"You still have time to call it off," Rafael suggested, and Al shook his head again.

"No, Kayla is quite right. We would look foolish if we confirmed and then cancelled again, and we'll never get another chance at this kind of public exposure. We are doing the documentary. But I need your attention to be everywhere because Robertson—might be focused on the wrong thing."

"Do everything myself. What else is new?" Rafael groused, eliciting one of his rare smiles from Al.

"Oh, but you do love it so. You'd feel left out if I failed to pile all of this work onto your lone shoulders."

Rafael extended his middle finger just a bit, pretended to study something at his nail, and rose.

"We'll get 'er done," he said and hid a grin.

"Oh, and Rafael?"

"Yes?"

"Those security sweeps of all materials in the building you mentioned? They might actually be a good idea. Even if we aren't expecting a chemical attack. Just to be—on the safe side."

***

Everyone at Perfect Cannabis Consolidated suddenly shifted into high alert and stayed that way. Security sweeps checked incoming and outgoing material and present inventory every single day. Rafael fine-tuned the security monitors at the doors, tinkering for days with the software.

He had been planning to install cameras all over the building, every major hallway and room. But HR went crazy with privacy concerns, and, eventually, even he realized when too much was too much.

The front and side doors would be monitored by cameras, and the interior would remain on motion sensors after hours.

He obtained pictures and CVs of every technician, cameraman assistant, and road crew member from the TV station and had Kayla's team research them. The station managers never had any issues with his odd requests. It probably added to their hopes that they would stumble over something truly horrible, Rafael thought.

Not on his watch, he vowed. If something bigger than an ant was coming into his building, he would know about it. And he could work on that ant thing too.

***

Outside of town, in a deserted part of the forest, loud laughter rang through a little clearing and a forest worker's hut.

"They're having a TV crew visit," Turner said hoarsely, rubbing his hands with glee. "A documentary—how precious. They're probably hoping for something really bad to come up. They don't know I can come and go as I wish. If they want something really bad, why don't we give it to them? If they are wanting to talk to a guy who has a death threat against him, we can make a bit of fireworks. I'll be there early!"

He laughed loud and long at his own joke, and if he hadn't been in the middle of the forest, someone might have suggested hearing a madman.

THIRTY-NINE

Rafael had a very detailed plan, and he had studied it over and over again the last few days.

Every member of the TV crew would walk through his newly constructed 'video gate' into an also newly set-up 'welcoming room'. Once there, a few of his carefully trained receptionists would hand out ID badges, offer coffee and other refreshments, and give the visitors the rundown on security and safety procedures, taking just long enough that Rafael's software would have enough time to verify everyone was indeed who they said they were, and to tag and memorize them.

Step one: he would know exactly who was in his building at all times and, thanks to a little RFID chip in their visitors' badges, also where they were located at any given time.

Kayla's research personnel had given him a dossier on every journalist, presenter, assistant grip, or cameraman who was scheduled to be there, and Rafael had studied them with a massive assist from Al's investigator friend, Sandro. No one on his list was related to Greg Turner, had ever worked for him, been a friend to him, or been connected to anyone who was closely related to Turner.

There was no connection. He was as sure as he could be of that. Again and again, he studied the reports, checked and double-checked late into the night, every day. Kayla watched him, deep lines etched into his face, and put a cup of tea beside him.

"Rafael, I'm worried about you. You're getting obsessed."

"I am not getting obsessed—I am obsessed," he corrected. "I'm obsessed with keeping Al and his brothers safe. And if our friend Greg Turner were sitting across from me just now…"

"Don't go there," she warned. "You'd end up in jail, and visiting jail once to see Barry Wentworth was enough to last me a lifetime."

Rafael well remembered and wisely shut up. Nobody was going to jail. This was just a giant puzzle titled "Keep Out Greg Turner," and if he hadn't been worried about the safety of his friend, he would have enjoyed poking into all the new developments in security systems, their uses and applications, and how they would make his life easier here at PerCan. Right now, all they had to do was keep out Greg Turner.

Barry Wentworth, on the other hand, had recovered his cocky swagger after a business magazine had crowned him the most successful fundraiser of all time.

He had sent a number of presentations to the board of directors, showing them how this TV documentary would impact their reputation, their share prices and their sales, and how marketing like this was the best way to turn PerCan into a household name as common as Kleenex.

Hand me the PerCan, will you.

***

The day of the documentary, there were to be no other visitors in the building, no contractors, or outside maintenance people, and only minimal delivery services. Rafael didn't want anyone to gawk at or interfere with the film crew, of course, but he also wanted to have a limited number of people to keep track of. The fewer strange faces, the better.

He installed himself in the security office with enough coffee to sink a battleship and began watching monitors as their guests arrived. He had become so involved in his task he barely noticed the door opening behind him.

"You know, we have staff to do that." Al peered over his shoulder at the monitors and finally put his hand on Rafael's shoulder. "I put you in charge of security, but that does not mean you have to do all of the work on your own."

"I know."

"Rafael. I have full confidence everything will be fine."

"I know." He pointed at the screen in front of him with a pencil. "There's Tim Verhoeven, the host of the show. He looks taller on TV, you know."

"Rafael." Al waited patiently until Rafael finally took his eyes off the screen and turned around.

"What?"

"You're obsessing."

"And you've been talking to Kayla."

"Amongst others. Everything will be fine. Now would you please let a tech do this job and come into your 'welcome room' with me to welcome our guests?"

"But isn't Kayla…?"

"Kayla is making everyone welcome, as usual, but it's time for the CEO to make an appearance. And, since this facility is what they are so interested in, I believe that calls for the director of facilities to be there as well."

"But nobody…"

Rafael looked back at the screen. Nobody had his eye for detail, he wanted to say, but Al shook his head.

"I've checked. Our best and most experienced security techs are on duty today. So, please come down and greet our guests with me."

He really didn't want to be anywhere else but here right now, but…

"Please? After all, if someone takes a knife out of their pocket, I would rather have you be there to deal with it."

"A knife? But we have metal detectors. I made sure… Oh."

He'd failed to see the broad grin on Al's face.

"There is no knife," Al said, smiling. "But it would look foolish if my director of facilities were absent and, even worse, incompetent, if said director had to spend his time watching security monitors."

"All right, all right, I'm coming already."

Grousing, he went along and down into the entrance to their welcome room. Kayla was busy charming Tim Verhoeven and his assistant, and the technical staff were already leafing through the promotional material that had been provided.

Rafael had watched Tim Verhoeven on his news segment, a snappy and quick-witted TV show host, with an infectious smile and a charming personality. He looked to be just north of 30, was always impeccably dressed in stylish suits, and still wore the ties everyone else felt were "so yesterday."

Tim was known for his fast-talking, sharp-tongued delivery that kept even Rafael entertained and engaged. He had a penchant for making sarcastic remarks and witty comebacks you just had to admire.

Despite his snappy and eccentric ways, though, he was a consummate professional who took his job very seriously.

"Al Ivers," Tim said, looking up. "What an honor to finally meet the CEO of this fantastic facility."

"Likewise, Mr. Verhoeven. Please meet Rafael Covin, our director of facilities. He's the one who makes all the magic happen around here."

"Oh, call me Tim, please." He stuck out a hand and blitzed his best TV charmer smile. "How are you doing, Mr. Ivers? I heard you were not well."

Here we go, looking for the blood, Rafael thought, but the smile never left Al's face.

"Al, please. And I am doing well, thank you. My staff and I are very proud of what we have accomplished here and extremely grateful that you have decided to feature Perfect Cannabis in your documentary."

"Cannabis, since its legalization both medically and recreationally, is a hot topic, naturally," Tim said, still smiling broadly. He looked up and saw another group of his technical crew coming into the welcome room. "Tell me, is your security always this tight or are all of these measures recent additions to keep you safe personally? I hear there are some issues."

Rafael bristled and wanted to take a step forward, but he felt Kayla moving in closer behind him. *Keep your cool,* she seemed to say, and indeed, Al's polite smile never wavered.

"We are manufacturing pharmaceuticals here. As such, safety is always at the top of our list. Ah, here is our Barry Wentworth, who arranged this documentary. Barry, won't you join us? I'm sure the film crew is about to start their work."

Taking his cue, Barry did what he did best. He wove his particular spell over Tim. He spoke of manufacturing pharmaceutical-grade marijuana, consistently and safely. He touched on their record as a medical company and their expansion into recreational use. He had facts, figures, and historical data at his fingertips as only he could, and, by the end of his little speech, Rafael would have invested in the company if he didn't already own a large chunk of it.

"I am impressed," Tim Verhoeven said, at a loss for words for once. "We'll have to get all of this into the documentary."

"Of course." Barry took the man's elbow and steered him to the far end of the room. "Let me introduce you to our head agronomists. Then we can get started with the film."

Rafael exhaled.

"You see, no knife," Al whispered beside him, and Rafael elbowed him gently.

"I know that," he said. "Just being careful."

"Thank you. Now, I believe everyone is here—we can start this show."

'This show' was a finely orchestrated event.

One-on-one interviews with Al, Dante, and Rafael took place in the privacy of the boardroom, in front of the grand window overlooking manufacturing, and they all spoke with pride and confidence. PerCan was one of the finest producers around, and they were not afraid to say so.

Barry sat in on every single interview and provided charm and little anecdotes Tim's viewers would find fascinating. Effortlessly, he wove in stories and facts that would come across well on TV.

Just like old times, Rafael thought. Barry could hold an audience in thrall, no matter the surroundings, no matter the circumstances. How like his father, the man who had been a TV preacher all of his life.

Tim Verhoeven broke for lunch and shook Barry's hand with a bold gregarious smile.

"Thank you. You made my job far too easy. If you're ever tired of raising funds, Barry, let me know. I think there's a TV show with your name on it that has yet to be made."

"Dear me, thank you for the compliment," Barry said, preening just a bit. "It is a talent, but I'm happy where I am."

"No false modesty for our boy," Rafael said to Kayla, and she elbowed him softly.

"Hush. The camera loves him to pieces, always has. For once, that is exactly what we want."

It was. Probably—likely—but Rafael still rolled his eyes.

The catered lunch had been delivered previously, and PerCan staff busied themselves serving. Al joined them, rubbing his palms together as if he were chilled.

"That went rather well. Remind me to thank Barry when he's done speaking to Tim. He did an excellent job."

"Thank him?" Rafael asked. "He was all but flirting with the cameras out there, I thought. A bit much perhaps."

"Exactly, Rafael. That is precisely what I asked him to do, his thing that makes everything look easy and magical. Sure enough. I wanted to take the light off me for a bit until my suits fit a little better again."

He still did look like he was wearing a rented suit, Rafael admitted, and opened his mouth to apologize. Just then, a random movement through the window down on the manufacturing floor took his eye.

His hands flexed automatically, and he stepped closer to the window, frowning. "Something wrong?" Al asked only a step behind him.

"I don't know. I thought I saw some movement down there where it doesn't belong."

They both stared for a long moment at the area he had indicated, and Al shook his head.

"Sorry, don't see anything. That's out by the receiving area. Chances are… somebody might be delivering something."

"Not today." Rafael squinted at the spot again—nothing.

There were no deliveries or pickups scheduled for this day, his own orders. As much as he stared, there was no one there.

"I seriously hope it is not some type of dreadful vermin, not the day of a TV show," Al said lightly, shuddered, and pulled Rafael by the elbow toward the food stations. "Somebody said not even a mouse could enter unobserved. And if one does by any chance, you may deal with it any way you wish—but tomorrow, please. Now stop worrying and get something to eat. You have a tour to lead in half an hour."

Maybe it had been a shadow, or a reflection, or an evil trick his mind played. Whatever it was, it was gone now. Rafael gave one last look to the area where he thought he had seen movement and let Al drag him away.

He had a quick lunch, joked with Tim and Kayla, and tried to forget that he thought he had seen something. He joined Barry at one of the standup tables and raised his mineral water to him.

"Just like old times, huh?"

"You know, I was thinking that," Barry said. "I always thought I wanted to run this cannabis company, but dear God, Al does a far better job than I ever could have."

"Did that storm mess up my hearing? Did you really say that just now?"

"You know me, Rafa. Administrative matters, not my thing. But you look utterly beat. Did something go wrong? Issues in the grow pods?"

"Just in case you had forgotten," Rafael looked around and lowered his voice a little, "Greg Turner? Still wants to kill all of the remaining Ivers men?"

"They will have him soon enough." Barry waved a hand through the air. "Do you remember, in the good old days, you could hide an entire secondary grow op at the end of the building and nobody noticed? Nowadays? The way you know this building and everything in it, the way you do these tours? I bet you would notice if one single broom were out of place in a janitor's closet somewhere."

"I'm not that bad."

"Pretty damn close." Barry grinned. "That's not a bad thing, you know. Way back when, when you and I thought about getting into this cannabis business, in a bar on a lark no less, I would never have dreamed of a five-star facility like this one. That's all thanks to you. You'll probably have to get me drunk to say it again, but I am deeply impressed with what you've done. You should be proud of this. I mean it."

He turned away without waiting for Rafael to recover his power of speech again. Tim Verhoeven was done with his lunch and had summoned him with a wave. Rafael still stood there, mouth agape, food half eaten.

Had Barry J. Wentworth—the Barry J. Wentworth—just told him he was proud of what he had done?

***

Rafael usually called these tours the dog-and-pony show. Al would lead them and explain the general area they were walking through and then either call on Rafael or Dante to go into specifics and details, before walking to the next area of the building.

They had done this a hundred times and perfected the routine, although by now, Al only led the tours for VIPs and ministry visitors.

Barry had carried the torch during the one-on-one interviews, but here, in the manufacturing space, Rafael called the shots.

He told the usual jokes, holding up a sterile paper suit, booties, and hard hat for Tim to step into on camera. He regaled them with the one about walking single file and not leaving your buddy behind amongst the cannabis plants. Finally, he relaxed. This was the stuff he knew. And whether it was a joke or not—yes, he would notice if there were a broom missing in one of the janitors' closets. Because that would mean it was standing around somewhere, waiting for someone to trip over it. Not funny.

He always started with the one thing everyone wanted to see the most: a room full of cannabis plants ready to harvest.

Normally, visitors would be barred from entering here and reduced to peering through a little window. National TV exposure had made them make a little exception. In they went, just a few steps, and Rafael grinned broadly when he found everyone's faces screwing up.

"This, ladies and gentlemen, is why they call it stinkweed or skunk weed. Stuff smells horrible unless you're used to it."

"Fortunately," Tim said into the camera and coughed discreetly, "they have not invented smell TV just yet."

Rafael showed them grow pods and equipment corridors, automatic controls for irrigation and fertilization. He showed them where CO_2 was brought into the growing rooms to encourage plant growth and people kept out.

When he was done, he realized Al looked about ready to fall down and cut his usual spiel a little short.

He watched Al wipe his face surreptitiously when the cameras were not on him and take deep steadying breaths through a balled fist. Not good at all. Quickly, he waved the group along, spoke a little faster, and glanced at Al now and then. He didn't invite additional questions, the way he usually would, didn't stop for idle chitchat, and only breathed a little easier when the group headed toward the exit again. Not their finest tour ever.

It didn't seem to matter. Tim Verhoeven all but glowed with excitement. Shortcuts or not, few people had seen a real cannabis production plant from the inside, and his show and ratings would surely go through the roof. Cannabis was just 'the thing' at the moment. It was finally legal, it was freely available, and, on the medical side, new uses and applications were discovered every day. Add to that the new trend toward 'natural' treatments and medicines, and people really wanted to know what it was all about.

"Every day, we receive inquiries and suggestions about new products," Rafael said gregariously. "We've earned our reputation as a manufacturer of consistently high-quality cannabis products, and consumers trust the name PerCan."

Cut to Rafael standing with a huge smile before his control panel, and Tim and Al shaking hands—and the film was done.

"This was fantastic, folks," Tim said. "You have amazing staff and directors here. We should have done this a lot sooner."

Rafael could see Al's polite smile slip a little bit and nodded at Barry. *Get to it.*

And Barry did. He approached Tim and gave his usual spiel about market share, investment and earnings potential and market positioning, all the while steering the TV show host back out into the main reception area.

Al reached for a ledge to steady himself when they were out of sight. "Thank you," he said. "I was afraid I might have to embarrass myself and ask to sit down there toward the end. Just what they were waiting for, no doubt."

"Perhaps you should not have exhausted yourself for the sake of this show. Shit. Barry has our friend Verhoeven under control. Now let me take you upstairs to sit down for a bit before you do any more hand-shaking and interviewing."

Gently, Al shook off his guiding hand.

"A breather is welcome, but nobody needs to take me upstairs, Rafael. Thank you for your concern, but I can manage."

"Are you…"

One quick flash of irritation from Al's eyes and Rafael bit off the remainder of the sentence.

"I think Dante and Roberto are up in your rooms for a bit. Why don't you join them, and if we need you again…"

"You know where to find me."

Al winked, took off the sterile protective cap and booties with measured, stiff movements, and walked off in the direction of their rooms. Finally, Rafael allowed himself to exhale.

They had done it.

They had pulled off this TV documentary without any incidents.

"Did rather well, if I might say so myself," he muttered and gave the control panel beside him a little good-luck tap with the side of his fist.

He wanted to make his customary rounds then, looking around for anything out of place, and quickly realized that everything was out of place. Things had been moved or prettied up to make room for the TV cameras and crew, and unless he spent several hours putting them right again… There was always tomorrow.

The caterers had another spread up there in the reception area, and he'd been told it was awesome. This time there would be wine—and likely a few other things they knew Rafael liked. Just the way to celebrate that they had come through this damned thing and done it well. Their little company—not so little anymore—in a prime-time TV documentary. Who would have thought it when they dreamed it up?

Some invisible pull kept him down there in manufacturing, walking from grow pod to grow pod, touching the monitoring screens and control boxes, but after five minutes of doing it, he shook his head like a wet dog.

"Damn nonsense anyway," he muttered to no one but himself. "Should be up there."

Kayla would be waiting up there, and Nick, who still walked on eggshells around him, as well he should. And, of course, Barry. Surprisingly, he realized, a lot of the bitterness he'd carried around when Barry disappeared and he'd been left holding the bag had gone.

How often had he cursed Barry and his half-legal deals, shady agreements, and last-minute pivots? *Damn Wentworth, I never know what to expect from him*, he would curse and try to keep up with Barry's latest 'change in plans.'

Somehow—maybe it was age—he realized he actually liked it. Pitting his knowledge and experience against the ever-changing circumstances and situations Barry presented him… it was a challenge. And complaining. There was always complaining about the chaos Barry was apt to cause to anyone who would listen. That was fun too.

"We are who we are," he muttered, gave one last searching look to his control monitors and decided to shut it down for now. He'd join them up in the welcome room and hoist a celebratory drink with his friend.

Rafael stopped and turned back, his hand already reaching for the door of the exit airlock.

Something had brought him out of his reverie and made him pay attention. A noise, perhaps? He listened, closed his eyes for a second, and tried to listen beyond the hum of the fertigation pumps, the CO_2 influx… Nothing.

"You're seeing ghosts all of a sudden, Covin," he muttered and reached for the door again, hesitating for just a second.

Something was back there, wasn't it? He thought he was sure something was back there, moving almost silently between the grow pods. Or was he imagining it? *Frigging seeing ghosts*, he thought, but still…

His phone almost gave him a heart attack pinging with a text message. Kayla.

You better not be hiding down in the grow rooms doing busywork. Come and join us in the welcome area.

He responded with a thumbs-up signal, nothing else. There was something…

I know these things are not your favorite. Just do it anyway. Please.

His eyes swept over the semi-darkness beyond, trying to pierce the shadows.

Just to do me a favor.

Rafael sighed. That woman had a way of asking.

On my way, he responded. *Just let me get out of the paper booties and hairnet.* He wasn't wearing a hairnet, but it got the point across.

Nobody was back here. All the TV personnel were in the welcome room again.

Kayla responded with the symbol of the praying hands—did that mean thanks? Damn those emojis anyway. Nobody typed a proper sentence any more.

He took his time, tidied himself up a bit, put on a clean sweatshirt with the company logo, and double-checked once again on the alarm systems for the doors into the manufacturing area. Wouldn't do to have a guest looking for a washroom wandering in there, right? And with all that done, he finally went back into the welcome area.

Kayla met him right behind the door, smiled, and handed him a glass of wine.

"Relax. You did it. Nothing happened."

"That we did. TV people are still here, I see."

"Yes. Turns out none of them has ever seen a marijuana operation from the inside. They can't quite leave yet."

"Few have."

"And they have a thousand questions."

"Only a thousand, huh? With their research background, I would have expected at least 50,000."

"Be nice to them."

She handed him a plate with all of his favorites and nodded toward the crowd. *Mingle.* For a moment, he stood and looked out over the crowd of visitors. They all still wore their visitor's badges, so he would know exactly where they had gone, when they left, and that they had left.

Nothing could happen.

Tim Verhoeven sidled up and involved him in a conversation about his isolated grow pods and his sophisticated automation system. Rafael gave a few lackadaisical answers but quickly realized the man was actually quite smart, and he explained the system to him.

A few of the techs wandered up to join the conversation, and before he knew it, his plate was empty, the wine had been consumed, and the gathering darkness beyond the windows let them know it was time to call this a day.

"Again, thank you so much for taking a day out of your schedule and for letting us be part of this." Tim offered a hand. "It's been a pleasure."

"Pleasure is all mine," Rafael said and shook his hand.

"Give my regards to Al Ivers, please. I wanted to say goodbye to him, but I haven't seen him since the end of the tour." Tim looked around the room with searching eyes and a little disappointment.

"Yes, he had an international phone conference. I'm so sorry it couldn't be postponed. But I will pass on your thanks."

Lying came surprisingly easy, he thought and chuckled. Why had Al not come back down? Too exhausted maybe?

"Yes, I heard you are expanding internationally. Congratulations once again."

When Tim Verhoeven packed his things, it served as a signal to most of his people. One by one in small groups, they said their goodbyes and left. Badges were to be handed in at the main security gate outside, just so he could be sure everyone had left. He hadn't left anything to chance.

"You do a very slick version of the old dog-and-pony show these days, you know?" While he was still ruminating, Barry had come up to stand beside him.

"You think?"

"Much better than our old 'and this is where we grow the cannabis.'" Barry handed him another glass of wine.

"I probably shouldn't…"

"Oh, for crying out loud, Rafael. Since when have you been

worried about the extra glass? It's done, it's over, all the TV guys are gone—celebrate."

Rafael grinned, took it, and toasted Barry.

"Man, I cannot believe you got us on national TV. That is—well, I, for one, find it hard to wrap my blockhead around it."

"Believe it." Barry grinned. "When that segment airs…"

"When that segment airs, we're going to be so busy I don't know what we'll do. But we'll figure it out. We always do. And there is all the international attention we are getting and people who want me to consult."

They stood together for a while, hanging on to their wine glasses and watching the TV crew folks leave.

The security guard at the door signaled to both of them, indicating that all of their visitors had left now. Their own staff had grabbed a bit of food and left. They were indeed the last people in the building, except for Al and his brothers. It had been a fantastic day, Rafael kept reminding himself. And none of the dreadful scenarios his mind had come up with had actually come to pass.

"Well then," he said, holding up his empty glass. "Here's to success. Time to head home. We hit it out of the ballpark today."

"We sure as hell did," Barry said, smiling. "I just want to give my regards to Al quickly. Walk with me? I never know when your alarm is going to think I'm an intruder."

"That's how I know it's working. I like to make sure. I think Al, Dante, and Roberto went up to their rooms to put their feet up and relax for a bit."

"I noticed that." Barry glanced around again and shook his head. "Everybody did. I'm a little surprised they didn't return to say their goodbyes. It looked a bit rude. Is everything all right?"

"Don't know why it shouldn't be. Al was beat from doing the tour, that's all." Rafael shrugged and raised his hands. "I offered to walk him upstairs, but you know him. 'Thanks—I can walk myself.'"

"Oh, I'm not blaming you. Perhaps he merely fell asleep, and he'll be mad to have missed the celebrations. It's just odd."

Barry frowned, tapped his fingers to his mouth, took a few steps away, and came to stand beside Rafael again. He opened his mouth to speak, and Rafael jumped right in.

"I got involved with Verhoeven and his group," Rafael said, a little irritated. "You know how it is when they ask you questions about something you know really well. Sorry—I didn't think."

Kayla, who had by now taken off her high heels and made sure there was no champagne going bad anywhere, joined them, swinging the offending pumps from a free hand.

"These look adorable, as long as you don't plan to stand up any time soon. Why do the two of you look like five days' rain? This event went fantastic. Did something happen I'm not aware of?"

"No," Rafael answered like a shot out of a pistol. "Barry here thinks one of us should have checked on Al, in case he wanted to join us but fell asleep. I'm just mad at myself because I got carried away and didn't think."

"He never came back down to join the remaining event. You're right," Kayla said, and Rafael rolled his eyes.

"Sorry, Rafael, but yes, it is a little odd. Al was as excited as we were about the event and the exposure for PerCan. He went through the whole day precisely and only because he knew it meant a lot to the company. Tell you what. I'll go check on him right now and say our goodbyes—and apologies for not waking him earlier."

Barry and Rafael watched her go, swinging her adorable pumps all the way.

"Damn virus," Rafael muttered. "I'll be glad to have him back 100 percent. Soon, too."

"Can't blame you." Barry peered deep into his empty glass and followed Rafael over to the bar, in search of remnants.

"And Roberto," Rafael continued. "There is a man I do not envy for…"

In the middle of his sentence, he stopped dead in his tracks so suddenly Barry plowed into him from behind, and Rafael held out a hand to steady him.

"Kayla," he called out, just as she started to open the door to the side tract. "Do not take another step. Come right back here to me."

He waved his arm, pointing at the floor beside him.

"But I was just going to…"

"Now!" he yelled, and the sheer panic in his voice made her drop the shoes in her hand and come back to the men.

Rafael stood in the middle of the room, staring.

"What?" Barry caught his equilibrium and followed Rafael's gaze.

"Fuck!"

"Clear me up, guys?"

Rafael pointed. There, by the giant double doors that led into the manufacturing and shipping area, was an alarm monitoring pad, installed there by Rafael many years ago so he could see at one glance when he arrived in the morning if there was a trouble area in the building anywhere.

He had rearmed the system when the TV crews had left the area; he knew it. And he'd gone to double-check it after he changed clothes. He knew this as sure as he knew his own name. But right at that moment, all of the lights on the panel were off. Off as in dead. Not alarm on, alarm off—but nothing.

"Maybe the panel's got no power," Barry suggested softly, advancing on the double doors step by step. "Electrical fault?"

"Nope, that would have triggered its own alarm."

"What does it mean?" Kayla asked and hugged her arms around herself, suddenly chilled in the warm welcoming room.

"It means somebody disarmed the system and took it offline. Dammit." He struck the palm of his hand with the fist of the other. "I had a feeling when I came out of the grow pods. I had a feeling like something was not OK, and I walked away. Didn't want to fuss about nothing and have people tell me I just didn't feel like this party."

"But surely, security personnel are still around?"

"Should be." Rafael nodded. "Two men at all times—day or night. But we put them on perimeter patrol. Damn, I wish I had listened."

"Where the fuck are the security staff then if they're supposed to patrol?" Barry's voice suddenly had taken on a bit of panic. "Nowhere to be found while somebody turns off the alarm? Didn't somebody mention this place was Fort Knox, just an hour ago?"

Kayla's fingers clamped around Rafael's forearm. "Can you call the police, Rafael, please? Robertson and his people must be out there somewhere watching the place tonight."

"Do that," Rafael said, still not taking his eyes off the alarm monitoring pad, as if it held all of the answers. "Barry, check the office areas right now, get anybody who is still in the building safely out of here, and then take Kayla once the police have been called. "

"And leave you alone in here? Not on your life, Rafael."

"Just do it. I don't know why somebody would be on the production floor. But if they went through all that trouble, they have a plan."

"And what about you, Rambo? You're going to walk around the building like the lone ranger? Guns drawn, defending your turf? That's what you're going to do?"

Rafael shook his head, still staring at the dead panel. "How?" he asked. "I designed that system to be foolproof."

Barry nodded at the alarm panel. "Let's get out of here. You said it yourself. Cops will be here in five minutes. Let them deal with it—with whoever."

"No."

"Rafael."

Kayla's voice sounded almost hysterical.

"Don't panic. I have no intentions of playing the hero around here.

I'm just going to get Al, Dante, and Roberto. Make sure they're OK—let them know what's happening. Then we'll all walk out of here. Failing that, we go to the boardroom and lock the doors. If anybody is on the production floor, we can see them from up there."

"I'm coming with you," Barry said, but Rafael shook his head.

"No, you go with Kayla, to the boardroom. Call the police."

"Fine, but I'm coming back."

"Then hurry. I won't wait for you."

Kayla trembled and covered her face with her hands. "Is that—is that even safe with an intruder here?"

"The back wall of the boardroom is against a firewall," Rafael said patiently. "And the glass front is triple-reinforced industrial glass. Anybody wants to get in there, they are going to need explosives."

Barry gave him a look as if to say *what makes you think they don't have any*, and Rafael shook his head.

"Just do as I say—please. If you want to come back and join me, that's fine, but I'm not waiting for you."

He approached the giant double doors and opened them as softly as he could. On his way back to the event, he had slammed that door with glee, knowing it made that dull, thumping sound if you didn't let it fall on the latch carefully. He loved that sound. It separated Manufacturing from the rest of the company, which he habitually called *admin bullshit*. A term HR tried to get him to stop using. Now he opened the doors carefully, inch by inch, so it would make as little noise as possible.

Beyond, all the lights had been shut down. Including the emergency lighting indicating the safe path around the place in case the lighting ever failed.

Rafael shuddered. He knew every corner of this place like the back of his hand, but what faced him right now was the blackest, most featureless darkness he had ever experienced. As if he had gone blind all of a sudden. Everything that should have glowed, blinked, or even flickered had been disabled. Rafael felt the dread in his stomach expand

and take over. He fought the impulse to call out and merely stood silently for a long moment listening into the darkness. Did he hear a rustle, footsteps even?

No, just his imagination. He felt more than saw Barry come up behind him, also staring into the darkness.

"Shit," Barry said softly, and Rafael could only echo the sentiment. Shit indeed.

FORTY

Barry had told him, Kayla had told him, their IR director had told him several times even—this documentary was important. The company needed the boost to its reputation, and this would provide it.

Usually, Al would have had Rafael and their IR director handle media appearances like this one. It was bad enough Barry had insisted he handle the PerCan news minute. Yes, people liked to hear and see the CEO. Yes, they were curious about Al Ivers, and no, he still hated to see his face in the media. It could have something to do with his father's checkered past, the parts of it that weren't made up anyway, or the media storm he had had to endure after Greg Turner shot Tadeo. Either way, he preferred to stay out of the limelight, thank you very much.

Let people like Barry Wentworth take the spotlight and enjoy it. Barry could charm anyone, but even Barry had said, *oh, no, you really have to do this one yourself. This is important.*

The show host, Tim, had insisted on having Al on air, and still, he'd been tempted to say no. After all, he was just getting over a serious illness, he reasoned. He'd been at death's door. Had knocked as a matter of fact and then turned around again. At the same time, someone had attacked his little brother.

Some disgusting excuse for a human being had sabotaged Dante's motorcycle and walked away, in the hope that Dante would crash and die in the resulting accident.

No one did that.

No one made an attempt on the life of one of Al Ivers's family and got away with it. The first few days after he woke up in the hospital, he'd been stewing in revenge fantasies. Greg Turner! He'd imagined all sorts of scenarios, how he would get to the man, what he would say to him and how he would…

After a few days, he had realized that he didn't have it in him. Revenge was an entertaining fantasy while you lay in a hospital bed, staring at nothing, spinning ever-evolving scenarios, but here, in real life, Al didn't really have the stomach for it.

Maybe that was the very reason his father had created all of these wild stories around his own persona, Al thought with a bit of regret. Maybe Tadeo had also realized that he didn't have it in him to strike out at someone, so he had built this fantasy, creating this character, Tadeo the criminal, who could keep the wolves of the strip-club business at bay.

Revenge was out, then, but there was still no way that he would give in to the terror of Turner's threats.

Never would he give Turner the satisfaction of making him hide in the shadows of a bodyguard. No thank you.

And he had insisted on that, until Rafael convinced him that he needed protection. He didn't really want it, but finally, he had allowed Rafael to build a safe space for him and his brothers here, at PerCan.

Rafael always said it was the safest building in town. It made sense to be here. He was close to the business, he was around people he knew and cared about, and no one could get to him.

And as much as he disliked the media, he wouldn't hide from Greg Turner. He would show his face on TV for once. *Here I am, Turner.* It was his way to let his father's killer know that he had not won and wouldn't win. He would never succeed in frightening Al Ivers—ever. It took a lot more than that.

What he indeed had not counted on was how physically exhausting shooting a TV documentary could be.

Stand here—walk over there—no, wait, the light's not right—do it again. Pretend to look at this panel or that, explain what it is you are doing. After an hour, he had fought the overwhelming desire to ask someone to bring him a chair so he could conduct the rest of the interview sitting down.

I am not going to show any weakness had become his mantra.

Even Dante had made a brief appearance, leaning heavily on his crutches, pretending all was all right, so Al could too. He'd been in a hospital bed long enough; he was exhausted, fatigued, and ready to drop, but he would not finish this show sitting down.

So, he'd pushed everything aside, made himself take one step after another, forced himself to keep his head high, speak loudly, clearly, and will all the confidence in the world in to his voice. Only Rafael had noticed. He knew him too well. Rafael had rushed through his usual tour and cut it a bit short. Perhaps noticing as the makeup people came around for the third time to touch up his face, because he looked pale—no matter, he had finished the show.

Rafael had even wanted to help him get upstairs. Well, that was overkill. He had finished—that was all he needed

Then exhaustion took over.

The moment he had sat down, he nodded off. Roberto sat at the computer, grousing about something or other, probably social media, Dante flipped through a magazine, and he was only vaguely aware of them as a kind of background noise, as he fell asleep.

Fallen asleep, for Christ's sake—how could he have? And why had no one come to get him? *Cut yourself some slack*, he reminded himself. *You've only just come out of the hospital.* It probably just meant everything was all right at the event downstairs. But as he woke up fully, he saw... nothing.

Nothing. Not an empty room, not the abandoned desk where Dante and Roberto had been sitting—nothing. Blackness, as if he had gone completely blind.

He groped around him on the cot. His phone had to be here some-where, but his fingers found nothing.

"Lights on! God's sake," but the supposedly voice-activated lights stayed off. But now, he heard something. A soft chuckle. A man who found something rather amusing.

Al sat up straight then, steadying himself with his hands left and right. His phone—where was it?

Somewhere in the room, a phone screen came to life, and he saw him. There, at the desk where Roberto had been reading emails just a little while ago, a man sat, his body and most of his face in the shadows, a dark hoodie pulled low over his face. He tilted the phone just so, and Al recognized him.

Greg Turner, and he held Al's phone in his hand, just out of reach. Al swallowed hard.

"Recognition setting in slowly?" the man asked, chuckling again.

"How in blazes did you get…?"

"In here? Al, that's such a dumb question. I worked for months to figure that out. I slept in the woods. I stole food and water, just so you would think you'd be safe and present me this perfect opportunity to strike."

Al wanted to ask *what do you want* but closed his mouth again. Turner wanted revenge—nothing else. Nothing he, Al could offer the man right then would be enough. He wasn't even entertaining the fantasy of fighting him off. But the hell if he was giving Turner the satisfaction of begging.

"Where are my brothers?" he asked instead, trying to see into the dark corners of the room, just in case…

"They are—safe."

"Pardon me if your kind of safe is not exactly easing my mind," Al said. "Where are Dante and Roberto?"

"Am I not being clear enough?" Turner asked, rose from Al's chair, and came a few steps closer. In addition to Al's phone, he held something else in his hand, something that made Al draw back just the tiniest bit.

"I see you recognize this," Greg said with a leer. "If you need more information, it's a Glock .45-caliber pistol. Bit heavy for my taste. But from what I'm told, it is the go-to weapon for—situations like this. For criminals like your father and your entire cursed family. You are likely familiar with it then."

"Not really," Al said dryly.

Turner pointed the weapon at Al and peered down its long barrel.

"You know, I'm actually a little impressed," he said. "I expected you to begin that long and boring process where you pretend to ask me what I want, and I pretend there is actually something I want, and then we both pretend to negotiate. It is rather tedious."

Al allowed himself a small smile, while his mind was clicking through possibilities. Physically, he was in no shape to attempt to attack Turner and have any hope of overwhelming him. Stall then, make time. At some point Rafael would wonder where he was and why he hadn't come back to the celebrations downstairs. If he managed to hold off Turner until then…

"What would the point be?" he asked instead. "I know exactly what you want."

"Oh?"

"Yes." Al sat back on his bed, folding his hands behind his head. "Of course I do. You left a very precise note behind after you shot my father."

"That was a mistake." Turner's eyes flashed with sudden anger, and he waved the gun in front of Al. "I should have just walked away and taken you out at the next possible opportunity. And then your dumb brothers."

"Oh, but where would the fun be in that, Greg? Nobody would know who had shot me and why. It would be confusing. People would think some nutjob in the cannabis space had done it. Oh, wait, that's exactly what happened."

"You might not want to get me mad," Greg snapped. "At least not until I tell you where your precious brothers are."

True. Al carefully composed his face as neutrally as possible and brought his fingertips to his lips.

"Revenge, Greg. That's what you want. Revenge. Because your father killed himself and left you to a less-than-stellar youth and upbringing. Am I right so far?"

"Wouldn't you have done the same thing?"

"I don't know." Al folded his fingers and raised his eyes to the ceiling. "Since you did shoot Tadeo, I'm assuming you chose this course of action because you thought he was a terrible person. I spent my whole life with him, so, would I shoot somebody because of that? Probably not. Then again—ah—it's just so hard to know what you would have done when you're facing someone holding a gun on you. I don't know. It makes it a bit difficult to…"

"Shut the fuck up."

Turner trembled a little, and Al kept his eyes on the gun. *Where are you, Rafael?* he thought. *I know I said I didn't want a nursemaid. That doesn't mean you can't check on me.*

"You talk way too much."

"Is that a fact? Usually, I'm told I clam up too much."

Turner jumped to his feet and paced the small room—one end to the other and back. Al folded his hands and forced the growing terror inside down. Where was Rafael then? Turner was nervous, and the hand holding the gun shook—why? Was it possible that he had spent all of his energy and imagination on getting in here, finding and confronting him… and thought no further? Was it possible that now, after what had to be months of preparation, he didn't know what to do?

"So why don't you do the talking? Tell me about your father and why you shot mine for him."

"You know exactly why—your father ruined mine."

Al shrugged. "Business…"

"He didn't have to ruin him. He could have—found another club, bought another building. Instead, he chose to ruin what my father had built, drive him into bankruptcy, and eventually…"

"Eventually into death, yes," Al agreed. "Would it make you feel better if I told you that I disagree with my father's methods? Of course, I was just a wee lad back then. I hardly knew the word disagree."

Come on, Rafael, Al thought again. *How long do I need to stall this man?* He estimated he had been asleep for about an hour. Given that he had told Rafael he only wanted to lie down for a brief nap…

"There's no use staring at the door, you know? Nobody is coming to check on you." Al cursed himself again for being so obvious.

"Oh no?" he asked, forcing a bit of levity into his voice. "You think they are so happy to be rid of me for a bit they'll just party on?"

"That documentary is a fucking joke," Turner spat. "Nothing but some media hype dreamed up by your pal Barry Wentworth."

"Wentworth does have oddball ideas sometimes. You're right on that score," Al said, forcing more levity into his voice. "Although I must ask you not to call him my pal. We do tend to disagree on most concepts of life and ethics, I have to say. As a matter of fact…"

"Didn't I ask you to shut up just now?"

"Of course. As you wish."

Al nodded and rested his hands in his lap. Turner was getting more nervous. For some reason, he was jittery and anxious. If he could just keep him here, contained, until somebody showed up to check on him… For God's sake, one of his people would have to realize something was wrong when he didn't show up at the reception area again. Just one. They would have to.

Yes, he had sent everyone away, quite angrily so, but Rafael was used to that. He always came back. He always checked on the people he cared about, didn't he?

And Dante and Roberto? Where were they then?

Of course, he had told Roberto to stay out of the way of all things

PerCan a little less than a day ago, he remembered. He'd even been quite snippy about it. *Do not make a mess of my company here, Roberto. You've ruined yours. Leave mine alone.*

Turner got up and put his ear to the door, all the while keeping his gun trained on Al. He opened the door just a crack, and Al sat up a little straighter.

"Say a word, Ivers, and the last thing you hear is going to be a big bang. Either way, I'm going to shoot you. You decide when."

Again, Al nodded and sat perfectly still, hardly daring to breathe. Time—he needed time. Time for Rafael to figure out something was wrong, time for Roberto…

Nobody was out in the hall. He could have told Turner that. Every single staff member in security had been on duty during the day, while the TV crew was here, and at this time of the evening, they would be down to a man or two, mostly patrolling the perimeter. Everybody was keeping an eye on the perimeter, as a matter of fact.

He remembered it too clearly. 'Once the TV fellows are gone, we can relax and breathe again,' Rafael had told him. 'Then we'll scale back security to perimeter again, as per normal.' Yet Turner—Turner had somehow managed to slip past them already. How? While everybody was looking at Verhoeven and his crew?

Kayla would have invited the remaining staff to leave early after the stress and pressure of the last few weeks. They had all figured they would be in the clear, once the day was over. They had been wrong.

"Let's go." Turner stepped back to the room and nodded for him to stand up. In his hands were a few of the long, sturdy cable ties Rafael used to keep wiring organized and out of the way.

"Where are we going?"

"Always with the questions—you'll find out in good time, Ivers."

"Then I am not going anywhere."

Al sat stubborn, straight-backed, hands folded in his lap. Maybe not the smartest move, but better than letting Turner here boss him around. He was getting a bit tired of it.

"Fine, then—if this little room is where you would like to die. I thought you wanted to see Dante and Roberto."

He brought up the gun again and poked it straight under Al's chin. Al could feel the cold steel, feel the pressure of it against his neck.

"No, wait."

The gun lowered again.

"If we are going to see Dante and Roberto…"

"Make up your mind, Ivers, will you?"

He roughly grabbed Al by the elbow, dragged him to his feet, spun him around, and tied his hands with cable ties, all without having to put the gun down even once. He gave him a hard push in the back and Al stumbled a little.

"You are weak—all of you Ivers brats are weak," Turner joked. "I was worried you wouldn't make it there for a while. Thought somebody else had got there before me and poisoned you. That would have been a shame if I couldn't shoot you. Wouldn't it be?"

He shoved Al again, and Al nodded.

"Then I figured out Roberto's dumbass move with the grow medium. So stupid. Really, really dumb thing to do. Jesus Christ, I'm surprised you didn't kill him yourself over it."

"Always with the killing."

Greg only chuckled.

"I thought it had been you with the grow medium, Greg. How did you figure out…" Al asked before he could stop himself. He didn't want to give Turner the attention he so obviously craved, but something told him to keep the man talking. While he was talking, he wasn't waving that gun around.

"Easy." Turner shrugged and gave Al another push. "Broke into his place, wasn't all that hard. Wasn't that hard to find the information either, once I knew what I was looking for. Do all of you Ivers goons think you are smarter than everybody else? Does it surprise you that a guy like me can figure out things? Is it because Tadeo had money and privilege?"

Al only shook his head.

"Let me tell you something. He might have had money, but he was a rotten-ass human being. You understand that, don't you?"

Al said nothing again, eliciting another push from Turner. "Answer me, Ivers. Do you understand?"

"I hear you, and I understand your words," Al said stiffly. "Whether or not I agree with you is my own affair and none of your business."

Turner opened his mouth to answer, shut it again, and only shook his head. Out in the hall, it was just as dark as it had been in his room. Turner appeared to have cut the lights in the entire building, including emergency lights. How in blazes could he do that—and moreover do it without Rafael noticing?

Then another thought occurred to him, and he felt as if someone had gut punched him. What if Rafael couldn't notice any longer, couldn't come to his aid because Turner had already dealt with him? What if...?

"Move."

Al put one step in front of the other, carefully, slowly, listening in the dark for any slight bit of noise, any sign that there were still human beings in this building. He'd walked these corridors thousands of times, during the day, at night. He should know what his own building sounded like, but walking in the dark was another thing entirely. Unbidden, an image of Rafael came to mind. *"I know this building so well I could find my way around any time, blindfolded and hobbled."*

Where are you now, Rafael? Where are you now?

"I said move." Turner shoved him in the back again—a little harder this time—and Al shuffled forward, reluctantly.

"Where are we going?" he finally asked, and Turner shook his head. "None of your business. Just walk."

If his sense of orientation had not taken a powder entirely, Al thought, they were walking toward the production areas. Good. The moment he discovered the cut lights, Rafael would come to find him, and no one knew the production areas better than he did. Usually, Rafael checked the damn security and his precious processes every 10 minutes, for crying out loud. Time—he just needed a bit of time. And he needed Rafael to be alive and well.

He stopped and pretended to have to catch his breath.

"Last warning, Ivers."

Turner pushed him in the back, and Al stumbled. Not entirely by accident, and not entirely planned either. It just happened. He tripped, stumbled, and fell, catching his elbow on the cement floor. He cried out with a curse that would have made Rafael proud and stayed down.

"Get up, Ivers. You don't want me to shoot you lying face-down in the hall, do you?"

"I prefer you not shoot me at all," Al got out, coughing and wheezing for good measure. "But I've just spent weeks in the hospital. I need a moment."

"You don't have a moment. My father didn't have a moment either. Now get the fuck up."

Al struggled. Greg Turner grabbed him by the scruff of the neck to straighten him out, and Al went limp, completely and totally limp. That Glock in Turner's hand—perhaps he could just… Turner fought to lift him upright, failed to do so, and all but fell down beside him, but the gun stayed out of range.

"Get—up—now," Turner screamed and put the muzzle of the Glock to Al's temple. Time was one thing, foolishness another.

Al struggled to his feet, considered briefly kicking at Turner's legs as he did so, and gave up on the thought again. Too risky, too little chance of success. Turner was unhinged already. A bit more might put him right over the top, and no one could know what would happen then.

He finally stood upright again, closed his eyes, and leaned against the wall for a minute. "Sorry, just one…"

"No more moments. You've had all the breaks you're going to get. We are not playing around here. Nobody is coming for you. Now move forward and don't try that again."

Turner walked behind him now and pressed the gun to Al's back. They walked in darkness and silence, Al orienting himself with his elbow against the wall, until he almost hit the metal wing doors at the end of the corridor. This was the airlock into the production areas.

"This is kind of my home, you know." Again, he could all but hear Rafael's voice in his head.

Greg Turner could not have done him a greater favor than dragging him here, into the production areas. Rafael would be there. He would come for him. He was sure of that. But where had Turner taken his brothers? He didn't dare to ask. He would find out soon enough, he thought, and a part of him was afraid what it was he would be finding out soon enough.

Turner gave him a little nudge in the back once again.

"Go on then," he said with a small amount of glee in his voice. "I'm sure you've figured out where we are. Walk on now."

FORTY-ONE

Barry took a step forward, and Rafael grabbed his shirtsleeve. "Don't."

"What do you mean don't?"

"I mean do not walk in there. We need a couple of good strong flashlights."

Barry flicked on the flashlight on his cellphone and held it up. It illuminated the entry lock and change areas to about five feet in front of them.

"Geez, Rafa. You'd think…"

"That's not gonna do it. That'll help if you drop your keys in the driveway at night, but not in our production rooms. There are no windows, and all the electric terminals are down. There is not going to be one speck of light in there. Not one."

"So? Don't you know this place like the back of your hand?"

"I do." Rafael cursed and pulled Barry back again. "Don't you think I want to run in there and find Turner and Al and his brothers, huh? But if it is indeed Turner who is behind all of this, I can almost guarantee you he's laid some traps for us out there. You want to stumble into something? You want to run right into his arms?"

"No, of course not. I understand."

The pressure against Rafael's hand lessened a bit.

"There are high-voltage cables in there too, chemical lines, water lines, the whole bit. Usually, they're secured so nobody can—accidentally step on or dislodge something. Turner? He's crazier than a hoot owl if you ask me. He could well have…"

"I said I get it, Rafael."

Barry stepped back and turned off the flashlight on his phone. "Now what? We call the cops? Security services, guards—what?"

"No, that would take too long." Rafael took off his glasses and rubbed suddenly tired eyes. "I'm going to go down to the security room and get two big flashlights. You find Kayla please. Tell her to stay put in the boardroom, no matter what happens, and call the police from there. That's the safest spot for her right now. Robertson and the cavalry should get here in moments—but do not let them into production areas before I've restored at least some lights. Is that understood?"

"Again, with the Rambo tactics." Barry rolled his eyes. "You want to be that hero, jumping through fire and explosions, is that it?"

"Please don't mention explosions right now," Rafael said and looked away. Barry grabbed his sleeve and pulled.

"Wait, what? What are you not telling me?"

"I don't want to go there."

"Well, you damn well better. What's out there you don't want me to know about?"

Rafael sighed, turned, and stalked off with giant steps in the direction of the security offices.

"Rafael!"

"What? Hurry and get to Kayla."

"Rafael!" Barry took two giant steps, grabbed Rafael by the elbow, and spun him around. "Rafael Covin, so help me God, I've known you for at least 20 years. And I know when you're trying to hide something from me. You suck at it. So, what's out there in that manufacturing area that you don't want me to know about?"

Rafael sighed and looked down at his shoes.

"Come on."

"Grow pod five has been giving me headaches for the past few weeks—maybe longer, actually. Always infections, always bacteria," he said, not looking Barry in the eyes.

"And?"

"And I finally had it with the thing. So I—sterilized—the whole pod, with gas."

"What the hell does that even mean?"

When he got irritated or nervous, all of Barry's nice manners could go out the window. And just then, he had no patience for niceties.

"Ethylene oxide, Barry," Rafael sighed. "It's used to sterilize heat- and moisture-sensitive areas, and I got tired of always battling issues in that pod. Regular treatments just weren't working. So, I flushed the whole pod with gas and let it soak. Figured I would vent it when the TV people were gone. Then it would be so clean in there you could perform heart surgery on our grow racks."

Barry brought his fist to his mouth and sighed. He waited a moment and nodded, letting go of Rafael.

"I take it that stuff—is kind of dangerous, isn't it?"

"Yup." Rafael raised his hands and mimicked a giant explosion. "Very. So, you understand why I don't want anyone stumbling around in there who doesn't know what he's doing and can't see his way more than a few feet. You cause a spark somewhere or an electrical short… I mean—it's contained to pod five, but…"

"Got it." Barry forked his hands through his hair and nodded again. "Got it. Go get those damned flashlights then, but I'm still not letting you go in there by yourself."

"But I will be just…"

"You'll be just fine, but two pairs of eyes still see more than one. You're going to get those flashlights and wait over there by that door while I warn Kayla and tell her to get the cavalry. Then we are going in—together."

Rafael acknowledged him with a tiny nod and went off in the direction of the security offices. Yes, he'd thought at the time, maybe it would be better to wait to work on the sterilization until after the TV crews were gone, but he'd done it anyway.

He'd been too damned impatient, wanting to come in tomorrow morning to a newly sterilized grow pod. This had been the last thing he wanted to try before tearing out the entire pod and rebuilding it from the ground up. Something about it had never quite gone right. Some design flaw in the structure, perhaps, some error when they put it up—who knew?

Should have listened to his gut. He'd known something was off, that someone had been there. From the moment he had found footprints of a running shoe in the manufacturing area. In his gut, he had known.

Footprints! That meant Turner had been coming and going as he pleased, maybe for weeks. He should have known. But like all human beings, he had this way of telling himself that he was imagining things, telling himself there was a logical explanation, because he didn't really believe in that intuition stuff. There was always a rational explanation—until there wasn't.

Could have, should have, would have. None of that was helping now. He needed to find and warn Al, Dante, and even Roberto, before that nutcase Turner did something to them. All this while keeping Kayla safe.

Oh, he was sure enough it was Turner behind the power outage and the fright he was feeling just then.

Wait until I get my hands on you, he grumbled as he touch-felt his way into the security office by the meager glow of his cellphone screen. *Just wait.* For a moment, it was entertaining to imagine what he would do to Greg Turner—but there was work to be done.

Kayla needed to stay put in the boardroom. Despite its glass front, he had built it with all manner of safeguards against potential disasters. Except, of course, for a madman being loose in the building.

And nothing was more dangerous than a man who wasn't thinking rationally, he thought, finally wrestling open the supply cupboard and digging out the flashlights. Heavy, rechargeable things, shielded against moisture, chemicals, electrical arcs. He didn't go cheap on safety equipment—or on alarm systems. So how in God's name had Turner managed to break in?

And where was his cavalry, Detective Robertson's crew?

He didn't want them to stomp around production like a massive herd of elephants, but he would have felt better knowing they were around.

No time now. Move, he told himself, grabbed a couple of flashlights, stuck an extra one in his belt—just in case—and took off again.

Barry was already waiting by the airlock and looked him up and down in the light of the welcome room, the only light source still available.

"Expecting anybody else?" Barry asked with a look at the spare light.

"No. But if I drop one, I can still use the other to whack that shiftless bastard over the head until he's unconscious."

"I don't think that's going to be necessary."

Rafael flashed him an angry look, and both of them relaxed again. Carefully, as he had before, Rafael pushed open the heavy metal doors and stepped inside, shining the beam of his powerful flashlight as he went.

Rows of lockers, gowns, shoe covers, hairnets—everything one needed to suit up for the sterile areas of the growing pods. Finding no one, he signaled Barry and walked as soundlessly as he could across the airlock to the second set of doors to actual production.

During the day, he never thought about those 20 steps across to the second set of doors. His eyes and ears would already be tuned to the sounds and sight of the operation. The hum of the air exchanges and the lighting generators would tell him those were running correctly. The soft swish of the pumps that routed water and fertilizer when and where it was required told him his plants were getting what they needed. Now, the entire place lay in darkness and silence.

Those plants are going to be toast, he thought, cursing himself at the same time. Who thought of a harvest of cannabis plants at a time like this? He did, of course.

He opened the second set of doors and stood, listening into the silence for a moment. Nothing. Less than nothing. He felt more than heard Barry behind him. Barry tapped his shoulder, pointed at himself, and signaled to the right. Rafael nodded and started for the left.

Step by step, they circled around the massive production halls. Every now and then, he stopped, closed his eyes, and forced his ears to pick out the slightest bit of noise. Did he hear someone walking? Did he hear a cough? Or was that Barry circling around the other way?

Jesus, if Turner really was out here, he could just follow their flashlight beams and know exactly where they went, he thought, and dropped his hand with the light so the yellow beam became at least a bit narrower.

The access halls between the independent grow pods and harvesting rooms were narrow and frequently made more so by equipment consoles sticking out from the walls. These screens were supposed to be lit so a technician could see at a glance what was going on. Rafael made a fist. Never mind. He'd bring his system back. He'd restore everything and bring it back better than ever, and then he would have independent generators powering these things.

He took a few more steps and realized he had come to another intersection between the outer access walks and the inner ones. If he turned off here, he would end up with the first row of grow pods. Right where his famous trouble spot was located—pod five. *Should I check it out?* he wondered. Should he check on that gas line, and the venting process? He could turn it off, make sure nobody could use it against them.

He took two steps, stopped again, and turned back. Recon first, then find Al, then deal with pod five. In that order. Even if he didn't want it to, it made too much damned sense. So, he continued his slow circle, waiting, watching, listening, and hoping he would find Turner. Hoping he would find Al and the whole thing would already be over. But with every step, he was faced with more silence, darkness, and nothing else.

Goddamned silence. Goddamned silence was unnatural and put his nerves on edge. He was just about ready to punch someone out.

Easy now. He hadn't lived through a hurricane and subsequent quarantine just to lose his marbles in his own production hall. But this goddamned silence made it difficult to form a coherent thought.

More steps, more listening and checking. And then he saw it—in the distance, straight ahead at the end of the hallway, a yellow pool of light grew. Every muscle in his body tensed, and he realized he was gripping the flashlight like a bat ready to swing, when he saw it was Barry coming his way.

Of course.

"Nothing," Barry said, shielding his light, coming to stand beside him. "You?"

"Nothing." Rafael shook his head. "Doesn't make any damned sense. Why go through all this and leave us in this triple fucking silence?"

A heavy hand rose and landed on Rafael's shoulder.

"To freak you out," Barry said softly. "Listen to yourself, swearing, jumping at every noise. You were ready to attack me back there. Don't lose it on me now."

"Easy for you to say."

"No, it's not. I just don't want to give Turner the satisfaction of playing his mind games. That's all he's doing—mind games. Don't let him into your head."

He'd raised his voice on the last sentence, and automatically, Rafael's eyes flicked around. Left, right, front, back—nothing.

"Don't, Rafael. He's here somewhere—hidden, probably playing with himself and getting his kicks watching us."

Again, Barry had raised his voice. Rafael automatically cringed, but watching Barry, standing at the ready, shoulders squared, automatically gave him a little boost. He was not alone.

"Well, come on out then, Greg Turner," Barry called out, slowly turning in a slow circle, scanning the darkness around them. "You wanted revenge—here we are. Are you going to hide in the darkness like a damned cockroach?"

Still, nothing happened. Rafael thought he heard a noise somewhere off in the far corner of the hall. By the way Barry cocked his head and looked in the same direction, he thought Barry heard it too.

"Turner?" he asked almost soundlessly.

"No," Barry called out louder than ever. "Couldn't be Turner. Because Greg Turner is crawling around in the dark, hiding like a cockroach."

"Turn it down with the roach insults, will you," Rafael said softly. "What are you trying to do—provoke him into coming at us, guns blazing?"

"That's if he has a gun. We don't know that. And there are two of us. So far, all he's done is turn off the power and spook everybody."

Moments stretched into infinity. Automatically, Rafael and Barry stood back to back, staring into the darkness.

"This is stupid," Barry called out all of a sudden. "I'm not going to wait around here for Turner to grow a brain and come out of hiding. Let's just go bring power back and let the police have at him."

"I wouldn't do that if I were you, gentlemen."

The voice came from everywhere and nowhere at the same time. Rafael frowned and flicked his gaze left, right, and back again. The PA system was old and basic, a leftover relic from a time when this building had been a manufacturing hall. He'd meant to tear it out at some point, meant to get rid of it—but there always was something more important to do. Until then, it wasn't bothering anybody.

But Turner—Turner had found it. Found it and commandeered it just like the power to the control systems, and the lights, and who knew what else. How? How did he move around as he liked?

"Well, what is it you want then, huh?" Barry asked out loud, turning in a slow circle again. "Because this is a stupid game—hide and seek in the dark."

Turner laughed. His laughter echoed through the silent production hall, sending shivers down Rafael's spine.

"What do I want? But dear Barry—or do you prefer Connor?—you know what I want. I want the Ivers men dead. And surely you of all people would welcome the world being rid of them, no?"

"No, I wouldn't," Barry snapped.

There was no way to tell where Turner was actually located. The security office perhaps? No, Rafael thought, that was too obvious. If he had hacked into the system, he could literally be anywhere… but there was one person he couldn't hide from. One person who could find him, no matter what hole he had crawled into. An idea grew in his mind and made his heart beat a little faster. Someone could locate Turner all right, and that someone might even be able to neutralize him.

Rafael signaled Barry to come a little closer and crouched down.

"Tessa," he whispered, cupping his hands over his mouth. "Tessa can find him. Maybe even neutralize him. Keep him busy."

Barry only nodded.

"Your war with the Ivers men is getting a little old, Greg."

He yelled and stood to shield Rafael with his body. Turner might be watching them, wherever he was, wherever he was hiding. No point in taking a chance.

They needed to get moving again—quickly. This building was massive, and anything they could do to keep Turner off-balance until the police arrived would have to do.

But first, he needed to get word to Tessa—somehow. Rafael and Barry had always wondered if she really had been a hacker at some point in her life, or if it was just a rumor she enjoyed letting people believe. Watching her fingers on her computer, it was entirely possible.

If there was anyone who could get into their systems, no matter what Turner had done or damaged, it was Tessa. She had the skills. And once she had him… Once she had him, pray to God she could lock him out, Rafael hoped.

The alternative didn't bear thinking about because it involved tracking down Turner on their own, on foot, room by room, before he got to the gas lines down by pod five. Did Turner know about the gas, or had he broken in here with the express purpose of just terrorizing? Did he even have a plan? And where were Al and his brothers?

And for God's sake, why were the police not showing up? Kayla had to have reached them by now. Told them it was urgent. What—*take a message and we'll get to you as soon as we can?* Shit!

Now what was he going to tell Tessa? She had gone home hours ago, surely had no idea what was going on at PerCan. He had only one shot at explaining things to her while crouching here in the dark with Turner possibly listening in. Unless he asked Kayla to call her. Kayla should still be hunkered down in the boardroom, with a working phone.

"First of all," Barry called out. "None of those three men ever did anything to you."

Again, the manic laughter echoed through the hall.

"Ah, but you were partners in crime with Roberto, Barry. Did you think I missed that? Did you think I didn't research how that information about Al Ivers and his criminal father came to me just at the time I was about to sign a merger with him? You just keep underestimating me! Just like the Ivers boys."

Somewhere in the building, a shot was fired, and both Barry and Rafael froze. Was that the cavalry coming to ride in now, or was it Greg Turner?

But Turner laughed again, the sound echoing crazily around the silent manufacturing halls. Barry and Rafael automatically ducked down.

"Precious," Turner giggled. "So precious. Did you wet your pants there? Or were you hoping it was the police coming to save your sorry asses? For your information, I wouldn't wait for them. I locked them out and us in. It's just us chickens in here."

Again, he giggled, and Rafael shuddered. He hid the screen of his cell phone and thumb-typed furiously, hoping to God that Kayla would understand what on earth he was thinking of, that she'd be able to call Tessa, and that Tessa would pick up. That sounded like a lot of ifs.

"You're right," Barry said, as if talking to a child. "I didn't like Tadeo

Ivers when he came to the company and wanted to call the shots. But Al is a different story."

"They are all the same," Turner insisted. "Never mind now. I will take care of them."

I will take care. Not *I already have.* Barry turned to Rafael and mouthed the words *I will,* and Rafael put his thumbs up. If he was correct, they still had a tiny bit of time—a chance.

FORTY-TWO

Al Ivers slowly sat up in complete darkness once again and blinked a few times. He brought his hand to his face and didn't see a single thing, until, somewhere close by, a cheap lighter flicked, illuminating his brother Roberto's face with an eerie orange glow.

"Aren't you glad I still smoke?"

"What happened?" Al asked. "Where are we? Where is Dante?"

"Dante is in the corner—still out. That sick fuck Turner cornered us when we were going back down to Reception, held a gun on us, and marched us down here."

"Where is down here?"

"Jesus, brother, don't you know your own plant? You spend all your time behind the glass upstairs? Far as I can tell, we're inside an empty grow pod. But you tell me."

An empty grow pod. Al's mind clicked away quickly. There was only one grow pod empty just now—pod five. The one that had had all the trouble with infections. Roberto clicked off the lighter.

"Got to save fuel for now, you know."

"Is Dante all right?" Al went into a crouch and tried to feel his way into the area where he had seen a crumpled heap on the floor. A crumpled heap that was most likely his brother, Dante.

"He'll have a headache when he wakes up," Roberto said dryly. "And without his crutches, he won't get far, but otherwise he's OK."

"Thank God." Al gently touched his brother's face and struggled to get comfortable. "What about you?"

"Me?" Al shrugged, forgetting that Roberto couldn't see him. "Same thing, I guess. One minute, I'm sleeping—next minute, Turner is marching me down the hall at gunpoint. Must have knocked me out when we got to the door and shoved me in here."

"Sounds about right," Roberto confirmed. "Now what? How the fuck did Turner get in here, with a TV crew and all of Rafael's security systems on high alert?"

"I don't have the slightest idea," Al snapped. He had reached Dante and confirmed his younger brother appeared to be breathing still. "You're the one of us who isn't injured. I don't know why you're sitting there doing nothing instead of trying to break us out of here."

"Brother, we're inside a grow pod," Roberto said darkly, and Al wanted to slap him.

"So?"

"So, I'm not Superman. I can't break a pod that's locked. Not the way Rafael builds them anyway. The only tools I have are a lighter and the nail clippers I used to get the cable ties off your hands."

Al rubbed his wrists where Greg had tied them. He could still feel the grooves the ties had left. "Thank you. But you could at least try."

They were quiet for a moment, and Al cocked his head. From somewhere, he thought he heard the faint echo of a voice—a voice that wasn't directed at him, but…

"Turner," he said, localizing the sound. "He must have got into the old PA system. Why?"

Roberto listened for a moment. "Could be he is just certifiably insane," he finally said, and Al heard him shuffle, as if he were getting more comfortable.

"Try and get us out of here, Rob," he said. "Please. If I know Rafael, I know he's trying to get to us. So, at the same time, if you would—please."

"I'm not even entirely sure where the door is, Al."

"Well, for God's sake, use your lighter."

Roberto chuckled, and suddenly, Al felt something cold creep down his spine. "Don't you think we should be a bit careful with that, brother? Emergencies only."

"Why? Why do you say that?"

"Don't you smell it?" Roberto took a noisy breath as if to show Al.

"What are you talking about?"

"You don't spend enough time in production, brother. Rafael has gas-sterilized this pod, I don't know when, and I don't know how much, but I do know we want to be a bit careful with an open flame around here."

"Gas-sterilized, my God! And you lit that thing anyway?"

Al was just about to turn and scream at his brother when the unmistakable sound of a gunshot brought them all up short. Even Dante stirred, murmuring unintelligibly.

"Better hope that wasn't one of your friends," Roberto said dryly, and Al wanted to hit him.

"Find a way out of here—now. Any way you can," he snapped and turned to help Dante sit up.

"It's not that easy."

"If it were easy, we would not have been locked in here, Roberto. Get to work." Al struggled to his feet and finally added, "Please."

He heard Roberto sigh and get to his feet as well. He turned back to Dante and put an arm under his shoulder.

"Are you OK?"

"Good as I can be," Dante grunted. "Please don't piss off Roberto now. We do need him to get out of here."

"I'm not pissing him off. I am just—urging him to come up with creative solutions that will get us out."

"I heard that," Roberto called out of the darkness. "And you are pissing me off, big brother. You always have. From the time we were little."

"Just find the door, please." Al felt around his neck. "My ID badge is gone," he said to Dante. "You?"

"No." Dante shook his head. "First thing he took off us."

"Well, that explains how he's getting around. I still can't figure out how he got in here without tripping any of the alarms and how he managed to get control of the electricity and lighting."

"And the backup generators, all of them," Dante added. "Don't forget that. No, the only thing that will do all that is an executive-level badge."

"If you're thinking of blaming either Rafael or Kayla…"

"I'm not saying they are to blame, Al. Jesus, I just said *if* he got hold of an exec badge, then he could have done all of this. Simmer down."

Al felt his hands clench and forcibly relaxed them again.

"Anything?" he called out instead in the direction where he thought Roberto should be.

"Yup, there's a door here." The voice came back at him from a completely different direction.

"Great—thank you for the information, brother. Now figure out how to get out of here. Every prison has an exit."

"I know that." Suddenly, Roberto was standing beside him again, and, again, Al had to force himself to relax and not punch him in the face.

"Well?"

"Your problem is Rafael."

"What would Rafael have to do with us being locked in here?" Al snapped. He opened his mouth to continue, but Roberto took his shoulder.

"Everything, big brother, everything. Rafael designed those doors to seal perfectly. Anything that shouldn't be here is kept out, and everything in here is kept in. In a perfect world, that's how it's supposed to work."

"But…"

"I mean a perfect seal, Al. There is nothing in this world that will release that, unless it's keyed up from the panel outside. It's a design feature—or flaw, I guess, in our case."

"Can't you—I don't know—break a hinge or something? This is ridiculous."

"Electronic locking hinges. Designed to lock down if the power goes down for a short period of time, usually until the backup gennies kick in. It prevents all these doors opening, letting in dust, dirt, and whatnot in the event of power fluctuations."

"You read Rafa's design specs."

"I read Rafa's design specs, and I told you a little while ago, Al—we are not getting out of here until Turner either opens that door or blows up the entire grow pod with us in it."

Al took a step backwards and bumped into one of the stainless-steel growing tables. He reached out a hand to steady himself and gripped the cold smooth steel.

Good God, he thought, but for once, he decided to keep his mouth shut.

FORTY-THREE

Kayla seldom yelled. At least she tried not to. But just then, she found herself screaming into the phone, using language she had not used in years. Barry and Rafael had gone down there, into the complete darkness of the manufacturing areas, relying on her to contact the police and to summon help. Immediate help. But suddenly, here was this random officer refusing to dispatch every man he could spare.

This was not how you dealt with Perfect Cannabis Corporation, and it most assuredly was not how you dealt with Kayla Montecito.

"We have a wanted criminal in this building, who is probably keeping several of our executives hostage. I expect you to…"

"We are working on it, ma'am, but we cannot just barge in there."

"You are already here, for God's sake!" Kayla yelled. "Does the right hand know what the left is doing in your outfit down there? Detective Robertson and a few of his men are right outside our building, keeping an eye on things. In a surveillance van. All you need to do is contact him and tell him…"

"I know that, Mrs. Montecito. Detective Robertson and his men are at your location, but they have been ordered to keep a safe distance for the moment."

Kayla blinked and grappled for an answer for a second. She stepped back, but the chair that should be there wasn't. Ordered to keep away?

"What do you mean a safe distance?" she growled. "What on earth are you talking about?"

"I can't tell you that either, Ms…"

His voice was trembling; she could tell even over the phone. Kayla took a deep breath, stuffed down the anger that was threatening to explode, and forced herself to take it down a notch.

"Listen to me. I am here, in this building. My fiancé and our CEO, Al Ivers, are in this building. So is Barry Wentworth, who is these days handling the fundraising campaign for the mayor's office. You follow me? The mayor personally. Good. Now please tell me why on earth Detective Robertson and his crew would be under orders to stand down? It is ludicrous."

The officer on the phone exhaled deeply and said nothing.

"Please," Kayla added, feeling her fingernails digging deeply into her palm.

"Get yourself out of that building if you can, Ms. Montecito. That is the only advice I can give you. We have had a credible report that there was an explosive device inside the manufacturing area there. If it blows…"

"A what?"

Kayla dropped into the chair behind her, swallowed hard, and gripped the edge of the desk. "What are you talking about?"

"Get yourself out of there if you can."

"But how do you…"

"We've had a call warning us of a bomb inside PerCan, Ms. Montecito. I shouldn't be telling you this, but—if you are inside, all of you, get out of there if you can."

"Wait, wait, wait just a minute," Kayla said. "I am inside, and there's no bomb here. There is a criminal. It's just a hoax—he made it up, to keep you away," She stared at the glass window into manufacturing and the impenetrable darkness beyond. "How…"

"It's not a hoax. And it wasn't an anonymous call. The caller identified himself as Gregory Turner, and the caller ID placed him inside the building there."

She swallowed briefly, relaxed her fist, and rolled her shoulders.

"Of course the attacker is inside this building, Officer," she said, clenching her teeth so hard her jaw hurt. "He is the one holding our executives captive. And as long as he is doing that, he won't blow the place up."

Unless Turner was crazy enough to want to end his own life, she thought. Unless he really had gone over the edge and did not care if he died along with everyone else. All of the Ivers men, and Rafael, and her right along with them.

Kayla swallowed hard.

"Ms. Montecito, are you still there?"

"Yes."

"We've called in reinforcements, officers who are trained to deal with explosives, but it will take them a while to get there. They—were at a nuisance call across town. Please. You need to get out of that building, now."

"I can't talk right now."

She hung up the phone and went to stand as close as she could to the glass window and put her palm against it. *What should I do, Rafael?* she thought. *Tell me what I should do.*

The glass felt cool and solid under her hands, but a shudder went through her nevertheless.

What if it blew up? What if the whole place blew up? she thought and automatically took a little step back from the glass wall. She remembered the day when she had first seen this room and heard Rafael's voice in her mind.

"I've designed that boardroom to be the safest place in the whole building. The wall is right against a solid firewall, there are steel I-beams underneath it, and the front might be glass, but it's the highest-rated, shatterproof, blast-proof glass anyone ever made."

She remembered Tadeo giving Rafael a hard time about the cost, and Al telling them all to ignore his father's angry tirades, and she smiled at the memory.

Explosives.

She picked up her phone and pulled up the text app and Rafael's name. *Cops just told me there are explosives in the building.*

???

They say they were warned. Get out of there.

The little dancing dots indicating Rafael was typing a reply moved for a moment, then stopped. Rafael didn't answer. Kayla stared at her phone and paced up and down the length of the boardroom. Beyond the glass wall, there was only darkness, but if she really squinted her eyes hard, she could imagine seeing Rafael down there. She wanted to reach down there mentally, grab a hold of him, and yank him out by the scruff of the neck if she had to.

Her phone finally chimed again. *Not without Al and his brothers.*

She cursed and hauled out with her arm, stopping herself just in time before she threw the phone against the wall. *Why on earth do you have to be so noble all the time?*

"Get out now!" She forced herself to type out the reply, even though she already knew it wouldn't do any good.

Not in this lifetime would Rafael save himself and leave the Ivers brothers and Barry behind.

Barry was still down there too. She could try and repeat the entire conversation with him, hoping he would drag out Rafael. Surely, Barry was not the type of man who wanted to go down with this building and Greg Turner. Maybe he would be able to talk some sense into him.

Her phone rang with an unknown number, and before she could think, she had answered it.

"Get yourself out while you can, Ms. Montecito."

"Who is this?"

"You know exactly who I am. I have no issue with you, so I'm giving you a one-time chance to get out of this building."

"Or what?" she spat, mustering a lot more courage than she actually felt. "Or you'll blow us all up? This is a state-of-the-art facility. We have safety systems and shutoffs in place. This is not happening."

"Do you now." Greg Turner laughed softly, and Kayla thought he really did sound mad. Dreadfully mad. "Well then. I control the lights and the power. I will leave it to you to imagine what else I might be in control of. Get out—now. Last warning."

Greg Turner hung up, and Kayla sat hard in a chair. "Rafael," she growled and struck the table.

How was she to know which system would work without power? How was she to know which vulnerabilities he already had or could exploit? Blueprints? Engineering drawings? Forget it—by the time she found them and understood them, the building could potentially be up in flames. Leaving what, exactly?

She jumped up and began to pace the boardroom again.

Maybe she should get out? Maybe caution was the better part of… *No thank you*, she thought, cutting herself off before her mind could go there. She would leave all right—at the last possible moment, when there was no chance and no hope of anything else any more. God help her to recognize that moment. She closed her eyes for just one second to center herself when her phone chimed once again. Rafael. Was he leaving?

She unlocked it with a touch and stared at the one word he had written: *Tessa*.

Tessa?

She tried texting back, but to no avail. But if he had texted her the name, then what? He meant to tell her Tessa would be able to help? Yes! If anyone could deal with Turner through cyberspace, she was the woman.

Kayla scrolled frantically through her massive contact list, hoping somewhere on her phone she would find Tessa's info. She didn't even know the woman's last name.

"Jesus Christ, come on, come on." She scrolled faster and faster, organizing contacts by first name, by company, by occupation—no Tessa.

"Help me out here," she screamed, ready to fling the phone against a wall again.

HR. The personnel department. They would have files. Would she be able to get in there? Where did they keep their files? Was it safe?

Her thoughts tumbled all over one another, her fingers shook, and then her phone dinged again. This time it was Barry Wentworth, and he only texted one line, a number. It had to be Tessa's.

"Thank you," she breathed and already opened her texting app, when another message from Barry came through.

Hurry.

How much time did she still have left? Enough to find Tessa and for her to get here while Barry and Rafael stumbled around in the dark, trying to find and stop Turner? How insane exactly was he?

Kayla sat down and unlocked her phone. Her fingers trembled so hard she could barely dial Tessa's number, hoping against hope the young woman was available, paying attention, and prone to answering a desperate call from an unknown number.

FORTY-FOUR

"So you agree with me—we think he's locked them into pod five?" Barry crouched down beside Rafael.

"Yep. And I'm afraid he might know all about the gas sterilization," Rafael said softly. "He's telling the cops and Kayla he's going to blow up the building and to stand back. Our cavalry is not coming to help. They're out there waiting for the bomb squad."

Barry put a hand on Rafael's shoulder.

"This would be the time if either one of us wanted to get out, you know."

Rafael only shook his head, even though Barry wouldn't be able to see it.

"Just saying, man."

"Go then if you want to."

"Rafael, how often have we been in a situation like this?"

"Trapped in a building with a madman, holding our friends captive, threatening to blow up everything? Never. I think I would remember."

"That's not what I mean, and you know it. With our backs against the wall."

Rafael only grunted assent.

"So? Then you know I am not leaving you behind either," Barry said, peering into the dark.

"Nobody left behind. Fine. We'll figure it out. Did you…"

"I texted her Tessa's number, and I told her to be careful."

Rafael crouched down a little lower and narrowed his eyes on grow pod number five. Nothing around it appeared to move. Nothing at all—but that didn't exactly put him at ease.

"This guy is so deep into our systems," he finally whispered. "When we get him, I'm going to break every bone in his body until he tells me how he did it."

The hand on his shoulder squeezed. "I think I just might help you with that. Now what?"

"Now we pray Tessa is on the ball and can get control of this building away from him. We have to assume he's watching pod five, hoping we come around, guns blazing, trying to rescue them. Go. Time to move again. Keep him guessing about our position. That's just about the only think we can do right now."

Both of them crouch-walked away to another access corridor, still keeping pod five in full view. For a moment, they sat in complete silence, until Barry adjusted his uncomfortable position on the floor. Rafael hunkered down and froze against the concrete floor. His body might have been screaming in protest at the unusual punishment, but he was going to fight Greg Turner—until the very last moment.

"I still don't see anything," Barry said, just to break the tension.

Rafael nodded in the direction of the pod. "See that pallet cart full of cardboard over there?"

"Yeah—it's a pallet cart. Loaded with packing materials. What of it?"

"Doesn't belong there."

"What do you mean it doesn't belong there?"

"Just what I'm saying, Barry. Packing materials belong in the shipping and receiving areas. No business being here in Growing. That means Turner put it there."

"I don't know, Rafa." Barry squinted at the area Rafael indicated. "We moved a lot of shit around today to make room for the TV crews when they needed it. Are you sure?"

"Might be what I would do," Rafael said softly. "Printed cardboard burns really hot if you want to light it. It also makes a whole lot of smoke, which is going to blind and disorient anyone looking for you. What do you think—is it easy to light?"

"Meaning he wants to start a fire, is that what you're saying?"

"Could be. He dragged it through half the building, so there's got to be a reason why."

"Jeez, Rafael, you only have good news for me today." Barry halted for a minute and closed his eyes. "Meanwhile, he tells the cops he has explosives? Is that his plan?"

"What do you mean?"

"He calls the police, tells them he has explosives inside the building, and instantly, everybody falls back? But think about it. Explosives are not exactly easy to come by, especially not if you're on the run, like Turner. But it is the one call every police station in the country dreads and will respond to in a very specific way."

"By calling in the bomb squad?" Rafael asked.

"Right again," Barry said. "By calling in the bomb squad—and waiting for them to get here. Meanwhile, you've bought yourself a few hours of noninterference. You light a big fire, do your shitty business, and disappear. Poof—but no bomb."

Rafael scratched his head. "I don't know. Got a point. But do you want to stake your life on that?"

"No," Barry said. "But I think it's awfully convenient that all of a sudden this man who's been on the run for months magically has explosives inside here. That's all. What if he's bluffing? What if he realized your gas-sterilization thingy there was actually a wonderful setup that played right into his hands?"

"Gas-sterilization thingy, Barry?"

"Oh, for heaven's sake, you know what I mean! He sees you have gas there…"

"Extremely flammable gas!"

"And he thinks great, bonus, nice big flame. I can call this a bomb—while meanwhile…?"

"Meanwhile, it's still highly flammable and still highly dangerous to the people we assume are in there, where the residue concentration of gas is still quite high, Barry. Let's not forget that."

"I know—I was fishing."

"So was I, Barry. I got you. I'm spending every second here, trying to figure out what his actual fucking plan is, and if he is messing with us, or trying to blow us up. Anything but what we are in fact looking at. I am trying. Fuck."

Barry's hand landed on his shoulder again and stayed there. A moment later, his phone vibrated in his pocket, and as he had done earlier, Barry shielded the lit screen inside his jacket and read. For the first time in the last hour, a slow smile appeared on his face.

"Tessa," he said softly. "Girl's on it—and she's armed."

FORTY-FIVE

Tess Goodwin didn't answer unknown phone numbers. Never. Way before it became a thing and fashionable, she had been the one to say, "I don't pick up unknowns," while everyone else still instantly reached for the phone, eager to have that nice conversation with some jerk who wanted to sell them a subscription or get them to buy into some scam. Dealer's choice. No thank you.

For her to reach for the phone and say hello when there was no ID bordered on a miracle, but her mind was keyed up that night, bouncing every which direction. She had watched the TV crews and Tim Verhoeven—whom she despised for his liberal views and attitudes—stalk around the building all day, and left PerCan as soon as humanly possible, without looking rude.

Small talk, social get-togethers, smiling at a slimy TV host—yeah, not really her thing. So, she made her apologies to Rafael and Barry and turned her back on the place.

She planned on buying a pizza and spending the rest of the evening playing a computer game she had acquired, which was so far kicking her ass. Progressing through the levels was far more complex and challenging than any other game she had played before, and that little fact both bothered and intrigued her.

She already knew the game had been designed by Ethan Sadler, the wunderkind programmer behind Joyce AI, and every online review she read was nothing short of glowing. And even though a former hacker such as Tessa didn't often go out and buy video games, actually spending money on them rather than downloading a pirated copy, this time, she had done so.

It was going to be a gamer evening, deep inside the virtual reality of the software, and she was looking forward to it. Her plan did not include picking up the phone and blowing off a boring, pushy salesperson.

And yet—she did pick up the phone.

"Yeah, what?" she said, cursing herself for picking up at the same time. Maybe she could just hang up again. She already dropped her hand to do so—when she heard Kayla Montecito's panicked voice.

The thing about Kayla: she was a tough lady through and through. In all honesty she kind of frightened Tessa. Never a hair out of place, never a stain on her always perfect outfit, and definitely never a swear word or excited tirade. She'd probably turn to stone if she ever said the F-word.

Except this time—this time, she all but screeched in panic.

"Tessa, Tessa, is that you? Don't hang up, please. We need you. Rafael and Barry need you. There is an intruder at PerCan—and he told the police he has explosives—and—I am up here all by myself—nobody is getting near the building—they're not helping, and Rafael thought…"

"Slow down," Tessa said, frowning, interrupting the torrent of words and unconnected yet alarming phrases. "Slow down, Ms. Montecito. It is you, isn't it?"

"Yes—yes—it's Kayla. Tess, we need you."

"Tell me what happened."

If she had one weakness, it was an inability to walk away once someone said, "I need you." But in this case Kayla sounded terrified enough she did not need to say so.

Her voice trembling, Kayla told a hair-raising story of what had happened after Tessa walked away. Tessa clenched her fingers around her phone, hard, and forgot all about gaming.

Somebody had hacked into the system past the barriers and safeguards she and Rafael had so carefully designed, past all security. That alone was offensive, but this—this dickhead was even now holding two of her oldest and closest friends hostage? Not with Tessa, you didn't.

"I'm on it," she said curtly and hung up the phone.

She shut down her game without bothering to save her progress and fired up another laptop, a very special one that had not seen any action in a long time. This particular model was loaded with a host of nonstandard software that would allow a talented and knowledgeable person to bypass most common software safeguards and go places, places where said person usually was not welcome. Tessa patted her old rig with three fingers for good luck.

"Let's see what you have done in my system, asswipe," she said as her fingers flew over the keyboard.

She shouldn't have to use her special setup to get into their own company's computer system, but automatically, she assumed that anyone clever enough to hack into the system would be smart enough to close the door behind him, to prevent someone like her coming in behind and undoing their dirty work. This particular jerk, however, had not.

She wanted to assume he wasn't very smart. 'He' because she also automatically adopted Kayla Montecito's assumption it was Greg Turner they were dealing with.

Turner had not bothered to hide his tracks very well, or cover up his hack. Her fingers froze on the keyboard when she realized why. Greg Turner had not hacked into the system at all; he hadn't needed to. He had walked in through the front door, bold as he pleased, legally and easily.

Tessa picked up the phone again and dialed Kayla. "Thomas Donnelly," she said.

"What? Who?" Kayla asked, momentarily confused.

"Thomas Donnelly, the guy you removed from the board a while ago. According to my computer trace, that is who is inside the PerCan systems at the moment."

"That's impossible," Kayla said flatly. "We fired him, I personally walked him out of the building, and HR disabled all of his accesses a moment later. He can't be."

"I'm not saying he's personally in the building. I am saying whoever is—Greg Turner or not—is using Thomas Donnelly's access codes."

"But we—no—he gave me his keycards," Kayla argued. "I handed them in at HR for destruction."

"Well, apparently not well enough," Tessa said, kicking herself for not auditing that particular security feature on a regular basis. "From what I can see…" Her fingers flew over the keyboard, ignoring the fact that the incessant clatter had to be murder on Kayla's ears through the phone. "From what I can see, he's been in and out of the building on a regular basis for the last three months. That's… Wait—what the hell?"

"What?" Kayla shouted, when Tessa fell silent. "What are you talking about?"

"This is weird. I have one signature trace here that shows two—two Thomas Donnellys in the building at the same time. How could…? Goddammit, I should have had an alert set up for exactly this kind of incident. I can't believe I never thought of…"

"Thought of what, Tessa? Stop being cryptic," Kayla screamed again, and Tessa blinked.

"It looks like Turner managed to clone Donnelly's access cards and then set up a second, hidden ID for himself. In essence, to the computer, it was Donnelly, but not Donnelly who was wandering around inside. Like a secret twin, get it? He must have stolen Donnelly's card at some point. But that should have been reported. Dammit—we never thought…"

"I have no idea what you just said, Tessa," Kayla said. "Just give it to me in short easy sentences. What does this mean to all of us, and more than that, what does it mean for Rafael and Barry?"

Tessa was silent for a long time and looked at the data on her screen. It was not pretty. This man, this Greg Turner, had access to everything, and he could weaponize every system within the complex PerCan structure.

At the same time, she felt cold fury rising inside of her. Not on her watch would anyone break into the system, endanger her friends and their company, and get away with it. Not on her watch.

"It means he has every available executive privilege within the network," she said tightly. "He can do whatever he wants, and none of us can stop him."

"Dear God."

"I don't think he's going to help us here, Kayla, but that asswipe did not count on me. I'm going to make his life a living hell over there."

"Can you not lock him out?"

"I can, but to undo what he's done will take hours. Hours we don't have. But if I go there—maybe."

"Please tell me you have a plan, and it has an actual chance of succeeding. Please."

"Stand by, Kayla. No—don't stand by. Come on down to the main floor and let me in about 10 minutes from now. I'm going over there. He's put all doors on lockdown, but I can unlock one side delivery bay, relatively unnoticed. By the time he realizes, I should be there. Meet me at the side, just in case."

"I have to tell you—he made a call to the police, warning he had explosives in the building? I'm assuming there are also roadblocks in place. If you don't want to risk coming here. I'll understand."

"I have no intention of being blown up tonight, Miss M. But if I am going to get him out of our systems and shut him down, I'm going to need to be there."

***

Rafael looked down at his phone again.

"Tessa is coming here," he said with a sigh. "I was hoping she would be able to help us—but at a distance. Isn't that what hackers do, dammit?"

"Come on," Barry said. "You knew she wouldn't leave you hanging for anything in the world. That's dedication, maybe not really smart. I wouldn't want her to…" His sentence trailed off. No need to put into words what they were both thinking.

"Didn't you just say you thought Turner was bluffing about five minutes ago?" Rafael reminded him, and Barry raised one eyebrow. "Now you agree with me? Now of all times." Rafael looked back down on his screen.

"I don't know what he's doing, but all of our wireless access points are down, and my cell reception comes and goes."

"Cell reception has always been shitty in this building. Too much steel or something."

"Bullshit." Rafael shifted, adjusting cramped muscles. "Whatever we do, we have to do it now. Who knows what kind of shape Al and his brothers are in? I can't imagine they went in there voluntarily."

"You don't want to wait for Tessa?"

"I don't want to wait to see what he's got up his sleeve to keep her out and us in, Barry. This guy is insane, OK? By the very definition, he's going to do something insane, and he will do it soon. Let's just get this over with."

"Easy." Barry's hand landed on Rafael's shoulder again. "I'm all for putting an end to this. I just want to work smarter, not harder."

"Management bullshit."

"Exactly. So, let's just…"

"I can see you." Turner's voice echoed from the PA system again, followed by raucous laughter.

Rafael wanted to jump to his feet, but Barry's hand held him a little harder.

"We're sitting in the dark, Rafa. If we can't see, he can't. He knows we're here—it doesn't really matter either way. He's just messing with your head."

Rafael only snarled, pushing Barry's hand off his shoulder.

"Don't let him get inside your head. You need to be cool now."

"Fuck being cool."

"All right, Rafael, all right. Back to our plan. We think he's holding Al and his brothers in in the pod, correct?"

Rafael opened his mouth to answer when he was cut by a massive, resounding boom that made the building shake around them. A white-hot glaring light bloomed ahead of them in the direction of the very grow pod they had been talking about. Rafael opened his mouth to scream, but a giant airborne fist picked him up like a ragdoll and slammed him down on the ground again, about six feet from where he had been sitting. He felt his body and head cracking against the hard concrete, and a searing, fiery mass roll over him, and then he didn't think anything any longer.

FORTY-SIX

Tessa approached the PerCan building, staying carefully in the shadows. She didn't think anyone had seen her sneak around the police roadblocks. A safe distance away, she could see a group of police vehicles huddled together and a man giving orders with massive sweeping hand gestures.

No point in trying the main doors. Even if those guys didn't grab her, she had seen them locked down when she checked the system, and even now, all of the security panels were dark. Not a spark of power to them. The only way in through those doors was a massive battering ram and a lot of firepower.

Fingers crossed Turner was busy with his revenge in there somewhere and didn't have the time to notice the one tiny delivery door she had changed from "locked down" to "open."

We'll come creeping up your ass in a few minutes, she thought bitterly as she tried the door handle. It moved downward, releasing the door. *Yes—score one!* Looking over her shoulder, Tessa slipped inside and stood still for a moment.

Kayla stood just inside the door, her back against the wall, her hands massaging one another restlessly, and Tessa looked down at her shoeless feet, cocking her head.

"I was wearing heels for the event," Kayla said quickly. "Maybe not the best thing right now?"

"I never did get the whole thing about heels anyway," Tessa said and put her hand on the other woman's elbow.

She looked around the interior of the PerCan building in wonder. It was one thing to see on a system schematic that all of the light sources had been turned off, quite another to stand in the pitch darkness.

Kayla turned on her phone and guided the way by the glow of her screen. "He must have turned off the power. There's no lights anywhere, except for the reception hall. That's how we didn't notice at first."

"It's a bit worse than that," Tessa said into the darkness, putting her hand on Kayla's shoulder as they walked, just so they wouldn't get lost. "There is power everywhere, as a matter of fact. Turner is just in control of what's on and what's off."

"How would he even know…?"

Tessa shrugged, before she reminded herself Kayla couldn't see her. "He used to have his own manufacturing plant, you know? Before he went bankrupt? He obviously picked up a thing or two."

They walked into the boardroom, dimly lit by the screen of a laptop.

"Rafael's." Kayla nodded. "I turned it on when the lights went out everywhere. Let's hope he has enough battery power till this thing is over or we'll be sitting in the pitch black too."

Beyond the window into the production area, only blackness met her, and Tessa shivered for the first time. Perhaps this had not been her brightest idea after all.

"Thanks for coming," Kayla said, and a trembling hand landed on hers. "Even if—well, thank you for coming to help."

"No worries," Tessa said. "I came here because he can kick me out once he notices I'm in the system—or if, I guess. His permissions override mine on an exec badge. But it's a lot harder to do when I'm in fact sitting here, where I can hard-link into anything I need to."

Tessa slipped her own laptop out of her backpack and sat at the boardroom table, next to Rafael's light-spending screen. *Hang in there,*

Barry and Rafael, she thought. *I am on my way—let's go and kick some massive butt here.*

She linked her own computer to Rafael's laptop and logged onto the PerCan monitoring system using Rafael's credentials. At least she'd be able to see what was happening, perhaps even stop it—if she got there early enough. If… What was Turner's plan—what could he be trying to do?

Carefully, she tapped from system to system. Anything she did could trigger an alarm somewhere, possibly letting Turner know an enemy had arrived. She tried to forget about Kayla pacing nervously behind her, or the very real possibility that Turner could actually kill them all. *This is just a game,* she told herself. *Just a big game.*

A player enters. Choose your weapon.

All systems currently down.

She felt defenseless, exposed even, and spread her fingers, hovering an inch over her keyboard. Wrong move and…

"He's disabled all safety systems," she said more to herself. "Security, alarm systems, emergency controls—even all of the fire-suppression systems are down. And he's… what?"

Her finger scrolled down an area on the side of her screen, listing available resources and status. Everything was greyed out.

"Fire monitoring system is down, and he's turned off the control valve to stop the water flowing into the piping system of the sprinklers," she said, frowning at her screen. "Fire? Is that what he means to do?"

"Explosive," Kayla said, her voice breaking with panic. "He told the police he had explosives in this building. If he does, and sets them off, if there's a fire and the sprinkler system is down—it will… Dear God, it will…"

"Cost a lot more lives." Tessa nodded. "But we can't go down there and open the valve again."

"I could," Kayla said, gripping the back of Tessa's chair. "I'm not helping here anyway."

"No, you can't, Kayla, and please try not to panic. You're freaking me out. If I make a mistake here, it'll cost both of us, all right? Please."

"But I could…"

"No, you can't. Believe me. The valves into the sprinkler are massive things. Neither you nor I could operate them. We just don't have the strength. If there is a fire…" She turned back to her screen and made a tight fist. "If there is a fire, we'll have to figure something out."

"A fire is a distinct possibility then, or Turner wouldn't have bothered with the suppression system. Rafael thinks he's holding them in grow pod five."

"I'm sorry, but that's also bad news. Rafael was gas-flushing that one earlier."

"Gas…?"

"It's a sterilization technique. Not great for your health. If they're in there, they'll be, at minimum, disoriented, dizzy. Probably more. It's flammable—it's bad stuff." Tessa shook her head.

"If I knew all you wanted to bring me was bad news, I wouldn't have called you," Kayla all but screeched.

Tessa flipped the lid of her laptop shut and put her hands flat on the lid.

"I'm trying to help here, Kayla, OK? I'm doing the best I can. I suggest you stop bitching at the only person who can maybe get us out of here in one piece."

For a moment, they both stared at each other across the white rectangle of Rafael's laptop. Then Tessa opened hers again and wiped her hands over her face. Kayla forked trembling fingers through her hair and sat down beside her.

"I'm sorry," they both said simultaneously, and Tessa smiled weakly.

"Sorry. I'm not—polite when things get intense."

"I don't think anybody is. Please do what you can."

"Yeah. All I got is this computer."

"That's more than anybody else has. Tell me more—about this gas that's down there." Kayla reached for Tessa's arm and hung on.

Tessa shook her head. "Not a big deal, usually. Just sterilizes everything. Then it settles out, and it's vented. On a regular day."

"On a regular day…"

"Yes. But that particular one—well, pod five was Rafael's problem child."

"Always an issue, I remember. Mold, infestations. Crops ruined."

"Yep." Tessa continued. "He told me—said, 'I'm going to flush it with a super concentration. Then leave it to soak and, if it's still an issue, I'll tear the goddamned thing down.'"

"Tear it down?"

"Yeah. One of the things he wondered was if something had gone wrong in the construction of that particular pod, the seals, the walls—whatever—and that's why…"

"I don't even want to know," Kayla interrupted. "There's a super concentration of gas in there. Just how dangerous can this get?"

"Don't rightly know." Tessa shrugged. "Guess you could always look up the MSDS…"

"The what?"

"Material safety data sheets. Off the cuff, I'd say don't smoke in there and don't be around it for too long, and no fire."

"Great—just great."

Kayla resumed her pacing. She hardly noticed any longer that her high heels had been left behind ages ago, and now paced in stockings from one end of the boardroom to the other. Back and forth—back and forth.

"Peachy, we have poisonous gas, we have a madman with a bomb—just another day at PerCan."

"Unless it's not a bomb."

"Did you find something?"

Kayla planted herself squarely in front of Tessa, who frowned at her computer screen.

"What if," Tessa said, "what if there is no bomb at all? And he just used this 'I'm going to blow the place up' trope to keep the police away?"

"That's a massive if, honey."

"Yes, but think about it. Why would he shut down the sprinkler system if he in fact had a bomb out there? A bomb is the ultimate level-everything weapon. Forget about sprinklers. There would be no point in going through the hassle of turning them off."

"That's also a big assumption for someone…"

Kayla just stopped herself in time, but Tessa looked down at her laptop and pressed her lips together tightly. *A big assumption for someone who doesn't have the life of a person they love on the line.* Loud and clear.

Kayla's hand landed on Tessa's shoulder, and her hand squeezed lightly. "I'm just worried about Rafael," she said softly, and Tessa nodded.

"I am too—both of them."

"So going with your assumption…"

"Going with my assumption, Turner saw pod five, realized what was going on with it, and locked them in there."

"OK. Then?"

"Then he thinks—great plan. There's not enough gas here to blow up the place, but there sure is enough to make a bigass fire, which will go up like in-sane, and then burn the whole place down in the process."

Kayla paled and shuddered visibly, and Tess reached for her hand. "Sorry for the visual. Didn't mean to freak you out."

"Keep going." Kayla clenched her teeth. "Might as well. So, you think instead of bringing a bomb, he just decided to make do with what was already here."

"Correct."

"Splendid. And neither the fire department nor the police will come near the place until they locate the bomb squad because Turner actually made an in-fact bomb threat. Just brilliant. We are sunk unless we can figure out how to stop him from igniting the gas in pod five—the very one our people are in—and causing an explosion, thereby burning the place down with all of us inside?"

"Basically…"

"Without the aid of fire-suppression systems or a sprinkler system, if I understood you correctly?"

Tessa sat back, cradled her head in her hands, and closed her eyes. "Now you know…"

"Why you were pissy earlier. Help me figure it out then—help me out. There's always an out." Kayla was pleading by now.

Tessa closed her eyes and leaned back, mumbling to herself. "There's always an out—always. Gamer theory. There's always a solution. Every game has a weak point. Except this isn't a game. Except there are no power-ups, no extra lives."

"Fire," she said. "Fire. Come on, come on, help me out here. If he's going to set a massive fire right in the middle of the production area, how are we going to extinguish it?"

"Fire extinguishers?"

"Not strong enough? Probably scattered."

"Sprinklers—turned off, though."

"What else?" Tessa asked. "What else do we have, Kayla? What could we use to fight a fire, what?"

"I don't know."

"There has to be something."

"I don't know!" Kayla screamed, and Tessa's eyes flew open.

"Water," she said. "We're going to use—water."

"Tessa! You just said he turned off the sprinklers. What the hell?" Kayla slammed both fists on the conference table, but Tessa's eyes suddenly burned with a fire of their own.

"Yes, he did! But." She flipped open her laptop, and her fingers flew over the keys as they rarely had before.

"I wonder if the bastard remembered that we have… Of course he did not, asshole. Now I have you—take this!"

Tessa pumped a fist in the air and looked up at Kayla. "Fertigation! He forgot that we have an automatic…"

Whatever she was going to say was drowned out by a massive resounding boom and blinding flash of white from down in the production area. The entire building shook, and, for a moment, everything in the room was illuminated in a hot white glow, and they both brought their hands to their eyes. Kayla felt the vibration from the window into the production area. *Rafael was right,* she thought irrationally. *The thing really is impervious to any and all possibilities.*

She took her hands off her eyes and screamed. One loud, reverberating scream of anguish.

"Rafael." She jumped to her feet and pounded the glass wall with her fists.

Down below, the only thing she could see was a huge, never-ending sea of fire, from one end of the hall to the other. Red-hot, greedy flames that roared as they rose up and greedily devoured everything in their path—everything.

"Get away from the window," Tessa screamed. "Now."

"Rafael." Kayla still stood, her palms flat against the glass as if she wanted to push through there and down into that sea of flame, where Rafael was. And Barry and Al and…

"No. No…"

She let her hands drop and turned around, and all at once the will to fight, the will to get out of there and to get Rafael and Al and his brothers out of there, left her, as if someone had taken a giant fist and slammed it into her stomach.

Kayla slid down against the wall and let her head drop between her knees. It didn't matter any longer. She should likely run—get out of there now—save her own life, and Tessa's. They still had a chance, right?

But it didn't matter any longer. Rafael, the man she loved, was down there in that sea of flames. Nobody could get out of there alive, nobody.

She remembered the first time she had seen the two of them, Rafael and Barry, who was calling himself Connor back them. Connor had been so captivating. He had this gift. He could spin a magical circle of words and stories that made you want to be part of that circle. It didn't even matter what it was he was selling, or doing. You just wanted to be part of it. And then he had just snuck out the back door and left her and Rafael behind to hold the bag, literally.

She'd thought it was over then, and she'd never feel anything again, other than that betrayal. Then Rafael had marched into her life and made himself at home.

Rafael. The man who built giant houses, who was the very opposite of herself. Impatient, sloppy, uncouth at times. Mostly unkempt, and often filthy, but always, always honest to a fault and true. And suddenly, they'd wanted a life together. Rafael had painted that magical picture, just get a few last things settled at PerCan, and semi-retire. Travel the world, maybe teach a few other people how to run a proper cannabis operation, sure. But mostly they were going to just—be together.

And now that dream they had spun would never be.

So what did it even matter if she got up and tried to run from the building, or, for that matter, if she just sat here on the floor in this boardroom that Rafael had been so proud of? What did it matter if the fire was coming this way?

It didn't matter one damn bit.

Kayla curled down even deeper. Some long-forgotten survival instinct screamed at her to get up and get the heck out of there, but she drowned it out. *I am not going anywhere.*

A thunderous crack shattered the air, followed by the tinkling of glass shards raining down. Kayla's heart raced as she instinctively knew it was the sound of the glass wall into the production room shattering.

A spray of tiny glass shards flew over her head and through her hair, and she didn't care to lift her head.

You're wrong, Rafael, she thought and laughed. *Fire can break that beautiful glass wall.* And she smiled to herself.

Just as she felt the greedy fingers of heat closing in on her, she heard a deafening hiss that drowned out even her darkest thoughts. Through the smoke and broken screen, she saw an unholy orange glow and felt the creeping fear that this was it. They had reached hell. Even the source of the hissing and gushing didn't matter anymore; it was all the same now.

The smoke curled around, thick and greasy, suffocating her with each breath, and the flames were getting closer. It really was hell, and she was right in the middle of it.

Someone grabbed a hold of her shoulder, and Kayla lifted her head a little more. Tessa stood in front of her, coughing and choking, a hand raised as if she wanted to slap her.

"Kayla, are you OK? Can you walk?"

The room around them was once again in complete darkness, and Kayla blinked.

"The fire…"

Her ears could make out a far-off siren wail, and she blinked again. Thick clouds of smoke still poured in through the broken glass wall, and she coughed violently.

"The fertigation system. I opened every valve to the tank with irrigation water. Now get to your feet."

Tessa grabbed her hand and pulled.

"We need to get out of here. I've alerted fire and police, but now it's our turn. We need to get out of here."

"Rafael—Barry…"

"I know, Kayla—I know. The fire department has to go in for them. Let's not tie them up looking for us."

"I don't understand…"

Kayla fought back. Her mind refused to make sense of the bits and pieces Tessa was giving her.

"For fuck's sake, move," Tessa screamed and finally dragged her to her feet, and Kayla obeyed.

She allowed Tessa to grab the sleeve of her expensive Gucci jacket with one sooty hand and drag her to her feet. Acrid smoke filled the room, making it hard to breathe, harder to see even. Kayla stopped when she stepped into something sharp and pulled up her foot.

"There's glass all over here," Tessa said and pulled on her sleeve again. "Sorry about that—no time to look for your shoes. Let's go."

Kayla remembered the sea of flames down in the production area, down where Rafael was. What did it even matter if she stepped in a few glass shards? What did it matter if she ever got out of here anyway?

"Go on without me," she said and tried to push Tessa away.

"Oh, you're not wimping out on me. I'm not going to be the one telling Rafael that I left you up here."

"But Rafael is…"

"Let's go—no time."

Tessa grabbed her sleeve again and tugged even harder this time. Massive chunks of glass dug into Kayla's feet, and still she refused to move. She was staying right here.

With a bang, the doors to the conference room flew open, and several men in dark suits and breathing masks entered the room. Tessa yelled something over a sudden roar, Kayla felt a wave of heat roll over her, and then, just like that, someone grabbed her, lifted her off the ground, and carried her across the boardroom littered with glass.

Out of the corner of her eye, she saw someone step on her expensive tote bag, the one Rafael had brought her from a trip last year. Then the smoke became so thick she could hardly see the floor, never mind taking a breath.

Things happened with frightening speed. The fireman brought her to a waiting ambulance and took off again. Someone slapped an oxygen mask on her face. Hands pulled off her stockings, and she wanted to scream when she felt each and every one of the glass shards pulled from her feet.

"What's your name? Stay with us—don't go to sleep now—Kayla…"

She heard shreds of sentences and words, as if through a pillow, just before a blessed darkness descended. Blessed gentle darkness that cradled her, and she didn't have to think any longer, didn't have to see that sea of flames spreading outward, knowing Rafael was right in the center of it.

FORTY-SEVEN

What might have been moments, hours, or days later, she sat up with a start and coughed violently, so hard she thought her insides might turn out with every hacking cough.

"Easy. Easy, Kayla, that's just the smoke. We've had a lot of it."

Kayla opened her eyes and tried to focus in the semi-darkness. Her hands clawed into bunches of sheer white sheets, and she could hear the beeping of the machinery all around her. A hospital then. Slowly, the room came into focus, and so did Tessa sitting on the edge of the bed, holding her hand.

"I didn't dream all of that, did I?" Tessa shook her head.

"Turner, he really did blow up PerCan. Al—Rafael. Dear God, Rafael..."

The memory of that white-hot flash of fire came back to her, and her eyes filled with hot, angry tears.

"You're going to be fine, Kayla, even though heels are going to be out of the question for a little while."

Heels? Kayla looked down at her thickly bandaged feet and wiggled her toes.

"The glass," she said. "That window into the production floor. Rafael's pride and joy. He said—he said nothing could ever break it."

"It's not like anyone expected a fire like that one. Combination of gas and massive amounts of packing materials." Tessa looked down at her hands and wiped them on the legs of her filthy jeans. Kayla sat up a little straighter and put her hand over the young girl's.

"You—saved my life," she said with a weak smile. "Thank you. I think. Even though I wanted to stay behind."

"That's bullshit," Tessa said and blushed a bit. "I mean, you were just—in shock or something. You didn't really want to stay behind."

"I did, Tessa. I saw the flames, and I knew Rafael was down there—and gone. And in that moment, I wanted to stay behind. I remember fighting you about it."

Kayla reached out and touched a bruise beside Tessa's left eye. "Wouldn't surprise me if I punched you there to make you let go of me."

Tessa lowered her head to hide her eyes. Angry tears spilled down her cheeks, and she didn't bother wiping them away.

"It's not fair," she choked out. "It's just not fair. Rafael—Al, Dante, they did nothing to Greg Turner, and yet."

Kayla nodded.

"Rafael Covin, Barry Wentworth, Dante Ivers, Al Ivers, and Roberto Ivers," she said, needing to mark the names of those she knew had been in the building, in the production area when Turner burned it down. "We'll make sure they are remembered."

"Remembered, Kayla? Remembered? I don't want them to be remembered. I want them to be here. Rafael never hurt a soul. And why were we the only ones in there fighting for them, huh? Why was Robertson and his task force not there? Why were they waiting at a safe distance? To see if the bomb threat was real?"

"I don't know, Tessa. I don't have those answers either."

Kayla gathered the young woman into her arms and leaned her head against her shoulder.

"It's not fair. It's just not fair."

Tessa, the girl who used to dye her hair blue-black, had piercings in her nose and more tattoos than Kayla had ever seen, cried openly now. Big heart-wrenching sobs that brought back her own grief again.

Rafael had wanted to send her home. He'd known it would be dangerous. She remembered him standing there, joy and pride shining in his eyes when he'd shown his production facility to Verhoeven.

God, the press, the TV stations, the papers, not to mention every online blog that wrote about the cannabis business. She could just see the headlines: "Half the City Gets High as PerCan Burns." Then there would be jokes and memes, and more lurid headlines, because people were people and they loved to watch someone else's grief. That's why TV had been there in the first place.

A fire in a cannabis plant—oh, God, how funny. Except that people had lost their lives in that fire, and people she loved would never come back home because of one man's revenge.

"It's OK," she said, hearing her own sobs. "It's OK to cry."

The door opened, and a nurse pushed in a cart with a chart, some meds, and a few bowls of Jell-O. She saw both women cry, and her face fell.

"Looks like the two of you are feeling a lot better," she said, forcing some levity into her voice. "We've had to treat all of the firemen for inhalation. You're lucky you didn't get a lot of that funny smoke. I tell you what, a fire in a cannabis plant…"

Kayla's withering glance stopped her dead in her tracks. "I mean—I didn't…"

"People lost their lives in that fire," Kayla said acidly. "Don't you think it's a little callous to joke around about that?"

"Yes, I heard about that," the nurse said and lowered her eyes. "Fire is a bad way to go. I am so sorry. It's just going around the entire hospital." She shook her head to clear the thought and forced a smile. "The good news is that both of you should be able to leave tomorrow morning." She smiled weakly at Kayla. "I'm afraid you'll have to wear flip-flops for a few weeks, sweetie, but everything is going to be just fine."

"Flip-flops?" Kayla looked as if the nurse had walked up and tweaked her nose just then. "You think I could give a rat's ass about shoes at a moment like this one?"

Beside her, Tessa covered a weak giggle because Kayla had said "rat's ass." The nurse scoffed, left her tray of Jell-O and soft fruit cubes between them, and told them to get more rest. She'd be back.

The silence spread between them, and Kayla took a bowl of grisly pink gelatin and pulled her spoon through it, just for something to do. Her heart ached, and her head felt empty. Completely and totally empty.

There'd be so many things she had to do tomorrow once they walked out of here.

Assess the damage, have an emergency directors' meeting, issue a news release, and make decisions about the company's future. Dear God, the major shareholders were dead. How did you make decisions in a situation such as this one? Was there even a company left?

Tadeo—Al—Roberto—Dante—four Ivers men, the last of this family line, lost because of the business, because of one man's need for revenge.

How—where did you start to process a loss such as this one? How?

"Fertigation, huh?" she asked after she had dragged her spoon through the gelatin so often it had turned into an ugly, broken-up mess. She put it aside again and looked at Tessa, really looked at her.

Tessa Goodwin had always been the Goth chick with the nose ring who knew far too much about computers, who had known Rafael and Connor—Barry longer than she herself had. She'd never liked Tessa. No, that was not entirely right. She'd never truly seen her, been aware of her, other than as that girl who worked for Barry and Rafael.

Now, her face was streaked with soot and bright tracks that would be tears. Her hair now hung around her face like a bunch of filthy strings. They could all do with a shower, once they were able to move.

"Yup." Tessa only nodded and pulled the bowl of fruit towards her.

"How did you do it?"

Tessa shrugged. "I just did. It was the only water source in the building that hadn't been shut off. Turner just didn't think of it. It was either that or flood all the toilets."

"But it brings water—to the plants, does it not?"

"Yup." Again, Tessa nodded. "But there are lines going toward every grow pod. They're above eye level. Rafael didn't cover them, for easier maintenance."

"So?"

"So I opened up every valve there was and put on enough pressure to break those pipes in a dozen places all at once. Water mixed with fertilizer. Not so healthy, but apparently, it does put out a bigass fire. Who knew."

Kayla said nothing and looked down at her own filthy hands. "That was pretty smart."

"Yup."

"Then that was the hissing I heard."

"You remember that?"

"That and the steam, and the smoke." Kayla smiled weakly. "I thought it sounded like we were at the gates of hell already, and those were the snakes and the demons of hell. God…"

"Yeah."

Tessa put the fruit bowl aside again, without having selected anything, and sat on her bed, her face buried in her hands.

"I meant to tell you," Kayla continued. "Thanks—for coming when I called you, you know. For dropping everything and for risking your life."

"'S'OK." Tessa put her head back and took a deep breath, followed by violent coughing. "Somebody was messing with Rafael's—with our—cannabis plant, and I wasn't going to let them."

"Still, thank you. You saved my life and prevented a worse tragedy. I will make sure this is not forgotten."

"With all due respect, Kayla, what the fuck? Prevent a worse tragedy? Really? How could it be any worse? Rafael—Barry—dead. The Ivers men—dead. So don't you go tell me about a worse tragedy because

I'm right with you with you. I wanted to stay behind. I don't think it could have been any worse. I might have saved a bit of property there at PerCan. Whoppy shit. If you need to go on with business, be my guest. I can't."

Tessa buried her head in her hands again, and neither woman said anything for a very, very long time. Kayla felt as if the space around them were made of glass, and the slightest movement on her part would just shatter it all to a thousand pieces—shatter it like it had shattered Rafael's precious glass wall.

Someone dropped a metal tray outside the room, and the clattering startled both of them out of their silent shock.

Kayla put her hands together and took a few steadying breaths, ending in a cough again.

"You've got it all wrong, Tessa," she finally said. "I don't want to get back to business. I just know—I know if I start talking about it—I am going to lose it, completely, once and for all, and that…"

She couldn't finish her sentence, as the tears welled up and choked her. With a sob, she reached for Tessa, who came into her arms, and together, they sat on the edge of Kayla's bed, clung to one another, and sobbed.

Their nurse came back into the room a good hour later, scolded both of them for not eating anything, and handed out little cups of medication.

"Something to help you sleep," she said, watching both of them to make sure they took the offered meds. "Not going to have the two of you up all night."

Kayla didn't want to sleep. She didn't want anything, but she didn't have the strength to fight anymore either. She took her meds without questioning them and dropped her head back into the pillow. She worried that if she fell asleep, she would dream—of fires, and explosions, and of the people she would now never see again. But she stared at the ceiling for a while, listened for the noises of the hospital ebbing and flowing around her, and finally drifted off.

***

She hadn't dreamed at all, or, if she had, she didn't remember it, because the next morning, she and Tessa were being woken again by another nurse.

Tessa started grousing about being woken up, when she looked at Kayla and shut up again.

"Hey. You alright?" Kayla only shrugged.

"Didn't mean to go on about…"

Kayla shook her head and waved her hand. "It's OK," she said softly. "One of these days, we'll have to come back to the land of the living—me included. Whatever."

"Yeah—whatever," Tessa said and looked away.

Their nurse chattered away, made a few notations on a computerized chart, and told them someone would be by to see about meals for the day. If everything checked out, the young woman told them, they'd be able to go home later on today, and did they want to make arrangements for someone to pick them up?

"Well, Ra…" Kayla started and closed her mouth again. No, Rafael wouldn't be around in a little while to pick her up.

She couldn't find her phone in the meager belongings that had made it out of PerCan and into the hospital and asked Tessa to see hers, but Tessa shook her head too.

"Sorry, not with my stuff, whatever little there is. Probably back at—back at PerCan."

Kayla nodded. "Yes, and your laptop and everything else. Sorry. We'll replace those, of course, as soon as—as soon…"

"Don't worry. It's probably all over the news this morning. What do I need a phone for or a laptop? Do you think I want to read that and go through it all over again? No thank you."

Kayla nodded weakly. Neither did she, really, but she was old enough to know that they would only be able to keep reality and the world 'out there' away for a few more hours, at best. Then she at least would have to go make statements, draft news releases, answer questions, and—deal with things. They had just a few more hours in this room, before they had to face it.

She lay back, stared at the ceiling, turned away any offer of breakfast, and finally dozed off again.

The respite was brief enough. It felt like minutes, although hours had probably passed. Someone knocked at the door and stuck in his head, and Kayla looked at Detective Sergeant Sean Robertson.

"You," she said dryly, sat up, and pulled the thin blanket a little tighter around herself. "What do you want?"

"I'm glad to see you well," the detective said and looked around for a chair. Kayla didn't bother telling him there was one pushed into their little washroom. Let the bastard stand.

"More or less well." She shrugged. "Much of this could have been prevented."

"Kayla—Ms. Montecito—we had a bomb threat called in, a credible bomb threat. We were under orders to stand down, not to enter the building."

"I was on the phone with your officers. I begged them to come in—begged them."

"I could not take that chance with my men. I am so…"

"Sorry? You let people die and you are sorry? That's just real gracious of you, Detective—thank you so much. Did it ever occur to you that Turner might be bluffing?"

"We could not take…"

"You could not take that chance. I heard you," Kayla spat. "You were watching the building, for crying out loud—this was a disaster from the word go. Your officers were there every moment of the event, and Turner managed…" She shook her head and just barely stopped herself from slapping the man. "Never mind. You failed. You failed all of us. Do you know who took a chance? Tessa Goodwin did."

Kayla pointed at Tessa, who had so far cowered down in her blankets and tried to stay as invisible as possible, in a hospital room with only two beds.

"Tessa here did take that chance, and she came in and opened the water valves and saved our lives at least. You failed—your entire department failed."

"Yes, well…"

"People died, Detective Robertson. Died. Because you failed in your sworn duty to protect us."

"Now look here. I warned you doing that TV show was too dangerous, and you did it anyway. If there is a bomb threat, it's my duty to protect my officers and people as well as you. You were asked to get out of the building as soon as possible. I know you were. So don't you…"

"You were not protecting anybody," Kayla spat. "You were playing into Turner's hands. Did you at least find his dead body as well? Did you?"

The door opened again, and their young nurse stormed in holding a digital notepad.

"Sir—ladies—we can hear you arguing all the way down the hall. This is still a hospital. If you cannot behave with a bit of decency, I suggest you leave, Sergeant."

She stood there, tapping her toes, and glared at Robertson.

"It's all right," Kayla said weakly. "The detective was just leaving anyway."

"I actually wanted to ask a few…"

"You're leaving," their young nurse said and took the detective by the arm. "I have other patients on this floor who do not need to hear you yelling about dead bodies, do you hear me? Insensitive, that is…"

"No—it's just one… I'm leaving. I'm leaving already."

She dragged him out, and Kayla dropped back onto her pillow with an exhausted sigh.

"You alright?" Tessa asked again, and Kayla just stopped herself before she snapped at the young woman too.

"People like him bring out the worst in me. 'We were under orders.' Just following orders, and nobody is taking responsibility. When I get back to my paper…"

"What was he talking about—it's just one?"

"What?"

"When Nurse Army Boots was dragging him out, he said, 'No, it's just one.' What was he talking about?"

"I don't know. One question probably."

Kayla closed her eyes again, waiting for somebody to tell her she could leave.

They were both checked, poked, and prodded once again, and Kayla refused to speak during the entire ordeal, even though kind and caring nurses and doctors asked over and over how she was doing.

The sooner she could get out of there, she figured, the sooner she could have her privacy and… And what? That was the big question. Fall apart in peace perhaps? Grieve the loss of so many people she had known, while at the same time wondering why she and Tessa were still alive?

Tessa turned on the TV at one point, and that was finally when Kayla opened her eyes again.

"Turn that off right now."

"But I just…"

"What did you say an hour ago? Do you think I want to see everything we went through last night on TV and live through it again and again? I don't. I don't need to see pictures of them wheeling us out of there, and after that…"

"OK, OK, I'm turning it off already."

Tessa made a face and snapped off the screen. She coughed gently and reached for the water bottle on her nightstand. Both of them still battled the effects of smoke inhalation. Kayla forced the best smile she could muster when their young nurse finally came back into the room.

"Please tell me that we can get out of here now," she said, and her face fell, at the answer.

"Well—your young friend can. You need to wait on a few tests."

"Why?" Kayla asked like a stubborn child, knowing full well she sounded as if she were whining. "We are both fine—surely, you can see that. I need to get back."

"Tired of our hospitality already?" The nurse tried her best to smile. "I'll see if I can put a rush on things, all right? It's just because of all of the cuts you received."

"I stepped into some glass is all."

"Shatterproof Panzer glass from what I hear." The nurse patted her hand gently and reached for the lunch tray. "Sure you don't want anything?"

Kayla waved her away and stared at the wall on her right. She heard Tessa sign a few forms and receive more paperwork relating to recovery. The nurse asked if she could call anyone, and Tessa said Ron, whom she assumed was a boyfriend.

"Take care. I'll see you around, I'm sure," Tessa said, and Kayla only nodded.

"Stay in touch, Kayla."

Then she was all alone in the hospital room. All alone with her thoughts, and with her grief and with her questions. She stared at the TV for a moment, tempted. Surely, last night's fire would be all over the local news, would it not be? Maybe they had found Turner. Some part of her wished he had been found dead, perished in his own fire, and with a shiver, she realized she didn't even feel bad about it. Without any kind of remorse, she could sit there and wish him death for what he had done to Rafael and to her, and to every single shareholder in Perfect Cannabis. And Al and…

"Am I interrupting something?"

She hadn't heard the knock at the door and spun around in her bed. She could only stare at the man who had walked into her room.

Her hand came up to her mouth covering it, and no words would come out. She wanted to speak and scream and instead coughed and sputtered for what seemed to be an eternity. Her heart raced, and her fingers clung to the man's hands even as he helped her sit up straight and gently patted her back, almost embarrassed.

"You? How?" she finally managed to say, and Barry handed her a bottle of water and held her hand as she drank from it greedily.

"I thought you were—I thought you were…"

She couldn't go on. Barry wore jeans and a sweatshirt, and his face and neck bore multiple bandages. His right hand and arm were bandaged up to the elbow, and his hair looked as if he'd mopped the floor with it. His eyes were red-rimmed despite the quirky smile, and he pulled up the one chair in the room.

"Thought I was gone? Trust me, for a while there, I thought I was."

"But how? I saw everything down there in Manufacturing go up in flames."

"Not quite everything. Rafael's sterilization gas did quite a number. Made a massive flash fire. I imagine it probably looked like hell's inferno from where you were sitting."

"It did." Suddenly, she gripped his arm in a viselike grip and let go when he winced. "I refused to put on the news. I didn't want to see. Tell me—just honestly tell me—did Rafael…"

Her face fell when he put his hand on her shoulder.

"Easy there, Kayla. Easy. I—I don't know. When they brought him in, it didn't look good."

"What about the others?"

Barry's face was a mask of stone. His eyes shut for a brief moment, and he took a deep, measured breath.

"Roberto is gone," he said, shaking his head. "He stood closest to the door of the grow pod when it blew, and it broke his neck instantly."

Kayla gasped and let out a little wail.

"Rafael—Rafael went in to get out Al and Dante. I think he carried Dante and dragged Al."

"Then they are…"

Barry shrugged and looked away.

"Last time I browbeat somebody into telling me, yes. But, Kayla, I don't know. They were not—all that encouraging. There's no good way to come through a fire like that."

"I thought they were dead—I thought all of you were gone. You are telling me that they might have a chance?" She struggled out of bed, without giving a thought to the fact that she wore a hospital gown and her feet were still bandaged all the way up to the knee. "They are alive. Dear God. Barry, they have a chance."

Barry J. Wentworth, the man who could talk himself out of, and you into, anything, looked down at his hands.

"We were both behind a pillar, Rafa and me."

Kayla cocked her head and sat back down on the edge of the bed.

"Then Rafael saw that Turner had piled all this cardboard by pod five, and he knew—he knew that asshole meant to start a huge fire, so he ran toward it, to get the Ivers men out if he could."

He shook his head and closed his eyes for a long moment. Kayla said nothing at all.

"I didn't." Barry finally continued. "I saw him running across the floor, and I thought, I really should go with him and help him, and I still didn't. I ran the other way."

Kayla took his hand and still said nothing.

"And all the while I'm thinking, if I had gone with him, if I had just gone…"

"I know this is hard, but…"

"No this is not hard, Kayla," he said, forking his good hand through his filthy hair. "This is fucking impossible. I keep…"

"Stop it, OK—just stop it. Do not fall apart on me now." She took his hand a little tighter and shook it. "You—Rafael—and Al. You were there from the very beginning. I am going to need you every step of the way when we get out of here. Me? I was only part of the company because of you and Rafael. I need you."

"The company?" Barry stared at her as if she had two heads, and his chin dropped to his chest. "You're talking about the idiot company? Do you even remember everything we did—in the name of the company? Are you not tired of it yet?"

"I might be. If it were me, I might walk away and kick that pile of ashes and say good riddance. But you just told me Rafael is alive, and it was his baby, that stupid plant. Everything he did, and thought about and wanted to do, it all eventually came back to PerCan. That man had better survive this, and when he does—when he does, I am not going to be the one who is going to tell him, 'Hey, we bulldozed what was left while you were out.' Do you hear me?"

Kayla got up off the bed and stormed into the little attached washroom, wincing when her feet hit the floor. Desperately, she splashed water into her face and patted at her grimy, messy hair until she heard a gentle knock.

"Kayla?"

"I'll be right out."

"Kayla, I don't think you should…"

"Should what?" She yanked the door open again and almost collided with Barry standing there. "Shouldn't get my hopes up too high? Few minutes ago, I thought Rafael was dead, and you. And I was never going to see him again. And now you are telling me he is alive and he has a chance. That's all I need. I know he is going to make it—I know he will—and I'm going to go tell him so."

"Whoa, whoa, Kayla." Barry took a step back and managed to catch her gesturing hands in his own. "I don't think they are going to let you walk into the ICU as you please, OK? Germ-free environment and all that. It's just not a good idea. Please don't."

"I suggest you stop telling me what not to do, Barry. I am going to wash up now, somehow, and I would appreciate it if you would run down to the gift shop and get me something that is clean, simple, and doesn't reek of smoke. Can you do that for me?"

"I—sure—but I really don't think…"

"Along with a pair of flip-flops or slippers or something—my Louboutin heels didn't make it back from the fire."

"Kayla."

Barry stood there as if lightning had suddenly struck him, blinking rapidly to clear his head. He stood there, eyes fixed on the woman in front of him, trying to make sense of the sudden burst of energy that had replaced the lifeless, depressed person he had found in this very room only a little while ago. Desperately, he pushed his fingers into the corners of his red-rimmed eyes and sighed.

"I will—try," he finally said, and took off as Kayla inspected the shower facilities in the attached washroom. It probably would have made more sense to go home to clean up, but that would only take time, and time was something she didn't want to waste. Rafael was alive—he was alive. Any chance he had, she would take it. It was better than what she'd been facing half an hour ago.

Hold on, Rafael, hold on!

A little while later, cleaned up a little and dressed in jeans and a garish "I heart our hospital" sweatshirt, she stood at the nurse's station that guarded the ICU and argued.

"No, you don't understand. I am his fiancée."

"I am sorry, ma'am. We can't let you in there right now. They are still in critical condition, all three of them, and we just can't take a chance. Out of the question."

"But that's why I want to be in there—to give him hope, to give him something to live for. I must—I really…"

"And my answer is still the same, ma'am. I cannot let you go in there. If you wait for a little while, perhaps one of the doctors will speak to you and give you an update."

Kayla narrowed her eyes and put her hands into her sides. Unwittingly, the nurse had used the term she hated most, *ma'am*. Mentally straightening up, she pulled out her last card.

"I am Kayla Montecito, from Montecito Publishing. Do you have any…?"

A hand landed on her shoulder, and she half turned to find Barry standing behind her.

"Mr. Wentworth." The nurse's face brightened, and she flashed her most charming smile at him. "How nice to see you again—it's been too long. How are you?" She scanned his disheveled appearance, and her face fell. "Oh, no, Mr. Wentworth, don't tell me…"

"Nothing life-threatening, Charmaine, I assure you. But the gentlemen in there," he nodded at the ICU, "are business associates of mine and Ms. Montecito's. I would really, really appreciate it if you would let us in there, just for a moment."

"I am so sorry." Charmaine looked down at her hands. "Strict orders. I cannot let you in. Any slightest bit of contamination might cause an infection that could do them in. Especially the older gentleman."

"Al? How is Al? I know he was so weak in the first place. Oh dear God, don't tell me he is…"

Charmaine looked down again and shook her head. "I don't know. But that's why it is so important to stay out of there." She smiled brightly again at Barry and nodded. "Wait just a little bit. I'll find someone to give you an update."

They sat on the uncomfortable plastic furniture that was ubiquitous in waiting rooms all around the world and waited. Kayla wanted to pace the length of the little area, but her torn feet wouldn't let her.

"Charmaine?" she finally said to Barry. "It has been so long? Old girlfriend of yours, or what?"

Barry smiled weakly. "Nothing so exciting, I'm afraid. I did a couple of massive fundraisers for this hospital last year, and they included staff events. That's all. I thought it might help."

"Yes—thank you. My saying I was from the press certainly did not and wouldn't have."

Barry smiled weakly. "You're welcome. I felt the need to stop you just before you said, 'Do you have any idea who I am?'"

Kayla rolled her eyes. "God. I can't believe I almost went there. When this is all over, Barry—when this is all over…"

"Yeah, when it's all over. And it will be—it will be."

Silence spread again, and Kayla lost herself in the memories of Rafael. Their trip to Denver to hire Nick Ambrose, building PerCan together, finally figuring out that the company was not the only reason they hung together so much. Rafael trying to clean up his vocabulary and manners because she mentioned he was always cursing. Rafael fighting with Tadeo Ivers. They had been through so much.

Whoever is up there in heaven, don't let it end here—please don't let it end here.

It felt like an eternity before a doctor finally had the time to spare more than two minutes for them. Much of the medical jargon went over Kayla's head, but one thing was clear to her: it was serious, very, very serious. And if either of those men had a living will, perhaps it was time to locate it now.

Her eyes filled with tears, even as she tried to deny it. No, she would not lose Rafael all over again, now that she had just found out he survived the fire. Not now, not again.

Barry took her elbow to steady her, and she leaned on him then. Any support in a storm.

Maybe it was that, or just Barry's presence and disarming charm, but at the end of the day, they were allowed to come in for just a few steps and to look through a window into the room beyond, where the three men lay.

She would never have known it was them under the tangle of tubes and cables, hidden by various bandages and supports. Her heart broke for all three of them and filled with unspeakable anger for Greg Turner. How could anyone have done something so unspeakable to another human being? Turner would pay for what he had done, she swore right then and there. He would not be allowed to get away—not while she had a single breath in her body and a few dollars left for investigators and lawyers and…

She put her palm against the window and mentally urged Rafael to open his eyes, but he did not. All three of them remained still and steady as the machinery around them did its thing.

I will be back, Rafael, she thought. *I will be back. In the meantime, you fight like hell to come back to me, you hear? Fight like hell. I know you can do that. Don't you dare leave me.*

Barry quietly took her elbow again and led her away to the cafeteria where he bought strong coffee for both of them. Neither of them wanted any food or drink really, and yet neither of them was ready to go home, to face the world just then.

"Thank you," she said, staring down at the cups on the table between them. "Thanks for using your connections."

Barry only shrugged. "Don't know if I did you a favor."

"He's alive. He is going to have to fight, and I know he can do that." With her fingertips, she pushed the cup left and right a few times and finally made a face. "I really need something stronger than this."

Barry grinned and looked around, and for a moment, she thought he would reach into his pocket and come out with a flask, but he only shook his head.

"They just let me out too, you know. I just can't—face the real world yet."

"Sorry, I wasn't suggesting…"

"No worries." He gently put his hand over hers. "Was just thinking I could really use a hit of the strongest bourbon man ever created. However…"

"However?" Kayla sighed and smiled at him. "It's strange, you know."

"What is?"

"You and I were together when this thing started. Back then, I didn't think I could hate anyone more than I hated you."

"Ouch!"

"You left me behind while you were on the run, remember?"

"Yeah, but I…"

"Water under the bridge." She squeezed his hand. "I just—can't get over how much older and smarter we all got in the past 10 years or so. It's not all about making massive amounts of money any longer, buying a helicopter, or vacationing in exclusive resorts."

"Speak for yourself."

Barry looked down into his coffee and stirred it with a lot more force than strictly required. His hair hung in lank, dirty strands, and, for the first time, she noticed that he was turning grey around the temples.

"Oh no, Barry Wentworth. You started this all when things were just becoming legal because it was easy and quick and everybody wanted to get into cannabis. People were throwing money at you to get the operation started, and you loved it. Every minute of it."

"Those were the days."

"And now look at you. You figured out that running an operation of this size is a complex and challenging thing that—doesn't really play to your strengths at all."

"No. I am a better fundraiser than operations person. Found that out pretty darn quick." He shook his head. "What are you trying to tell me?"

"You're the best there is. And we're going to need you. Now more than ever."

"Huh?"

"Barry, I don't know how much there is left of PerCan. I imagine when we get there to look at it, it'll be pretty bad. It looked like a war zone when they were dragging me out of there last night."

"Same here. I imagine—I imagine it's a pretty bad wreck in there."

"So? When has that ever stopped either one of us? We'll need to rebuild. For the sake of Rafael, and Al and Dante, and in memory of Roberto—we will have to rebuild. I don't think either one of us is ready to just walk away, saying, 'Hey, it's been a scream.'"

"Don't you want to wait first to see if…" Barry hugged his arms around his body as if he had caught a chilly draft all of a sudden, and his teaspoon clattered to the green plastic table. "You know…"

"See if they survive, you mean?"

He only nodded, looking away, to the bored staff at the counter—at anything but her face.

"Barry, they will—they have to." She grasped his hands with both of hers now. "Whatever we have to do—whatever it takes, you and I will make it happen, do you understand? Whatever doctor, whatever hospital, whatever treatment—we'll make it happen. That's what I am going to do. Please tell me you are on board. You and Rafael have been friends forever, and I know you're no fan of the Ivers family, but…"

"That's not it, Kayla. That's not it at all, but seeing them in there… I don't know as there will be anything we can do. Roberto… he was a big guy, remember? Stronger than anything, fit, athletic. And now he's just—gone. One second to the other…" He snapped his fingers, and his hand fell onto the ugly, scarred table again. "Just gone."

"I know—I am sorry. I forgot for a minute he was your friend."

"Not a friend exactly. It was complicated. He hated his dad for keeping him out of the cannabis business. For a moment, we had identical agendas. My point was just—if you had lined them all up, I would have picked him to survive anything. And now?"

Kayla tried not to remember the sea of flames she'd seen the night before. Surely, she wouldn't lose Rafael all over again. Surely…

"Hey—whatever it takes," Barry said finally, with a crooked smile. "We'll do it. Whatever it takes."

"Whatever it takes," Kayla said and squeezed his hands as hard as she could.

FORTY-EIGHT

Suddenly, they couldn't wait to get out of this hospital, go home, and clean up. Friends and associates of Barry's had been calling him nonstop, even though his phone was on silent, and he made a face as he looked at it.

"I really have to go—there are enough messages here to keep me on it for a week. And these are people who don't even know I was there last night!"

"I need to get back too. I still have a publishing house to run. People are probably wondering where I am and why I am not picking up the phone, whether I am OK, and Rafael… I need to get a new phone, I need to get cleaned up, I need to go out and check on the building. Jeez—I don't know why I am sitting here."

"Because you are human." Barry rose and put out his hand to help her up. "Are you ready?"

"I don't think I will ever be ready."

"Cut yourself some slack. We are human, and there are lions, tigers, and bears and a whole lot of questions waiting for us. Let's go."

He called cars for them to pick them up and take them home, he arranged for a courier to deliver a new phone to her—four hours or less—and he made sure someone would meet her at the house with a key. For the moment, Kayla was content to let him take charge.

Finally home, she spent a good hour getting cleaned up, washing her hair over and over in the sink until she finally felt she didn't have the scent of smoke in her nose any longer. She changed, exchanged her ugly little flip-flops for a cute, bedazzled pair, and finally unlocked her new phone.

The message count instantly raced upwards, into figures she'd never seen before, even back when Barry had been arrested and everybody in the world wanted to know. Besides her own family and friends, there were messages from the staff at Montecito, other journalists, Rafael's friends and neighbors, business associates. Too many to count. And everyone wanted to know the same thing: what the heck happened last night? And was she OK?

It had been all over the news. A massive fire and suspected arson at Perfect Cannabis Consolidated—several executive members said to be trapped in the blaze.

Could she—would she—give a statement? Who were the people who had been trapped? Did they make it out? What was their condition? Questions piled on top of questions. She was already tired of repeating herself over and over, and it had only been half an hour.

Quickly, she wrote a statement for her staff and had someone distribute it at Montecito. *Thank you everyone for your dedication and concern. I am safe and mostly unharmed. Please continue in my absence as I have some pressing matters arising from the fire to attend to.*

No more. Of course, everyone wanted to know how Rafael was. If he had been there, if he had been one of the executives mentioned.

In the meantime, she suddenly had a need to see PerCan. She needed to go out there, needed to see… Dear God, what if the entire building had been reduced to a pile of smoking rubble? All of Rafael's work and dedication! It wouldn't—it couldn't…

She had just decided to call a car to take her to the site when someone knocked at the door. Jesus, had the newshounds followed her home already? Just as she tried to figure out how she would get down there without having to run a gauntlet of questions and reporters—her phone pinged with another message.

I'm at your back door. Want to go see PerCan? B

She opened her door and pulled him inside quickly.

"I thought I'd left you at the hospital—with a ton of stuff to do."

"Yup."

Barry too had showered and changed, looking mostly human again. If you looked past assorted scrapes, scratches, cuts, and bruises. Kayla did not.

"You got banged up pretty bad too. Why are you wandering around playing the heroic helper?"

Barry shrugged.

"I see. And you just happened by my house on your way to…"

"No, actually, I drove here specifically. I have a ton of shit to do, but for some reason, I can't get to it. My mind isn't there. I have to go see the building, and I thought…"

"You thought I would feel the same way?"

"Uh-huh."

"Aren't you the mind reader then? That is exactly where I was going when you knocked."

Barry pulled a keychain out of his pocket and dangled it in front of her eyes.

"Rental. Your chariot awaits."

***

They drove across town in silence, each of them following their own train of thoughts. They were likely similar, Kayla thought, *God, I wonder what I am going to find,* and *I hope the whole thing hasn't been reduced to rubble.*

She watched Barry as he drove, his jaw firmly set, his hands clamped down on the steering wheel so tightly his knuckles were white.

Their security forces already patrolled the area at the perimeter of the fence that surrounded the site again, and Kayla craned her neck. What was it they were still keeping safe? How much of it was still there?

There was the building. Large parts of it looked like it always had.

Their chief of security recognized them and guided them into the parking lot, where, the day before, TV crews had stood preparing to tape a show, where Kayla's own car still sat abandoned, along with Rafael's Mercedes in the far corner of the lot.

Her fist automatically tightened, and Barry smiled weakly. "Don't look now," he said.

"Easy for you to say. You must have had a car and driver last night, before—before everything happened."

"Uber." He shrugged. "I knew you had ordered a buffet and some excellent wines."

"Jesus, Barry." She elbowed him in the side, but he had made her laugh. For the first time since the lights went out last night.

He smiled, but it was a ghost of the brilliant charmer she knew and was used to, designed to make her think everything was OK. It was not, and it would be a long time before she could even think of saying it.

Their chief of security, Lance Monaghan, held the car door for her and helped her out.

"Perimeter security has been reestablished," he said, nodding at the workmen by the fencing. "Emergency techs made a mess of it last night. Our CFO already hired a disaster recovery team."

"Has the building been cleared?" Kayla asked, and Lance shook his head.

"Not anything down in Production. Cops are all over that still. Admin, you are good to check it out."

Kayla shivered and hugged her arms closer to her body. "What's it look like?" Barry asked on her behalf.

Lance looked down at his feet, brought his hands together up to his mouth, and sighed.

"You were there, Mr. Wentworth. It's a mess. A complete mess. What hasn't been directly affected by the fire was affected by the water the fire department brought in. Grow pods seven through nine are still standing and unaffected, I believe, but…"

"But Turner cut the power last night," Kayla said, fought against the shiver that shook her once again, and straightened up. "And we flooded the fertigation lines. So the crops in those pods are gone anyway, no matter what."

"That's about it. I'm so sorry, Ms. Montecito. I heard you were there, and our Tessa…"

"Yo, all I did was open the tap, OK? No need to make a big fucking deal out of it, 'kay, Lance?"

Kayla spun around and saw Tessa coming toward her, hands shoved into the pockets of her jeans. She looked a little disheveled still, a bit worse for wear, but cleaned up, her hair bundled up in a messy bun on top of her head, and her dark makeup firmly in place once again. Her eyes red-rimmed and unreadable.

"Couldn't stay away, Tessa?" she asked and put a hand on the girl's shoulder.

"Yeah, well, I had to see for myself, you know. Plus—my laptop is still in there."

"Yours, was it?" Lance said and rolled his eyes. "Cops were all over that thing thinking it might have belonged to Turner. Dear God, you gave those men a tough nut to crack."

"Don't tell me they took my rig, Lance, please." Tessa took two big steps toward their chief of security and grabbed his hands. "I've been through a big fire last night, so this is not what I need, right now."

Again, Lance rolled his eyes. "Do I look like I would do that, Tessa? You ought to know me better than that. No, I told 'em it looked like yours, and it's in that trailer over there awaiting you confirming that it is in fact yours."

That was what relief looked like, Kayla thought, looking after Tessa, who took off for the trailer by the building as if someone were chasing her.

"What's with that trailer?" she asked of Lance, who looked a little embarrassed.

"Cops put it up this morning, to serve as their command center while they went through the building. They've cleared the office areas by now, like I said, but…"

"It's fine, Lance. It's fine." She took a deep breath and carefully zeroed in on the questions she really wanted to ask. The one she needed to know above all of them. "Any—er—sign?"

"Of Turner, afraid not." Lance shook his head. "If he'd have been still in there, and I'd have found him, I would—I would have…"

"Easy." Barry put his hand on the man's elbow. "The cops are going to find him. They absolutely will. Meanwhile, our job around here is to rebuild the way it was before he—um, before he…"

"Came around?" Lance finished helpfully, and Kayla nodded.

"Exactly. Rafael, Al, and Dante are hanging in there at the hospital. For them, if not for the remaining company and the shareholders, we need to come back. We need to do this and rebuild."

"Count me in." Quite suddenly, one of the security people checking the fence stepped up to the group. "Sorry, couldn't quite help overhearing. Rafael is a fine man—if we are rebuilding for him, count me in, anything I can do, anywhere I can help. I got two hands. If money is tight, no problem. I'm flexible."

"No, wait—I wasn't about to ask anyone here to…"

The man raised his hand, shook his head, and called out to the other men with him who were inspecting and checking the high-tech security fence. They joined the group, chatting amongst each other, and Kayla heard Rafael's name—again and again.

These people loved him. God, if she had thought she was the one suffering the most, she was an idiot. These people respected and adored Rafael. Suddenly, it became hard to swallow past the knot in her throat, and Barry and Lance took charge quite automatically.

Barry took her arm and gently led her into the building. The gagging smell of smoke still hung in the air, making her want to turn around and run right back out, although she could already see teams from the disaster recovery contractor setting up their equipment and tools to get to work.

The girls who usually sat at Reception huddled in a corner and came running the moment they saw Kayla.

"We heard."

"We're so sorry."

"Oh my God, Kayla—oh my God. Anything you need. For Rafael—for Al—for Dante. Anything you need."

"Anything."

"Just ask if there is a need. I am always available."

She heard it over and over during the next hour.

People she hardly knew, and whom she had only seen when she came into Production to meet Rafael, suddenly came up to give her a hug, and told her to give him their best. People who had just been coming to work previously suddenly stood together, shook her hand, and told her to count on them. People whom she had collectively thought of as 'staff' suddenly told her to count on them.

Kayla was humbled and fighting tears—humbled and embarrassed at this collective force of caring, directed at her.

She all but clung to Barry's arm as they walked through the building. The boardroom, Rafael's pride and joy, looked like a war had been fought here, and her grip on Barry's arm only became tighter.

The massive glass pane had been shattered on the right-hand side, and what remained hung blackened in the frame, like a massive rotten tooth. Workmen had swept up the glass shards and were busy trying to remove the remains from the frame to move them into makeshift dumpsters.

Two of them were trying to stop her from doing any more than peek into the room, but she swept them aside with a determined gesture.

"I almost died in this room last night," she said hoarsely. "I have to see it."

There was not much to see any longer. The boardroom table was being dismantled. What was not singed or broken was scarred from flying pieces of glass. How had she and Tessa ever made it out of there, without being cut to bits, Kayla wondered, just as her feet reminded her she hadn't. A few chairs remained; others were mangled and bent in a massive pile in the corner of the room. The whiteboard still held smeared notes from the last meeting, and, on the credenza, miraculously unharmed, stood a crystal decanter and the water glasses Al preferred. There was even an inch of water in the decanter, and Kayla choked back hysterical laughter. Barry's steadying hand on her elbow stopped her just in time.

"Why don't we leave them to what they are doing?" Barry said, just as Kayla spotted one of her high-heeled shoes in the trash pile. It had lost its heel, and the soft cream leather was singed and torn across the toe. Kayla shuddered.

"Yes, let's," she said softly. "I just had to see it."

Rafael's office was mostly undamaged, other than that pervasive smell of smoke that had crept into everything, from the carpets to the wall coverings, and she collapsed into his favorite office chair, clamping her hands onto the armrests. Finally, she picked up a picture in a little frame: Rafael digging a spade into the foundation of one of his first buildings.

"He had this in my office for a while," she said, her voice tight and choked. "While they were building this place, when Tadeo…"

"When Tadeo was in charge," Barry finished. "Yes, I remember. He would say it reminded him where he had come from, and how he should never get so big as to ask anybody to do a job he wouldn't do himself."

"That, and a hard hat that said 'da boss' on it." Kayla smiled and looked around, but she couldn't spot it anywhere. Perhaps it had been lost over the years.

"I did not expect all those people to come around and…"

"To stand behind Rafael like that? Oh, he has a way with people. You know that. Somehow…"

"He cares about people, that's why." Kayla rested her face in her hands for a minute. "Guess if we had any doubts about rebuilding, right there, we have our answer."

"I think the board might want to have a word or two, but you're right. Without committed people, nothing will ever happen around here, but we seem to have those."

"You sound like you're ready to swing a hammer with them down there, Barry."

"I don't know." Barry shrugged and grinned. "But I guess if a hammer needs swinging—I probably can do that."

"Rafael and I were getting ready to retire, take it a bit easier, do some travelling, see the world. Besides, I don't even know if they will…"

Survive. She didn't want to say the word and checked her phone instead. She had left strict instructions to be called if there was any change in Rafael's, Al's, or Dante's condition. Nothing.

"They'll survive," Barry said, rising. "Meanwhile, I'm going to organize a phone conference with the rest of our board, make some plans. We'll have to get the insurance involved. They will not be happy. I don't know how much of this place the police have cleared yet, but I think you should speak to the staff, and to the press, if you're up for it."

Kayla was up for it. She took another few minutes, mentally willing Rafael to get better, then assembled the staff in the great lobby.

She thanked everyone for their compassion and concern, in the name of Rafael, Al, and Dante.

"Keep them in your thoughts," she said. "If anything, they will need your prayers and your good thoughts, now more than ever before."

She spoke of Roberto, and how he had lost his life in Greg Turner's mad revenge plot, while trying to free the others.

"We will make sure he is remembered," she said softly. "Once Perfect Cannabis has been rebuilt, we will make absolutely sure he is remembered."

Applause greeted her, but Kayla raised her hand, stopping them.

"Greg Turner killed a man and injured three others," she continued.

"Why? Because he wanted to take revenge for something that happened many years ago, that none of these men had a hand in. Greg Turner is a sick man, and yet he escaped from this hellish blaze he caused."

She wanted to stop there, but suddenly found she could not.

"He needs to be found," she said. "Found and brought to justice for what he has done. He may have escaped the fire last night, but he cannot hide forever. Make sure you know what he looks like, make sure you remember it well, and if you see him anywhere on the street, out in nature, or even on your security cameras or on social media, call the police. We all here—all of us," her arm swept around the room, "all of us have to become another eye looking for him. Thank you."

Now the applause thundered. People came to shake her hand and hug her again. Kayla could feel herself needing to sit down. It hadn't been that long since she'd been in the middle of that fire, but she gritted her teeth and made sure to talk to everyone this time, to thank them.

An arm pulled her away a little while later, and she found herself face-to-face with Detective Sergeant Sean Robertson.

"Really, Kayla? You just hired everyone in this room to the police force? Are you insane?"

"Don't you talk to me about being insane, Robertson. If you had done your job last night, or over the last few weeks looking for the mentally unstable person in this story, Greg Turner, well, none of this would have happened."

"I told you we…"

"He called in a bomb threat, and you were under orders to stand down. I heard it. And I might even understand the logic behind it, but Turner has evaded you for months now. Somehow or other, he managed to sneak in this building—more than once."

"What are you talking about?"

He maneuvered her into a quiet corner of the lobby and pulled out a chair for her. "Sit. You look like you're about to fall down."

"So happens I was in a massive fire last night, if you hadn't heard or were busy with something else."

"I know—you're not happy with me. Now tell me what the fu— what the heck you are talking about. Turner was here more than once?"

"Weren't you wondering how he got in here, Detective? How he managed to turn off the electricity to everything with the exception of what he needed? Didn't you ask how he might have gotten past our security systems, which, by the way, are some of the best available in this country?"

"I just thought…"

"You thought maybe Rafael's security concept was flawed, and Turner exploited that."

"I don't have enough of an understanding to make that decision." Robertson took a step back and mustered Kayla, head to toe. "Well? You going to tell me or what?"

"Or what," Kayla spat. "Gregory Turner managed to clone the access cards of an executive I had dismissed—Thomas Donnelly. I have no idea how he did it. But that gave him executive-level access to every single system in the building."

Robertson blinked a few times in rapid succession, whistled, and looked around for another chair. "Cloned," he said incredulously. "But how do you…"

"Yes. Cloned. And I don't know how he did it, but Tessa saw him in the system yesterday, as Thomas Donnelly."

"And Donnelly couldn't have…"

Kayla waved him away. "No," she said flatly. "We had our arguments, but nothing that would cause this level of destruction. Most likely, he was just a weak link Turner exploited."

"Jesus." Robertson forked a hand through his hair. "That explains a lot."

"And if you had found him before…"

"Ms. Montecito, I told you already…"

"How many cameras are out there, do you know? It creeps me out sometimes—every major intersection has a traffic camera, every store has video surveillance, every bank, every ATM, and, lately, every doorbell has a camera in it. You think if you had taken Turner's picture and started to search, you would have found him? Before he destroyed our grow operation? Before he killed Roberto Ivers and seriously injured Dante and Al, and Rafael? Think about that for a minute."

"I'm not arguing that the technical possibilities would have been there, Ms. Montecito," Robertson said, getting more exasperated with her by the minute. "But you can hardly expect that I would have compelled every doorbell video in the city to see if Turner had walked by."

"Really?" Kayla held up her cell phone. "Because I just did a smaller version of that."

Robertson took a few steps away from her, folded his hands behind his head, and came back.

"About that. We'll be wading through half-baked accusations and wild tips for weeks now. Valuable police resources are going to be wasted because somebody doesn't like his neighbor and thinks that's Greg Turner in disguise."

"Meanwhile, I am planning to hire a private investigator to help out. Maybe he or she will succeed where you did not. One person already died, Detective. God forbid anything happen to either Rafael, Dante, or Al. Because I don't intend to sit back and say, 'That's just the way it is.'"

As if her outburst had given her a jolt of fresh energy, she got to her feet, pushed away from Robertson, and walked away, leaving him standing in a corner of the reception area, dumbfounded.

In the hall that led down to the personnel offices, she stopped, steadying herself against the wall, and took a deep breath. She'd never get the smell of smoke out of her nostrils. She looked at her phone. Her office had sent her a message—their social media accounts were blowing up with responses to her call for action. Greg Turner's picture started showing up. *Be on the lookout.* Her own people congratulated her for her courage and promised to be there for her.

And she'd only spoken half an hour ago. Maybe it hadn't been the wisest thing, setting everybody she knew onto Turner's trail, but it was the only thing she could think of. Besides, it was her business, was it not? Making the news.

***

Large portions of the building were still blocked from access as damage was being cleared and safety concerns checked, but when she looked out into the lot in front of the building, she saw another giant trailer being delivered and set up. More employees started to gather out there, and Kayla secretly smiled and made a fist.

Gregory Turner better be on the lookout.

She checked her phone obsessively, unlocking it when she'd just put it away, hoping there would be a message. Despite all of the encouragement she received from staff at Montecito and at PerCan, from friends, neighbors, and even casual acquaintances, she still waited for that one message that Rafael had woken up.

Please God, let him be OK, she would repeat in her head, and then feel guilty, because the last time she'd actually prayed was likely as a kid in Sunday school, and Al and Dante were in the same hospital room, but it was Rafael she was waiting for.

How did Barry manage, she wondered? Where did he get the energy, after having been through the same fire she had? Because half an hour later, he wandered into the room and spread his arms.

"You now have a temporary office trailer and command center out there. Phone and internet have been hooked up. I really don't think we should be in here right now, until everything's been cleared."

"Thanks." She took his hand and rose. "I really don't know how you do it."

"Magic." Barry shrugged. Then he hesitated, cocked his head a little in that way he had when he wasn't quite sure, and asked, "Any news?"

393

No need to ask what news he was looking for. Kayla shook her head. "Nothing. I think I might just take a drive out there."

"Don't." Barry put his hand on her elbow.

"You're not going to do them any good sitting outside their hospital room, fretting."

"But I need to be there."

"No," Barry said and gently but surely guided her out of the building and into the trailer he had set up. "You need to be here for our people. You need to be here making sure that building is ready for Rafael, so he can wander around grousing about how we did everything wrong when we cleaned up, and if we had only waited for him, he would have started completely differently."

"You know him so well." Kayla smiled and took a seat at a hurriedly installed round table, where the disaster recovery team already waited with updates and requests.

Hours went by, reading through damage reports, issuing orders, and speaking alternately to the media, concerned employees, and contractors who needed instructions.

Fire inspectors and forensic experts searched through the charred remains of pod five and confirmed what Barry had already told her: Turner had used all of the available cardboard he found in the shipping docks to create a massive fire, hoping to kill everyone he had locked into the pod. The sterilizing gas Rafael had used only played into his hand, making sure the fire burned hot, and spread rapidly before anyone could get in to try and save the men.

If Tessa had not come out to PerCan, if she hadn't logged into the system and opened every single watering and fertilization valve in the building, none of them would be standing here today, giving orders to restore the building.

Tessa. Tessa herself was there, with a new laptop and their chief of security, checking through every inch, every element of the IT system, running diagnostics, calling out findings. Kayla had only a rudimentary understanding what they spoke about, but every now and then, they'd look up from their work, Tessa's and Kayla's eyes would meet, and they'd smile in a shared understanding and memory.

They had both been there. They'd never forget.

The day passed, and still there was no new update from the hospital. Kayla wanted to scream. Was she the only one, who…?

Then Barry showed up with a car service to take them to the hospital. How he was still on his feet, she didn't know, and, when she asked him, he only shrugged.

Again, she stood at that little glass window, looking into the room where Rafael, Al, and Dante lay. And, again, she put her hands flat against the glass and willed them to come back.

You have to make it, you hear me? I am bringing your bloody production back for you to come back to, so you have to make it. That's all there is to it.

That night, the doctors were just a tiny bit more encouraging, just a smidgen more hopeful, she thought—or maybe she was imagining it all because she couldn't let her mind go to that place where they didn't.

She went home, put down her new bag, and wondered how she would get through the night without nightmares about fires and Greg Turner, but, in the end, exhaustion simply overtook her, and she fell asleep without another thought.

FORTY-NINE

The nightmares didn't come, but they crowded in on her thoughts the moment she opened her eyes the next morning. How had Rafael fared overnight? Was he any better? Had anyone come up with a tip about Turner?

She cleaned up awkwardly, dressed, and had a car take her right back to her temporary little trailer at PerCan, where she found Tessa and Barry at work already. The three survivors.

She smiled when Barry hugged her.

"Any change?" he asked, and Kayla shook her head.

"No, but they are stable, all three of them. I think the way his doctors put it was 'cautiously optimistic.'"

"Cautiously optimistic is good. Any optimistic is good."

"Damn right it is. Have you heard from our friend Robertson?"

Barry handed her a cup of coffee from a tray of many. "Negative. I am hoping that means they are simply busy with tips...."

Kayla sat down, curled her fingers around the hot cup, and stared into the dark liquid.

"I had dozens of messages this morning. So many want to help, want to make sure Turner doesn't get away with what he has done. The more sympathetic ones want to make sure he gets help for his mental issues."

"He won't get away with anything. Trust me."

"You're so sure about this? He roamed about this town for months undetected, hiding in the shadows, God knows where, while all of us carried on without knowing that he had gone over the edge."

Barry looked at her without speaking then, and she saw something in his eyes that made her shiver just a bit. Something she had never seen before in the always jovial, good-time Barry J. Wentworth. Perhaps it was determination, but if she had to guess, he would have said hate. Straight up, cold-edged hate.

"Not while I have anything to say about it, he won't get away," Barry said quietly and turned around to speak to a contractor who had just arrived at the trailer with rolled-up plans and supply lists.

Kayla hugged her arms to her body and reached for her phone. Everyone she knew was by now on the lookout for Turner. He couldn't hide. Meanwhile, she knew she had to keep busy with the restoration of PerCan, or she would go out of her mind, checking her phone for messages for updates on Rafael.

Instead, she coordinated arriving supplies and made a few conference calls with her publishing office. Anything—but the distraction never lasted. Every time she realized she'd been working on something for longer than 10 minutes without checking on either Rafael or the progress of the search for Turner, she panicked and checked her phone.

Barry, she noticed, came around every few minutes as well.

She was in the middle of counting how many dumpsters filled with debris had been hauled away when the door to her little trailer flew open, and Detective Robertson pounded up the stairs and inside without pausing.

"Are you happy with yourself?" he snarled and slammed the door shut behind him.

"Probably, if you tell me why I shouldn't be. Are you happy with the progress the search for Greg Turner is making, Detective?"

Kayla flipped her laptop shut and folded her arms before her chest. "And about your manners storming in here?"

"Every single one of my detectives is busy chasing down leads about

Greg Turner, Ms. Montecito. All stations are inundated. Jammed up from here to next Wednesday."

"Good. Then it won't be long before he is found."

"It also won't be long before the real criminals realize we are busy chasing our own tails, and there will be nobody available to stop them."

"The real criminals, Detective? The real ones? As opposed to the phantom that tried to blow up PerCan?"

"Sorry, that came out all wrong."

He dropped into a chair and dragged his fingers through his hair. "It's been nonstop from the moment you told everyone."

"To be on the lookout—I know."

Again, the door opened, and Barry bounded in. "Any news?"

"Not yet." Kayla nodded at Robertson. "The detective was just about to tell me how I overloaded his police force and the real criminals are getting away."

"The real…"

"Bad choice of words, I told you. Listen, the both of you." Robertson straightened and refused to back down from Barry's angry glare. "Will you please stop getting involved and let us do our job? 300 fake reports and Greg Turner sightings—that's how many I've been dealing with since yesterday. And each one of them needs to be followed up on and checked. It's not like I have an army at my disposal."

Kayla looked down and said nothing for a moment. "Fine."

"We're on the same page here, Ms. Montecito. We all want the same thing. We want him caught. And if a bunch of civilians are running around playing detective, somebody is going to get hurt, understand?"

That one made a modicum of sense, and Kayla nodded. "Yes, I understand."

"Good. Then stop having your office send out 'have you seen this man' messages promising a reward. Please."

"I was only…"

"We're trying to help," Barry said and put his arm on her shoulder.

"We were attacked. This company and us personally. With all due respect…"

"Yes, I will do my best." Robertson raised his hands. "That should be self-explanatory."

He got to his feet and left the trailer just as abruptly as he had entered it, leaving Kayla and Barry staring after him.

"Now he's doing his best," she muttered. "After months of telling us there's nothing to be done about Turner."

"You posted a reward?"

"Damn straight I did. You think I was going to sit here twiddling my thumbs waiting for Robertson and his crew? Turner hurt Rafael. What if—what if…"

Her voice cracked, and she fanned her hands against her eyes to stop the tears.

"Don't go there." Barry opened his arms. "Come here, take a step back, and take a breath. It will work out fine. Everything will…"

At that very moment, the door blew open again, and Robertson pounded back into the trailer, yelling into his phone.

"Where—what area, what time?"

He listened for a moment and motioned for Kayla and Barry to come in closer.

"You got eyes on him? Right now?"

Kayla's hands froze and balled into fists, and she couldn't move as time slowed down around her. Robertson said, "Yes," and "I got it. Be right there," a few times and finally finished his call.

"What?" she yelled, feeling as if she wanted to grab him by the shoulders to shake him.

"We have a sighting—this time, it appears to be a credible one."

"Where?" Kayla and Barry spoke almost as one.

"Not too far." Robertson suddenly checked himself. "I can't tell you that. What I need you to do is stay here, stay inside this trailer and wait, just in case he is headed this way. Can you do that?"

No, of course not, she wanted to say. *Finally, you have eyes on this maniac with a revenge fantasy, and you want me to stay here? You want me to sit back and wait?* She opened her mouth, and Robertson raised one single finger.

"Armed and dangerous," he said slowly, enunciating like a first grader. "You know what that means? Good. I have to go, but I need to know you will stay here and not go running around there, searching for Turner, filled with crazy ideas of your own. Please. This is no game. Can I count on you to stay right here?"

Hell, no, she thought and looked at Barry. Barry narrowed his eyes and said nothing.

"Say it."

"What, are we in first grade?" Kayla snapped, and finally, Barry nodded.

"Yes, Detective, we will stay right here."

"Good. Make sure you do. When I give the all-clear, you can take Ms. Montecito home. Until then, I don't have the manpower to spare to protect you."

"Understood."

The detective left, and Kayla automatically ran to the window to watch him jump into his car and peel out of the lot.

"Now what do we…?"

"Kayla." Barry took both of her hands. "I don't like him any more than you do—but I just promised Robertson to keep you right here and safe."

"But we can't just…"

"Yes, we can. For once, let's just sit back and let them do the heavy lifting. We have enough on our plates right now with the disaster recovery and worrying about Rafael. When was the last time you called the hospital?"

"This morning." Kayla looked down at her shoes.

"You can check in with their nurse then. Maybe there's good news by now."

"They would have called."

"Look." Barry gently led her back to the desk she had vacated a few minutes ago and pulled out a chair for her. "It's taking all I've got not to run to where he was seen last, find him, grab him, and ask him what the hell he was thinking going after my friend. Then I want to take a baseball bat and beat the living…"

He exhaled and looked down at his shoes.

"Anyway, you get the picture. But I know Greg Turner is mentally unstable and extremely dangerous. And I also know, we—all of us here—do not want another person in the hospital we have to check up on. Or worse."

"You're right." Kayla sank back in the chair and side-eyed the windows. "When did you get so annoyingly smart?"

"I know what revenge can do, Kayla. Revenge killed Tadeo Ivers. Sometimes I wish I'd never teed up Turner to destroy that merger with Green Technologies way back when. None of this would have happened. But I can't undo any of it. So please—please. Stay here, stay safe, and let Robertson handle it."

Kayla steepled her hands before her face and sighed. Her carefully tied ponytail was coming undone, and she had to shake strands out of her face. She'd never heard Barry talk about regrets, or guilt. And now two people were dead, and the other three…

"Fine then," she said softly.

"I'll make sure I have a baseball bat handy. Plus, they'll have him in a little while anyway." The dark moment dispelled, Barry grinned his usual, uber-charming grin again. "There's nothing really here for him to come back to. He's burned down most of PerCan, he knows Rafa, Al, and Dante are in the hospital, and you and I… I don't think you and I even make his radar. All the same, I'm going to stick to you like glue, just so you know."

Kayla stared at the window for a long moment, not really seeing anything outside, and tapped her fingers on the desk.

"I will go insane if I have to sit here doing nothing. So—what did the disaster recovery team say? How bad is the damage to the grow area anyway?"

Barry blinked, and pulled up his report. "Well, office and admin areas and the big boardroom should be OK within a week or two."

"Two weeks?"

"Yeah, I hired Rafael's old construction company. If the police had let them, they would have been here this morning.

"Growing area is a different story," Barry continued, checking the notes on his tablet. "Pods three, five, seven, and nine are a total write-off. The remainder need massive restoration work the closer they are to five. The only workable ones would be one and 11—except the fire knocked out or destroyed all of the environmental controls and ferti-gation, and the expert on all of that is Rafael. So, when he's back, that will be the first thing he has to work on. Until then, most of what we do will be removing debris and damaged materials."

"Thank you." Kayla looked down for a beat and smiled. "Also for saying *when* he gets back."

"No problem."

"Then let's get to work again. I'm going to make a quick call to the hospital. Then you and I should do a walk-through, and make an initial plan. Here is what I am thinking…"

***

And so the afternoon passed. The nurses and doctors still had no further updates, except that the men were still alive, still fighting for their lives, but a cautious optimism was warranted. Dante would never use his right leg again, and might end up losing it altogether, Al was still the weakest of the three, and Rafael—Rafael had inhaled so much smoke and chemical debris it would remain to be seen how much damage that had caused. For long, critical moments, his brain had been deprived of oxygen. One would simply have to wait and see.

Kayla made a fist. *Don't even go there*, she thought. *Don't think of it. At least he is alive.* Nick Ambrose had to be out of his mind, and, come to think of it, she hadn't seen him at the site yet. He might never be able to be in the same room with her. It was because of her that Dante had come back.

Don't think of it—don't go there.

***

Rules, lists, and schedules were the backbone of the publishing industry, and so she clung to those, walking through the building with Barry, Tessa, and Pam from HR, making lists and notes, assigning calls and schedules, and signing off on purchasing orders.

Purchasing orders that right then were a simple piece of yellow legal paper with the words Purchase Order written on it.

Barry wouldn't leave her side, as he had promised, but he trailed behind by a few feet, talking to insurance adjusters, bankers, and investors on the phone all afternoon.

Somehow, once they had made that decision, it had never been a question at all: *we will rebuild.*

The afternoon wore on, as employees dropped by and offered to help, wanted to shake her hand, and give their best wishes to Rafael. Kayla had to dab her eyes every single time, until Pam finally offered to speak to staff. Kayla shook her head and continued.

How could one man have affected so many lives with his straight talk, his earnest efforts and hard work, and genuine, caring manner? Easily, apparently, if that man was Rafael Covin, and that was only part of why she had fallen for him.

Not that people didn't ask about Al or Dante, but it was Rafael they seemed to worry about the most.

"You ever wonder how he does it?" Barry asked as they both returned to the trailer.

It had gotten late, and he had to turn on the single bare bulb light they had inside their little field office.

"Oh, trust me, I know how he does it." Kayla loosened her hair, shook it out, and retied it into a ponytail. "He cares. He cares about everyone. Listen—it's been one hell of a day. Are you sure we can't go home?"

Barry looked down at his phone, scrolled through a few messages, and shook his head slowly.

"Last I heard from Robertson was that they are on his tail and to still sit tight until he gave the all-clear."

"Aaagh." Kayla threw up her arms. "So we sit here, in a construction trailer, waiting? How long did he say?"

"He didn't."

"Fantastic. Just what I always wanted. On top of everything, I'm getting hungry. Can we order some food?"

Kayla tried to pace up and down in the trailer, which proved to be impossible. She checked her email and her most-often-used news feeds obsessively. Nothing. She really wanted to check in with Rafael's nurses again, but the annoyance she'd heard in her last call told her not to. It had only been a few hours, and she could almost hear them saying, "Every minute I spend on the phone with you…" No. Maybe just before she went to bed. Which was a few hours yet.

Again, she tried to pace and, again, failed.

Barry slouched in a chair, feet on the table, casually scrolling through his phone. Annoying. "Anything?" she asked.

"Hm?" He looked up and shook his head as if he'd been in a completely different mental space.

"Anything new?" Kayla asked, well aware that she was snapping at him.

"No. I'm reading something—totally different."

She went to the tiny, single window of the trailer and peeked out. The PerCan building now lay in darkness and silence, with the exception of security spotlights. Several dumpsters had been lined up to haul away debris, many of them already full. Everything else was quiet. She turned on her heel and glared at Barry, already immersed in his reading again.

"They must have him by now." No answer. "Turner. They probably caught him by now, you know."

Barry sighed and put down his phone.

"Kayla. They will call us the moment they do. The moment, OK?"

"You don't have to get so snippy with me. I'm just saying—it's been hours. Maybe Robertson forgot. Or he went straight to interrogate him. Maybe they think we went home or something."

"I don't think so. He was pretty adamant for us to wait."

Barry picked up his phone again, and Kayla almost felt her patience snapping right then and there. Who the hell were these people, telling her to hang out in a construction trailer all bloody night?

Nobody was doing that, and besides, she had things to do and needed to prepare for tomorrow. She still had a publishing house to run. Staff—employees—important decisions.

"You know what," she said and looked around for her jacket and purse. "It is late. I'm hungry. I'm going to call a car to take me home. I can wait for Robertson to update you just as well there as I can here. Where's my phone?"

"Kayla. Robertson thought…"

"Yes, I do know what the good detective thought. He thought we should wait here until everything was taken care of. That was hours ago, when he assumed he would go out there and catch Turner right then. That didn't happen. So now I am going home."

"Please don't."

"Why? Because Robertson said so? Good for him. I'm leaving. You can stay here if you want. If they don't call you until tomorrow, you can even sleep here. Don't worry—I'll wake you in the morning."

She found her jacket and shrugged into it with short jerky movements, located her phone on a sideboard, and scrolled for the number of her car service.

"All right, all right, hold on." Barry got to his feet and shook his head. "You are the epitome of a stubborn female. I should have remembered. At least let me take you home."

"Stubborn? Did you just call me stubborn? I have my car service on speed dial."

"And I have a car sitting right out there." He pointed at the window, and for a second, she thought she saw a shadow moving outside.

"Oh, I well remember how stubborn you are. I've known you for a very long time."

Barry opened the door, and a gentle evening breeze came into the trailer, and she could see the leaves blowing around out there, throwing shadows. A set of metal grate stairs led from the door down, and she had to grab the railing for a moment. Walking anywhere was going to be a challenge for a little longer.

"I'm fine," she said, waving away Barry's helping hand. "I've been walking around all day. That's all. Just lock up that darn trailer and let's go already."

Barry's car sat a short distance away, closer to the dumpsters they had ordered. It was the last car left in the lot, and Kayla rolled her eyes.

"You see? Everybody else has gone off already."

"Yes, dear, of course, dear," Barry mocked and let go of her elbow to pat his pockets. "Now where are my keys?"

"Barry—I really think I should…"

It didn't matter what she thought she should because the air was knocked out of her lungs quite suddenly by a dark shapeless shadow that had slipped out from between the dumpsters, hitting her full force in the chest. Kayla screamed even as the force of the impact slammed her backwards off her feet and into the ground.

Her fingers grappled in the gravel below, and she could feel someone grabbing her shoulders. Frantically, she tried to make sense of what was happening. The man standing over her, roaring with sheer wordless anger.

And then there was another sound, a single scream. Kayla scrambled on the ground, getting to her knees, feeling gravel digging painfully into her shins and hands.

Barry's rage had erupted like a volcano as he seized the man who had assaulted Kayla. He bellowed with fury and hurled him against the metal dumpster with a bone-jarring impact. The man's head ricocheted off the unforgiving surface, making a deafening clang that echoed through the lot. Kayla trembled with fear and disbelief. Could that really be Greg Turner, straightening now, and rounding on Barry? The sheer brutality of the assault made her stomach churn with revulsion and dread.

Kayla finally made it to her feet and stumbled back a step. Surely… Another scream. Turner spun around, raised his fists, and charged Barry. The security spotlight glinted off a lethal-looking switchblade in his hand as he swung for him.

"Get out of here, Kayla."

Oh God—why hadn't they stayed inside that trailer? Why hadn't she listened?

"You," Turner yelled, squaring off to Barry, the light glinting off the blade. "You are everything that's in my way."

"Run, Kayla."

Kayla stood frozen. For the second time in so many days, she was watching people she cared about being attacked. For the second time. Not again.

Where was her phone? Her heart raced as she scrambled toward the little grey rectangle on the ground, the sound of the scuffle behind her growing louder with each passing second. She could hear the metal clang of the blade against something hard and the thud of bodies hitting the pavement. Kayla's hands trembled as she fumbled to pick up her phone, her eyes darting between the screen and the fight unfolding before her. Suddenly, a shadow loomed over her, and she looked up to see Greg

Turner towering above her. He'd knocked down Barry, turned toward her with lightning speed, and caught her with an elbow around her neck.

"Want to call for help, do you? Call all you want. There is no help."

Kayla desperately twisted in his grip, but she could feel it—the sharp cold blade of the knife against her throat. She clawed at Turner's arm, desperate for air, but he only squeezed harder. Barry charged forward, and Turner spun around and kicked him in the gut, sending him stumbling back. Kayla's vision was starting to blur now, her limbs growing weak. She couldn't die like this. Not at the hands of some psychopath. All of her senses suddenly became hyper aware. There was Barry, his mouth open in a scream. There was the smell of Turner, dirty and acrid, the smoke of the fire from the previous night overlaid with sweat and desperation, and Barry's furious, primal scream.

And then—Turner's grip loosened.

Greg Turner laughed, a long and mad cackle that made shivers go down her back, and then it stopped as suddenly as it had started. His hands let go of her, and the knife dropped from her throat, drawing a tiny bead of blood on the way.

Barry was a mere blur. Kayla saw a flash and something in his hand. Something long and heavy. Greg Turner screamed as she had never heard a living being scream.

Kayla trembled uncontrollably now and sank to the ground, scooting backwards until she hit the metal dumpster behind her. Barry kept coming. In one motion he had grabbed a metal pipe that had fallen out of one of the dumpsters, and he swung with angry, lethal strength, again and again.

Blows rained down on Turner as if they would never stop, unloading everything that had happened in the last few weeks—perhaps even years. Kayla whimpered, pulled her arms around her knees, and rocked back and forth. This could not be her reality. And then, somewhere in the distance, she heard the sound of a siren.

Lights flashed. A pipe dropped on the ground beside her, and gentle hands took her shoulders.

"Kayla, are you all right? Please be all right, please…"

Barry. His face now a mask of concern, even though his eyes still shone with the wild fury she had seen moments ago. Gently, he shook her shoulders.

"Tell me you're not hurt."

His voice came through a long, endless tunnel. So far away. Then she heard tires crunching on gravel and voices, so many voices talking all over one another. *Over here,* somebody yelled, and another siren wailed somewhere. More hands on her shoulders trying to lift her, when all she wanted to do was close her eyes and let go. Just let go.

"It's all over—look…"

That sounded like Rafael. It was Rafael's voice, but where was he? With an effort, she raised her head, and then, with a pop, as if a bubble had quite suddenly burst, reality returned.

Kayla let out a scream and tried to back away even more, against the dumpster behind her.

"Easy—easy. It's all over, OK? Are you hurt?"

"Barry," she said softly, and it was the only word she could get out.

"He's over there, being taken care of. He's fine. What about you? Are you injured?"

"Barry." She tried to scramble to her feet, her shoes sinking into soft gravel. "Barry."

"He's fine. Easy."

The unknown police officer trying to help her gently held her shoulders and asked her to stay down, but Kayla pushed him away with a ferocity that surprised even herself. She stumbled to her feet, her legs shaky with adrenaline and fear, but determined not to stay down. She was not going to be a victim again.

Where there had been only empty darkness before, the lot was now teeming with vehicles—police cars, ambulance cars, a fire truck somewhere in the distance, and unmarked vehicles rolling in and stopping haphazardly, as people jumped out and joined the growing group around her.

"Barry," she called out again, and a figure detached itself from a group.

"I'm here, I'm here—I'm fine."

Barry came toward her and hugged her close, and, finally, the tears she had been holding in came out. Great heaving sobs that tore her apart. She didn't dare to look down, down by the dumpster where she knew…

"Here, it's OK, it's OK," Barry murmured, but she could feel his hands on her shoulders shaking violently.

"What happened—what on earth happened just now?"

"He was threatening you, and I—lost it," Barry said softly, and she could hear some uncertainty in his voice. "I'm not even totally sure."

A car crunched to a stop somewhere close, and Detective Robertson jumped out without bothering to close the doors. With several giant steps, he was by their side.

"Barry? Ms. Montecito? Are you all right?"

"More or less," Kayla said, hating how her voice trembled. "All I wanted to do was go home."

"Didn't I tell you to…?"

Barry raised a hand and stopped the detective with that one gesture.

"Can you lay off the guilt trip for just a minute? We were not sure what was going on or how long this would take, but we couldn't spend the whole night in that trailer either, all right? I take responsibility."

"Barry, you don't have to…"

"What about Turner?" Robertson glared at Barry. "We were tracking him. We were closing in, and now…?"

"You can collect him over there," Barry said with a cold, hard edge to his voice and cocked a thumb over his shoulder. "He was threatening Ms. Montecito, holding a knife to her throat."

Robertson only stared at Barry.

"I took care of it." Barry shrugged. "A piece of metal pipe that had fallen out of the dumpster. He was threatening Kayla, OK?"

Robertson still didn't speak. He turned away, to where medics now surrounded the crumpled form of Greg Turner, and exchanged a few words with them.

Kayla took Barry's hand and clung to it as if her very life depended on it. "I thought—I thought I had…"

"Hush," he said softly. "It's over. I don't know if Turner will survive, but I can guarantee you he will not harm any of us again—ever."

Robertson came stomping back and grabbed Barry's elbow, trying to pull him away. "What are you, some sort of ninja warrior?"

"I was mad at him." Barry shrugged. "Look, can we go now? Ms. Montecito is cold, half starved, and somebody just tried to kill her—again."

"We'll have to ask a few questions."

"Well, ask them after we've had some food and a hot shower, OK?"

Meanwhile, a medic wanted to look at the cut on Kayla's throat, declared it not particularly dangerous, and treated it with disinfectant and a bandage. Someone handed her a cup of hot, sweet tea and wrapped a blanket around her shoulders. And moment by moment, she felt her insides warming up and the release of the terror she'd been feeling for the last hour.

Finally, she straightened her back and gave herself a little mental shake.

"Barry was defending me, Detective," she said, her voice strong and clear once again. "Which is something I was expecting your force to do. How on earth did Greg Turner manage to slip away from you to threaten us here? That is what I want to know."

"I told you to…"

"Yes, you told us to stay here, Detective—right where Turner was able to attack us. Pretty good advice, I can see that."

The detective looked down at the ground and rubbed his hands over and over.

"Why was he even here, and why did we not know about it? If you were tracking him, surely, you knew he was headed for this building."

"We lost him in the downtown core," Robertson said. "We had no idea he was going to come back here. It makes no sense to come back."

"Presumably, that is exactly why he did it." Barry shrugged. "Probably thought he could spend the night there amongst the construction debris and move on in the morning. Why would anybody look for him here?"

Robertson nodded. "And then." He cocked his head toward the dumpsters, where the paramedics were now loading him on a stretcher and into the waiting ambulance.

"Then he saw us getting into my car, and his mind took a bit of a left turn, I guess," Barry continued. "He babbled something about how we were everything that was left in his way and…" he shrugged, "held a knife to Kayla's throat."

"And you just…"

"'I beat the living crap out of him' is the phrase you are looking for." Barry tightened a fist and pressed his lips together. "As anybody in my situation would have, I am sure. What kind of shape is he in, do you know?"

"Gee, Mr. Wentworth, somebody beat the living crap out of him. What kind of shape do you think he's in? He's going to need an extended hospital stay—but fortunately, you prevented the attack on Ms. Montecito. Thank you."

"Can we go now?" Kayla asked again, and Robertson shook his head.

More questions needed to be asked, more photos and tests taken. Photos of the cut on her neck and her hands and her phone that had flown out of her hands and the jacket Turner had torn when he grabbed her.

Kayla stumbled awkwardly back into the trailer and sat at the desk she had vacated—had it just been a couple of hours ago? She wrapped the blanket tighter around her shoulders and closed her eyes for just one second only to open them again with a shudder. She could still see Barry rounding on Greg Turner, the pipe in his hand. She could still hear Turner scream.

"Are you all right?"

Kayla thought it felt like every few minutes someone asked her that question. Was she all right? No, not really, and it would likely be a while before she would be anything close to all right. And that voice she had heard—just as the police and medics arrived.

It's all over—look.

That voice—*deep breaths now,* she reminded herself. Kayla took deep breaths and blew them out, folding her hands tightly.

Somewhere in the room, a phone rang, again and again. Kayla looked around. Barry stood in the corner and checked his but shook his head, and then she realized it was her new phone, that Detective Robertson had picked up and brought inside—as evidence.

Never mind evidence. If that phone rang, it could only mean one thing. With trembling hands, she picked it up and answered the call.

"This is Kayla."

"Ms. Montecito? I have some good news for you."

Kayla smiled, and warmth and joy flooded her entire body. In one moment she knew what had happened, knew whose voice she had heard in her head, just as Barry was defending her from Greg Turner. Rafael Covin had finally woken up, and his first thought had been of her, and his first question had been if Kayla was all right. Yes, yes, of course, she was all right now.

EPILOGUE

"Were you not told that you should be taking it easy?"

"Maybe." Rafael moved awkwardly, using a cane as he couldn't quite put all of his weight onto his injured right leg. He hated the cane, really, and constantly groused that it made him look old, but construction sites were hard enough to get around in on two perfectly healthy legs. Besides, the cane was proving to be quite handy when he wanted to point at things, or nudge someone who definitely was not moving fast enough. Lots of people were not moving fast enough. What were they thinking? Did they really imagine that rebuilding a cannabis facility was something that happened all on its own if you just gave it enough time?

"Grow pods don't grow on trees," he called out to somebody. "Don't you have equipment to unload from that trailer out there?"

"I know that, Rafael," the worker in question called back and turned to him with a huge smile on his face. "I am unloading it now. Shouldn't you be sitting down somewhere?"

"I am not sitting down!"

"You're a bit rough on them, are you not?" Kayla took his elbow and watched the uneven ground. It was still hard for her to get around, with roomy boots the only footwear she could wear, but she wouldn't miss a day of the rebuilding for anything.

"You, young lady, should be wearing steel-toed safety boots—and they're construction workers. I'm merely being straight with them."

He wore a Covin Construction Corp hard hat and wrapped his free arm around her shoulders.

"Did I tell you how proud I am of you?"

"Only every other day."

"I cannot believe how much cleanup you got done while I was in that damnable hospital."

"You mean while you were recovering from almost burning to death and inhaling all manner of smoke and chemicals?"

"Oh." Rafael waved a hand. "Not nearly as tragic as all that. Be good as new in no time. Few cool scars maybe, that's all." He pointed toward an enormous boom crane lifting what appeared to be a thick pane of glass. Right then, it looked blue and opaque covered in safety film, and the sight made her shiver with the memory. Rafael tightened his hand a little more.

"Look—the new window into the production area is going in today."

"I see that." Kayla only looked for a minute and back at the bustle in the production area. All of the blackened remains of grow pods had been removed by now, and the concrete below and the walls cleaned of all debris the fire had left behind. "Are you so sure that is a good idea—another glass window? After everything that happened, I mean?"

"No, this one is even stronger than the one we had there last time. All but bulletproof."

"Rafael. Do me a favor and don't use words like *bullet*."

"No, but you see—it will be able to withstand…"

"Sometimes I wonder if there is something seriously wrong with you," she said, shaking her head.

A soft hum announced Al Ivers arriving in a small electric scooter. Al parked with a flourish and awkwardly climbed off the little car.

"The only man I know who gets excited about construction matters in the presence of a beautiful woman. How are you, my dear?"

Gallantly, he took Kayla's hand, only to envelop her in a massive hug. He still looked so gaunt and frail a strong puff of air might blow him over. He had survived by a sheer miracle and his own tenacity, after all of the fine physicians at the hospital had shaken their heads and told them not to get their hopes up too high.

"I'm just fine, Al. And you too should probably be at home, resting and recovering, don't you think?"

She frowned and looked down at the little scooter he had arrived on. "Did Rafael fit that thing with offroad tires?"

"Well, if he wanted to check on the arrival of our window today, he sure needed them," Rafael said and hugged Al as well. "This is a serious construction site. How are you feeling, Al?"

He winked at his friend and nodded toward the scooter.

"You might as well sit again. We're not big on ceremony around here."

Al sat obediently on his scooter and looked around. "I really cannot believe…"

"How much they got done? Unreal, isn't it? We're ahead of schedule. All of the electrical equipment is arriving today, and the new pods will go in by the end of the week."

Kayla took Rafael's hand, squeezed, and shook her head.

"I'm happy to see you out and about. I can't imagine rehab being any fun. And—and…"

For a long moment, neither of them spoke, and finally, Al looked up at them and smiled.

"Before you get all embarrassed wondering if it's OK to ask about Roberto and Dante, let me relieve you."

Kayla made a fist and pressed her lips together—hard. The memory of that night still visited her in her nightmares, with the image of the men inside a burning grow pod, helpless. Roberto, trying to open the door…

"We will hold a memorial for Roberto next week," Al said softly. "He died giving his life for the three of us, trying to open the door so we could escape, just at the moment when…" His voice choked, and Rafael put a hand on his friend's shoulder.

Al swallowed a couple of times and pressed his lips together. After a few tries, he straightened his shoulders with an effort and sat up straight.

"We will hold a memorial," he said. "Out at Pride Cannabis, the company he built and was so proud of."

"At Pride? But that's…"

Kayla interrupted Rafael and beamed. "That's a lovely idea, Al. Roberto was exceptionally proud of everything he had built there, and his men—his men were the people who helped us out when we needed them most."

"Thank you. Now. The man nobody here wants to mention is Dante."

Kayla and Rafael didn't speak. Dante was not doing well, and no matter how often they had visited him in the hospital, he didn't appear to be getting any better. The one-two punch of a motorcycle accident and a massive fire had been far too much for his body, although Kayla suspected the ongoing rift between herself and Nick Ambrose, and the arguments it was causing between the two of them, couldn't possibly help matters any.

At a minimum, Dante would never be able to use his right leg again, and there was still a possibility he might lose that leg entirely. He fought that decision and wouldn't speak to anyone. What she knew, she knew from Al. Kayla shuddered when she thought of it and clenched her hands even tighter than they already were.

Al only smiled gently.

"Kayla, I understand this is distressing for you. Dante specifically asked me to reassure you that you bear no guilt or responsibility for what happened."

"He would say that," Kayla said, choking back the lump in her throat. "But Nick and he, and that—that mess. That was all on me."

Al reached out and took her hand and gently unclenched her fingers.

"Dearest Kayla, please do not torture yourself. That is not why I am telling you this story. Neither of us are blaming you, especially not Dante. You did what you had to do—end of discussion."

Kayla only nodded. It was all she could manage at that point, but Al would not let go of her hand.

"The reason I'm telling you all of this…" He turned his scooter around a little to include Rafael, who stood staring at the busyness of his construction site, his lips firmly pressed together. "The reason I am telling you all of this—and this includes you, Rafael, even though you are standing there right now pretending nothing bothers you and you are all cool."

"I am not… Yeah—it's rough when I think about it. That's why I don't."

Al only chuckled. "Right. You do not fool me for a minute, Rafael. No, I am telling you this because Nick and Dante have decided to rebuild and run Roberto's Pride Cannabis together, and I've told them we would support them any which way they need, or are comfortable accepting."

"What a lovely idea," Kayla said, and Rafael scowled.

"It's their way of honoring our brother, and I hope you understand that."

"Sure," Rafael muttered and looked down at his shoes.

"I know this will leave a huge gap in our production and continuity as a company, but I also know you will manage, Rafael. You always do."

"Usually," Rafael said and shuffled his feet. "When one of you Ivers men tells me I have to."

"Splendid. I knew you would love the idea. To tell you the truth, I was not even all that keen on rebuilding PerCan myself, but the board seems to have outvoted me on this matter, and I was not up for a massive fight, even though I own most of the shares."

"But you might have…" Kayla said, and Al put a finger to his lips.

"Shh—it's been decided. So be it. Besides, you would have to find something else for Rafael here to do all day long without his production area. I'm sure he would be very difficult as a retired person."

"I heard that!"

Rafael had walked away a few steps to peer closely at a freshly poured cement pad.

"Well, he'll have to start getting used to it," Kayla said. "I already made him promise to start taking it a lot easier once this rebuild here is done. Perhaps, God forbid, even take a vacation here and there. One without tornadoes in it."

Rafael came back and sighed. "I will. I told you I will—but first you will have to let me rebuild my plant. These people can't even pour cement properly if I don't show them what to do. Can you imagine them installing the new grow pods on…? Anyway," Rafael peered at the two of them for a moment. "By the way, they have finished restoring your office, Al. All of the smoke damage is gone. They've even put in a brand-new coffeemaker, so if the two of you want to have a bit of coffee and donuts…"

"Is that your way of saying 'get the heck off my construction site,' Rafael?"

Rafael only grinned. "I would never… But first you have to tell me what's happening to that horrible, insane, and triple-damned…"

"Greg Turner," Kayla finished and shivered hard, reaching for Rafael's hand again. Al folded his hands in his lap and said nothing for a very, very long time. He sighed, raised his head, attempting that quirky little sideways smile Kayla had always teased him about. But that smile didn't reach his eyes. They were cold, flat, and dark. *Pure and undiluted hatred,* she thought. Hatred so strong and powerful that, if he ever let it out, it would be an unbeatable force of nature.

"Greg Turner," he said, his voice curiously unaffected, as if he were a guest on one of those true crime podcasts everybody was listening to just now. "Greg Turner—yes. The man who tried to wipe out my entire family."

Again, Kayla shivered hard.

"Despite the fact that your friend Barry tried his best to beat the lights out of him—literally—he will in fact survive. And let me just say this one thing. This just may be the one and only time I fully and wholeheartedly agree with Barry J. Wentworth."

"Damn straight," Rafael muttered. "And if I hadn't been in the hospital…" He gave Kayla's hand a reassuring squeeze.

Al raised a finger and continued. "Let's be grateful you were. Now. As I said, Greg Turner will in fact survive—a little worse for wear, I would assume. Even the detective mentioned Barry did not have to beat him quite this severely. Be that as it may, he will survive. But the reports I'm receiving about his mental state are not entirely encouraging."

"How is that kind of information even public already?" Kayla asked and met Al's cool dark gaze. He said no more, and she swallowed hard.

"Right. You have your own information channels."

"The mental health professionals in charge of his evaluation don't really agree about much, I hear," Al continued, as if she had never asked the question. "But there is one thing they are in full and complete agreement on."

"Crazy as a hoot owl," Rafael said, and Al smiled thinly.

"Indeed. Although I presume their medical terminology is a little more refined than that."

"So, he's going to get off by reason of insanity," Rafael said, kicking at a bit of loose gravel. "That is such utter and complete bull. He can't just get away with it."

"Your concern is quite touching, Rafael. Trust me. No one will in fact get away with anything. Mr. Turner will be remanded in the care of a psychiatric treatment facility for the duration of his treatment, at the conclusion of which he will have to serve the full term of whatever sentence will be pronounced upon him for double homicide, attempted homicide, and the destruction of all of this."

Al waved his hands around the production hall and buzz of activity within.

"I still don't like the thought of that—that man lounging in comfort somewhere after everything he has done to your family, and tried to do to Kayla."

"That is not going to happen, Rafael." Again, a hard edge of steel came to his eyes and voice, and he straightened his shoulders a little. "Trust me. I will use my considerable influence to make sure of it."

Kayla rubbed her hands and shivered again at the dark turn their reunion had suddenly taken, but she need not have worried.

"Well, hello everyone! I see the gang's all here. I didn't know this was going to be a party."

The double doors into the office areas had opened, and Barry wandered in, smiling and waving at the workers around him as if he were a celebrity on the red carpet. Which, in many ways he was, as the story of how he had overwhelmed Greg Turner had been told again and again amongst the workers and staff. With every telling, Turner became just a bit madder, and Barry a bit more heroic, so he might have had something to do with the storytelling himself.

Now he looked tanned, fit, and pampered in a custom-tailored light suit and perfectly polished new shoes—handmade, no doubt. Kayla grinned and gave him a huge hug.

"Where have you been? You look like you came off a cruise ship or something."

"God forbid cruises. Wash your mouth with soap, woman. Just a quick jaunt to the Bahamas for some much-needed R&R. I extended the trip a bit because—well—my parents felt the need to stop by and tell me how happy they were I survived the explosion. You know." He waved his hand. "We're finally in a good place again, all right?"

"Nice. You look good, bro." Rafael slapped Barry's shoulder, and they turned again toward the boom lift hoisting the new window into the frame above.

"Another window, huh? So, the board members can look down and watch everything happen once again."

Rafael just opened his mouth to answer, but Al awkwardly struggled out of his electric scooter to stand with the three of them. Kayla had to fold her hands to avoid trying to help him stand. He looked thin enough she imagined seeing blood vessels and bones beneath his papery skin. Al stood and rested his hand on a beautifully carved cane for balance.

"Well now," he said. "Now that all of you are here, I wonder if I could make a small suggestion."

Rafael raised an eyebrow, and Barry half turned and cocked his head. "Sure. What's on your mind?"

Al smiled and looked out over the production hall that was once again coming together, just the way it had been before. Before all of it happened.

"It seems to me," he said, "that at the very beginning, there was a dinner. And a fundraising event at some highly expensive restaurant in town which is surely gone now. And there was you, Barry, and Rafael and Kayla and me."

He smiled, and Kayla watched all of the anger and the resentment leave his face, and the room.

"We, all of us, have gone through a lot since those early days. There have been accusations, and wrongdoings, and resentments and horrible, horrible revenge. But through all of it, we always found our way back together for the good of the company, for the good our products do for so many people out there."

"Hear, hear," Rafael said softly.

"People suffering from pain, or PTSD, or a host of other diseases who are receiving care and relief from the products of Perfect Cannabis Corporation."

"Of course," Barry said. "That was always our main…"

But Al raised his hand to interrupt him. "Hang on for a minute, Barry. You'll have your say when I'm done."

He reached out and took Barry's elbow for a moment, and let go of it again.

"For the last few years, we four have witnessed what anger and revenge can do to people, so I would like to suggest that, A, we bury all of our grievances with one another here once and for all and start fresh."

"Agreed." Kayla didn't even have to think, and Rafael and Barry nodded assent.

"And B," Al continued, smiling again, "with Dante and Nick gone to run Pride Cannabis to honor Roberto's memory, I'm going to suggest to our board we bring Barry Wentworth on as a director going forward. I just wanted to make sure that I had your agreement here."

He smiled at them, and nobody spoke. Barry stood with his mouth open, at a loss for words for perhaps the first time in his life, Rafael grinned broadly and made a fist, and finally, Kayla reached out and hugged Al.

"I see I do," Al said when he had regained his footing. "Then what say we call a meeting and make it all official, and let's see if we can run the best cannabis producer in the country together, shall we? I know Irv Moody is still burning to get involved. He gave me a call to see what was what. He seems to have leads about a few good, capable people. And we can use all the hands we can get. So—let's go, people."

And he sat in his scooter again, led the way toward the boardroom, and left the others to follow him, just as the crew snapped the final fasteners on the great glass pane above that would hold the window into the production area of Perfect Cannabis products.